E. HOFFMANN PRICE'S
EXOTIC ADVENTURES MEGAPACK®

E. HOFFMANN PRICE'S
EXOTIC ADVENTURES MEGAPACK®

WILDSIDE PRESS

COPYRIGHT INFO

Table of Contents

A NOTE FROM THE EDITOR

Welcome to *E. Hoffmann Price's Exotic Adventures MEGAPACK®*! Wildside Press, in association with Mr. Price's heirs, is dedicated to making the extensive body of work of this pulpsmith extraordinaire accessible once again to the public through our line of *MEGAPACK®* collections.

Edgar Hoffmann Price (July 3, 1898 – June 18, 1988) was born in Fowler, California. A graduate of West Point, he served in World War (followed by military duty in Mexico and the Philippines) and was a champion fencer and boxer—fellow pulp author Jack Williamson referred to him as "a real-life soldier of fortune." Hoffmann was also something of a polymath—a Republican and a Buddhist, he was also an amateur Orientalist, and a student of the Arabic language.

Price's first fiction sale was in 1924 to *Droll Stories* magazine and over the years he befriended, corresponded with, and personally met many authors of the pulp era including Robert E. Howard, Clark Ashton Smith and H.P. Lovecraft. He wrote hundreds of stories for many pulp magazines (including *Weird Tales*) in varied genres like horror, detective, adventure, fantasy and science fiction. Wildside Press is proud to make his work available to readers again. Due to the inaccessibility of much of Price's work (he kept no manuscript archive and so we must resort to those original publication copies we can track down) we have decided to package the material into themed Megapacks, highlighting specific genres he worked in. Later volumes will be released as we gather further material (any collectors interested in aiding our endeavors by supplying photocopies from their collections are strongly urged to contact Wildside

E. Hoffmann Price's Exotic Adventures MEGAPACK® contains 11 stories and short novels set in a wide range of locales: Europe, Polynesia, Asia, the Middle East, etc. Their settings also range chronologically, from historical adventures to contemporary thrillers and were all published between 1935 and 1945 (with an outlier from 1971 as the finale). These are full-blooded, two-fisted tales of warriors throughout the ages, seeking glory and triumph.

We hope you enjoy these rip-roaring tales of adventure and daring-do. We will be releasing additional collections of Price's work in the near future. These include:

E. Hoffmann Price's Two-Fisted Detective MEGAPACK®
E. Hoffmann Price's War And Western Action MEGAPACK®
E. Hoffmann Price's Fantasy & Science Fiction MEGAPACK®
The Tenth Golden Age of Weird Fiction MEGAPACK®: E. Hoffmann Price
E. Hoffmann Price's Fables of Ismeddin MEGAPACK®
E. Hoffmann Price's Pierre D'artois: Occult Detective & Associates MEGA-PACK®

—Shawn Garrett

WORSE THAN DEATH

(Also published as "Man Hunt")

Originally appeared in *Spicy-Adventure Stories*, September 1935.

Even though business was rotten in Damascus, Ibrahim the dragoman found it more and more difficult to keep his mind on his work. Sitti Ayesha, reclining among a heap of cushions, looked like a cigarette ad come to life; her olive-tinted curves smiled tantalizingly through the shimmering silk that caressed her nicely rounded hips.

And whenever Ibrahim managed to deflect his gaze from somewhere south of the broad jeweled girdle that encircled her slender waist, he was dazzled by the warmly tinted flesh that led up toward breasts concealed by hammered silver brassieres; but he finally abandoned his ponderings on force vs. persuasion, and regarded his lovely client's dark eyes and petulant, crimson lips.

"But they really are *sheikhs*," he declared. "Aristocratic Arabs from the desert."

"They remind me of goats," declared Sitti Ayesha, her nose wrinkling in disgust. "And I'm not just referring to their looks."

The conversation was in English. If you took time to look at Sitti Ayesha's passport—one of her concealed assets—you would learn that she was Amelia Burns, of White Horse, Oklahoma. Her olive skin and potful of money were both inherited from an Indian grandfather who had pitched his teepee next door to an oil well.

She had everything but romance—hence her masquerading in Damascus, and her disappointment at finding that the *sheikh* of song and story is an odoriferous old gentleman badly in need of bug powder.

As for Ibrahim: a dragoman is a tourist's guide. The term comes from a Turkish word that originally meant interpreter, and now means gyp artist. Ibrahim, moreover, had lost nothing by spending a dozen years in Manhattan learning American language and customs.

"But you said you wanted to meet a *sheikh*—"

He made a despairing gesture, and for a moment forgot his worries long enough to wonder whether Sitti Ayesha might shift enough to give him a view of points thus far concealed by the baffling draperies trailing from the broad, jeweled girdle. "Though they'd not care a lot for you. You're entirely too thin."

Sitti Ayesha's dark eyes blazed indignantly at the dirty jab. She jerked herself upright. The concealing wisps of silk hitched up and apart.

"El hamdu lilahi!" gasped Ibrahim. "Praise God!"

His strategy had worked.

The view, though momentary, was enchanting. And before Sitti Ayesha knew what was happening, the dragoman had her in his muscular arms, trying to convince

9

her there was no use importing romance from the desert. She was caught off guard, and for a moment the divan looked like the fourth down and one yard to go! Her silver brassieres clattered to the tile floor; but Sitti Ayesha's henna-tinted nails raked the dragoman until he looked like a tom cat returning from a tough week-end.

Yet Arab valor persisted, and though Sitti Ayesha did manage to keep her opponent at elbow's length, Ibrahim was getting the better of the engagement. The girl from Oklahoma was weakening…"

"Ibrahim," reproved a caustic, feminine voice from the doorway, "is that any way to treat a client?"

The flurry of silk and amber tinted legs subsided. A plump, rather nice-looking Syrian woman in her middle thirties reproachfully eyed the badly clawed dragoman: Ibrahim's aunt, who was acting as Sitti Ayesha's maid. Her presence was decidedly discouraging.

"If Miss Burns doesn't like *sheikhs* from the desert," continued Aunt Fatimah, "maybe we can have her meet that Afghan prince, Muhammad Nadir Khan. He's awfully handsome and wealthy."

"Oh, that'd just be splendid," enthused Sitti Ayesha. Then, reproachfully regarding the dragoman, "Why on earth didn't you tell me about him?"

"Well, you said a *sheikh,"* protested Ibrahim. "A prince is something else!"

"Fix it up right away."

Ibrahim flashed his aunt a deadly glance, and said to Sitti Ayesha, "But that will cost $500 extra. An Afghan prince is sort of special."

"I don't care if it costs a thousand," declared Sitti Ayesha. Oil heiresses are that way.

She fumbled among the cushions and found a handbag. "Here's a down payment. But if he's as crummy as those *sheikhs,* the deal is off. I came to Damascus for romance."

Ibrahim made a nose dive for the money, bowed profoundly, and left the house.

"Ya Allah!" he groaned, eyeing the fistful of cash. "May God curse all aunts!"

His face lengthened until it looked like a coffin. He might have found a suitable *sheikh,* but an Afghan prince—! The nearest one he knew of was in Kabul, two thousand miles away. But something had to be done.

Arab wit went into a one man huddle. After three cups of coffee, and a pipe at Marouf's *loquanda,* Ibrahim began to brighten up. But it was not until he approached the American consulate that he really saw daylight. The broad-shouldered, lean, hawked-nosed American in expensive tweeds who was stepping to the street was his inspiration. Money, and lots of it. A rakish, adventurous seeming fellow. Sun-tanned, and athletic. Just the type but he wasn't wearing the right clothes.

As the American pocketed his passport, the dragoman stepped directly in front of him and bowed half way down to his knees.

"Welcome, your Highness! God bless you! Back in Damascus again, praise Allah!"

As he spoke, he seized and kissed the American's hand.

"What the hell's all this about?" the American demanded, jerking away his hand.

"Doesn't your Highness remember old Ibrahim?" The dragoman was pained and grieved.

"Where do you get this 'your highness' crap, anyhow? I'm Harrison Kane, from New York."

Ibrahim eyed him sharply, stroked his moustache, and shifted his skull cap back towards his left ear.

"Mr. Kane, if you're not Muhammad Nadir Khan, you ought to be. You're a dead ringer!"

Harrison Kane, hearing an Arab speaking Americanese became interested and sympathetic. Ibrahim explained.

"It's this way, Mr. Kane. I'm working for a Circassian girl with a coal scuttle of jack, and she's stacked up like the front row of the Follies."

"Interesting, if true," was Kane's skeptical comment.

"By God, it's more than that," assured Ibrahim, lowering his voice to a confidential whisper. His next few words were for Kane's ear only: and they dealt with the charms of Circassian girls… Kane stroked his chin and listened…

"Anyway," resumed Ibrahim, "she's got a crush on Prince Muhammad Nadir Khan. Half a dozen years ago she saw him riding through the streets of Kabul and took a heavy tumble. And now that her father is dead, and she's inherited all his dough, and she heard the Prince had moved to Damascus, she packed up and here we are. Only—" And Ibrahim's voice became husky, and great tears gleamed in his eyes. "Only, the Prince got killed in Egypt, and jeez, I just ain't got the guts to go back and tell the poor kid. I didn't hear about it till I just now passed the Prince's house."

The dragoman sighed like a locomotive blowing off steam, and wiped his nose on the sleeve of his dejellab. An old Arabian custom.

"By God, that is tough," Kane agreed. Beauty in distress always is.

"But when I saw you," continued Ibrahim, "I thought someone was kidding me about the Prince having croaked. Honest, I did. So how about you meeting her. You could take his place. If you like her, okay. If not, just beat her up a couple times, and she'll get her fill of Afghan princes—but it won't be like learning her childhood romance is pushing up daisies in an Egyptian graveyard."

It was sorrowful, but Kane said, "Nuts! Even if I do look like Prince Whoozis, she'd tumble in a minute. I can't talk this native lingo. I was just looking for an interpreter—one of these birds they call a dragoman."

"Praise God, you met me!" declared Ibrahim. "The dragomans of Damascus are a bunch of crooks. Me, I'm an American citizen—lived for years in New York, just came back to the old country, and got this job with Sitti Ayesha—that's the gorgeous girl from Circassia."

"An honest to God Circassian girl?" Kane was becoming interested.

"Sure. You know the kind—you read the Arabian Nights, ain't you?"

Kane nodded and smiled reminiscently. Twenty years ago, he had snitched the key to the locked cases in his father's library and had read most of volume one of an unexpurgated edition before mother had caught him.

"This'll be better'n you read about," assured Ibrahim.

"But this matter of language," reiterated Kane.

"Simple. She talks only Circassian, and about a dozen words of Arabic. And the Prince speaks nothing but Afghan, and hardly any Arabic. Get it? Just make yourself pleasant, and if she says no, you won't be able to understand, so just go ahead and make her happy."

It sounded screwy, but Kane remembered his Arabian Nights.

"It's a deal," he declared. Then, reaching for his wallet: "How much do you get?"

"My dear sir," protested the horrified Ibrahim. "I'm just trying to save a lovely girl from a broken heart—"

He sighed, and wiped his eyes.

"Lead on," said Kane.

"I'll meet you at your hotel, as soon as I can pick up some Afghan clothes for you," proposed the dragoman. "Then I'll teach you a dozen words in Arabic."

"Right," agreed Kane.

Ibrahim lost no time finding the necessary masquerade then he hailed a taxi and dashed out to the Salahiyeh suburb to break the good news to Aunt Fatimah so she could prepare Sitti Ayesha for royalty.

That evening Ibrahim arrayed Kane in a voluminous turban, an embroidered *kaftan,* a silver hiked tulwar, and riding breeches with English-made boots.

"You look more a prince than he did himself," declared Ibrahim. "This'll be a cinch. Now let's see how much Arabic you can remember."

"*Ana ul amir*—that means I'm the prince," recited Kane. "*Ruh*—get the hell out! *Shufi andak tashrab*—what have you got to drink—"

"Damn good Arabic," approved Ibrahim. "Let's go."

"Wait a minute," Kane frowned. "How would you ask her—"

"Don't ask her! It's the same in any language."

Half an hour later a hired Rolls Royce drew up in front of Sitti Ayesha's house in the Salahiyeh suburb. Harrison Kane, hitching his belt so that the scabbard of his *tulwar* did not tangle up with his spurs, emerged from the glittering car, and approached the massive door of the white stone house. Ibrahim headed for the servants' entrance.

Kane pounded the heavy brazen knocker. A Negro doorkeeper admitted him and led the way across a courtyard, and then down a long vaulted hallway. The servant gestured for him to wait, then faded down a cross passage. Kane, peeping through the grating that pierced the door before him, promptly forgot his lines.

Sitti Ayesha was a glamorous, gleaming length of warm, olive-tinted flesh stretched out on a Kashan rug. Her toenails were stained with henna, and heavy golden bands accentuated the slimness of her ankles and the fine long curve of her legs. The transparent, caressing fabric that clung to her thighs tantalized Kane's questing glance, and the inward sweep of her waist was an invitation to squeeze her until she gasped.

The peacock plume fan that Aunt Fatimah was slowly waving made the gauzy veil about her breasts ripple and then snuggle, closer.

"That nigger must have fallen into a hole," muttered Kane, impatient at the delay. "I'll announce myself."

He pounded the door. It slammed open.

"*Ana ul amir,*" he proclaimed.

Sitti Ayesha, startled by his abrupt entrance, reached for a scarf to drape about the points of interest, but in her confusion missed both places and succeeded in masking only the broad jeweled girdle about her waist. The enchanting flurry of olive-tinted limbs raised the amir's blood pressure fifty points.

"*Salaam aleikum, ya amir,*" greeted Aunt Fatimah as she reached for a cloak and draped it about her mistress' exposed fascinations.

Kane had forgotten the answer; but he did remember something. He gestured toward the further doorway and said, *"Ruh!"*

Orders are orders, coming from a prince. Aunt Fatimah dusted for the exit, which left Kane with a clear field, and wondering what to say next. There was only one remark he could remember.

"Shufi andak tashrab?"—but his mind wasn't on drinking by any means.

The girl from Oklahoma was in a tough spot. The Afghan's simmering glance had left her quivering and shaky inside. So instead of making an answer that might betray her imposture, she leaned back among the cushions, smiled dazzlingly and flung aside the cloak that masked her fascinations. She had counted on the distraction giving her a moment to collect her wits.

But it didn't work out that way. Her pert breasts were more than any honest Afghan could see without doing something about it.

Kane's flying tackle was a classic. Instead of a sonnet to her eyebrows, and a plaintive Kashmiri love song to the tune of a *sitar,* the Afghan prince was not even pausing to discard his *tulwar* or boots. He had her in his arms before she could use a single one of the tricks that enable a nice girl in Oklahoma to stay nice and still have lots of fun.

His kisses scorched her lips, and sent thrills and shudders racing down her spine. The medals on his *kaftan* were gouging into her breasts, but she couldn't think of enough Arabic to tell him that it would be nicer if he took off his coat. Sitti Ayesha dared not protest lest she betray her imposture, and since she couldn't say a word, she couldn't effectively resist.

And as the Afghan's exploring hand probed the silk that still separated them, she shivered, snuggled closer, and decided that it was too late to protest.

Her breath sighed in his ear. She relaxed and clung to him like a shadow.

But before Prince Muhummad Nadir Khan could make it a home run, the door burst open. The fun was over. Six Arabs came plunging into the room. As Kane bounded to his feet, they closed in.

He drew his *tulwar,* and lashed out; but the treacherous haft turned in his grasp. The blade struck flat-wise, sending one of his assailants to the floor, knocked silly instead of beheaded. A club sizzled through the confusion, crashing down on Kane's shoulder.

He leaped back, slashed again with his *tulwar,* but just missed splitting one of his opponents lengthwise. The blade was knocked from his hand. Kane ploughed in, fists hammering. He gave a good account of himself. The room was a milling confusion of grunting Arabs, flailing limbs, and spattering teeth knocked loose by the American's pile driver fists. Sitti Ayesha's screams drowned Aunt Fatimah's riot call from the hallway.

Smack. Another Arab knocked end for end. And then a club crashed down across Kane's turban. And as he sank to the tiles, groggy and goggle-eyed, three Arabs muffled Sitti Ayesha in a cloak. He struggled to his knees, but another club probed the confusion, catching him squarely across the head. Lights out for the amir!

When Kane's scattered wits re-assembled, his head seemed the size of a bass drum, and he felt as though he had passed through a rock crusher. Ibrahim was anxiously regarding him.

"What the hell! How come?"

"*Harami*," replied the dragoman. "Bandits from the desert. They sapped me and then—"

Ibrahim glanced about the disordered room. He stepped to the door to which a scrap of paper was pinned with a dagger.

"It's a demand for ransom." Then he translated: "*In the name of Allah, the Merciful, the Compassionate! Ibn Marouf, to all whom it concerns, greetings and peace. Bring two thousand pounds Egyptian to the oasis at Wadi Firaun and we will surrender Sitti Ayesha unharmed. If you delay or notify the authorities., we will collect our tribute from Sitti Ayesha. And when we have taken our pleasure, we will send her to Mecca to be sold in the slave market.*"

"Two thousands pounds Egyptian," muttered Kane. "Over ten thousand bucks."

"Ten thousand dollars," echoed Ibrahim. "After all only a trifle, to save her from a fate worse than death. Just think, that lovely girl in the hands of forty bandits."

Remembering his own sensations when he naught his first glimpse of Sitti Ayesha, Kane shuddered at the thought of the forty greasy Arabs.

"By God, they can't get away with it!"

Ibrahim shook his head. "Unfortunately they can. The French Governor would be afraid to send troops that far into the desert. The bandit's spies must have been fooled by your resemblance to the Afghan prince. They know that ten thousand dollars is nothing at all to him."

The longer Kane thought of what he had missed, the more certain he was that it would be worth double the ransom to get another chance at Sitti Ayesha.

"You know the way out to the oasis?"

"No, but I can get a guide," answered Ibrahim.

"Let's go." Kane headed for the door. "Maybe I can rout out the American consul. He'll help me raise the money in a hurry."

They set out for the city.

* * * *

Ibrahim waited at the door of the consulate. Presently Kane emerged and announced that he had to present his letter of credit to the Governor General of Syria, who would have the cash available at once. In the meanwhile, Ibrahim was to get transportation.

"On my head and eyes," assured the dragoman. He missed the grim light in Kane's eye and the determined set of his jaw. It was not until the American emerged from the French General's residence an hour later, that Ibrahim began to wonder. Six grim-looking ruffians accompanied the synthetic Afghan prince. They were armed, and each one carried a heavily laden haversack.

"Just a little bodyguard," explained Kane. "So this bandit won't try to hijack the ransom."

"Then you've got the money?"

Kane nodded, jerked a thumb at one of the haversacks, and said, "I've got something there that'll open their eyes!" He edged Ibrahim toward a battered but serviceable Cadillac parked in an alley near the General's residence.

"You sit up there with the driver," ordered Kane. "All right, Ali. Step on it."

The Arab chauffeur headed out for the Salahiyeh suburb, then swung left to the Palmyra road. After half an hour's drive, he left the highway and cut eastward toward the Syrian desert, pounding at a terrific clip across the moonlit wastes. Forty minutes later the Cadillac was laboring down a *wadi* that finally opened out into a flat, desolate expanse. Far ahead Kane noted a dark clump on the horizon.

"That is the oasis," said Ibrahim. "Better let me go on ahead and tell the bandits that you have the ransom. So we won't all be killed before we can explain our purpose."

The chauffeur braked to a halt and snapped off the headlights; but as Ibrahim stepped to the running board, Kane caught him by the shoulder.

"Wait a minute!" he commanded. "If you think I'm giving any greasy Arab bandits ten thousand bucks, you're all wet. We're getting out to fight on foot. And I'll split ten thousand bucks among this crowd after we've ganged up on that bunch of petty larceny snatchers."

"Ya Allah!" groaned Ibrahim. "We'll all be killed. I'm going back."

Kane jammed a revolver against his ribs.

"You're leading the advance. Or do you want to go back to Damascus labeled 'opened by mistake'?"

Before Sitti Ayesha could fairly realize that a handful of invaders had broken into her house in time to keep an Afghan prince from giving her high, low, jack, and the game, a camel-scented burnoose enveloped her head. A dozen strong hands hustled her out through a side door, and jammed her into a waiting car. Judging from the goaty aroma, it was loaded with Arab sheikhs. Gears clashed, and the machine headed out a road that seemed to be paved with monstrous waffle irons.

Presently the verminous *burnoose* was removed from her head. They were tearing across the open desert. Her captors made no effort to hold her. They were busy hanging to the coat rail to keep from being pitched out of the open car as it bounded like an Ibex from crag to crag, as the old saying goes.

Aunt Fatimah was wedged next to Sitti Ayesha.

"Oh my God!" moaned the girl from Oklahoma. "What happened—what do they want—did they kill the prince—?"

"They're bandits," answered Aunt Fatimah. "Probably holding you for ransom. Though maybe they're thinking of pleasure. Even a bandit needs a bit of home life once in a while."

"Oh—" Ayesha's tender flesh crawled as she shot long side glances at those bronze, villainous faces. "I'd rather die first."

"Well, maybe the prince will ransom you," suggested Fatimah. "That is, if he isn't dead."

Sitti Ayesha heartily regretted that Muhammad Nadir Khan had not arrived earlier.

"They probably won't touch you," consoled Fatimah. "Unless the prince refuses to send a ransom."

Another half hour of pounding across the desert, spectral in the moonlight. They were approaching a constantly expanding blotch of darkness straight ahead. Ayesha caught a flickering gleam. An oasis, and the black tents of the Arabs. Four men, gathered about the fire, advanced to meet the car as it crunched to a halt. They escorted their prisoners to the middle tent. The chief approached and addressed them in Arabic.

"He'll give you two days to raise a ransom," Aunt Fatimah translated. "Ten thousand dollars."

"Thank God!"

Ayesha sighed and sank to a rug stretched on the sand. It was bitterly cold, and her scanty silks were no protection against the penetrating night air. One of the Arabs brought her a woolen burnoose. It left her debating whether it would be better to freeze or to be eaten alive…

Night in the desert…the black tents of the Arabs…though Oklahoma might be lacking in romance, they had steam heat and mattresses…

But despite the chill and the creeping things, Ayesha dozed. She was too weary and nerve racked not to. She awoke with a start. She heard the drumming of hoofs, a ragged volley of rifle fire, a bedlam of yells. Bullets whistled through the walls of the tent.

Flattening to the sand, she lifted the flap. The bandits were dashing towards the fringe of the oasis, but their escape was cut off by a semi-circle of horsemen that was closing about the encampment. Steel gleamed, bursts of orange flame probed the darkness, and the thunder of hoofs and guttural yells of the horsemen drowned the frenzied screeches of Ayesha's captors.

She saw a lean, hawk-nosed, bearded Arab on a white horse wheel and slash home with a curved scimitar. One of her captors dropped, sheared from shoulder to hip. He lay twitching in the moonlight, a ghastly quivering heap of rags and gore. Another drew a pistol—but before he could level the weapon, an automatic chattered like a machine gun. He doubled up as though kicked in the stomach.

The survivors raised their hands. The Arab on the white horse shouted a command. Half raised blades were sheathed, and pistols lowered.

"God in heaven! What's happened?" gasped Ayesha.

Fatimah's placid countenance was tense. She eyed the man on the white horse, then she said in a low, trembling tone, "That's Nuri Sultan—the wildest outlaw in Arabia."

A bandit was a bandit. Ayesha was bewildered by Fatimah's sudden terror.

"After all, we're no worse off—"

"These are real bandits," moaned Fatimah. "They'll kill all the men, and as for us —"

"Real bandits?" italicized Ayesha.

Fatimah, dragging the girl from Oklahoma back into the tent, blurted out a partial confession.

"The first crowd—those that broke into your house," she concluded, "were just some dragomans trying to get the Prince to pay off a big ransom for you. But this is awful! Oh, my God! Nuri Sultan! Even the French are afraid of him."

And then Fatimah sent out a screech that shook the tent pole. Nuri Sultan, vaulting from his white horse, had heard their voices, and had seen the flurry of legs and arms as they ducked for cover. Before they could slip out under the edge of the tent, the flap was jerked aside, and Nuri Sultan stalked into the tent.

Ayesha was moving fast, but the bandit had wings. His hand closed on her shoulder, jerking her back into the tent. Her shriek brought half a dozen of the bandit's men on the run.

"Mashallah!" they gasped in unison, seeing by the camp fire glow what their leader had discovered. Ayesha had worn little when Kane first saw her; and now she wore less. Her disarrayed hair trailed over her shoulders. Her pert breasts peeped

through the twining blue black strands. Her shapely legs were something to dream about.

She still wore her jeweled girdle, but only a few sorry tatters of gauze hung from it. Ayesha's heavy hair did not quite reach her hips—hence the chorus of "Allah be Praised!"

"Get out!" shouted Nuri Sultan, one arm pinning Ayesha to his side as he whirled to face his men. "And if you want to make good use of an idle hour, take her friend out of here and see what she is good for."

As he spoke, he indicated Fatimah. She looked uncommonly good to the Arabs who had been dazzled by Ayesha's youthful curves. The ensuing rush was like a subway jam. And before you could say Allah be praised, Fatimah was the center of a gathering that was diving for the oasis.

Nuri Sultan caught his lovely captive in both arms. She had thought for a moment that he was going to keep her unharmed and hold her for ransom; but it was now apparent that he first had to find out how much she was worth.

"Don't! Stop—please don't!" she shrieked as the Arab's arms closed about her.

Ayesha, facing something worse than death, forgot every last word of Arabic she had learned, and the bandit captain didn't understand English.

"Don't—please don't. I'll pay you anything—"

She was an armful for any man to handle; but Nuri Sultan knew what he wanted. And by the time she had raised the bid to an even twenty-five thousand, the horseman from the desert had the advantage. Her breath was coming in panting gasps, and her struggles were subsiding…

"Thirty thousand—"

That impressive sum trailed off into a sobbing, despairing wail.

* * * *

Harrison Kane, leading his squad of city Arabs into the desert, finally distinguished three black tents pitched somewhat to the left of an oasis. He called for a halt to explain his plan of attack; and then Ibrahim learned what the haversacks contained.

"We'll sneak up and toss a hand grenade out to the further edge of the camp. When they come running out, we'll hose them with our pistols and give them the rest of the grenades. Then when—"

But the field order was interrupted by a low groan and a guttural cursing. Half a dozen dark figures were crawling toward the huddle. Kane jerked his pistol into line, but before he could fire, Ibrahim caught his wrist.

"Don't shoot!" said the dragoman. "That's my cousin, Habeeb!"

"Habeeb, hell!" growled Kane. "Let go or I'll—"

"*Ya* Ibrahim!" gasped a voice. "Run for your life!"

A gargling of Arabic; and then one of Kane's men translated: "These fellows aren't bandits. They're dragomans from Damascus."

In a moment Kane had the story: "Nuri Sultan raided our camp. Then he slashed the soles of our feet and turned us loose, so we'd have to crawl back to town on our hands and knees. He's just keeping the women…he's going to take them to the slave market in Mecca to sell them."

Kane began to understand. He caught Ibrahim by the throat.

"Cough up—or by God, I'll take you to pieces by hand!"

The half-throttled dragoman confessed that the original kidnapping of Sitti Ayesha had been fake; but he forgot to mention that she was from White Horse, Oklahoma.

"Let's go!" commanded Kane. "There's not more than a dozen of them, and we'll surprise them."

He had scarcely resumed the advance when he heard a shriek that speared the desert silence like a fire siren. A woman's voice. A woman crying out in English. Kane stretched long legs toward the oasis. He covered a heart breaking two-twenty —"An American girl!" Kane growled between gasps. "Shake it up!"

The oasis however was further than the sounds indicated. The desert air is deceptive. He heard her cries, clearly, but seemingly no closer. She was vainly pleading, and struggling to repel a bandit.

Nuri Sultan, raider and slave trader, had snatched an American girl as well as Sitti Ayesha. Kane, desperately hoarding his rapidly failing wind, pressed on, wondering if he could reach the camp before it was too late.

And then blackness swallowed Kane and his men. Too late, he saw that he was on the edge of a *wadi*. He recoiled, but lost his balance and plunged headlong down the steep wall of the ravine. His followers, equally at loss in the treacherous desert, piled after him. The opposite wall was too steep to scale. They lost precious minutes dashing along the rocky bottom.

And when Kane finally emerged on the open plain, there was no longer any outcry coming from the oasis.

He was battered and bruised, and he had lost his haversack of grenades; but exhausted as he was, Kane was in better shape than the city Arabs who painfully hoisted themselves clear of the ravine. He reeled for a moment, dizzy and panting. He heard the neighing of a horse; but the camp seemed deserted. There was no one at the flickering fire near the middle tent; no sign of bandits.

And then Kane heard a sound that froze his blood, and made his brain explode in a red flare...

He dashed like a madman across the rocky waste, leaving his exhausted followers far behind him. As he ran, he cursed in panting gasps, jerked his pistol from its holster, and hoped that he had misinterpreted what he had heard.

Great God! It couldn't be—

The sounds now seemed to come from the oasis, and not from the central tent. He tried to tell himself that it must be his own panting breath that he heard as he forced himself onward. But as he reached the edge of the camp fire glow, Kane was beyond reason.

Without waiting for his men to catch up, he recklessly bounded toward the middle tent, tore aside the flap. He had no ears for pounding footsteps of the followers he had outdistanced, and he did not hear the yell that came from the oasis. He was aware of nothing but the occupants of the tent.

He could not see the girl's face, but her bare legs and arms gleamed white in the glow of the camp fire. The American girl! She was sobbing and moaning, but she clung to the Arab who had her in his arms...

Kane's pistol snapped into line. He had never shot a man in the back, but it was a good time to start. Yet despite his wrath, he restrained himself: the heavy .45 slug would kill the girl as well as her assailant.

And then the seemingly deserted camp flared into an uproar. Shouting men charged from the oasis to meet Kane's squad. Pistols crackled. As Kane bounded forward, the Arab tore himself from the girl's embrace. His bearded face was clawed to mincemeat, and his flowing *djellab* was torn to ribbons. The blast of Kane's .45 shook the tent, but the Arab, seasoned to surprie attack, ducked and scooped up the pistol that lay at the edge of the rug.

"You damn'—!" raged Kane, jerking another shot. The Arab recoiled, fired wildly. Kane's weapon snapped back into line. It jammed; but the American's wrathful charge carried him inside the enemy's guard. Dropping his useless automatic, he snatched the armed wrist, wrenched it, and bodily flung the Arab crashing against the heavy tent pole.

And then from without came an ear-shattering blast, the scream of iron fragments, a howl of dismay. A grenade had cut loose. Pistols chattered. Another bomb shook the encampment.

Kane, ignoring the battle, leaped forward to pin his enemy to the earth; but as he closed in, he saw that the Arab lay in a grotesque huddle, his head lolling at an unnatural angle, his face distorted, his eyes staring.

"Broken neck," growled Kane. "He had it coming."

He turned to the girl. *Sitti Ayesha!* Recognition was mutual.

"Thank God—but where did you learn to speak English?" she gasped. Then she remembered that he had arrived too late, and tried to rearrange the few sorry tatters of silk that still clung to her.

"In a convent," Kane bitterly answered. "So you're the American girl I heard? Circassian, hell! If you hadn't pulled this flim-flam game, you wouldn't have—"

He spat disgustedly and prodded Nuri Sultan with his boot.

Sitti Ayesha, née Burns, had no chance for words. Kane's city Arabs came bursting into the tent, Aunt Fatimah at their heels. The show was over. The survivors of Nuri Sultan's gang were dashing across the desert, on foot. Aunt Fatimah eyed the girl, the dead bandit chief, and Harrison Kane's grim face.

"Oh, I wish I was dead," sobbed Sitti Ayesha.

"Don't be foolish," consoled Aunt Fatimah. "There may be things worse than death, but so far, I doubt it—"

Sitti Ayesha through her tears regarded her maid and saw that she also had been thoroughly pawed.

"Oh, did they—"

Aunt Fatimah nodded and said, "Well…yes…but—"

Kane, noting her contented sigh, recognized a philosopher. He helped Sitti Ayesha to her feet. She was bedraggled, but nevertheless…

"I still don't know what your idea was, posing as a Circassian," he said, "but let's go back to town and talk this over." Then eyeing the dead bandit, he added, "After all, consoling widows is a white man's duty."

GAMBLE WITH THE GODS

Originally published in *Top-Notch*, September/October 1937.

One Hindu priest murdered ; one Chinese temple burned; a Buddhist pagoda stoned; five small riots, and then some really first-class street fighting. Just about that time, the Moulmein *Times* hinted that the authorities were disturbed by an outbreak of what seemed to be religious conflicts.

Without doubt, both of Moulmein's newspapers knew the truth, but the district commissioner did not encourage engaging frankness. Yet his reticence had not handicapped Denis Ward. As that American's rickshaw pulled away from the jetty on Tiger Street—he had hurried from Penang by speed boat—he heard shouts and shrieks from the Dawezu Bazaar. He was not too late; the difficulty hadn't been settled. Then he shook his head, and thrust the Moulmein *Times* to the cushion. "Why the hell don't they admit that some one looted the Vishnu Temple on Washerman Street?"

They might as well have, though Ward did not expect the papers to give the name of the thief and the exact location of the little green image of Vishnu. That would leave him nothing to do.

Though it would not much more than fill a cigar box, Vishnu's statuette was encrusted with splendid, emeralds and ancient, blazing rubies. This was rich loot, and its return should net him a neat reward. As for the risk of being knifed or taken to pieces, by hand, before he could convince the priests that he intended to surrender the image—well, a lot of people had made a glaring failure of vivisecting Denis Ward, freelance adventurer.

He was somewhat larger than Ling Fu, the valet whose rickshaw was some paces to the rear. Denis was wiry and inconspicuous, with a face that was indefinite except when it became squarish and grim. His eyes were somewhat bluish, with hints of gray, and his hair had never decided whether to be sandy, straw-colored, or brown. No one ever noticed Ward.

The rioting at the Dawezu Bazaar was improving every moment. From the post office, where Ward pulled up, the view was inspiring. Hysterical Hindus, chattering Chinese, bearded Arabs, and coal-black Tamil coolies were mixing it up. Staves thwacked; knives flashed. Women and bareheaded Buddhist monks fled from the disturbance—and then a squad of turbaned Sikhs approached at the double.

They impartially booted, thumped, clubbed the rioters, and, in doing so, completed the destruction of the market stalls where fruit and fish and sandals were trampled under foot with pots of pungent sauces and freshly baked *chupattis*.

"Pretty, eh, Ling Fu?" said Ward, as his valet pulled up alongside.

"Impressive," agreed the little Cantonese. He could, in a pinch, press his master's tropical ducks, and he could, likewise, handle a razor—but Ward shaved himself.

Ling Fu's use of edged tools was much better in a hand-to-hand, with all rules suspended.

"Very religious town," continued Ling Fu, effortlessly shifting just enough to duck a durian that a rioter had hurled at a policeman. And, always statistically inclined, he added, "Twenty monasteries—nine Mohammedan mosques—two Chinese temples—six Hindu shrines—"

But before he enumerated the fifteen sectarian schools and calculated the religion *per capita* in a town of sixty thousand, Ward roared, "Hey—cut that out—"

Ling Fu looked pained. The master usually liked to learn things wherever they went. Then he saw that Ward was bounding toward a tangle on Dawezu Street.

It centered about a *ghari*. The shaggy pony was squealing and kicking. The red-faced man in the solar topee was turning purple and cursing in a foghorn voice as he tried to ward off the staves wielded by four Hindus. And the blond girl in the blue silk print screamed and tried to take cover by crouching against the dashboard of the *ghari*. It was her lovely, frightened face that drew Ward into the fracas.

And as he tackled an oily Hindu, tumbling him headlong into a heap of offal, Ward decided that he wanted a look at the girl when she wasn't screaming and trying to dodge clubs. Then the red-faced man was jerked to the street. Ward plowed in, and his fists reddened from the teeth and noses he hammered out of line. A knife slashed his white coat from shoulder to hem. He wrenched the fellow's wrist and booted him over backward.

But Ling Fu's flank attack turned the tide. The frail Chinaman had a knack of laying large people out with torturing twists. And the arrival of the Sikhs cleared the deck, though they did not take any prisoners. They were too busy helping the red-faced sahib to his feet, and wondering whether Ward's scratches were serious. Fie said, "Tell the lady the fun's over."

But the lady knew that, and as she tried to pat her disheveled hair and ruined hat into shape, she smiled dazzlingly and said, "I do believe you enjoyed it! But thanks —"

"Save some for Ling Fu," said Ward. "He dissects them by hand when it's not tactful to use his carving set."

Ling Fu beamed, and assured Win Hampton that he was a Christian Chinaman. That gave Ward time to notice the thin, hook-nosed Arab who, from a distance of some paces, was smiling ironically and stroking his beard. His narrowed black eyes missed nothing, but despite his interest, he had not taken sides.

"Seeing as you're new in Burma," began Ward, after acknowledging Marley Hampton's thanks, "you and your daughter might—"

"And how do *you* know we're new?" Win Hampton interrupted.

"Papa's sun helmet just fresh from Chow Kit's, in Penang"—Ward grinned, offering the retrieved headgear—"doesn't prove a thing. But you've not developed a sun squint, and who ever saw a complexion like yours in Moulmein?"

"I'm so glad you like me!" she mocked. Then her blue eyes became somber, and for a perceptible pause she scrutinized his face, as if wondering whether its squareness was a reflection of the man behind it. "And I'd love to have you call at the Winthrop for tea—"

"That's handy," he cut in. "I'm staying there myself."

He wondered at the sudden tension of the slim hand she had offered as she leaned from the *ghari* and added, "Tomorrow?"

Ward watched the Hamptons drive away. If they were sight-seers, he was a Buddhist monk! Marley Hampton looked like money; so did his daughter, if one had an eye for costly simplicity. But while the girl had quickly recovered from the shock, uneasiness had surged back in a wave that mirrored her father's perturbed expression.

* * * *

But Ward, once in his room at the Winthrop, had to get back to this matter of the Vishnu temple loot. He was not taking the obvious course of interviewing the priests. Detective routine was not his game, and, moreover, it was not working. The reticence of the papers proved that. But Ling Fu's hints in Penang had given him his plan.

That evening, he called on a man on South Pagoda Road, a Chinese merchant who owned an interest in an opium shop. And there were things about Tsang Li that were not so commonly known: such as his reputed membership in the secret society of the Sa Tiam a guild of thieves who would not consider an old pair of shoes too small, or a war elephant in full regalia too large to steal.

Ward did not assume that the Sa Tiam had had a hand in the looting; but very little can happen without the Chinese underworld getting word of it. The only catch was interviewing members of that society. To get a word with Tsang Li required a fine hand.

A touch at least as smoothly silken as the servant who did not blink an eye when Ward addressed him in Mandarin; as delicate as the compliments which Ward exchanged, some moments later, with the frail little man whose dove-gray tunic rustled as he bowed, clasped his own two yellow hands, after courteously removing his spectacles.

"The high-minded and resplendent excellence of Tsang Li," began Ward, "has aroused this dull person's admiration to the point of unwarranted intrusion."

"This uncouth dealer in cheap commodities is embarrassed by undeserved honor," asserted Tsang Li.

"Precious commodities," countered Ward, "seem cheap to a superior person, especially when he has them in dazzling profusion. I am abashed—"

He fumbled with a small parcel, glanced down as if dazzled by the fine old lacquer and porcelain that enriched the room. "This trifle is not a worthy gift."

As a matter of fact, the tiny bowl of jade was of that rare, true green that made it worth more than its weight in gold to a Chinese connoisseur. A mandarin would have coveted it.

Tsang Li's smooth flow of honorifics did not falter when he saw the three brass coins that were in the bowl. But when he resumed the courteous cross examination that included queries as to Ward's age income, and health, he said, "Where are you from?"

"From the east," answered Ward.

"Has your mother any old iron?" Tsang Li's voice took on an edge as curious as the question itself.

This was ticklish ground. Few white men knew the complete ritual of any Chinese society, and Ward was not one of them. His answer seemed to satisfy the Honorable

Tsang though his host would not be discourteous enough to correct him, then and there. Later, perhaps, a knife would remind Ward that less than a hundred percent was a fatally low score.

And in response to an inquiry as to his caller's business, Ward answered, "I am looking for rare bits of Hindu art. Even if the Honorable Tsang cannot be bothered with such trifles, this illiterate person would appreciate exalting advice."

Tsang Li delicately fingered the ends of his wispy mustache and said, "To speak in haste betokens ignorance. I will ponder."

Then he called a servant, who presently returned with an exquisite lacquer casket about the size of a cigar box. He handed it to the master, who presented it to Ward, all the while deploring its crudity and flaws. In truths it easily matched the American's jade bowl. And when the servant wrapped it in a large red silk kerchief, Tsang Li called for tea.

He noted, without seeming to do so, which of the several cups Ward selected from the peculiarly arranged set, and how his fingers were placed. And when Ward left, Vishnu had not been directly mentioned.

But some street vendor might accost hint that night, or the following day.

His speculations, however, were abruptly ended as he passed Malay Street, near the Mayongon Bazaar. Its odors, blending with those of the water front, were compelling. But even more overwhelming was the solid thump against the top of his rickshaw.

Unfortunately for the man who had dropped down from an overhanging balcony, Ward understood the process, having seen several unwary travelers thus knifed in Singapore. He hurled himself forward in time to avoid the downward-licking blade.

The entire balance of the fragile vehicle having been upset, the assailant was spilled backward. Ward whirled, groping for a conveniently loose cobblestone, but the rickshaw coolie caught him about the knees, and down they went.

"There it is!" yelled the coolie, as Tsang Li's gift spilled from the tipped vehicle.

The man with the short, deadly kurki lunged for the prize. Ward heaved the stone, but missed. Yet even in the half gloom, he saw that the man who seized the parcel was a Hindu. And having his prize, he did not stay to fight.

He vanished toward the water front just as Ward kicked the struggling coolie into the gutter. But the fall had wrenched his leg and before he was fairly under way, Ward knew that he had not a chance of overtaking the thief. When he retraced his steps, the coolie was gone.

"Anyway"—Ward chuckled—"I owe him for the fare. And I bet that Hindu's going to look sour when he finds out that Vishnu isn't in that package."

At the best, this was no more than a hunch. But Ward's welcome to Moulmein had contained too many elements that fitted too well for coincidence. And the attack on the Hamptons was one of them.

Chapter II

The attack by the Hindu, Ward reasoned, could very well arise from resentment caused by his interference in favor of Win Hampton and her father; but the seizure of Tsang Li's gift gave the encounter an added significance. The parcel was large enough to have contained the image of Vishnu.

"The priests think I got the loot from Tsang Li," Ward told himself as he prudently walked down the center of the street. "I'm on the right track."

That the police had made absolutely no progress in tracking down the thief was not amazing. The devotees of the god would purposely withhold information, so that they themselves could execute vengeance. Ward shivered. Now that he was a suspect, death lurked in every shadow. The priests would hardly strike in person, but there were men of all races who would wield a knife for gold from Vishnu's vaults.

Gold? He chuckled grimly at the thought of such extravagance. A few rupees would buy a man's life. From behind barred doors he heard the coin-hungry voices of gamblers. They were playing *main po* and fan-tan by the flickering flames of peanut-oil lamps. And a gambler always needs money. In the next block he caught the pungent scent of cooking opium—the reek of hashish. A man who needed a few silver pieces to buy his day's drugs would kill though he knew not even the name of the god whose wrath he served.

A drunken Malay reeled down a dark alley. The tang of arrack lingered. And a Mohammedan low enough to defile himself with forbidden liquor would slay for another drink—

Then Ward laughed softly, and devils gleamed in his eyes. "Hell—this'll be fun— finding a kidnapped god to save my own neck!"

The round-faced Bengali clerk at the desk offered a servile salutation as Ward entered the lobby and felt a fictitious coolness of muggy air stirred by the long-bladed, lazily whirling ceiling fans.

The lift carried him to the third floor. He had scarcely covered half the distance to his room when a door opened, letting a muffled rumble of voices swell into an angry rumble. A lean Arab came catapulting out. He landed against the opposite wall, almost at Ward's feet. His mouth sagged, his eyes were glassy, and one thin, muscular hand twitched, making fumbling, futile motions toward his belt. This was the bearded man who had so intently watched the mob close in on the Hamptons, at the Dawezu Bazaar.

And Marley Hampton, flushed and breathing audibly, stood at the threshold. "Get out—and stay out!" he boomed, dusting his hands. The knuckles were bleeding. "You damned fraud I'll—"

"That's bad, Mr. Hampton," reproved Ward, smiling wryly. "I believe you hit him —and with your fist."

"Uh—sure I did! The four-flushing scoundrel!" Hampton was too angry to know just how to tell the newcomer to mind his own business.

And by that time Ward had edged into the suite. Win emerged from her own room and faltered a greeting. The encounter had agitated her; that was apparent.

"What do you mean?" resumed Hampton, jerking the door shut.

"It's none of my business," apologized Ward. "But you should have killed him."

"Uh?"

"Yes. You'll have to. Or he'll do as much for you."

"See here—what do you know about Mahmud?"

Ward shook his head and smiled wryly. "Nothing. Except that he's an Arab, and you struck him. To keep his self-respect, he'll have to kill you." Hampton blinked and regarded his bruised fists. Then he repeated, "But I just hit him, with my hand."

"You might," Ward very patiently went on, "have pulled his beard. For a moment, I'd forgotten you *could* have done worse." He turned toward Win, and said, "Forgive this intrusion. I just felt I ought to warn you."

"Thanks!" snapped Hampton, noting Ward's disarray. "But it looks like you've been smacking people around yourself."

"Hindus don't count. Good night." Mahmud was no longer in the hall. Ward went to his room feeling a bit foolish. He was still sure that Hampton simply did not understand, and could not forget that the very best people, back home, pop each other with fists and then shake hands and have a drink.

When he entered his room, Ling Fu bowed and said, "Honorable master, this unworthy person begs leave to remind that it is not wise to walk unarmed." He produced a .45 revolver. The weapon was freshly oiled; it testified to Ling Fu's loving care.

"What's the idea?"

"Slight bloodstains and disarranged coat," said Ling Fu. "Pardon neglect in failing to offer necessary reminder before now. There was an Arab watching with too much interest at the bazaar?"

"Bad guess!" Ward laughed grimly. "It was a Hindu. And he got away with Tsang Li's gift."

"He will not live to enjoy it," predicted Ling Fu. "But his days would have been less if the honorable master had been armed."

Ward reproved, "You know I can't run around shooting people, even in self-defense. I've told you a number of times we shouldn't be conspicuous."

"I am abashed," apologized Ling Fu, without a trace of penitence. Then he said in English, "For inconspicuous obliterations, place thumbs under subject's ears, with palms against checks. Exerting suitable pressure at base of skull frequently causes death in twenty seconds."

"You would be statistical!" grumbled Ward. "But show me that trick again. How do I stand?"

"Position irrelevant."

The wiry little Chinese moved like a ferret. He evaded his master's instinctive gesture of defense; nothing less than a quick shot from the revolver could have blocked him. Before Ward realized what had happened, a vise grip that exactly answered the description closed on the back of his head. The room reeled, spun dizzily; red spots blazed before Ward's eyes, and his ears roared and buzzed as he vainly tried to shake off the practice attack. It was as though a tomcat was clinging to him—but it was deadlier than a leopard's stroke. He made croaking sounds during that endless drop to the floor.

And then, after an interminable period of blackness, Ling Fu's voice reached his ears: "Three seconds very helpful, but not fatal."

"For a Christian Chinaman," said Ward, "you're a whiz."

And for the next half hour, they took turns practicing defense and attack. Ward was blowing like a spent horse, but Ling Fu was scarcely ruffled. The American was learning—but he still had a long way to go before he could discard the noisy and only a little more deadly weapons of his own country.

The next morning Ward was out early. His purpose was to prowl in the bazaars, and tune in on as much native gossip as he could. The inscrutable East is garrulous in the extreme, and no one would credit him with tinder-standing the crossfire of surmise and guess and half truths in a dozen dialects. By piecing enough of them together, he could learn more than the priests of Vishnu, or the police. However they disguised themselves, their presence would be sensed and chatter would cease.

He hardly hoped to get the image from Tsang Li. Even if that shrewd old fellow did acquire it, the price would be too high to leave any chance of taking a profit from its owners. Since Ward very definitely was not out to sell stolen goods, the compensation for wits was painfully limited.

He had scarcely reached the lobby when he saw that Win Hampton likewise was out early. The moment she recognized him, she impulsively extended her hand, and said, "Yes. I've been waiting. I simply had to see you. You seem to know this country."

Her blue eyes were troubled, and her gay little smile was hardly more than a mask.

"I'm flattered silly. Shall we sit here?"

"Over in the corner would be better," she suggested. "Just in case dad comes down."

That did not surprise Ward. He had purposely indicated a conspicuous seat, and her reaction gave him a hint.

"He's so stubborn," she went on. "I want him to leave at once. First those Hindus —then the Arab last night—"

"Which Hindus?" frowned Ward.

"In Penang, a week or two ago. They had marks on their forehead—three strokes, yellow on each side, and white in the center."

"Like a trident?" he hazarded.

"Of course. Does that mean something?"

"Just a caste mark, you might call it," evaded Ward. There was no use telling her that that was the symbol of four-armed Vishnu, who holds a conch shell, a chakra, a club, and a lotus flower; Vishnu, who some day will ride forth on Kalki, the white stallion, and with his drawn sword carve a new world out of this sorrow-laden one. "But what—"

"Dad had a furtive-seeming talk with them, and then we came to Moulmein, of all places. And you know what happened. We'd been here only a day. And now that Arab, Mahmud—"

"Funny," said Ward, "how he fits in."

"He"—she lowered her voice—"offered to sell some temple treasure. Dad promptly called him a fraud and told him to take his trickery somewhere else. That's nearly as I could understand. I was in my room, and Mahmud's English was rather sketchy."

"And he wouldn't deal with the Arab?"

"Of course not! We may be tourists, but we know you can scarcely set foot in the Orient without being offered supposedly stolen or smuggled or illicit treasures. In Egypt it was scarabs taken from a Pharaoh's tomb. Outrageous prices, and they're invariably fakes!"

She poured that all out in a breath, then regarded him with wide eyes. Ward was thinking fast. He wondered if she realized what she had told him.

"Why tell me?" he queried.

"Because—Oh, Lord. I'm worried silly, what with rioting, and your warning last night. Will you do me a favor? Talk to dad when he's not all wrought up. I think we're in danger of some kind. I can feel it."

"So can I," was Ward's wry response. "Score one for feminine intuition. But wouldn't I look pretty, advising a grown man to leave Moulmein because some Hindu picked on him during a general riot, and then an Arab made him a phony proposition?" Then, suddenly, he said, "What's your father up to? Teak? Petroleum? Plantations?"

"I don't know," she answered, very slowly. "We're tourists, though he may have business in the background. But I wish you'd join us at dinner to-night, instead of at tea. If he became acquainted with you, I know he'd have confidence in you."

"Such as you have?" he queried.

She steadily regarded him for a full moment. "Exactly. Just as I have."

"Thanks." Then he shook his head. "But I can't, not to-night. Though I don't see what I could do unless he just demanded advice. And something tells me he doesn't often do that."

Win sighed. "I guess I shouldn't blame you. And you've turned me down so flat, I'm just wondering—"

"To-morrow," Ward cut in. "Sure as death and taxes."

Chapter III

Ward's prowling along the water front, mingling with the pilgrims who thronged the stairs leading to the pagodas that crown the two highest hills in Moulmein, and poking his way through the bazaars netted him nothing but muttered contempt. There were too many towering Sikh policemen to give a riot any chance of developing.

That evening he headed for South Pagoda Road and Tsang Li's gilded door. Once more the bland gatekeeper admitted him to the spacious garden with its tiny bridges and pool, and the same silk-clad servant escorted him into the master's presence.

The interminable exchange of courtesies ended when Tsang Li said, "There is no well deep enough to hide a stolen pagoda."

In English, that would mean, "Vishnu's image is entirely too hot for you to handle." But when Ward hinted that a thousand-mile journey begins with a single step, Tsang Li became very frank.

"Every guild, particularly that of thieves, needs a counselor and a protector. It has come to me—though I may be wrong—that the thieves of Moulmein have been warned by their advisor not to touch the treasure of Vishnu."

"And so, of course, they will obey?" Ward was not ironic.

Tsang Li shrugged and smiled that vague smile which seemed to be more with his hand than his lips. "Who will pay a pension to the family of the disobedient fool? Who will defend him when he is arrested on some other charge? Who will attend his funeral, even though he dies of extreme old age? Who will send gifts for his son's wedding?"

And Ward's heart sank. He knew that not one member of the Sa Tiam would touch the jewels of Vishnu, nor any part of them. He also knew why the thieves' guild existed: by refraining from dangerous loot, they gained tolerance for minor ravages. Government is the same the world over.

Tsang Li's smile was kindly and regretful. He was about to call for tea, which would end the interview. Ward was murmuring compliments. The ancient Chinaman knew that even a foreign devil who could acquit himself according to the book of rites was a superior person.

And then the sleek servant entered, begging pardon for the intrusion. "Exalted and honorable master, an Arab named Mahmud begs leave to present his respects."

Ward's sharp glance and distinct interest were in violation of etiquette, but he said, "Your tea would be more savory if I took it after this visitor has departed."

Tsang Li's smile was a yellow riddle. He gestured toward a teak screen paneled with dragon embroideries. Ward backed toward it; and in another moment, Mahmud entered like a striking falcon.

He could not speak Chinese, but Tsang Li had serviceable Arabic. So Mahmud, despite his aversion to an eater of unclean pork, was somewhat mollified. Yet by Chinese standards, he was perhaps abrupt in coming to the point. Compliments exchanged, he drew a parcel from his *aba* and unwrapped it.

Ward, peeping through a crack in the screen, saw four-armed Vishnu, his great emeralds and blazing rubies all splendid in the glare of the cut-crystal chandelier. Its magnificence put to shame the descriptions that had filtered from Suez to Surabaya; this could be no less than the very loot that had cost a priest's life, and the lives of those slain in street fighting. The four arms of Vishnu seemed to menace the two who surrounded him, and Ward's heart began hammering.

Would Tsang Li, despite his saying about no well being deep enough for a stolen pagoda, buy the treasure? No doubt that the old Chinaman was amazed; that he had not expected this, though he may have suspected Mahmud of being Ward's competitor.

Ward was sweating. He could not buy from Tsang Li except at a price so high that no honest profit could be taken from returning the treasure. Neither could he seize it from Mahmud; such a breach of etiquette would follow him all over Asia. Where the Sa Tiam did not flourish, their cousins, the "Family of the Queen of Heaven," or the deadly Ghee Moon Society did.

But Tsang Li slowly shook his head. "Cousin of the prophet," he said, using titles to which the Arab had no right, "and pilgrim to the holy cities, I am too poor to buy this."

"Only a hundred thousand rupees," repeated Mahmud.

Fifty thousand would have taken it. Tsang Li delicately stroked his scholarly mustache. Ward's nails sank into his palms. Then he felt as though he had heard exalting music; that was when Tsang Li gently said, "Not at any price, O prince! Some one has deceived you. Those be not true rubies from Mogok, but *balas* of great beauty and little worth."

That was a deliberate affront, and Tsang Li had intended it as such. The Arab's face darkened, and the muscles near his ear twitched. He was beaten. But before Ward had fairly relaxed, or Tsang Li had picked his next phrase, they were both caught off guard.

Mahmud was quick as a striking cobra. *"Ya humar!* O thou pig and father of pigs and eater of pork!" His curved handjar flickered like summer lightning.

Tsang Li's cry ended in a futile gesture and a cough that brought up blood. Ward, kicking the screen over, was halfway across the room when servants came trooping in. One of them fired a pistol. Another ran to aid the master. They blocked Ward's charge, but he plowed through, scattering them right and left.

He hurled himself. Mahmud wheeled, drawing a second dagger. The first still jutted from Tsang Li's dove-gray tunic. Crouched, teeth white in a snarl, the steel licked out—but Ward, trying to sidestep, went down when a rug slipped beneath his tread.

The point glanced from his shoulder blade. The pain sickened him, but he knew that his wound was not bad. Teeth set, he lurched toward the window, and cleared the sill just too late to pin Mahmud to the ground.

They raced across the garden, but the lean, unwounded Arab had the advantage. His legs were longer, and fury was driving him. Rebuffed by Hampton—rebuffed by Tsang Li—his rage had exploded. Each had affronted him, called him a fraud. Ward, desperately pursuing, understood it all: Hampton, coming to Moulmein to buy the emerald Vishnu, had unwittingly kicked the vendor out! And those men whom Win had described as being marked with the trident of Vishnu were priests, warning Hampton.

The Arab's stride broke as he hurdled a pond. He barely scaled the wall before Ward dropped after him, and into the street. But the half darkness was alive with moving figures. Robed men in massive turbans blossomed up like tombstones in a Moslem graveyard. Sikh policemen, cropping out of the dark alleys they had been patrolling, came forward on the run, drawn by the shrieks of Tsang Li's gatekeeper.

The howling Hindus swept down on Ward and the fugitive. The clamor drowned his voice. Feet belabored him; and hands probed his pockets. But before he went down, he caught a glimpse of Mahmud, darting snakelike through the press. Incredibly, the Arab had escaped!

When the thick-headed Sikhs finally kicked things into a semblance of order, the Hindus shouted Ward down, and swore that he had been clutching the Vishnu treasure as he cleared the wall. And the bearded policemen were convinced that when Tsang Li died of his wounds, their captive would face murder charges.

But, very oddly, the Hindus, whose incredible bungling had prevented the capture of Mahmud and the treasure, somehow vanished on the way to the station. Thus there were no witnesses against Ward when he faced the sergeant. The Hindus, having picked the wrong customer, saw no reason for bragging about it. But they would seek him privately, to redeem their two failures.

Chapter IV

The police barely concealed their disappointment at not finding weapons on Ward's person. He heard the Sikhs swearing in Punjabi that certain Hindus had accused him of having the emerald Vishnu in his possession; but from lack of complaining witnesses, the sergeant had to center on the attack on Tsang Li.

It was a heart-breaking hour before the old Chinaman's major-domo came to the station to exonerate Ward. His story was that a fanatic Arab had broken into an interview between the master and his American friend, and that Ward had valiantly pursued the slayer. There was not a whisper of the Vishnu loot; and since Ward himself had stoutly denied ever having seen the treasure, there was no contradiction of evidence to warrant his detention.

29

The case against him slowly crumpled. The deputy commissioner, who had been routed out of his club, came into the private office, frowning and tugging his straw-colored mustache.

"Ward," he snapped, "we've watched you for the past few years, all over Malaya and Burma. We've never found anything wrong with you. But by some damnable coincidence, you're always Johnny-on-the-spot when there's trouble. Either you did have the temple loot—you and the late Tsang Li—and it was passed to a confederate, or else it's just the skittishness of the natives doing you a blasted injustice."

"That's right, sir," was Ward's unruffled answer. "A blasted injustice. I'd have been armed, wouldn't I, if I'd been gunning for loot?"

The official snorted. "That's all, Ward. And if by any chance you are not on the level, better make good use of this fluke."

"Good evening, sir," Ward said. "And thank you kindly."

But he knew that being exonerated did not relieve him of suspicion. Ever since his return from the Shan Hills, he'd been conspicuous by reputation, if not by sight. And official notice would play hell; he'd have a C.I.D. man on his heels from now on. That meant that if he should track down Mahmud, he'd be nailed the moment he seized the loot—and be convicted of theft, as well as of murdering the priest who had died defending the treasures of his god.

When he reached the street, two Chinese were waiting. One was Tsang Li's son, Tsang Yat; the other was the major-domo. The former said, "I am grateful for your attempt to aid my revered parent. His *tong* brothers will avenge his death, but they will wait until you have fulfilled your mission."

"Thank you," acknowledged Ward. "I shall no longer stay at the address I gave your highly enlightened and very learned parent. It is possible that you will not recognize me the next time we meet."

"Wisdom drips like pearls from your mouth," said Tsang Yat. "You anticipated my advice."

And when he was alone, Ward telephoned Ling Fu, to whom he gave certain instructions. Then he was connected with Marley Hampton's suite. He said to Win, "You were more than right this morning. But from the looks of things, I'm suspected of carrying the ball. So your father shouldn't be in any danger, unless he asks for it. And I'm sorry, but I can't dine with you for another day or so." Then, before she could question him, he added, "Read the morning paper carefully and you'll understand."

He met Ling Fu in the Chinese cemetery at the head of Washerman Street. And there, in the walled enclosure where gilt inscribed tombstones marked the graves of Chinese buried until their bones could be exhumed for shipment back to their ancestral cemeteries, Ward stripped down and put on the secondhand garments which Ling Fu had purchased at the all too appropriately named "louse bazaar."

When he emerged from the cemetery, he appeared to be a Syrian Arab. His grayish eyes were not inconsistent with his pose; neither was his nose entirely wrong. And juice from several bottles of pickled walnut—the British sahibs import them from London as an accompaniment to curry—stained his skin. It was all very nicely done, except that his scalp had been nicked in a dozen places when Ling Fu shaved his head, as befits a Moslem.

Presently he was creeping up an odorous alley whose mouth gaped at the entrance of the Vishnu Temple. Somewhere inside a taper cast a wavering light. There was no outward sign of life, yet the shadows of the temple were vibrant with animation that was unseen and unheard; the great pile of ornately carved masonry seemed sentient, waiting to swallow up and destroy.

For him to enter in the guise of an Arab would be as perilous as though he came as a white man; but Ward, now that he knew Mahmud's part in the game, was using his disguise for more than avoiding observation by the local police. By offering himself as bait, there was a possibility of playing hide and seek with the Hindus who had been waiting for him at Tsang Li's house. He was playing for a chance to draw the pursuit from Mahmud, and to himself.

The Hindus, having failed to find the treasure in Ward's possession, had, of course, decided that the Arab must have it. Thus, if Ward's approach worked, he would deflect their pursuit and so win time enough to pick up Mahmud's trail.

"And that," he told himself, as he worked his way to the temple entrance, "will just about level off for the way they tried to pin me to the back of my rickshaw!"

The humid air of the courtyard was sweetened by the lingering fumes of incense, but the reek of sacrificial blood became heavier as he skirted the wall. It was like the stench of a slaughter house. It reminded him that those dark gods craved blood; that when Vishnu returned to recreate the world, his white stallion would be red to the fetlocks.

He heard a subdued, chilling shiver of bronze. It was the muted, eerie clang of a gong in some deeply buried crypt, and the shuddering sound sent frost racing down his spine. A vagrant breeze brought faint rustlings from the leaves of the jasmine in the corner, but the sweetness that swirled toward him was still foul with scent of stones soaked with the blood of centuries. Somewhere, men were chanting. It was more like the somber mutter of drums than human voices.

Someone was intoning a *mantra* in the sacred Sanskrit. The priests were in conclave. And later, they would discuss what they had learned of the night's disturbances; nor would they have missed much. Ward snaked forward. If he could add their suspicions to his own, he would again have the lead—unless a knife first found him or Mahmud.

Invading the holiest crypt of the temple was an insane venture, but Mahmud had done it, and returned. Ward brushed the sweat from his forehead, licked his dry lips, and paused for breath before skirting the lotus-dotted pool—

Then, without any warning, soft, clinging folds of silk enveloped, him. The gloom behind him blossomed with cunning hands. Wiry and desperate as he was, Ward had not a chance to struggle. The dismaying unexpectedness of the attack, coming from behind him, from ground he had just explored, had for an instant robbed him of the split-second swiftness that might otherwise have leveled the odds. But iron fingers sank into his muscles, probing nerve centers and constricting them so that he was paralyzed. Thumbs sinking into his carotid artery made his senses reel. Twenty seconds or less would bring certain death—

As roaring blackness enveloped him, and he himself seemed to be an immeasurable distance from his body, the irony of it stabbed him like a hot blade. He was dying from that same relentless hold which Ling Fu had tried to teach him. It leaves not a mark on the victim—

The next sound he heard was a singsong voice. Before he realized that he was back in the alley that faced the temple entrance, he understood what Tsang Yat was saying, "Esteemed friend, this violence was necessary. We could not risk startling you. You might have cried out in surprise, or perhaps killed some of us."

"The Honorable Tsang Yat," Ward's servant interposed, "had extremely up-to-date statistics. So this awkward person recommended publishing same, with speed and privacy."

A gulp of *ng ka pay* fairly cauterized Ward's tonsils, but the pungent stuff revived him, and he listened to Tsang Yat continue, "One of my late father's servants was quick-witted enough to follow the Arab, while you were wrestling with those Hindus outside our gate. But he could not enter the house. And it is forbidden for peaceful Chinese to incriminate their *tong* by being involved in suspicion of temple robbery. Later, when the loot is restored, there will be dealings with Mahmud."

From the viewpoint of the Sa Tiam society, this was reasonable enough. To intervene at present would compromise the entire guild of thieves, whose protector and legal advisor Tsang Yat had become; but to kill Mahmud, later on, would be purely a family matter, and thus entirely ethical. So Ward listened, and finally he said, "Ling Fu, I'll handle this myself. You better stay out. It's just me plus one Arab."

Chapter V

Mahmud's house was near the Alir Mosque, not far from the Kyaikpane Wharf. To the right, as Ward headed north, were several rice mills; to the left, the government timber depot, where patient elephants would, at dawn, begin their daily task of stacking teak logs that came floating down the Salween. But now there was no activity, only a treacherous gloom above which towered the gilded peak of the Kyaikpane Pagoda. Beyond it were the innumerable masts of Chinese junks, house boats, swift Malay proas. These Ward could not see as he advanced, but yet he knew that they were there; he could smell them, their cargoes and their inhabitants, and the salty tang of the tidal inlet that meandered through that low-lying, marshy ground.

He identified Mahmud's place by the adjoining rice warehouse. And, empty-handed, Ward made his first move against a man desperate enough to slay Tsang Li in his own reception room. Shadow-silent, he scaled the palm-stake palisade of the warehouse. Somewhere, a watchman was snoring. But the corrugated iron roof did not betray Ward's progress. Presently, he was creeping along the crest of a stone wall, whose height commanded the Arab's squat, two-storied home.

There Ward listened, strained his eyes; but his nostrils warned him of his peril. The stale, acrid odor of hashish blended with the smell of the house. No wonder Mahmud was savage as a tiger, insanely daring in theft and slaying. While he might now be in a comfortable stupor, he might equally well have senses abnormally sharpened, and be deadly as half a dozen normal men.

It was only Ward's grim persistence that drove him on, inch by inch. Once accustomed to the gloom, he perceived the parapet of the roof top, which he could reach by letting himself down the face of the wall until he had scarcely more than a foot to drop.

For a moment he clung there, startled by some one's dry, racking cough. The sound seemed to come up from the trapdoor that opened from the flat roof to the second-story rooms. No mistaking the cough of a hashish smoker.

It was repeated. Ward's knees bent as he absorbed the drop. If Mahmud was sod-denly drugged, searching the house would be easy. But concentration on the apart-ments below distracted Ward from the snares of his own level. A cord, stretched an-kle high, almost tripped him. He was still recovering when earthenware shattered to bits in the courtyard below. He had stumbled across a primitive burglar alarm.

But what cut off his retreat was the woman whose scream stabbed the darkness. He recoiled from the trapdoor just as a broad-bladed parang whipped by and clashed against the parapet. The steel flicked his robe, and the air stirred by its passing fanned his cheek. Ward groaned, pitched forward, and lay there gurgling and thresh-ing.

"Oh, dog and brother of a dog!" The girl was young, her voice tense with terror, and the shock of an apparently successful killing. A shudder rippled through her ex-ultation as she came nearer, reviling his religion and ancestors. "Pigs befoul thy grave and thy father's grave, thou profaner of a true believer's harem!"

He could have retreated. Her outcries had not aroused Mahmud. But that was not Ward's game. Once he fled, his quarry would be warned; nor was there any certainty that the loot was actually in this house. So he played his next card.

"*Ya sitti*! Praise Allah that the blood of one seeking sanctuary is not on thy head!" His voice was now normal, and not that of one mortally wounded. The girl recoiled, and in the perceptibly thinning darkness—the false dawn was at hand—he could just see the gleam of her great black eyes, the whiteness of her teeth, and the contours of her unveiled face. "Enemies hunt me. Where is Mahmud? Quick—tell me where he —"

Without waiting for her to recover, he plunged toward the trapdoor, staking all on one bold move.

"My father is—is—below."

"And hasn't heard this noise?" Ward turned his face so that he could not see her unveiled.

His speech, and his claiming sanctuary, which any Moslem may demand of an-other, gave her confidence. Mahmud's daughter struck a match, whisked a veil over her face, and regarded him over its edge. By the wavering flame Ward saw a jar of water, and a tray with fragments of half-eaten cakes of bread.

"Eat," she invited; not because she thought he was hungry, but because that morsel of food would make him a guest, and Mahmud's protected.

Unwittingly, she had thrown the issue squarely to him. He knew the Moslem code and respected it for the sake of many a true believer who had been his friend; and though Mahmud was a renegade, Ward could not put himself beyond the pale by ac-cepting the food of the man he was hunting.

"Not until your father invites me," he declined. Pride was in his voice and tone. The girl knew that this was not one who would deal with a woman. "Where is Mah-mud?"

"Come with me." She turned toward the stairs, and he followed. "But I fear his wrath if I awaken him. He is weary."

At the foot of the stairs she turned down a passage. He could barely distinguish her trailing white garments in the gloom. Then she halted. A hinge groaned. The girl said, "Wait—I will call him."

If Mahmud was as soddenly drunk with hashish smoke as his muttering indicated, he should be easy to handle. The girl's unexpected presence was a serious obstacle, but Ward was devising a plan to get Vishnu's loot out of cover, and without violating the laws of hospitality. As for Mahmud and the law—that was no concern of Ward's. Tsang Li's men would settle him if the police did not.

So he crossed the threshold, but confidence trapped him. In mid-stride, she thrust him between the shoulders and one bare foot kicked out to trip him. He lurched, recovered, but too late. The door slammed heavily, and a lock clicked.

Ward's laugh was low and bitter. His refusal of bread had aroused her suspicion, and here he was, caged until Mahmud sobered up enough to take things in hand himself. And if the criminal investigation department men had any clues that led to this house, it would be bad for Ward, if he lived long enough to be snared by them. Worst of all, Ling Fu would literally obey orders; the master had said it was to be a lone hand, and that settled the matter. Which is why Chinese are at once the best, and the worst of servants.

And as true dawn followed the false, Ward surveyed his prison. It was a stout-walled cubicle, and judging by the lurking scent of musk and sandalwood, it had once been part of some Arab's harem. The iron-barred window with its *jalousies* confirmed his opinion.

Moulmein was waking up. From afar he heard the trumpeting of elephants taking their morning bath, and the cries of their mahouts as they prodded the great beasts to work. Fishermen added their voices, and from the Alir Mosque the muezzin called true Moslems to prayer.

"*A-a-a-a-a-alahu Akbar! Al-l-l-l-lahu A-a-a-akbar!* God is most great! Come to prayer—prayer is better than sleep and—"

Somewhere, priests of Vishnu were greeting their god. And below, Mahmud was muttering and cursing. Otherwise, the house was silent. Ward, alternately tugging at the bars, then circling the room in search of some rafter he could dislodge—though both endeavors were equally futile—was wondering how an empty-headed captive would face a passably sober Arab who was murderously handy with a knife.

Leaning against the sill and wiping the sweat from his forehead, Ward glanced between the *jalousies* and toward the front of the house. The door opened, and Mahmud's daughter, basket balanced on her head, stepped out into the vague grayness. Her anklets tinkled as she went to market.

Ward was soon aflame with thirst. He had sweated himself dry and as the sun rose, its fierce heat made a furnace of the small, locked room, whose door kept the sea breeze from circulating.

His fingers were bleeding and riddled with slivers. Bit by bit, he was enlarging a chink between the withes which, laid athwart the ceiling joists, supported the layer of earth on which the roof tiles were set. He was not quite tall enough to reach from the floor. Perched on the sill, leaning inward as far as he could, every muscle was strained in keeping himself in position. Thus a task none too difficult under favorable circumstances was an almost useless misery; he could not apply his strength.

And what urged him on was that Mahmud's daughter remained away long after marketing time. His first thought was that she had gone for reinforcements to help her half-drugged father; but as that possibility dwindled, he struggled for release so that he could nail Mahmud and thoroughly search the house. His successive changes of strategy had each time gotten him further from his goal, but he had finally gained one move. The master of the house did not know that he had a captive.

But long before the day was done, Ward was dizzy from hunger and thirst. Mahmud cursing at his daughter's absence, stirred about below. At last, apparently finding food and drink, he settled down to sleep in hiding. He was prudently keeping out of sight until last night's violence became an old story.

* * * *

The sun set at last, and the slow return of coolness revived Ward. He was too weary even to curse her strategy. When he did think of it, he scarcely blamed her. And he envied Arab wit.

Then, as night settled, Ward saw men emerging from the shadows. The shape of their turbans identified them: Hindus, and they approached Mahmud's door. One knocked. There was no answer. Finally, one said in a low voice, "Let us in. Your house is surrounded. Let us in!"

Mahmud challenged. "Break in, and I'll slice you crosswise."

He could do that, and they knew that he would, if they rushed him. And in the meanwhile, there was no doubt that he could slip out and escape, no matter how many lurked in the shadows about the house. But the Arab's chances went a-glimmering when the spokesman of the Hindus said, "We know that you have Vishnu's treasure. That is why we set the police on that other meddler. And since you were stupid enough not to leave town at once, we have you—"

"Come and get it," invited Mahmud, "and the loot is yours."

His voice was like the low snarl of a panther about to strike. Ward, about to escape through the hole in the ceiling, paused long enough to hear what followed. A free-for-all would give him his chance, unless it drew the law.

"You are too anxious," mocked the Hindu. "We expected as much, seeing that we are no more anxious to meet the police than you are. So we seized Aminah, your daughter. Perhaps you've missed her?"

The vain fury of Mahmud's curses made Ward wonder if the Arab might not go amuck and attack them; but without doubt he anticipated what the speaker added, "Therefore, bring us the treasure, or she dies in a way you will not like."

Long silence. Then Mahmud said, "Allah curse thy father and his father! Sons of lewd mothers, what proof have you?"

"Her absence is enough. But if you doubt, we will leave her bracelet at your door." What followed was a muttering that Ward could not understand ; but he sensed that in giving Mahmud the address, the spokesman had instinctively lowered his voice. His farewell, however, was audible enough. "And if you make trouble or try to break in a knife will find her, at the first disturbance."

They left him with his wrath. It was wiser to parley with Mahmud in their rendezvous than in his house.

Chapter VI

Ward managed to squeeze through the irregular opening he had clawed and poked into the time-weakened roof. Now that he was an escaping prisoner, he had no qualms about the food and water he had declined when Aminah offered them: but he ignored the bread. There was time only for a gulp of water, and no more than a short one. But it refreshed hint, and so did the prospect of slipping up on Mahmud as he took the Vishnu loot from concealment.

With the emptied jar as his only weapon, Ward stole down the stairway. Once back at the level of his prison, he paused to listen. Mahmud was cursing, and in a good many tongues in addition to Arab. The fellow was talented. There were several Ward could not understand.

His progress to the ground floor was slower. A chink in the wall or a hole in the floor were the usual places of concealment. But when he reached the murky gloom of the lower apartment, there was no light except the glow of a pipe. Mahmud was smoking, taking gurgling draughts of hashish. He squatted on the floor, and Ward could just distinguish his hawkish face. The Arab groaned. "Aminah, in the hands of those infidels!" Then he spat and growled, "Allah blacken me if I don't rip their guts out!"

Only his white turban was visible as he set aside his hookah. He was stirring in the gloom. Steel gleamed dimly. He must be sheathing a dagger. He stalked toward the front of the house, and Ward crept breathlessly after him.

But Mahmud did not excavate in the front room. A hinge screeched, and he was on the street. His stride was fluent as a tiger's; and while Ward cautiously followed him, Mahmud did not look back. Despite the threat the Hindu renegades held over his head, they had not defeated that fierce Arab. Ward could sense that from his gait, and the hand poised on a dagger haft.

A small earthen pot was no weapon for the impending encounter, but Ward had nothing better. So he stalked his game toward the Alir Mosque. He was positive that Mahmud had not picked up any parcel in the darkness of his house. First a pipe had filled his hands, then steel.

Mahmud swaggered toward the arched entrance of the mosque, whose minaret towered over the water front. Within, burning wicks floated in several bell-mouthed glass bowls. The wavering oil flames sent long shadows chasing across the walls. Ward, huddled in the darkness between two closely spaced columns, watched Mahmud stride purposefully among beggars who lay snoring on mats spread here and there. The house of Allah is the poor man's house, and during the day, it is his club.

Mahmud passed the fountain in which a true believer must at least ceremonially cleanse himself before prayer. He had not even removed his shoes. And then, somewhat closing the gap between them. Ward knew that he had mistaken the Arab's reason for visiting the mosque. It was not to pray for his daughter's safety, not for vengeance.

Mahmud was kneeling in a far, dusky corner, but he did not face toward Mecca, nor was he making the familiar genuflections. There was the muted ring of steel, a *click-scrape-thump*. He was getting at something concealed in the masonry of the mosque, an ideal hiding place. Not even the law would lightly profane this place, and the Hindus who had trailed Mahmud—doubtless members of some sect who despised Vishnu as much as they did Allah—would be torn to small and ragged pieces if they as much as approached the sacred enclosure.

Ward lost sight of Mahmud for a moment, when he swiftly rose and ducked into the gloom of a colonnade. The unexpected completion of the probing had caught him off guard. His heart was thumping, and his teeth clenched as he considered the chance that his quarry might elude him. Then, making all the haste he dared, Ward emerged from the mosque. He caught a glimpse of Mahmud, silhouetted against the mouth of a narrow alley.

To slip up on Mahmud and smash the earthenware jar over his turban and then snatch the loot was no more hazardous than his previous maneuvers; but the Arab's daughter complicated things. Such a course would condemn her to death. Ward could scarcely do that out of necessity, much less for profit.

Other free lances might shrug it off by reasoning that she was just another Arab girl, and the daughter of a thoroughly worthless father; but Ward was squeamish about women, regardless of race. Though Aminah had neatly tricked him, he could not resent her loyalty and quick-wittedness in behalf of her father. Moreover, Ward had caught the despairing note in Mahmud's lurid oaths as he set aside his hookah, swallowed his avarice, and set out to extricate Aminah.

And knowing how deeply greed is burned into the heart of the average Arab, Ward could not remain unmoved by that ruthless fellow's sacrifice. Thus, as he trailed him, the American was racking his wits for some way of saving the girl's neck and also seizing the plunder.

But the next instant jerked Ward from thought to action. The Arab yelled as a patch of shadow detached itself from the gloom and for a moment masked his white turban. A descending knife glittered, and the alley echoed with wrathful Cantonese. Yet, despite the surprise, Mahmud was defending himself before he had fairly pitched to the ground.

Ward dashed forward, yelling at the top of his voice, "*Ya mumineen!* O true believers! Help, in the name of Allah!" He made that dark quarter ring as though a full-blown riot were in progress, and some of the beggars in the mosque, aroused from their sleep, heard the cries of a Moslem in distress and echoed it as they came reeling out toward the excitement.

Ward hurled the jar. It spattered to pieces against a wall. Mahmud's assailant broke away before the disguised American could close in. The Arab regained his feet, took a step, then collapsed ; but though he did not overtake his assailant, that made no difference. The fellow dropped, groaning and gurgling. His knife had bitten deep, but he had also eaten steel.

And as true believers came pouring into the alley, Ward was at Mahmud's side, supporting him as he said. "He is done, brother."

"There is no god but Allah," said the Arab. "*Ay, wallah!* Here is the slayer and the slain, and there is neither might nor majesty save in Allah, the merciful, the compassionate!"

His wound had sobered him. He heard Ward solemnly say, "Brother, all things come from him! Verily, power is his!"

Mahmud's bloody fingers relaxed from the dagger hilt and sank into Ward's wrist. Then be gasped, as robed figures closed in about them. "There is a parcel near me—I dropped it as I fell—swear that thou wilt take it—to—those who hold my daughter—Aminah—captive. It is the price of her life—"

"Where?"

"Deliver it—" said Mahmud.

"Allah will reward thee. And so—will my purse—and if the girl pleases you—you are a true believer—she is yours and—"

"Allah, by Allah, and again, by Allah!" Ward swore. "But where?"

The bloody foam that drooled from the Arab's mouth dripped down on Ward's hand. Mahmud was fighting for breath. The crowd of spectators, some carrying torches, were babbling and chattering. And the police were approaching on the run. But despite the confusion, he managed to understand what Mahmud coughed in his ear. It was an address on Great Pagoda Street.

Ward, under cover of lifting the dead man from the mire and setting him near the wall from whose angle his assailant had bounded, managed to snatch the parcel that Mahmud's robe had half concealed. He groaned, bewailed the shattering of his jar, cursed as he knelt on a sharp fragment—and managed to hide the package in his own sash. It was hardly larger than a cigar box.

And then the law closed in. The presence of the Moslems Ward had summoned kept the Sikh policemen from concentrating on him. He had obviously tried to save a true believer, yet he was no more involved than any of those others—all of which he had in mind when he gave the alarm.

Yet endless moments passed before he knew that he would not be jockeyed into the awkward position of star witness; that his incoherent, muddle-headed report made him blend into the crowd, neither more nor less than any of his outraged fellow's. But what clinched it all was the body of the Chinese assailant. Ward recognized the late Tsang Li's gatekeeper; and while the Sikhs who patrolled the warehouse district did not realize the significance of this, police headquarters would. Until then, it was just another case which death had conveniently closed.

Ward sighed his relief when, making the most of a chance, he unobtrusively slipped from the indignant throng. He had to work fast, before the identity of the dead Arab was broadcast, and all the mysterious, clashing factions of Moulmein's underworld interpreted the doubly fatal encounter.

"Tsang Li's gatekeeper," he reasoned, "lost face for admitting an assassin into the master's house. So, regardless of orders about postponing vengeance, this fellow struck. He must have been watching Mahmud's house. Damn lucky he didn't harpoon me by mistake—"

He headed for the mosque near the railway jetty. There he washed Mahmud's blood from his hands and garments, and ventured a look at the contents of the silk-wrapped parcel. It contained the miniature image of Vishnu, and its jewels were intact. He had a fortune in his hands—and also, a woman's life.

A freelance had no business with qualms. He had learned that in the Shan States. And this was a richer prize. But Ward's mind was made up when he set out for the house on Great Pagoda Street, leaning on a stout, staff-shaped stick he had picked up along the water front. Whether the Hindus recognized his imposture or not, there was more than a chance that they would try to knife him, just to get a dangerous character out of the way.

A rickshaw turned the corner and into Great Pagoda Street. A man in whites and a straw hat rode in it. Ward shrank into a doorway, just as a second rickshaw overtook it. By the dim light that came from a Chinese shop window, he recognized the passengers of both vehicles: Marley Hampton, overtaken by his daughter as his own driver slowed down to look for an address.

Hampton angrily exclaimed, "Win—what the devil are you doing here? Go back home!"

"I won't!" Her voice was low but tense. She leaned from her rickshaw to seize his arm. "Not unless you do, dad. I know what you're up to. You're crazy—you'll get killed—"

Hampton's heavy face tightened with wrath. "Win," he said, "you're a grown woman, but by Heaven—I'll—I'll—"

She recoiled from his expression, more than his half-striking gesture. She slumped wearily, and choked a sob. Hampton tossed her coolie a coin and a curse, ordered him away. Then he growled at his own man who moved on. But Win, suddenly regaining her spirit, halted her coolie and half hysterically cried after her father's advancing vehicle, "I know where you're going. I'll call the police—"

Then Ward slipped from cover, and before she could repeat the half-coherent threat that her father had either ignored or misunderstood, he was at her side. She froze, audibly gasped at the sudden apparition. The neighborhood was none too savory at that hour.

"It's all right," said Ward in English. "Go home. Win. I'll keep him out of a jam."

"Oh—Mr. Ward—Denis—" She could hardly believe her ears.

"Right. Go back. It's my party. And I'll finish it."

"But he'll be killed. So will you. I read all about what happened before you phoned me. You're reported as probably murdered, and—"

"I told Ling Fu to spread that," Ward improvised. "Now run along, please. And do pull yourself together." Then he said to her driver, in the vernacular, "Go by bright streets. I've got your license number, and I'll cut you lengthwise if any one says even a word to her on the way. The Winthrop, and quick!"

She could not understand, but the iron of his voice assured her, as it put fear into the coolie's heart. Like most of Moulmein, he had heard of an Arab who would rather mince flesh than words, and before she could say more, her rickshaw was on its way.

That left Ward to carry on. Dimly ahead of him he saw Hampton alight from his vehicle and dismiss the coolie. He was swallowed by a doorway near the one that Ward was seeking.

"That damn pig-headed pilgrim! He's asking for it. And he wouldn't, if he had half Win's sense!"

Chapter VII

The door Ward approached was shadowed by a deep archway. He knocked, and announced in Hindustani that mimicked Mahmud's voice, "I am here, and if you have harmed her, I will eat your hearts."

A hashish cough made it doubly convincing. The door creaked open. A palm-oil lamp flickered in a far corner. Wavering shadows obscured Ward's lace as well as the oily features of the two men who came forward to join the one who had admitted the dangerous caller. A slender Arab girl lay bound on the floor, in the light of the floating lamp wick. This must be Aminah, whom he had only seen passingly, by the false dawn. She was now unveiled, and a Hindu, squatting beside her, was ready to slice her throat with a broad-bladed kukri if she cried out, or her supposed father made a false move.

"Where is it?" demanded the spokesman, extending a pudgy hand.

Ward growled, "Let her speak first. Perhaps—Allah strike you dead—it were better for her to die, after being in your hands!"

Aminah's eyes widened. She had sensed the false note, and knew already that this was not Mahmud. Ward half exposed his parcel. There was an instinctive craning of necks as he fingered the wrappings. Aminah's guard let his glance shift from his captive, and his kukri moved out of line.

That was when exposed rubies glowed redly in the dim light. Ward shot the statuette forward with a straight-arm move that launched it like a bullet. It smashed the girl's guard squarely in the face, so that blood from his forehead blinded him and the impact stunned him. Then he lunged between the three, who were too close for effective stabbing. He whirled, smacking his staff across a hand that darted forward with a knife. The blade skated across the hard-packed dirt floor, and a man howled from the pain in his shattered wrist. Aminah screamed, her supple body whipping like a serpent, so that the blind slash of her captor did not quite reach its mark.

Her bound legs upset the primitive lamp. The wick flared high, guttered out as Ward side-stepped a licking blade. He flailed his cudgel, and heard it snap in the dark. An inner door smashed open, just as one of his assailants tackled him in the dark, bearing him to the floor.

Light poured through the opening. Ward, kicking a bare foot into the stomach of the man who was crawling toward him with a dagger, saw Marley Hampton and two Hindus charging in. Their foreheads were marked with Vishnu's trident. Hampton's face was blank with alarm; he looked as though a rabble had suddenly burst into a board of director's meeting.

But the two whose triple-streaked brows identified them as devotees of Vishnu lost no time in getting into action. Ward, however, was quicker. He wrenched the knife from the grasp of his stiffened opponent, jerked clear of the one whose thrust was on the way, and leaped for the door.

They recoiled. Mahmud's reputation made them hesitate. And in the howling confusion, no man's voice could be distinguished. The American sidestepped before either could urge the other to take the lead. He seized the small table about which they had been sitting, and hurled it athwart them.

One went down, cracking his head against the jamb. And then there was a hammering outside, at the door through which Hampton must have entered. Heavy voices boomed in Punjabi ; a squad of Sikhs were breaking in. The other devotee of Vishnu yelled and turned on Hampton, whom he seemed suddenly to suspect of treachery, of having baited a trap.

They rolled into Aminah's prison before Ward could intervene. The street door was splintering under the attack of the police. Ward plunged into the darkness after Hampton and his assailant, and seizing the bolt of the connecting door, he jerked it shut. He slapped the bolt home just as the Sikhs charged into the adjoining house; and above the uproar, he heard English voices.

Ward closed in on Hampton and his assailant. The American's coat ripped. That was all he needed to pick one from the other. He hammered a hard fist into the Hindu's face, drove him end for end into a corner.

"Cut it out, Hampton! This is Ward! You're clear—get out—"

"How—what the hell—" Hampton groped, hearing the welcome voice of a countryman.

"Strike a match!"

Hampton groaned; from the adjoining building came the confused rumble of raiders' voices, Punjabi and English. They were at work at the connecting door. Then Hampton's match flared.

He was thoroughly shaken, and he clutched his side, where his coat had been ripped by a glancing knife—a long slash that could not be serious, as it must have grazed his ribs instead of sinking point-on.

"Get out!" growled Ward, "before you're pinched for being mixed up with the Vishnu treasure. Some one tipped the cops, and you're sunk. Give me those matches!"

"Where—how—Lord, they're hammering at the street door—"

"The window!" Ward boosted him to the sill. It was unglazed, and there were no bars. "Plow through. Maybe you'll make it—"

He struck a match. The emerald Vishnu lay near Aminah and the captor who had been knocked out when it bounced from his forehead. The girl had worked her wrists free of her bonds, but her ankles were still secured.

"Sahib," she cried, extending her hand. "Here—"

"They won't hurt you—it's the police," was Ward's answer. He ignored her appeal, snatched the temple loot, and headed toward the window.

But he had lost too much time, even in those scant seconds needed to get Hampton out of the way, and find the prize. The bolt hasp suddenly tore out, and the door crashed open. Flight was now hopeless; they'd jerk him from the sill, if they did not shoot him for resisting arrest or club him senseless.

Ward lurched face down, letting the statuette tumble as it would. It had barely come to rest against a half-conscious Hindu when flashlights blazed, and the police plowed in. Ward, faking exhaustion to gain a few seconds, saw that white officials had accompanied the raid, and that the sergeant, who had two nights previous questioned him at headquarters, was in charge.

"Find my father. Oh—they've killed him. I knew they would—"

That was Win Hampton. Ward now knew that instead of going back to her hotel, she had turned out the Moulmein police in force.

"They didn't," said Ward from the floor. "You must be mistaken, Miss Hampton. Your father isn't in this place at all. I came here to get the Vishnu temple loot from the man who had it."

And that English speech, coming from a battered Arab, won him the center of interest, until a Sikh caught the gleam of rubies near the man he was trying to boot to his feet.

"My word!" groped the sergeant, and it was echoed by a deputy commissioner's secretary. "That is the statuette that—"

Then Ward went into his dance. For lack of another few seconds, he had lost his prize. He laughed wryly as he concluded his story of having come from Penang to gamble his head against the chance of finding the treasure whose loss was keeping Moulmein a hotbed of racial and religious animosities.

"I had it," he concluded, "when Mahmud, the thief, was cut down by a servant of Tsang Li. But the dying Arab told me that his daughter's life depended on giving this bit of cut glass to the Hindus who had her prisoner, and I couldn't let her face the music."

"Too bad, Ward," consoled the secretary. "We're not authorized to pay you any reward, though I personally think you deserve it, even if your methods are—ah—highly irregular. And you may be sure the priests of Vishnu won't."

"Probably not." He grimaced, glanced about, and wondered why Aminah, whose ankles had been unbound, was so intently regarding him over the edge of her improvised veil. But he knew why Win Hampton's glance blended penitence and gratitude. "I'm holding the bag—a very empty one. But aside from thanks—which I might save up and find useful the next time I'm in a corner—I wish some one would tell me how those lads with Vishnu's hash mark on their foreheads fit into this, and why they're putting them in irons for trying to rescue their own property."

"I don't mind telling you," explained the secretary, "that this is more important than you realize. This Vishnu cult has for months been suspected of being hand in hand with that uncommonly troublesome Gadar group in India—the Independence party, you know. They need revolution money, and from Miss Hampton's remarks when she asked us to save her father, I'd judge that Vishnu's own priests were selling the god's jewels in what they considered a sacred cause."

That cleared up a lot. No wonder the priests of Vishnu had secretly conferred with Hampton in Penang. No wonder they had claimed the treasure had been stolen. That was a plausible way to account for the loss of the emerald Vishnu; though such a story would arouse his outraged worshipers to rioting, it at least would not expose the true motive. And Mahmud, seizing the god, had made their false story all too true!

"Denis," said Win Hampton, while the police were waiting to take him to headquarters for an official checking of his story, "I'm so sorry I spoiled your game. Will you ever forgive me?"

"Think nothing of it," Ward said with a blitheness he did not feel. "Aminah crabbed the business before you did."

The Arab girl, innocent of her father's crimes, was not a prisoner, though she also was bound for headquarters. Yet on the plea of thanking her benefactor, the man who had heard her father's last words, she approached Ward just as Win Hampton turned to rejoin the secretary.

"Sahib," she said, fingering a golden chain at her throat, "let me give you a present. Whatever my father said, we were not poor."

Ward could not wound Arab pride by refusing. "Damn it," he said in English, being somewhat embarrassed by a gift he did not want to take, "I guess I've got to."

"Right," said the white police officer, who had understood the girl's plea. "Why not?"

Aminah fumbled the chain. Ward stooped to pick it from the floor. As he rose, he felt her hand brush his pocket. The gesture, serpent swift and between them, could not have been seen by any of the spectators. He stepped back, held the golden links in his two hands, and commended her father to the mercy of Allah. Then he went with the police.

And it was an hour or two later before he learned what she had slipped into his pocket; her real gift, the one which she had not dared to keep to offer him later on.

It was Marley Hampton's wallet, blood-smeared, knife-slashed, and stuffed with a bale of large bills. Hampton's coat, torn and cut, had, during his break for the window, fallen near Aminah. That was what she had tried to offer Ward, and he had mistaken her cry and gesture for a plea for escape. A sahib's wallet, even though glimpsed by match light, had appealed to her quick eye as a rich find, though she could hardly have realized just how much it did contain.

"If I kept it all, it'd teach him a lesson." Ward grinned, heading for his hotel. "Gambling with the gods takes an expert. And he'd have been in a pretty mess, if he'd been nailed with temple loot in his hands."

Then he remembered that he had a dinner engagement with Win Hampton; so he compromised by deducting only his usual fee for getting a wandering deity back to his shrine.

KISS OF DEATH

Originally published in *Spicy-Adventure Stories*, November 1937, under the pseudonym "Hamlin Daly."

A courier had carried the letter on foot through the Malay jungle to the Tuan Besar mine. Ken Hartley's grey eyes narrowed as he recognized the familiar script and the New York postmark. His glance shifted to the photograph on the living room wall.

Why the devil was Irene Byrne writing now, after all these months? Why had they quarreled in the first place? Each time he tried to destroy her picture, those smiling eyes reminded him of kisses by moonlight. He cursed wrath-fully and opened the letter.

Irene, he read, had for the past year been secretary to Carlton Forest, vice-president of Transpacific Industries, Incorporated.

> "...*Forest is on his way to the Malay States to corner all the little mining concessions and plantations. I don't know how he's going to do it, but be on guard...*"

She still cared enough to warn him—but not enough to hint that he could stage a comeback.

The snarl of the dogs brought him to his feet. He heard a woman in the compound, breathless and terrified. Ali, the labor foreman, was trying to question her in Malay. Hartley seized a flashlight and bounded to the veranda.

The girl was uncommonly lovely, a glamorous, dark-eyed creature. A crepe slip hung in tatters to a slender, amber-tinted body. Her black hair streamed to her hips, half veiling pert breasts that peeped from the remains of her only garment. She was barefooted.

Hartley's long months of loneliness claimed their tribute. His blood raced at the sight of those sleek hips and shapely legs.

"Bandits!" she gasped. "Benson's plantation—!"

Ali stepped aside. The girl crumpled, a pathetic huddle of thorn-raked flesh. Hartley carried her into the house. She was warm and soft and clinging. It was all he could do to keep his mind on his neighbor's peril. A slug of brandy gave her command of herself. She was Dolores Wong, Mrs. Benson's Eurasian maid: a new one, he thought, though he rarely saw his distant neighbors.

"They raided the plantation—I escaped to get help—hurry—!"

"Ali, saddle up! Turn out the mine crew!" commanded Hartley. Then, to Dolores, "I know the way. You'll be safe here."

He thrust on his boots, seized cartridge belt and rifle, and bounded across the compound. There he mounted his long-limbed chestnut and galloped down the wagon trail that wound through the jungle.

Half an hour later he reined his winded horse at the crest of a knoll. Down in the valley he saw a lurid glow.

The planter's house was ablaze. The whiplash crackle of a sporting rifle answered the boom of muzzle-loading *jezails.* A horde of dark figures was swarming toward the palisade that surrounded the house.

Ali and his men clattered up the slope. Hartley yelled and charged on alone; but as the firing ceased, he knew that he had arrived too late.

The raiders were rushing the compound gate. Benson had run out of ammunition.

A woman screamed, just once. Hartley savagely spurred his chestnut gelding. Leaning across the beast's neck, he hosed the straggling bandits with lead. They wheeled to return his fire.

Slugs nicked him, spears raked him, but he was going through. There might be a chance. Then his horse wavered, pitched in a heap—dead. Hartley flung himself clear. His pistol was empty. He jerked his carbine from its holster. He fired from the shelter of his dead beast. Seeing that he was alone, the bandits closed in.

He leaped up, firing from his hip. The hail of slugs beat them back; but he had no time to shove home a second clip. A long *parang* whistled down to split his skull. He struck it aside with the smoking barrel. He whirled the carbine, smashing the butt across a bandit's head. It became a desperate slaughter by torchlight—

And then Ali and his men emerged from the clearing, yelling and shooting. That turned the tide. Hartley brushed the blood from his eyes and leaped into the compound. The raiders were in full flight. The Malays were cutting down the stragglers.

Hartley found Benson and his wife. The planter was hacked to pieces. The blonde woman near him still held an emptied pistol. Her other hand was clenched as if still trying to pluck the spear that projected from her breast. She was young, and shapely…like Irene…though Hartley had never seen as much of Irene as he now saw of that woman whose gauzy night gown was blood-stained and smoke-soiled. Horror mocked beauty.

Hartley carried the victims out into the open. It was only then he noticed that the raiders were Chinese. And when his victorious men returned to plunder the fallen looters, the tragic evening presented another riddle.

Each bandit carried with him three brass coins wrapped in red paper, and a square of red silk inscribed in Chinese.

Hartley mounted a laborer's pony. Ali followed, bringing the bodies of the planter and his wife on a bamboo litter.

They had scarcely reached the mine when the earth shook, pitching Hartley's nag to its knees. There was a heavy, sullen rumbling. Flame and nitrous fumes poured from the shaft. A blast had demolished the mine entrance. Falling rock spattered about him.

He dismounted at the powder magazine. The lock had been broken. It was empty.

"Good God!" he groaned. "That's curtains!"

Unless Hartley could prove that the blast had not been the result of storing illegal quantities of dynamite in the drifts, the Warden of Mines would have to cancel his lease. But how prove his case? The ruin spoke for itself.

Asia was in revolt. First a planter, then a miner.

Once in the living room, he slumped into a chair and poured himself half a tumbler of brandy. His head was whirling. He ached from a dozen raking cuts.

He heard a stirring behind him. He turned. Dolores was emerging from the hall. She smiled somberly and said, "I heard. But you tried to save them."

Hartley laughed bitterly.

Dolores seated herself on the arm of his chair. She wore borrowed Malay finery now, and her hair was piled high on her head.

"There's something odd about that raid." He caught her arm. "Tell me—did Mr. Benson have any trouble with Chinese laborers? What are these red silk tickets and coins?"

She shook her head.

Could this be part of Forest's campaign to rout out small concessions?

"Did anyone try to buy Mr. Benson's plantation?"

"How should a servant know his business?"

He poured himself another drink. The brandy burned into his black mood. He began to remember that a man's life wasn't made up entirely of mining. The woman who leaned against him was young and fragrant. She was half white, at least; and Hartley was beaten and lonely.

He drew her closer. Her gasp forced her breasts against him. They were firm and vibrant, reminding him of Irene, of what the jungle isolation had withheld.

For a moment her eyes widened. She tried to evade his embrace. But when he kissed her full on the mouth, she relaxed. Her lids drooped. He felt the sudden pounding of her heart. Her lips were warm and hungry now. The next kiss was long and clinging. She was trembling, and her breath came in short gasps...

Dolores slipped to her feet and took his hand. She knew her way about the house. But Hartley carried her in his arms.

* * * *

Dawn, and the splashing of water ladled from the earthen jar in an adjoining bathroom awakened Hartley. Presently Dolores entered his room, fresh and radiant. By daylight he could see more clearly where her soft flesh had been raked by thorns as she fled from the plantation.

Dolores had arrived barefooted—*yet her feet were not marred or bruised*!

He caught her arm, wrenched her bodice half off.

"Damn funny the thorns skipped all the soft spots! And your feet—they're too small for any *ayah* that runs around without shoes."

Her color faded. She ran to the door. There she halted, tense and desperate.

"By Allah, *tuan*!" rasped Ali, bounding from the living room. "Thou hast sharp eyes—"

Dolores screamed. Hartley leaped to the doorway. Ali was reaching for his heavy knife. No chance to stop him.

Hartley lunged for his pistol. The blaze of powder blended with the flash of steel. The knife was blasted from the wrathful Malay's grasp!

"She's worth more alive than dead!"

Hartley slapped her into a corner. "Who sent you to trick me away from the mine?"

She lay huddled on the floor, moaning and quivering. "Can't talk, eh? All right, Ali. Maybe you were right. But take her outside to do the job. Don't want blood on the floor."

The hard-bitten Malay grinned, and retrieved his knife.

"Don't let him kill me!" she pleaded. "It's the Triad Society—trying to force mine and plantation owners out of the country—so an American—Carlton Forest—can buy up all the properties—they abandon. Those red silk squares are membership certificates."

Hartley saw how he had been tricked.

But for hard riding, he would not even have had a chance to fire those futile shots in defense of the besieged planter. Dolores had skillfully timed her arrival so that the other party of raiders could stealthily destroy a place they could not capture by force.

His only move was to go to Singapore and convince the Warden of Mines that the blast had not resulted from criminal carelessness. Then land on Forest!

"Ali, pack up at once. This woman is going along."

* * * *

It was forty miles to the head of the highway, and the village where Hartley had stored his car. That meant two days wallowing through the jungle.

At the end of the first day's march, Ali led Dolores to Hartley's tent. She could not escape, alone and barefooted, into the jungle.

"Allah forgive me, *tuan*," he apologized. "But she has hounded me all day. And you forbade me to slice her lengthwise."

She was an Eurasian, scorned alike by European and full-blooded native. The world forced her kind into trickery. Hartley was half sorry for her.

"All right?" he snapped. "Now what?"

"The Triad Society will kill me, even if I am in the hands of the police."

"Am I supposed to cry about it?"

"Ken—I'm terribly sorry. I didn't know they were going to murder those people. I didn't know you—that I'd like you the way I do—."

Her penitence was getting under his skin. He remembered those kisses and soft whispers in the dark. "I can't let you get away with it. That makes me an accessory after the murder."

"But you could forget it until we get to Singapore. You're the only one who's ever been nice to me."

"Well..." He hesitated.

She turned toward the lamp and blew it out. She fingered the edge of her sarong. It seemed to slip, then lingered, but it would take little to make it cascade about her ankles. He could just distinguish her warm contours in the gloom. Her bosom was a shapely blur and her legs gleamed in a vagrant moonbeam...

He tried to thrust her away, but a resilient curve tricked him. He cursed his folly, and drew her closer.

If she insisted on his being affectionate though she knew he had full knowledge of her treachery, then putting her under guard in the morning—

"I love you." She laced her arms about him. "They'll kill me, anyhow. I only wish..."

47

"Yes?" He could no longer fight off this jungle madness, with her fluttering breath so warm on his face.

"I wish…you could *kiss* me to death…" she murmured.

He'd never heard of such a sentence, but he tried…

* * * *

Later she smiled and nestled close for a moment in parting.

"Tell Ali the prisoner is ready. Didn't I promise you I'd not try to beg off?"

He rode at the head of the wagon train. He wanted to get as far from her as he could.

His problem, however, was solved that evening. Dolores was gone. On the bottom of the baggage cart was Hartley's penknife, and the withes she had clipped from her ankles and wrists.

"The damn' little tramp!" he growled. "That's why she wanted to be kissed to death!"

And when he checked up he found that the brass coins and squares of red silk were gone. Not a bit of evidence to back his theory! He now had a pretty story to tell the Warden of Mines! With Forest's powerful opposition, Hanley was well out on a limb.

Instead of resting in the village, he removed his car from storage and began the long drive to the railway.

* * * *

Upon arriving in Singapore he made a rapid tour of the leading hotels. Forest was at the Wellington. Hartley registered there, then called on the Warden of Mines.

Mr. Blount-Quinby was coffin-faced and skeptical.

"Absurd! The Triad Society has been suppressed for a dozen years. Now, if you only had that Eurasian girl and those certificates. There's been too much careless handling of explosives all over Malaya. But we'll investigate, and you will benefit by whatever the commission finds in your favor."

An epidemic of accidents? The Triad Society now seemed part of a fake to hide Forest's hand.

Hartley returned to his hotel and bad his luggage transferred to a room across the hall from Forest. He left the door just ajar and waited.

Presently a tall, ruddy man in tropicals emerged. Hartley had seen enough news reel views of Forest to recognize him.

As Forest stepped into the elevator, Hartley phoned the desk.

"Send the valet up to get the clothes I laid out. Have them back before I return for dinner. Right away. No, of course I can't wait to let him in!" He gave Forest's room number and hung up.

Presently a Chinese "boy" was at Forest's door. He turned the pass key in the lock. Hartley's flying tackle helped him over the threshold. One gasp, and the Chinese was silenced by a popping fist.

Forest had a luxurious suite. The sitting room contained a desk and a portable typewriter. Hartley pounced on a well filled brief case.

He fumbled with the catch. Taking the stuff would warn Forest. Better go through it, and leave the contents intact.

An instant later he realized his error. A pistol prodded his back.

"Raise your hands!" A woman was behind the gun. Her voice was flat and tense. "Now step to the telephone and say exactly what I tell you."

Sweat trickled down his forehead. This would finish him in Malaya. Someone else was spying on Forest; but Hartley would take the rap.

He lifted the receiver. He waited for her next order. From the corner of his eye he saw a slim chance. He side kicked, knocking over a tabouret and bottle of Scotch. Tray and glass clattered to the floor.

She started. The pistol shifted. As Hartley whirled, a jet of flame seared his ribs; but he caught her wrist. The little .25 dropped from wrenched fingers. Hartley stared. The girl returned it. Recognition was mutual.

"Irene—for God's sweet sake—!"

"Ken—" Her laugh was hysterical. "Since when have you gone out for house-breaking?"

"Sit down. While I tell you things. And ask you a few. About your letter."

"When I wrote, I didn't know he'd have me come along—"

"Kind of clubby, hanging around his rooms, eh?"

Irene's lovely face flushed. "This is a four room suite. I was coding some cables when you broke in."

The Chinese was reviving. Irene convinced him he'd gotten the wrong number, and a five dollar note clinched that. Then she listened to Hartley.

"Let's go into my room," she interrupted, leading him through the suite.

Irene's things were there. And she wasn't wearing a negligee.

"So I'm on the spot," he concluded. "What are his plans?"

"I can't sell him out," she protested. "I know he's not behind those murders—"

"Hell of a friend you turned out to be!"

"Ken, darling. Let's not quarrel," she pleaded. "I'm so glad to see you—"

"You act like it." He thrust her from him.

"Ken—" Her arms evaded his repulse and closed about him. "Do be reasonable. Don't you see, I just can't."

He compromised by drawing her to the couch beside him. He bent over and kissed the hollow of her throat. She tried to break away, but only succeeded in hitching her skirts well over her knees. He caught a glimpse of white flesh above her hose tops, and the froth of lace.

He presently found that he could hold Irene with one arm. Her protests were now inarticulate. If her heart didn't stop pounding, it would hammer something through her gown...judging from what was pressing his chest. His kisses smothered her objections. She was quivering now, and panting, with emotion.

* * * *

"That brief case," she whispered, a long time later, "oh, help yourself. I've missed you so—"

Hartley stepped into the front room; but he had scarcely opened the briefcase when a key grated in the door. He bounded toward the clothes closet. He made it just as Forest entered the room.

"Irene!"

The man glanced about, peeled off his coat.

49

She emerged, drawing together the edges of her negligee. Her knees were dimpled, and there was an entrancing glimpse of white, between the folds of that froth of chiffon that clung to her hips.

"I'm going to call on an important official," said Forest. "Come along to draw up the contract when we decide the terms. Can you be ready by the time I've changed?"

His hand closed on the knob of the clothes closet.

"Must we go tonight?" she sighed, releasing the edges of the blue chiffon. Forest forgot the doorknob. When Irene sighed, she made a job of it. The lift of her bosom was—

Just revealing enough to set him on fire.

"I'm blue and homesick," she murmured.

"Poor little girl—"

Forest caged an armful. But he could not see that Irene's lips moved soundlessly as she looked over his shoulder. Hartley however did. He slipped from cover.

As he moved, he caught a glimpse of Forest's free hand. Though the sway of Irene's hips was faked, it thoroughly burned him. He tripped over the bottle on the floor. It clattered against the brass tray.

Forest whirled. His glance included the opened brief case.

"So that's why you suddenly got playful! Lucky I got wise to you before you learned something important, you damn'—"

"And you're another!" flared Hartley. The repartee wasn't so heavy, but his fist was.

"You're fired!" croaked Forest, scrambling to his feet.

"There's a job waiting across the hall," chuckled Hartley. "Let a bell hop move your luggage."

She followed him. But when the door closed behind her, she flung herself across a divan and sobbed. "Ken, we *are* in a jam! You should have left. Now he can identify you."

"Second guess is usually best," he ruefully admitted. "But the way he was fooling around distracted me. Anyway, where was he bound for?"

"Probably Hong Wu's residence," she answered. "The sultan's financial secretary. Why?"

"Something's rotten, or he'd not have piped down so quietly. He should have hollered about sneak thieves—get it?"

She did. Hartley headed for the door.

He casually strolled out a side exit, then walked around to the rental cars parked at the main entrance.

"Wait here," he instructed the driver.

* * * *

Hartley was reckless and desperate. No use trying to evade the law. Hiding or slipping out of Singapore Island is impossible for any but natives. Hartley had to make his case in a hurry, or else—

Half an hour later, Forest emerged; and hailed a rental car. Hartley's chauffeur followed.

Forest headed out toward Moulmein Road, beyond the gas house. That was odd. Hong Wu lived east of town. Maybe Irene had been mistaken. Lucky he had tailed

Forest instead of going directly to his supposed destination.

Hartley ordered his driver to snap off the headlights. They would betray him in the darkness.

For half a mile he tailed Forest. Then came a screech of brakes, followed by a crash of metal and the splintering of wood. Forest had cracked up.

Hartley heard a babble of voices, then a yell. Black figures were silhouetted against the headlight glow of the stalled car. Steel gleamed. A man in white bounded to the highway: Forest, attacked by natives.

"Step on it!"

But Hartley's chauffeur whipped the car about. Hartley jammed his pistol against the fellow's back. That straightened him out. He tramped on the gas.

Forest was running and making a job of it. A streak of steel flashed over his shoulder. He stumbled. Hartley leaned out to fire at the assassins. The chauffeur saw his chance and swung the car into the ditch. The impact flung Hartley over the front seat. The door swung open, piling them both into the swamp. A kick knocked Hartley's pistol from his grasp.

No time to dive for it. He snatched a the iron from the floorboards and scrambled to the road.

Forest was surrounded. He had picked up a club and was flailing it about.

Hartley, bounding into action, bent his iron across a skull cap. A hurled *kris* grazed his shoulder. Forest was down but still fighting. Hartley ploughed home, parrying a stab and hammering home with his fist. He knocked a Malay end for end. Then he lunged, his shoulder driving in like a battering ram—

But not in time to check the *kris* that pinned Forest to the road. The surviving raiders fled. Their work was done.

Hartley had instinctively rushed to defend a white man assailed by natives. Now he realized what a calamity Forest's death was. At least a month must elapse before Transpacific Industries could send another agent to Malaya. Until then, Hartley could not continue his quest for evidence to offer the Warden of Mines; but desperation prodded his wits.

He searched Forest's pockets. He removed a thick manila envelope. In the back seat of the car which had crashed headlong into a carabao cart, he found a briefcase. By the glow of a surviving parking light he scanned the contents.

"Got it! Better than trailing Forest—*I'll impersonate him!*"

The letter of introduction indicated that the sultan's financial minister did not know Forest.

He set out on foot. His chauffeur had fled. At the fringe of the native quarter he purchased a fresh suit of tropicals. He could not risk returning to his hotel.

Presently he hailed a car and headed for Hong Wu's palace.

A Chinese servant admitted him. The Honorable Hong would be pleased to see Mr. Forest at once.

A moon-faced dignitary in dove gray silk received Hartley. For half an hour they exchanged compliments. Then the American played his cards. They had to be good, and before Forest's death was discovered.

"Honorable Hong, my unworthy corporation authorizes me to bid three million dollars," said Hartley.

Hong Wu held out for five. They finally agreed to split the difference.

"Since we agree, Elder Brother, let us draw up the papers."

Reasonable, but that sunk Hartley. His hasty scrutiny of Forest's papers would not carry him through such a test. Then he snatched at his only chance.

"But before we do that, Honorable Hong, tell me how His Highness, the Sultan proposes to confiscate all those small leases without running afoul of the British Government?"

All he needed was the answer to that query.

"Ah…that *is* relevant," admitted Hong Wu. "I will ring for my secretary! Be pleased to send for yours. My car is at your disposal. While they are drawing up the papers, I will explain. The Sultan has arranged everything. Your company need not worry."

He tapped a small gong, then gestured toward a telephone. Hartley stepped to the instrument. With Irene as a witness, it would be easy to convince the Warden of Mines. He had it in a bag!

He called his own room by number, not name. Irene answered. She recognized his voice. His claiming to be Forest left her puzzled, but she risked no questions. She sensed that a heavy game was on.

"Very well, then, Miss Byrne. Be ready when Mr. Hong's car calls!" he commanded, and hung up.

"And now," said the Honorable Hong, "kindly raise your hands."

His pistol covered Hartley. Half a dozen coolies emerged from behind the dragon-blazoned draperies. Something had slipped!

Hartley ducked behind a table. Hong Wu's shot shacked into the wall. Hartley catapulted his barricade athwart the rush of coolies. He flung himself toward the door.

It was bolted; and the rush overwhelmed him. They trampled and booted him to the floor. Strong hands wrenched his limbs. Heavy bodies knocked him breathless. Finally they held him upright, battered beyond resistance.

"Very clever imposture, *Mr. Hartley,*" mocked Hong. He turned toward an inner door and said, "That is the name, isn't it?"

"Just as I told you," answered a woman: Dolores Wong. "But though Forest's secretary warned him, this is more than I expected."

For a long moment Hartley eyed the Eurasian girl he had failed to kill with kisses. Hong Wu laughed softly and said, "One of the men you drove away returned just in time to see you go through Forest's pockets. So we strangled the Honorable Hong. I took his place to find out how you fitted into this game. Imposture for an imposter."

"Who the devil are you?"

"The grand master of the Triad Society. My borrowed identity should suffice during the short time names will interest you. I recognized you from Dolores' description."

"How does my—his secretary fit into this?" Hartley demanded.

"Very simple," said the self styled Hong. "The girl's letter to you betrayed her employer. You followed to slay him and take his place. This proves that you are no petty miner, but Forest's rival. I am holding you and your accomplice for questioning.

"Centuries ago, the Triad Society expelled the Manchu invaders from China. Today we are more ambitious. We now aim to expel all foreigners from every part of Asia. Our first move is to keep Americans out. Thus when the day of vengeance arrives, there will be no American intervention in their favor. Though Asia is rotten ripe, we can not survive if your country stepped in."

"Lovely," mocked Hartley. "But where do I come in?"

"You and the girl will explain Forest's plans, so that I can notify my secret agents in America. Transpacific's next representative will then die before he leaves San Francisco.

"Tsang Lee, take him to headquarters. This house is dangerous."

Tsang Lee clubbed him across the head. Just once, but it sufficed.

* * * *

When Hartley's wits returned, he was bound hand and foot, and lying in a gilt and vermillion apartment invaded by the stenches of the native quarter.

Irene was beside him and regaining consciousness. She had been taken by surprise. Her garments were not torn.

Hartley explained how he had been tricked into trapping her.

"And we're sunk," he concluded. "Your letter—Dolores read it—"

"Which was more than I expected," Hong Wu purred from the doorway. "She made the most of your touching sentiment. Had I been your age, I would have kissed her to death."

And then Dolores, clad in Chinese silks, appeared beside her master. Her smile and Hong's mockery gave Irene the story; but she laughed softly, and said, "It takes more than her to turn me against him."

"Ah…but bamboo slivers driven under your nails will make you talk," murmured Hong Wu. "And you, Mr. Hartley—you will speak when you tire of her screams."

He clapped his hands. Two coolies entered with a stout chair, and a table equipped with a wooden vise whose horizontal jaws were grooved for the victim's fingers. A third had fine slivers of bamboo that would torture sensitive flesh more than any needle.

Hartley shivered, and wondered at the strange gleam in Dolores' slanted eyes, his folly mocked him. She had kissed him to death!

Hong Wu would never believe that Hartley and Irene did not know the intricacies of Forest's plans.

They bound Irene to the chair, clamped her fingers in the vise. Hartley sickened, watching her strain against her bonds as the savage little fibers slipped into the quick of her nails, gently forced home—almost bloodless torment no man's nerves could endure. But she would not speak.

Before she fainted, Hartley's sympathetic muscular contraction had stretched his bonds. Hong Wu did not realize that Irene's agony was whipping him to inhuman strength.

A draught of *ng ka pay* revived her. Then Dolores intervened: "Some women are that way, Honorable Hong. But I will make her speak…"

She glided from the doorway, halting between Irene and Hartley. Then she stretched languorously, and peeled off her outer tunic.

"He loved me when you scorned him," she whispered. "He will love me again. Save yourself wasted misery… He will not die. Only you."

She shed another tunic, and her sleek silken trousers. What remained was a gauzy witchery, and though her breasts were bound flat in Chinese fashion, she revealed more than enough to compensate.

Hartley was winning his fight against his bonds. There was a chance—

"He knew I was his enemy, yet he loved me. Did he ever want to kiss *you* to death?" she mocked.

Another heave—and then Dolores twined her gleaming self about Hartley.

Hong Wu and his torturers were breathing audibly. Her exposure offended Chinese propriety, but at the same time its effect robbed Hartley of a chance to escape.

"Tell, and you both live," urged Hong Wu, reluctantly turning to Irene.

Not a chance of escape until Dolores moved. Then Hartley felt the chill of steel between his wrists. The cords parted!

"Tell him," he croaked, catching Irene's eye. He hoped to distract the Chinese.

But Hong sensed the change. He whirled as Hartley seized the blade. He yelled. The torturers leaped, drawing knives.

Hartley hurled himself, tripped, sprawled on the floor, helpless for the damning instant he needed to free his ankles. A streak of golden flesh blotted out a flash of steel. Dolores screamed. Long nails slashed Hong's face, blinding him with blood. And then Hartley's feet were free. He crashed home with shoulder and knife.

Hong Wu collapsed, throat ripped open. Hartley's next opponent was empty-handed. His knife was hilt deep between Dolores' breasts. She had flung herself against its point. She was tugging at the haft as Hartley ploughed into the melee. She hurled the red knife, checking an armed assailant.

Then he understood Irene's frantic cry. Her pistol—the tiny automatic her brassiere held in place. He made a dive for it. The vicious little slugs cleared the deck. The last of Hong Wu's men collapsed in a doorway opening to a side street.

The arrival of a bearded Sikh policeman prevented a counterattack. Hartley ran back into the house.

"I had to give Hong Wu those things I took from you," Dolores coughed as he knelt beside her. "So he would not suspect me. Then I could help you. But I didn't expect this—trouble—tonight—no one else—ever was—nice to me—and maybe she —will forgive you—if you—kiss me to death…"

And when Hartley rose, wiping that red kiss from his lips, he knew that Irene had forgiven him.

"But I'll love you at least half that much," she whispered. "Now let's see the Warden of Mines. I'm staying in Malaya."

TWO AGAINST THE GODS

Originally published in *Golden Fleece*, December 1938.

The slanting light that reached into the little room brought golden glints from Oello's tawny skin and brought a cool green glitter from the emerald collar that circled her slender throat. Her face remained lovely and untroubled as she turned from the narrow window, but all the splendor that Felipe's kisses had coaxed to her dark eyes was gone.

"Ten more llamas," she sighed, "and loaded until they can hardly walk."

Francisco Pizarro's interpreter somberly regarded the caravan that was adding to Atahuallpa's ransom. In another few days, Oello and all the other wives of the captive Inca would go with him to freedom.

"Suppose Pizarro does turn him loose?" Felipe challenged. "You and I can go to the coast. Atahuallpa can't reach us, there."

Oello did not answer. Felipe caught her arms and drew her from the sill. He repeated, "Pizarro and the Inca can do without us!"

He was an Indian from Tumbez, but only his crisp black hair and swarthy skin marked him apart from the Spanish invaders whom he served; he wore a purple doublet and hose, none the worse for having been discarded by Ferdinand de Soto, who was second in command. A sword and a wine colored cape hung across the foot of the low couch.

The Inca's wife regarded her lover with widening eyes. He was about the age of Atahuallpa, and though his features lacked the fine modeling of the sacred Inca clan, he had a strong face and resolute mouth. His chin thrust out as he sensed Oello's blend of dismay and horror.

Felipe answered her unspoken exclamation: "He may be the Child of the Sun to you people of the mountains. But in Tumbez, Atahuallpa's a conqueror who sends Inca nobles to tell us what to wear, what to think, what crops to raise."

She was young and shapely. Beneath her flowing mantle of silk-soft *vicuna* fleece she wore a skirt and blouse of fragile cotton. The embroidery that enriched the frail fabric was heavier than the garments themselves. And though the heartbeat of her close pressed body whipped his own pulse, Oello's beauty could not distract him from his wrath.

The heightened color of her olive tinted cheeks, the misting of her long lashed eyes confirmed his resolution. As their lips parted, he said, "Atahuallpa's an upstart. Huascar's the lawful Inca. You know that."

Oello smoothed her rumpled blouse, then flung back her heavy black braids. Stolen kisses were in themselves a high crime against the Inca; but somehow, outright desertion seemed even more sacrilegious.

Outside, a trumpet drowned the wrangling and gambling of the Spanish soldiers. Felipe picked up his cloak and sword and said to Oello, "There's a way of doing this. I'll tell you more tonight. Now, you'd better go back. The officers will be meeting Pizarro."

* * * *

Ferdinand De Soto, the only one of that hard bitten lot who had any pity for Atahuallpa, spent each afternoon rolling dice and playing chess with the captive Inca. But now that the trumpet summoned Pizarro's officers. Atahuallpa would turn to the wives who had accompanied him in captivity. It was time for Oello to leave.

Felipe watched her slip stealthily down a shadowy passageway. If Atahuallpa died before he won his freedom, Oello would have no further qualms.

Later, the interpreter saw his chance. There are more ways than one to kill a captive king. But neither tall Pizarro nor his assembled captains knew what a stake Felipe had in this deadly game of gold and kingdoms.

Torchlight gleamed on their full armor. Ever since that fatal half hour in which Atahuallpa had become a prisoner, Pizarro's small force had slept under arms, lest sudden revolt catch them off guard.

"The Inca," said Pizarro, "says we ought to turn him loose."

He spoke slowly, weighing every word. His thin face was strengthened by a long, straight nose; a slow, patient man, immovable and remorseless as the Andes. Though born a swineherd, and for all his sixty years unable to write his own name, Francisco Pizarro commanded the respect of *hidalgo* and ruffian alike.

"Turn him loose? *Por dios!* You're crazy if you don't kill him!"

A short, one eyed man waddled forward a pace. Diego Almagro had spoken it all in a breath. Standing beside the handsome Ferdinand de Soto, Almagro seemed more toad than man. His broad shoulders and stocky legs made him appear shorter than he actually was. A twisted nose, somewhat the worse for having been broken and crudely set, combined with his one protruding eye to make him the ugliest man of the army.

"Blood of God!" seconded several others. "Almagro's right! The quicker you kill him, the sooner we can go to Cuzco."

Pizarro gravely stroked his beard. De Soto's generous mouth hardened. Felipe's eyes brightened. Thank God for Almagro!

Finally de Soto found a lull. He said, "Don Francisco, the Inca has paid for his freedom. He has done us no harm, only favors. You can't kill him, after accepting the biggest ransom ever offered by any king."

"*Caballeros,*" resumed Pizarro, "when reinforcements arrive from Panama, we can march to Cuzco. And safely release the Inca. Right now, we can't risk it with our small army, going so far inland."

"Sangre de Cristo!" Almagro raised a warty fist. "You've hogged all the first loot, just because my men weren't here when you blundered into Cajamalca to grab the Inca, mainly by fool luck! Listen, Don Francisco! I've got two hundred men—good ones, and more than you have. We're marching to Cuzco, whether you do or not. How do you like that?"

Pizarro's face did not change, yet his presence abashed all but the volatile Almagro. "That is foolish, Diego. If we divide our force—even if we went together, through those dangerous mountain passes, the Indios could ambush us to the last man, and rescue the Inca."

"That's why," stormed Almagro, "you've got to kill him!" He turned to his own captains. "What do you say?"

"Por dios, you have already said it, Don Diego!" Then Felipe's smile faded. Ferdinand de Soto took the floor. Though not yet thirty, he was grave and lordly; even self-sufficient Pizarro respected the young lieutenant-general.

"This is a crime you plan! Worse, it is needless. God gave us the right to capture a pagan king, but murdering him is something else. Now, listen to this, *Caballeros y muy señores!*

"Huascar, the lawful ruler, is locked up in a fortress somewhat north of here. Atahuallpa is very much hated in some parts, being an usurper. Thus we can deal with Huascar, who is now the captive of a captive."

"What do you mean?" grumbled Almagro. "That's a bun for a loaf!"

De Soto's slow smile made Almagro redden and stutter. "Don Diego, perhaps I can make this clear. If we liberate Huascar, he will pledge allegiance to the King of Spain. He will be bound to us by gratitude. Huascar will make things easy for us. Half of Peru hates Atahuallpa; all Peru will obey Huascar!"

"Santiago!" Pizarro's somber eyes gleamed. "Don Ferdinand, you have spared me an unpleasant necessity. How did you hit upon that idea?"

De Soto gracefully declined his chief's compliment. "It was simple enough, playing chess with the prisoner, to piece together enough casual remarks to learn where Huascar is kept under guard."

* * * *

From that moment, Felipe hated the man whose rich garments he wore. Atahuallpa, though deposed, would go free with all his wives.

He came forward, saying, "Don Francisco, there is more to this than *Señor* de Soto realizes. With all respect, he does not as well understand the Quichua language as a native would. Atahuallpa and the nobles who wait on him are plotting revolt. An army is gathering in Huamachuco, making the most of the sixty days you gave Atahuallpa to collect the ransom."

"Por dios, I told you!" Almagro cut in.

"Name me the nobles who discussed this with the Inca," de Soto demanded.

Felipe met de Soto's stern challenge, and readily: "My lord, even I do not pretend to know the names of all the Inca's officers." Then, to Pizarro, "When I hear more, I will report."

He was glad enough to be dismissed by his chief. Felipe did not like de Soto's unspoken questions, and the suspicion that clouded his eyes.

On his way from the officers' conference, Felipe took heart. Almagro and the two hundred men who had not shared the initial loot would overwhelm de Soto's pleas for the captive emperor...

That night, Felipe slipped back to the cubicle where he and Oello had exchanged so many stolen kisses. Finally, when moonlight crept across the three cornered plaza, and reached in through the narrow window, he heard the soft tinkle of her anklets.

Felipe caught her in his arms, and his kiss cut short her murmur of endearment. Then, suddenly, she broke from his embrace.

"I shouldn't have met you again. We can't see each other anymore."

He laughed softly. "I've found a way to free you."

She sat bolt upright. "But—why—that's impossible!"

"It isn't. They're going to depose Atahuallpa, and put the Huascar on the throne. He'll wear the sacred red *borla*, and so Atahuallpa won't be Child of the Sun. It won't be sacrilege if you leave him then!"

That was plausible, particularly in these troubled times. Before the civil war which had reached its gory conclusion some months before Pizarro arrived, such logic would have been impossible; but now, many tribes did mutter against Atahuallpa, calling him an usurper. Moreover, if the Gods had not forsaken Atahuallpa, Pizarro could not have seized him. Oello wavered; being one of many wives, she had never until now known one man's undivided love.

Felipe, moreover, though not of the lordly Inca clan, was a friend of the conquering Spaniards who could lay violent hands on the Child of the Sun and yet not be blasted by divine vengeance.

"But how can we stay in the clear till we're out of reach of Atahuallpa?"

Having made up her mind, she was practical.

No Indian had ever dared form a plan like Felipe's. He had learned from Pizarro's daring and grim purpose. He said, "It's easy. You can get clothing for me, so I can go as one of the Inca's personal couriers. No one will dare question us."

"I'll have all that by tomorrow night." Oello's voice trembled from the enormity of the venture. "Now I'd better go."

But Felipe detained her. He sensed that she would weaken. As he drew her toward him, he said, "No one'll miss you tonight."

"No," she said, trying to break from his embrace. "I'm afraid. I've been afraid, these last few days—" But she could not overcome his insistence...

* * * *

The moon patch had not quite shifted from Oello's golden beauty when the lovers realized how sound her qualms had been. There was a sudden metallic sound, and a glare of torchlight from the low doorway. Had Oello's Indian nerves retained their usual steadiness, all might have been well; but dismay brought a cry from her lips as she bounded to her feet, wrapping her vicuna mantle about her.

Ferdinand de Soto and one of his soldiers blocked the way. He recognized Oello's high rank; her jewels and the fine fabric that only an Inca was allowed to wear betrayed her.

That one cry of dismay echoed down the dark hallway. Then de Soto said, "So this is how you learn Atahuallpa's secrets? You misbegotten dog, a king is a king, even if he is a captive!"

Felipe said, "All you fine lords have women of your own! I warned Pizarro of an insurrection. See if he condemns me!"

Oello stood there, lovely and motionless. Her one cry was beyond recall. As de Soto groped for words, sandaled feet made soft, slapping sounds in the hall.

Yupanqui, one of the Inca's officers, had arrived on the run. Another dignitary was on his heels. When they were able to believe what they saw before them, Yupanqui said in broken Spanish, "Kill him. Kill her."

De Soto interposed. The unarmed officers, knowing him as the Inca's friend and seeing his wrath, made no move to pass him. They bowed, then retired; but what they said in their own language made Felipe's mouth tighten.

De Soto said to his orderly, "Get Don Francisco's orders at once." Then, to Felipe: "Maybe you can save yourself by giving all the details of that revolt. When you came forward to contribute your bit to my plan, I smelled a native perfume on you, and I began to understand. No common woman uses such a scent."

Moments dragged. The guard came, and marched the two prisoners into the Inca's reception room. There Atahuallpa sat, and Pizarro with him.

The Inca's eyes blazed from beneath the long red fringed *borla* that reached to his lashes. He was tall for his race, and somewhat swarthy. This was the first time within the memory of man that anyone had dared look at a woman of an Inca's seraglio; yet his face was placid. Being a god in human form, he did not display emotion as men did.

"You saw this, Don Ferdinand?" he calmly asked. When the indignant officer assented, the Inca turned to the nobles who knelt, barefooted, before the chair on the dais. "Yupanqui? Sinchi?"

"We could not believe this thing," they answered, "without seeing. We beg pardon for having seen."

Atahuallpa brushed aside the red fringe of his *borla* and turned to Pizarro. "They should both die."

"The interpreter," Pizarro said, mustering up his command of Quichua, "is mine. The girl is yours to do with as you please."

"*Sanctissima madre!*" de Soto's courtesy reached its limit. "You take that dog's part? You deny the Inca his just vengeance?"

"Felipe," was the deliberate answer, "is my man."

The captive king understood enough to know that one of the lovers would escape him. He said to his officers, "Take her out, and do what is fitting."

Oello knew well what that meant: having offended the Sun, she would be buried alive, so that his rays could no longer bless her. Being one of the sacred Inca clan, her blood could not be shed. She cast one glance at Felipe: this was farewell, without any hope.

The interpreter bounded forward. "Don Francisco!," he demanded, "this woman is mine! She has become a Christian. I have converted her to your faith and mine. The Inca has no more claim on her!"

He had said that in Spanish. He turned to Oello and demanded in Quichua, "Is that true? Haven't you denied the Inca? Make this sign as I do—"

Scarcely understanding, she imitated him as he crossed himself.

Pizarro raised an imperative hand and said, "Father Valverde will be glad to hear of a new convert."

That settled the matter. When Felipe turned to face the Inca, Atahuallpa looked the other way.

* * * *

The following day, Felipe's plans went all awry. True, he had saved Oello from the Inca's vengeance. But Ferdinand de Soto had gone out with a picked troop to reconnoiter in the vicinity of Huamachuco and determine whether there was or was not a concentration of troops awaiting the word to swoop down on Cajamalca to annihilate the Spaniards. Worse than that, a courier was on the way with a message from Atahuallpa to the officers who guarded Huascar; the captive was to be brought to Cajamalca so that Pizarro could judge between him and the usurping Inca.

"*Cristo del Grao!*" Felipe sat hunched and frowning, studying it out. Oello watched him, sensing that this was no time for kisses. She did not know that he was thinking, "Almagro and Pizarro have snapped at the idea of putting Huascar on the throne and using him as a dummy. But de Soto will be back, saying there's not a sign of revolt anywhere. Atahuallpa's going to live through this."

Felipe was not afraid of any immediate peril. Yet he knew that, sooner or later, Atahuallpa's loyal retainers would stealthily seek him and Oello; the officials who had seen the affront put on their lord would not rest until they reported the death of the offenders.

To protect Oello and himself, Felipe had condemned Atahuallpa to death.

But to execute that sentence was another matter. Finally he looked up and smiled. "We still have to leave. Being Christians will not save us from secret vengeance. Get the clothes we need."

Although she did not understand his plan, she realized her peril and his. "While you're attending to your part," she answered, "I'll attend to mine. But I'm terribly afraid of horses."

He thrust out his chest. "I understand them. I rode de Soto's, once."

That evening, Felipe went to Pizarro's quarters and respectfully saluted him, "The holy saints alone know what *Señor* de Soto will learn about this revolt. It is possible that Atahuallpa will secretly send fast couriers to have the Inca soldiers leave Huamachuco, to deceive us.

"But the worst is this—"

Diego Almagro raised his ugly face from a flagon of wine and cut in, *"Por dios, what could be worse? Sending de Soto away from here!"*

"Don Ferdinand," Pizarro slowly said, "is usually well advised."

Almagro spat. "That he may be, *verdad!* But me, I'd rather have him here. Where he can't be ambushed in the mountains. Where he can team up with us if we are attacked."

"We considered all that," Pizarro patiently replied. "Now, Felipe?"

"With your permission and Don Diego's—" The interpreter's courtly bow included them both. "Atahuallpa is insane with rage—"

"About your way of making converts, eh?" Almagro laughed gustily, and Pizarro's thin face relaxed in a carefully weighed smile.

Felipe went on, "I am the faithful servant who kisses the hands of Your Excellencies. More than that, I have been foolish and the cause of Atahuallpa's anger—"

"We can put up with *that!*" Almagro gulped some wine and chuckled.

Felipe continued, "I do not deserve your kindness. What I mean is this. For the affront he received in…ah…this matter of making converts to the True Faith, he is too angry to be sensible. He did send for Huascar, as you ordered. But I am afraid that Huascar won't get here."

Almagro rose so suddenly that his paunch tipped the table. The flagon crashed to the floor. "By God and Saint Jago! He'll kill Huascar just to spite us. The way he shut up, last night—he was too mad to shout. *Compadre,* you had better do something about it!"

Pizarro dismissed Felipe with a gesture. He said to Almagro, "Send a courier after de Soto. Tell him to go to Huascar's prison and guard him closely, all the way to Cajamalca. He's too valuable to lose."

But Felipe did not hear this. Having planted new suspicion, he was eager to leave before he was too closely questioned as to details; though it was logical that the high tempered Inca, about to lose even the shadow of power, would stop at nothing to prevent Huascar from regaining the throne.

Almagro's greed and Pizarro's natural fear of a general revolt that would and could overwhelm his small army were Felipe's allies; yet a man's wits must at times direct destiny.

Indian stealth enabled the lovers to slip past the guards. Felipe had secured a horse; and at the start, he wore his Spanish costume. A mile beyond the walls of Cajamalca he met Oello, who had gone ahead to wait.

She emerged from hiding. A bundle was balanced on her head. It contained not only Felipe's disguise, but all the finery she had discarded in favor of the coarse, alpaca gown of a peasant woman.

"He won't hurt you," Felipe reassured her as he reined in his borrowed horse. "Give me that bundle—put your foot in the stirrup—up you go!"

She made it, somehow. Her awkwardness at that unaccustomed exercise made the restive beast paw and snort. But Oello clung to her lover and maintained her seat behind the high cantle of the saddle. Though a clumsy rider, Felipe's triumph gave him confidence. The horse sensed that this man was not afraid; so he subsided. That Felipe could ride at all made him splendid in Oello's eyes.

Finally she relaxed; it was now affection and not fear that kept her arms about Felipe. He half turned in the saddle, caught a swift glimpse of her beauty in the moonlight. His heart rose and choked him. No man from Tumbez had ever dreamed of such a woman!

Presently Felipe turned from the paved post road that reached twenty-two hundred miles, north and south, paralleling the one that skirted the sea.

"Hang on," he cautioned, leaning forward as the panting beast lowered his head and dug into the nasty climb up a trail that followed a gloomy quebrada.

"What's the matter?" Oello was puzzled. "This isn't the way—is someone chasing us already?"

Felipe evaded, "Just to make certain." There was no use telling her too much. Only those vague Christian saints could predict the outcome of his venture. They must be more powerful than Inca gods, and Felipe wished he knew them better. For luck, he muttered a prayer to Pachacamac, who was greater even than the Sun.

Before dawn, Felipe halted. Oello, cramped and shaken, slid stiffly to the ground. "Aren't you going to put on those clothes I brought you?"

He shook his head and smiled. "Not for a while. Now rest up because we're going on, as soon as the horse gets his strength back."

Toward the end of the second day, Oello recognized the foaming Andamarca, far below them. But before they reached its banks, they would have to go afoot. The horse, improperly cared for and carrying double, had little strength left, so Felipe led the beast, and Oello trudged along, holding a stirrup for support.

Ahead was a suspension bridge that swayed in the wind. Its cables were made of osiers and maguey fiber. They supported the narrow catwalk that crossed the thousand foot cleft which gaped beneath. Due to the sag of the cable, the drop was steep, and so was the ascent to the opposite lip of the ravine.

It took an hour of struggle to get the horse past the center. Pizarro's cavalry knew a few tricks that Felipe had not learned. Then, beaten and frantic, the beast bolted, shouldering Oello off balance. Clawing for support, she slowly slid back, and between the guard cables. Each oscillation of the bridge robbed her of a bit more than she had gained.

Felipe, flung in the opposite direction, yelled hoarsely. "Quit kicking! Flatten out!"

He recovered enough to drop belly down. His toes laced in the strands that bound the floor boards. He caught Oello's wrist; but her weight, mainly unsupported, threatened to pull him loose with each deadly sway of the long main cable. They were facing each other from the edges of a devil's hammock. They had outwitted a god; he had made a toy of Pizarro's suspicions; but the mountain wind and a horse's panic mocked all that success.

Sweat made his fingers slippery. He could not risk trying for a better grip. Oello had ceased kicking in her efforts to get a knee back over the edge.

"Let go," she sighed. "I'll pull you with me. The gods hate us."

That was Indian fatalism. She was right. Felipe knew that, but he had marched with Pizarro, in whose iron heart was not one grain of resignation to fate.

A flash of that thin, remorseless face for an instant blotted out Oello's relaxing features. Felipe cried, "Wait till the next swing, you little fool! *Hold on!*"

The pendulum dip now tended to spill him through the guards; but the rise of the opposite edge supported Oello at the waist. He let go her wrist. His hand moved, an eye-tricking flicker during which he was slowly sliding back.

But he made it; he caught her braided hair. That gave him the advantage he needed, and likewise freed her hands, so that she could use them to draw herself back over the edge.

They crawled up the slope. When they reached the abutments, they crumpled against the cold rocks, panting and quivering. Later, when Felipe recaptured the horse, Oello said, "The Gods tried us, and you did not fail."

But Felipe did not hear. He was peering into the sunset haze, and toward the highway that ran north and south a thousand feet below. Oello clung to him, and wondered what could draw his thoughts so far away.

"Quick," he said. "Open that bundle. I'm becoming an Inca courier."

He seated himself on a rock at the opposite side of the trail and unbuckled his sword belt. He tossed her the weapon and said, "Hide it carefully along with the rest of this truck." He flung his doublet after the blade. As a second thought, he corrected, "And find a hiding place for yourself."

"For myself?" Her eyes became dark and troubled. "Why—"

"There's something down there I want to look into," he evaded.

Then Oello saw the black spots that moved along the highway right where it skirted the Andamarca's bank.

She caught the gleam of bronze lance heads, the ruddy glint of copper loaded maces, the glitter of gilt against the quilted armor of Inca soldiers.

"Oh—" She began to understand. "We're near the fort where Huascar was locked up." She stood there, sword and scabbard in hand. "But don't worry. They're going south. Do you know, I'm certain that must be the convoy that's taking Huascar to Cajamalca. They won't notice us."

"Maybe," said Felipe, smiling oddly, "Huascar is with that convoy."

He was struggling with his boots. Sweat made them cling. Oello, her back toward the bridge, still strained her eyes, trying to identify the devices on the gaudy pennons the troops displayed.

"It must be Huascar! His standard—he'd fly it, even as a prisoner."

But Felipe's smile froze. He whirled about, hearing a clank of steel, the ring of horse's hoofs, the tinkle of curb chains. A deep voice shouted in Spanish, "You, there!"

Oello turned. On the other side was Ferdinand de Soto, splendid on his horse. A dozen men were behind him.

They were about to cross the bridge. The girl moaned, "Runners from Cajamalca told him to chase us!"

Felipe, neither in nor out of his boots, pitched in a heap. His untethered horse, some yards off the trail, bolted at the crash of brush. There was no chance of flight. De Soto's skittish stallion shied from the bridge, but the lordly Spaniard wheeled him for another trial. He would make it, Felipe knew.

As he struggled with the damning boots, Felipe did not know whether to pray to Pachacamac or to the saints. De Soto repeated his shout, but the wind distorted his words; neither fugitive could understand.

Oello defiantly screamed, "We won't come back!"

Her legs stretched in a bound that brought her skirt swirling about her hips. She had the sword out of its scabbard. On the other side, the Spaniards muttered in amazement. Too late, they understood. An arquebus jerked into line, and another. "Fire!", shouted de Soto.

The keen blade chopped into the cable. The arquebuses coughed flame and smoke. Slugs spattered about Oello. Felipe cried, "Get back—I'll cut it!"

As he hobbled toward her, one foot half shod, the other bare, two soldiers dismounted and dashed toward the bridge. "Back, you fool!" de Soto shouted.

A crackling had followed Oello's final cut; then a popping, as each snapping cord put greater strain on the others. The audacious soldiers dropped their arquebuses and fled.

The cable parted. Though the other held, the bridge was impassable except to a man with the courage and strength to crawl down its dip, and then up.

"We've gained hours," said Felipe. *Por dios,* who'd think Pizarro would pull de Soto from reconnoitering and set him to trailing us?"

Oello did not know. She was too happy to care. Twice in an hour, the gods had helped them out of peril.

* * * *

The purple shadow of the Andes had blotted out all details below.

Camp fires now winked from the darkness of the highway. Huascar Inca was eating, and his respectful escort was drinking *chicha.* He would be happy, going from prison to a throne…

An hour...two hours descent of a crude trail. Then Felipe said, "Wait here, while I find out whether this is a searching party, or Huascar's escort."

Darkness and firelight favored him when he approached the sentries of the camp. Both officers and common soldiers were bivouacked about the rest house beside the highway. This assured him that the building must be reserved for Huascar.

He presented the wand that identified him as one of Atahuallpa's personal couriers. Though the lowest peasant came with that token, he was for the moment entitled to the respect of the Inca's own presence. The sacrilege of imposture made deception inconceivable; but Felipe had learned from Pizarro.

The man who approached to bow before the sacred symbol was tall and sharp faced and commanding. The golden discs in his ears were so large that they made the lobes touch his shoulders. He was one of that sacred clan that could do no wrong; there was no life he could not take, no woman he could not demand, and yet be beyond criticism. But even he would be bare-footed when he approached Atahuallpa; he would have on his shoulder some small burden as a token of servility.

And that stately man in the crimson *vicuna* robe listened respectfully. He accepted the wand that made him the Inca's hand, for the execution of that order. He said, "It will be done as Atahuallpa commands. Runners will go at once to tell him that the body is in the river. And that we return to our starting point."

He did not question Felipe, nor offer him refreshment. He knew that Felipe, who could command whatever was needed, was leaving the camp because there were duties other than witnessing the strangling of Huascar. "Only Pachacamac or the saints," mused Felipe, "could take an Inca woman, and put a king to death."

That thought made him light headed. The whine of the mountain wind became exalting music. When he rejoined Oello, he had to steady his voice to say, "It is well with those soldiers. But it is better that you and I return to Cajamalca. I didn't expect de Soto to hunt us in these mountains, for the sake of Atahuallpa. Pizarro and Father Valverde are our best protectors."

"But the assassins who'll kill us for offending the Inca?"

He smiled, patted her hair as she helped him into his Spanish garments. He said, "He will have no one touch us. It has come to me, suddenly."

Intuition could give her no details. She knew only that Felipe had become more than a man. That he had ordered the soldiers to retrace their course proved that.

"Isn't Huascar going to Cajamalca?" She was diffident now.

"He is not. I forbade that, also."

She was almost afraid when she kissed him. The divine Atahuallpa had never been half as much a king of men and a child of the gods.

So they rode to Cajamalca, not knowing that Ferdinand de Soto had not even recognized them, or known of their flight. Nor could they know that de Soto, finally finding another bridge, had crossed the stream and was now hastening to find Huascar's escort.

Felipe was weary. Oello was too ecstatic to be aware of fatigue. The runners who went to report Huascar's death to Atahuallpa were far swifter than the jaded horse that carried double...

When Felipe and Oello approached the Valley of Cajamalca, sunset reddened the white walls, and long golden lances of light reached out the clouds that swathed the *sierra*. Drums rolled, and the mountains flung back their thunder. Trumpets brayed;

then the notes became shrill and soul shaking, so that Oello shivered, and Felipe's pulse began to hammer.

The barbaric sound beat and stabbed him; it was tragic, it was exultant, and strangely, it brought tears to his eyes. Yet for all the whimsical feeling that this fanfare welcomed him, apprehension made him flinch.

Oello whispered, "I'm afraid of that sound."

The trumpets ceased as suddenly as they had spoken. For moments, the lovers waited, and the ruddy glow became lavender and eerie before their eyes. Then a mumble of voices came from the city.

Felipe and Oello were troubled as they went on; nor did they know why.

"I'd think someone had died," she whispered.

"Maybe someone has," said Felipe. It had happened sooner than he had believed possible. He was dazed, now that it was done.

No one noticed the two who came into Cajamalca. The wailing of women tore the sullen silence. Two musketeers stood watch beside a stake in the center of the plaza.

A man was bound to that stake. His head slumped to his chest. There were faggots heaped about his legs, but there was no odor of burning. A soldier passed by with a flaring torch. The momentary glow revealed the plumes of the sacred *coraquenque* which the man at the stake wore in his headdress.

"Oh…" A quavering exhalation, and Oello faltered, "Atahuallpa's dead. They've killed him—strangled him—"

"As he would have done to you," Felipe told her.

They were entering the quarters of the Spaniards when Almagro boomed from the door of the officers' salon, "*For dios!* It's time you came back, you and your wench! Death and damnation, if we'd not had another interpreter, we'd have been let down nicely at the trial."

Horses' hoofs were drumming in the distance. A platoon of cavalry rode hellbent. De Soto must be returning. Felipe wanted to keep out of his sight. He said, "*Señor.* I was afraid of Atahuallpa's wrath—I—"

"Bring him in, Diego!" Francisco Pizarro was now speaking. "Since we're in trim for court proceedings, we might as well try this loafer!"

The monotonous wailing of Atahuallpa's widows was for a moment blotted by the clatter of horses slowing down to a walk as they were reined in on the flagstones of the plaza. Sentries challenged, purely as a matter of form; a familiar voice answered, "De Soto and his troop!"

The guard turned out. The sounds gave Felipe the picture. His lips were dry, and he could feel the sudden fear that gripped Oello. No one kept her from accompanying him as he slowly advanced toward Pizarro's table at the far end of the hall.

Then Pizarro smiled. "Here, here! Don't look that way, man! Almagro's just having his fun. But if you were a soldier, I'd have you flogged." He eyed Oello; she was lovely, despite her fatigue. "I don't blame you—"

But that pleasantry was cut short when de Soto stamped into the hall.

"By God—you, Francisco! You Diego—" His outthrust arm was like a lance ready to impale the two leaders. "The saints forgive me for serving with you assassins! The minute my back's turned, you murder Atahuallpa! Reconnoiter—Christ's blood, there wasn't a sign of insurrection!" His blazing eye nailed Felipe. "Your trickery, you son of several dogs!"

Almagro's one eye fell before de Soto's accusation. Pizarro stuttered, "He was legally tried and condemned. Diego insisted."

"I? *Señor*—"

"Condemned for stirring up insurrection, and ordering the death of Huascar," said Pizarro, regaining his self-possession. "But since he became a Christian, he was not burned at the stake. And if you were not his friend, moved by grief, I would hold you accountable for your unmilitary conduct."

"Why," demanded Almagro, "didn't you guard Huascar, as you were ordered?"

"Why," countered de Soto, "didn't you give Atahuallpa at least a dog's chance? He was a king. Only our lord, the King of Spain, could try him for the murder of Huascar. This night's work makes me ashamed of my fellowship with you. How do you know Atahuallpa ordered his brother's death?"

Pizarro answered, "A runner came to tell Atahuallpa that his orders had been obeyed. That Huascar's body had been thrown into the Andamarca only a few minutes after the courier who ordered the execution had left. And then the escort moved north, as ordered. Does that answer you?"

"*Sanctissima madre!*" de Soto bitterly exclaimed. "If you were not my chief, I would question that. God forgive me, had not a frightened native cut a bridge under my very feet, I could have saved Huascar. And so saved Atahuallpa, a king and a friend who served us well!" He bowed his head. The grief that displaced his wrath distracted every man's eye from Oello. She stood so close to de Soto that she could reach the dagger that gleamed from his belt.

No one saw her draw the weapon. Her eyes blazed with red fury. She screamed, "It is my fault that Atahuallpa died!"

She spoke Quichua; but every Spaniard saw the flashing blade, the swift motion of body and arm as she turned on her lover. The dagger cut over his fending arm and bit home. It tore his throat, then sank into his chest.

As she followed him to the floor, she screamed, "You ordered Huascar's death—to strike at Atahuallpa—"

Too late, Felipe knew that to Oello, it was one thing to betray the love of a god, another to take his life. Choking and coughing, he tried to fight; but his wounds, and her insane rage were too much.

Almagro's blade was out. It had killed many a woman and unarmed man before now. And Oello was Atahuallpa's widow, going berserk. He struck before de Soto could intervene.

The lovers were in each other's arms; a quivering red huddle in which little life remained. Almagro's warty face twisted. "*Por dios!* She might have killed a couple of us."

"He'd have been a good interpreter," Pizarro finally said, "if he'd had sense enough to leave women alone."

He gravely shook his head, and wondered why hot headed de Soto stalked from the hall without reclaiming his dagger. But Almagro's thoughts went further. "Buck up, Francisco!" he chuckled. "With both Incas dead, we've got Peru in our pocket, and it'll be easy sacking Cuzco before these disorganized Indios get over the shock!

WOLVES OF KERAK

Originally published in *Golden Fleece*, December 1938.

"Look, *sidi,* a girl from Feringhistan—fit for the harem of a king—and only a thousand *dinars*—a thousand—"

The auctioneer's bleary eyes shifted toward a lean Turk who was licking his thin lips. "Nine hundred?" he wheedled. "Nine hundred, and Allah make you happy?"

The Turk shrugged. Captive women were plentiful as fleas in Cairo since Saladin had carved his way to the throne of Syria and Egypt. Though this one was different, in her white, frozen loveliness.

Hussayn, the auctioneer, whisked the mantle from the girl's shoulders, leaving her clad only in her unbound hair. It trailed to her hips, a red-gold veil that almost hid her white breasts—though their roundness was kissed by the late afternoon light that lanced past the minarets of the El Azhar Mosque. The ruddy light gilded her sleek legs, accented the exquisite modeling of her face.

She was too proud to shrink from the eyes and hands that would go over her loveliness as though she were a horse put through its paces.

"Eight hundred?" pleaded Hussayn. "The daughter of an infidel prince, Allah burn him! Taken from a galley bound for Akka!"

The buyers were dubious. Her haughty green eyes warned them that she would be a handful to manage.

"Bound for Akka?" rumbled a broad-shouldered man whose peaked helmet towered over the kinky heads of the tall Sudanese guards. His hawk face was bronzed and arrogant. The eyes that narrowed beneath his dark brows were granite gray, not the smoldering black of the lean Arabs about him.

"Ay, wallah! The galley of Henri de Montfried."

The tall man thrust himself a pace forward, and the auctioneer pleaded, "Seven hundred dinars, my lord emir! See those white arms—a mouth like a pomegranate blossom—"

Poetry dripped from Hussayn's lips, and fire raced through the veins of Jehan de Courtenai, the tall spy from the Crusaders' outpost at Kerak. Her beauty was like exalting music, making him almost forget the chatelaine whose fickle fancy had sent him to find oblivion in the Holy Land. And she was a Christian, this girl on the auction block, stripped for the eyes of greasy merchants, rapacious money lenders, grim-faced *mamluks* of the sultan's guard.

Jehan de Courtenai's duty was plain: to move on, continue his gaming, drinking, jesting, listening to voices of Cairo to learn what troops El Adel was sending into Syria to join Saladin. But he could not so easily abandon this red-haired girl.

"Five hundred, and you are robbing me." After five years in the service of fierce old Raynald de Chatillon, he had learned enough about the East to bargain. Immediate acceptance would have betrayed him.

"Six hundred, and my children starve," groaned Hussayn.

But the payment of even sixty *dinars* would have left de Courtenai without a *dirhem* for the next day's bread. He had a horse and arms. He could sell them, ambush some drunken *mamluk* and get fresh equipment. And he could leave Cairo that very night; he had El Adel's plans—

"Done, and Allah blacken you!" He dug into his purse. "Take this—in earnest—I bring the rest tonight—"

The auctioneer fondled the gold pieces. A step brought de Courtenai to the girl's side. He spoke a few words in *lingua franca*—a coarse jest that the crowd relished. Under cover of their laughter, he whispered in French, "Tonight we go to your father's friends in Akka."

He saw understanding in her green eyes. She knew now that he was a countryman, not an infidel Kurd.

He turned toward the arched gateway of the court, but it was blocked by veiled women and turbaned men who ran down the narrow street. The roll of kettle drums drowned their clamor, and a file of half-naked Sudani swordsmen filed around the corner. Tall runners struck right and left with their staves as they shouted, "Way for the Sword of the Faith, Abu Bekr the son of Ayyub of the House of Shahdi!"

These were the titles of Saladin's brother, El Adel, the governor of Egypt. He rode a black horse, and his jet robes made a dark tall splash among the yellow tunics and chain mail of his Turkish guards. De Courtenai salaamed with those who had taken refuge in the gateway. His voice swelled their applause.

Then the column turned, and the heralds cleared the gate. De Courtenai, though forced back against the jamb, could not hear what El Adel said to the tall *mamluk* who rode with him, boot to boot; but the Turkish officer's answer was plain enough: "She is here, in Hussayn's slave pen. On my head and eyes, *ya sidi!*"

She. De Courtenai's heart froze. The hoof beats of El Adel's horse ceased. A curb chain's tinkle broke the silence. Then El Adel demanded, *"Ya* Hussayn! Where is the Feringhi girl—?"

"In the corner, my lord!" the *mamluk* cut in.

"Ay wallah!" said Hussayn. "This way, redhead."

El Adel's words seemed like clods dropping into a grave: "Send her to the palace —to Sitti Zayda's apartments." A tinkle of gold. The prince cut off Hussayn's flood of thanks. "And veil her, father of a dog!" Drums rolled, and the black-robed horseman spurred his splendid beast through the gateway. Mail jingling, the yellow clad *mamluks* poured after him. El Adel resumed his march to the mosque.

Hussayn whined in de Courtenai's ear, "Sidi, your money—there is no bargain when the brother of the Victorious King buys. But I have other women—"

"Shaytan blacken you!" De Courtenai stalked down the street.

Who could oppose Saladin's brother? Certainly not a spy who dared not court notice. But this red-haired girl was more than just a Christian captive. De Courtenai's promise had revived her hope. He could not fail her now.

He stepped into the nearby *serai,* where his horse was waiting. "Saddle up!" he commanded to the groom. "Have him ready!"

Sitti Zayda was Saladin's sister. In the morning she was leaving with the caravan bound for Damascus, eight hundred miles away. That much de Courtenai knew from bazaar gossip; nor was the rest difficult to guess. The red-haired girl, sought out by El Adel himself, would go with the caravan; perhaps as Sitti Zayda's serving maid, perhaps as a hostage whose life would be bought with ruinous concessions from her friends.

There was still a way. The way of death and madness.

"Raynald has sent other spies who didn't return!" De Courtenai's laugh was iron as he rode that night toward the palace.

Hard men served Raynald. He could have no other kind; not in that hawk's nest southeast of the Dead Sea, perched on a high hill as a bulwark against the Moslem tide which relentlessly tried to engulf the long, narrow strip of Palestine that the Cross still held against the Crescent. Saladin's power grew day by day, and Raynald cursed the four years' truce which kept him from raiding the caravan trails.

Slowly, cautiously, not a link of his mail complaining, de Courtenai crept to the shadow of a bastion. Wrapped about his waist was a coil of silken cord. With infinite patience, he dug his dagger into the mortar, gouging toe holds. The moon rose above the domed tombs of the Khalifs as he reached the crest of the wall that girdled El Adel's palace.

But the shadow of a minaret reached out with a black band to hide him as he crouched, knotting the cord about a crenellation. And a moment later he was picking his way across a fragrant garden.

The spray of fountains mingled with jasmine. From afar, he heard the call of sentries walking their posts on the walls of the citadel. Presently de Courtenai slipped into the shadow of a pointed archway.

It seemed unguarded. From far within came the wavering light of flambeaux. Then a harsh voice rasped, "Back, *ya emir!* Are you drunk?"

A long-faced eunuch accosted him, blinking, scarcely crediting his eyes. An armed man in the quarter reserved for El Adel's women!

De Courtenai made no move for his blade. He regarded the eunuch as he might some curious insect. "Maybe you'd like to ask El Adel what I'm doing here. Quick, brother of a dog! Where's your chief?"

The eunuch's eyes dropped. There was no fear in this man, nor had he touched a weapon. He could not be an intruder. His bearing accorded with his gilded mail and silken *khalat*.

"I'll get him, *sidi.* On my head and eyes."

An easy way out. Let the chief eunuch be responsible. But de Courtenai interposed, "Get *al-asfarani*—the yellow haired daughter of the infidel. El Adel won't risk taking her across the desert. She's to go by boat. I'm in a hurry—it sails at once!"

The tall Kurd spoke with authority.

The eunuch had no mind to confess ignorance of El Adel's plans, and for all he knew de Courtenai had entered through the guarded gate. "Wait, sidi. I'll see if she is ready—"

"Tell her to get ready, pig!" snapped de Courtenai. He dared give the eunuch no time to think! "Hurry—or I'll skin you alive!"

His voice made echoes rumble. It was not until the fellow had hastened along the passageway that de Courtenai shivered from the sweat on which a breeze blew coldly. He muttered a prayer. Moments dragged…

From somewhere in that luxurious pile of masonry came the notes of an eight stringed *oudh*. A woman was singing.

There was another voice; a man's. And the only man in this building must be El Adel.

A white shape blossomed in the dark arch of a cross passage. The tinkle of bracelets startled de Courtenai. He turned. It was a woman.

She hurried to him, slippered feet whispering across the tiles. As she came into the torch glow, he could see her splendid figure outlined by the frail fabric that clung to every curve.

"I'm Elinor de Montfried—I heard your voice." Her breath trembled in his ear, and her red hair caressed his cheek. "You're as good as dead—go! While you can! Maqsoud will find out—El Adel is taking leave of his sister—I'm going with her—he said so."

"With me!" He caught her hand. "Over the wall—"

Elinor clung to him, fingers sinking into his wrist. "You can't—good God—they'll miss me any minute—"

"You're not going to Damascus!" He lifted her from her feet. She was tall and shapely, but she gasped at the ease with which he swung her to his shoulder. "Hang on. That rope'll—take us both—"

It would, but it was too far away. From within came a babble of voices. It swelled and echoed. Women scurried about, chattering and screaming with excitement. A man shouted, and others answered. Their armor rang, their feet thudded against the tiles. The alarm was out!

De Courtenai, carrying the girl, raced across the garden. Torches glared in its further depths, and steel gleamed. He ducked into the shadow of a plane tree, hoping the search would sweep past him. But the file of *mamluks* wheeled and their drawn scimitars were crescents of silver.

Elinor slipped to her feet. He said, "The rope—over there—I'll hold them—"

From the corner of his eye he saw the white flash of her legs as she ran. So did the pursuit. They divided, and as de Courtenai's sword drew sparks from a peaked helmet, another squad came charging from his right.

They came at his flank. He leaped back, blade whirling in hissing arcs. The captain dropped, his neck mail shorn, and his throat with it. A scimitar splintered to shards against de Courtenai's guard. But the weight of the attack was bearing him back.

Beyond his assailants he saw Elinor's white body writhing in the grasp of four men at arms. Her cape yielded in the struggle. Then a circle of mail engulfed her. But one bare arm reached out, and above the ring of steel and the panting of his enemies, de Courtenai heard her scream, "The gate—the gate—go—"

He had to. He could not cut down a company of *mamluks;* not while his life was valuable to Raynald de Chatillon. He whirled, dodging the tips of the crescent of blades that was swooping to surround him. He struck in passing, shifted swiftly, leaped clear.

Elinor's captors were dragging her into the palace. De Courtenai was separated from her by a wall of swords. And then he saw what she had meant by "the gate." It was open. Another squad of mamluks, summoned by the sentries, was rushing in from outside. They had him caged, or thought so; but if they had known him for one of Raynald's men, they would not have been so sure.

He moved faster than his first assailants could follow in the treacherous light of moon and torch; the newcomers did not recognize him for an enemy until he struck with his flailing blade.

Surprise helped; wrath drove him, and the strong arm behind his heavy scimitar cut through. For a moment the sheer weight of steel against casque and shoulders seemed to crush him to the ground. But the enemy were in each other's way. Chain mail yielded to his savage slashing; tall, wiry men scattered before his charge.

De Courtenai, battered and sword-seamed, cleared the gateway. He cut a horse-man from the saddle, took the dead man's seat as the milling footmen poured out af-ter him.

Then de Courtenai raced down the avenue toward the citadel. A sentry challenged him. Cairo was awakening. But the swift desert horse swooped falcon-like into the wastelands, in and out among the tombs, and toward the Mokkatam Hills...

At the first oasis, he mounted a racing camel whose owner's lance had been no match for de Courtenai's blood browned sword...

* * * *

Late one night, the sentries at the outer works of the Castle of Kerak challenged a solitary rider. They could not understand his answer. His camel collapsed and his peaked helmet gleamed dully as he sprawled in the sand near his beast.

"Another infidel trick—"

But they called the captain of the guard.

"De Courtenai!" The officer recognized the hawk's beak; the rest was grimy parchment drawn over bones, and a beard caked with dried blood. But when they gave him a flagon of wine, the returned spy spat the dust from his lips and croaked, "Where's Sieur Raynald?"

Presently, supported by two men at arms, he faced his grim chief and reported, "El Adel's armies are marching to Kurdistan. To compel the atabeg of Mosul to join Sal-adin. A holy war is brewing."

"Well done, de Courtenai," approved Raynald, but as he turned, the spy detained him.

"A moment, sir. I raced Saladin's caravan from Cairo. It's bound for Damascus. On the road that passes not far from our eastern boundary. We can seize it. El Adel has a captive. Elinor, the daughter of the sieur de Montfried."

Raynald cursed, shook his grizzled head. "Can't do it. That damned truce! I'd like to help you. With that moon calf look of yours, when you ought to be thinking of food and rest. But forget it."

Then de Courtenai played his last card. "Wait—there's something else I forgot. Sitti Zayda, Saladin's sister, is with the caravan."

"God's death! Are you certain?" Raynald caught the other's shoulder.

"Learned that in El Adel's palace. But the truce, Sieur Raynald?"

It was now a horse of a different color. "Truce—body of God!" Raynald stormed. "*I* didn't make the truce! That pagan-loving Raymond of Tripoli—that weak-kneed King of Jerusalem—they made it! What a chance! After thirteen years in a Turk's prison!"

Raynald paced the flagging like a caged tiger. His sword-seamed face was exalted. "Get some rest! You, Guilford, send out scouts! Don't worry, lad—we'll get that girl for you. But if Saladin's sister isn't in that train, I'll hang you by your heels!"

Kerak was already buzzing. The *snick-snick-snick* of whetstones on steel was the last sound that de Courtenai heard as he flung himself on a pallet of rushes. That, and the brazen blare of trumpets, was the first sound he heard, a full day later, when he stretched his aching limbs and tottered to his feet.

All day he scanned the shimmering horizon. Late in the afternoon, a white cloud rose toward the brazen sky. Many camels...fast camels—Saladin's camel, and Satan take all truces!

As the sun set, the iron men of Kerak rode down the steep hill. De Courtenai now wore his cross hiked sword, and the visor of his flat-topped helmet masked his face. He rode beside Raynald, and behind them came all the other wolves of Kerak; fierce Franks and lean Arab nomads who plundered all men alike.

Neither drum nor trumpet sounded. These men knew the desert and its warfare. They were intent on surprising the camp whose fires were a small winking red in the distance. There was only the muted voice of armor and curb chains muffled to avoid any betraying clank. And later, a muttered command passed down the column.

The nomad free lances swung from the troop. De Courtenai's heart hammered beneath his hauberk; hammered as it never had since his first battle. Time dragged as he pictured the nomads making a vast circle, looping back to the caravan's further flank—

Time unending...and then he heard it, a far off yell, the rush of camels' padding feet, the drumming hoofs of desert horses. He lowered his lance, leaned forward in the saddle.

"Hold it, fool!" yelled Raynald. "Wait till they're sure the nomads are running— wait—"

But de Courtenai's beast stretched long legs. Devil take strategy! The caravan guards were already in triumphant pursuit of the nomads. The camel train would not race into the darkness with its precious cargo.

He charged into the glare of waving torches, riding down the Negro footmen. Arrows rattled against his armor. A platoon of horse, about to take up the pursuit of the nomads, wheeled about at the howling. Scimitars whirling, marl agleam in the light of a blazing tent, they swooped into the oasis.

De Courtenai's lance cleared a saddle. Another—and splintered as it swept a Kurdish horseman to the sand. He pivoted, and his sword flailed into the pack that enclosed him. A blade licked up from the ground. His horse lurched hamstrung.

But the yell of triumph was drowned by the rumble of hooves from the rear. Women screamed. Fallen torches set other tents aflame. Grooms galloped frantically across the desert. The wolves of Kerak had arrived.

They swept the camp clear, reformed and met the main guard that came from its phantom chase across the sand. De Courtenai, again on horse, rode through the confusion to join in the last stroke of destruction. But as he passed a broad silken pavilion, a squad of Turkish guards charged out. In their center was a veiled woman, and beside her was one whose red hair trailed like a banner in the leaping flames: Sitti Zayda, and Elinor.

El Adel's *mamluks,* whom no alarm could draw from their loyal mistress! De Courtenai spurred his beast athwart their path. Scimitars danced against his shoulders, hammered his casque. Lances tore into his hauberk, and blades licked at his maddened horse. But he stood in the stirrups, wedged in the heart of the pack. Sword gripped in both hands, he whirled it, and the chaff from his mill was red. Then the rear guard troop from Kerak poured in. De Courtenai's dripping blade waved them away from the captives. Elinor slipped from her horse and to his saddle bow. One arm steadied her; his other hand seized the veiled woman before she could bolt.

It was all over except for guards beyond the fire glow, fighting back to back until thirsty blades cut them down. And that had scarcely ended when Raynald returned from his red work at the further fringe of the oasis.

He reined in, eyed Elinor's white loveliness, and boomed, "God's blood, de Courtenai! I don't blame you. But I've found something sweeter!"

He leaned over in the saddle, reached for the Saracen girl's gold embroidered veil. De Courtenai's protest was too late. The frail fabric yielded, and her cape came with it in Raynald's great paw. Bare faced and bare headed; lustrous black hair all agleam with great rubies; pearls shimmered against her olive tinted throat, and a pearl pendant nestled in the hollow of her breast.

In the eyes of a Moslem, this was exposure shameful as the nudity of the slave market.

"My lord the wolf." Zayda's voice trembled with fury, and the glow of cheek and breast was more than the fire's reflection. "Saladin's own hand will cut that arm from your body."

The Lord of Kerak laughed gustily. "Let him seek me, any day."

"Sieur de Chatillon," interposed de Courtenai, impressed by the girl's proud bearing, "it's not her fault, your thirteen years' captivity."

Elinor caught Raynald's arm. "As a favor, let her be veiled."

Raynald shrugged, gestured to the trumpeter. Recall rang above the dying crackle of the flames, and soon the wolves of Kerak were marching across the desert with their loot.

Elinor refused a horse. Arms twined about de Courtenai's blood splashed neck, bare shoulder leaning against his slashed hauberk, she whispered, "Take off your helmet. So I can see you. Every minute, as long as I can. It's so wonderful—I can't believe it—I heard in Cairo that father escaped—"

He doffed his battered casque, drew her toward him till she gasped from his fierce embrace. Then in the moonlight he saw that her eyes were tear-gleaming, and sorrowful as her face.

"I'll send a message to your father. He won't worry long—"

"It's not that," she explained, "this raid will mean war. It's my fault—"

"A dozen wars!" he laughed. "This is worth them."

"No. It's the end for the Crusader's power. The holy fire has left them. In Cairo I heard that. Saladin is uniting all the infidel tribes who used to fight each other instead of us. The King of Jerusalem is an oaf. Count Raymond of Tripoli is more Saracen than Christian. We'll be swept into the sea—"

"We'll go back to France, you and I!" He kissed the qualms from her red mouth, but not the fear from his own heart. Elinor was right. Not this year, or next, but in the end. Islam had become a consuming flame.

The rising moon welcomed the wolves to Kerak. Sieur Raynald ushered Elinor and Sitti Zayda to apartments in an isolated turret in the great black castle. He relished his vengeance and said, "Lady Elinor, I give you a king's sister to dress your hair!"

But the smoldering eyes of the Saracenic princess did not brighten. She knew the lord of Kerak and his undying hatred for her race.

"Rest while we drink," was de Courtenai's final word at the massive door. "Vengeance is sleep for Sieur Raynald. But you won't hear the splash of wine up there in the turret."

"Try and break away," whispered Elinor.

"You'd better bolt the door," he warned, knowing that she would not.

Down in the somber acre of dining room, Sieur Raynald and his wolves feasted and drank. Circassian girls from the caravan poured their wine. Flickering torchlight kissed their unveiled beauty, brought fire from their gilded hair. Syrian slaves with languorous black eyes sang to the music of pearl inlaid rebeks.

"Bring out that wine from Samos!" roared Raynald, pounding his flagon against the board. "Out of the deepest cellar! What we can't drink now, time will lap up! Dry dusty time—time that makes old men of me and Saladin—puts a white beard on my vengeance—"

"You've brought him out of his hole, Sieur Raynald!" boomed hook nosed Guilford, and others shouted, "Here's your war, Father of Wolves!"

So they drank and planned. War it must be, for they had seized a caravan that their overlord, the King of Jerusalem, had given protection.

But de Courtenai's thoughts were in the far off turret... He watched the dancing girls from Hindustan, part of the royal loot. Their breasts were masked by hemispheres of gold, and their writhing stomachs were pale gold in the torch glow. The jeweled pendants of their broad girdles winked with the sensuous sway of their hips, and their black eyes seconded the passionate voice of the *sitars.*

When the table was cleared, half the wolves of Kerak were beneath it. Wine blazed in their eyes and dripped from the beards of those who were still in their chairs. They pounded their flagons as the nautch girls from El Adel's train swayed down the length of the table. Their slim legs twinkled, smiled through the frail scarlet skirts that swirled with their turning, rising hip-high, settling faster than the eye could follow.

The planning for war was over. The Syrian slaves left their corners, joined the girls from Hindustan. Their lips were ready for any master. Sieur Raynald slapped de Courtenai on the shoulder, nearly knocking him from his chair. "Go to the turret! *Pardieu!* She's waiting for you!"

He welcomed his dismissal, and laughed as Sieur Raynald reached for the nautch girl de Courtenai had thrust aside. As he stalked through the halls, he regretted a frayed doublet and patched cape, the last of his once rich wardrobe.

She was waiting, eyes aglow—until they misted from his kiss. He carried her to the massive bench set into the turret's overhanging gallery. The poison sweetness of oriental perfumes no longer tainted her outlandish borrowed garb. In the shadows, all he could see was whiteness that reminded him of home and far off France.

He had kissed many women in many a mad Syrian night. But Elinor was a wonder that made him feel awkward and unworthy. To have her beside him was enough.

Or so the thought was in his wine dizzied brain, until her nearness inflamed him, and she whispered, "Don't ever leave me! Love me as long as you can—there's war to-morrow—I'll be in Tiberias, waiting—"

And that was heady logic...

"I don't care why you left France...whose husband you killed," she murmured finally. "Father will let me marry you. After last night—"

But a cry cut into their kisses; low, wrathful, like the scream of a panther. It was Saladin's high spirited sister. "Dog and father of many dogs—"

Glass spattered. Cloth ripped. A triumphant laugh raised bellowing echoes. Sieur Raynald was seeking vengeance. De Courtenai leaped to his feet. Elinor followed, seeking a taper from a far alcove.

Zayda it was, and Sieur Raynald's powerful hands were more than full. Her gown hung in shreds to her slim waist, but her hennaed nails were raking his face.

"My lord," shouted de Courtenai, seizing Raynald by the shoulder, "you're drunk —this isn't man's vengeance—"

The wolf of Kerak whirled, flung Zayda asprawl. He was weaving on his feet, yet cat-quick for all of that. De Courtenai flung up an empty hand to strike aside Sieur Raynald's dagger slash.

"Stop!" screamed Elinor. "She was good to me—as she could be—"

Sieur Raynald lunged, raging.

Zayda scrambled to her feet. "Saladin's own hands will cut the arms from you!" But Elinor settled it as de Courtenai grappled with his wrath crazed chief. She smote him over the head with a candlestick, and he dropped.

"By God!" panted de Courtenai. "He's dead—"

The three eyed one another.

But Raynald was too drunk to be killed easily. He grunted, came to his knees, well sobered. "Maybe you're right, de Courtenai," he said thickly. "Take her away. Take them both to Tiberias. If that heathen wench is untouched, we can bargain with Saladin. Win time for that thin blooded King of Jerusalem to collect his wits and prepare for war."

He reeled, blinked. "Tonight, de Courtenai. Before the news spreads and the marches are thick with Saladin's men."

"But you, Sieur Raynald?"

"I stay to hold Kerak. Until those fools on the coast need me!"

* * * *

So that dawn, de Courtenai and a fairly sober squad of the wolf's pack set out for the black gorge of the Dead Sea.

As he rode, de Courtenai said to his men, "This infidel girl is Lady Elinor's maid. The first man who noises it about Jerusalem that she is Saladin's sister gets his skull split to the chin!"

And the wolves knew their captain.

Sitti Zayda said to him, "Why do you do this for me, *ya emir?*"

"For her sake, King's Sister," he answered in Arabic. "Because of you, not her, the wolf of Kerak made his raid. You were her fortune."

"Allah does what he will do!" Zayda answered, shrugging her cape closer about her. "It was written."

And de Courtenai began to know why the holy fire of the crusades had dimmed. For a century, between battles, the invading Franks had rubbed elbows with the Moslem. They could no longer as fervently hate these people who accepted any turn of fortune as the unquestioned will of the One True God. The Crusader was no longer certain as he once had been; like himself, the Moslem revered Christ as a prophet.

King Guy of Jerusalem blustered and trembled when, days later, he received de Courtenai's report. The grim Templars brightened. Their Grand Master, iron hearted Gerard de Rideford, caressed his sword. But swarthy Count Raymond of Tripoli pulled his sharp face into sombre angles.

"This is not well, de Courtenai. We had two more years of truce. Two more years to prepare against Saladin's growing power. And with diplomacy—"

"Christ's blood!" growled the wolf's cub. "Were diplomats sent to hold Kerak? Sharpen sword, *monsieur le compte*! We've got—"

But he checked himself before he blurted out that Saladin's sister was a hostage. He could not betray that high spirited girl to this lukewarm pack; each night on the long march with Elinor had made him more grateful to Zayda. His Moslem disguise had been more than skin deep; Arab-like, he felt that Zayda was part of Elinor's *kismet*.

"We've got," he resumed, "the advantage of assembling before Saladin gets the news."

As he turned on his heel, Count Raymond detained him. "Raynald should be hanged by the heels, the hot-headed fool! But take a message to my wife in Tiberias. If you will be so good, *monsieur.*"

"At your pleasure, Sieur Raymond."

"King Guy's council," said the Count of Tripoli, "has appointed Nablus as the rallying point. Tell her to send messengers north from Tiberias to Tripoli. And to Antioch."

At dawn, de Courtenai's party left Jerusalem.

"I'm afraid," shuddered Elinor. "God can't bless our love. It's causing war—fresh war, when there could have been two years' peace—"

"But war in the end, just the same," de Courtenai finished.

"There is no God but Allah," murmured the veiled maid-servant who rode the ambling jenny. "He does what he will do, and may he give my brother the right arm of Raynald!"

* * * *

When de Courtenai left the banks of the Jordan to skirt the western shore of the Sea of Galilee, he overtook villagers heading northward. Dust rose as far as he could see the road, and dust clouds trailed down the vine clad slopes, cut the dark green of olive groves, the ripe gold of wheat in the flatlands. The country was alive, and each beast of burden was heaped mountain high; not with farm produce, but with household goods.

The countryside was heading for Tiberias, and de Courtenai could taste fear in the very air. "Oh Uncle," he shouted to a grizzled Syrian bent double with the burden he carried, "what festival brings you from the hills?"

"Saladin has come to harvest!" moaned the woman at his side, stumbling from the naked children that ran at her heels. "The Turks come down from Damascus—last night we saw the flames of villages—"

They were on their way to Tiberias and the shelter of its walls. De Courtenai cursed, gestured at the gray towers and walls of the city and the blue of the sea behind, where it bowed out to Mejdel. He had lost too much time. Some survivor of the caravan had ridden north. Saladin must have received the news in Damascus!

They ploughed on through the stream of peasants that blocked the road. They were caught by the vortex that poured into the gates of Tiberias that evening. The walls were manned, and knights with fresh crosses sewed to their surcoats spurred about, directing the men at arms who carried rocks and oil and sheaves of arrows to the parapets. It was stale news that de Courtenai brought to Eschiva, Count Raymond's wife and chatelaine of Tiberias.

"*Madame*," said de Courtenai when the countess received him in a hall all astir with her clanking captains, "I bring you greetings from *monsieur le compte*. But instead of giving you his message, I will take your news to him."

The blonde chatelaine thanked him, called for food and wine for his weary party. Then she said to Elinor, "Your father reached Tiberias, but his wounds are—"

She checked herself.

"Tell me!" Elinor's nails dug into her palms.

"He died praying for your safety." Eschiva drew the white-faced girl to her side. "But you are welcome—to whatever war leaves us."

Elinor swallowed a sob, smiled bravely. She caught de Courtenai's hand and said, "It has brought me Jehan, *madame*. It will leave me with him. And this pagan girl who was kind to me during my captivity."

Eschiva's weary eyes brightened. "Sieur de Courtenai, the priests will soon be too busy with the dying. But there will be time for them to do a happier duty."

Elinor turned from the chatelaine's arm.

"Jehan," she said, "I'm so very much alone—and if you can love me, after the ruin I've caused—"

His kiss cut short her words of self-reproach. Then he turned to bow to the countess. *"Madame,* where is this priest?"

The countess laughed softly. "De Courtenai, give this poor girl a chance to get over that long march! And you're dying on your feet. Tomorrow—forgive me, but these officers are enough to drive one woman crazy!"

She turned to the captains who came to report. A steward ushered the travelers to their quarters. The countess was right. De Courtenai was perishing of weariness; but his last thought was that with a night's rest, he could handle Saladin and all his armies...

* * * *

At first it seemed that a far off storm was brewing. Still half asleep, de Courtenai gained his feet, saw the gray of dawn against his window bars. Then knew that the sullen rumble was the voice of saddle drums. Trumpets shook the city, and the shouts of men on the walls drove de Courtenai toward his armor. The hoofs of Saracen cavalry were shaking the earth. Saladin's advance guard had ridden day and night to strike before the city was prepared for siege.

He bounded to his door; Elinor's trembling fingers buckled his hauberk, laced his helmet. Sunrise reddened the Sea of Galilee. Leaning from the window, they could see the gleaming helmets of the advancing horde. A crescent of steel was enveloping the landward side of Tiberias.

"Fate rides fast," said the girl in de Courtenai's arms. "God—look at them—"

It was lighter now, and she could distinguish the black standards of Islam, the dirty brown of camels and the brown robes of Bedouin lancers who followed the wave of cavalry. "No! Don't go—not yet—"

He could not shake her loose. "I've got to join them." He gestured toward the squires who helped armored knights to their horses in the court below; to the horse and foot that already sortied from the city gates, pennons a-flutter and field music blaring.

"No—it'll be a siege—you're worn out—" she begged. "Tomorrow—there'll be days aplenty for that!" Her lips sapped his resolution.

But Elinor recoiled from his arms when the chatelaine's quiet voice broke in, "Sieur de Courtenai, she's right. I'm recalling the hotheads who just left without orders. But you can serve us all. As no one else can."

"How, madame?"

"Ride to rallying point at Nablûs. Warn my husband and the king. More than the advance guard is surrounding us. A messenger arrived before dawn. It's the main body of Saladin's army."

Her slender arm reached beyond the embrasure, indicating the turbaned men who were unloading parts of siege engines from the backs of camels, and assembling the fitted beams.

"You can get through, disguised as an infidel. No one else could have done what you did in Cairo."

"No one," echoed Elinor, lips suddenly gray as she thought of one man, and that man her lover, facing Saladin's horde.

"I can," said de Courtenai, removing his flat topped helmet. "By slipping to the lake. Getting beyond their flank."

"Zayda," Elinor whispered fiercely, close in his arms. "Couldn't we make her buy them off?"

"No woman could stop that army! She's your luck. Don't betray her."

Then de Courtenai followed the Chatelaine to choose a Saracen's weapons from the armory…

* * * *

Later, a patrol filed from a sally port, fanned out, charged at the besiegers. Dust and the wide line of steel blotted the enemy from de Courtenai's eye. When the charge of the Franks melted before a hail of Turkish arrows, he was afloat, unperceived by Moslems who followed the retreating horsemen to the very walls.

Miles south, his swarthy Turcople boatmen set him ashore. De Courtenai had no horse, nor was any to be found in that deserted lakeside. But a mule grazing beyond an abandoned village served his purpose. So he rode, turban wound to hide his helmet, a flowing cape to conceal his chain mail and scimitar.

The Wolf of Kerak was at Nablus when de Courtenai gave the message to the council. "I left soon after you did," he laughed, "to prod these cattle into the field.

But where's that heathen hell cat?"

"In Tiberias." This unexpected encounter with his chief left de Courtenai no other answer. Had he chosen a lie, he could not have convinced Sieur Raynald that Zayda had escaped. "But the Saracens won't raise the siege on her account—it's gone too far for bargaining."

The strategy of the Crusaders was direct enough: go north at once with what forces had gathered, menace the Saracen flank and block their southward march. In the meanwhile, the rest of the Franks could assemble and then join the advance guard.

The column of horse and foot set out the following dawn, an iron serpent that wound across the sun drenched plain. Heat devils danced ahead, and low hanging dust lingered behind. Armor speedily became blistering hot. Sweat blackened leather jerkins, foam whitened the horse gear—until the fierce breath of Palestine dried out both man and beast, and bitter dust burned eye and lip and nostril.

Slow, relentless, massive; giant men, ponderous mounts, heavy lances, going north to meet lean horsemen who swooped like falcons across the desert's face. De Courtenai put pebbles into his dry mouth and husbanded his leather flask of brackish water like his chief. He had but one thirst: for battle beneath the walls of Tiberias.

Scouts came and went. Rumors were thicker than the dust. Tiberias had capitulated... Saladin had died in battle at Antioch, and victorious Franks were hurrying south to join their comrades...but that night, the blaze of looted villages winked from far off hilltops.

A second day. Then the third: a baking, stifling hell. Footmen stumbled over the furnace-hot, rocky terrain, and horses fell beneath the weight of armored riders. But at last they reached the shade and cool water of the springs at Seffuriyeh.

"Another day's march!" De Courtenai unlaced his helmet.

"The wolves of Kerak," growled Sieur Raynald, "could go tonight and strike at dawn!"

But there was no advance in the morning. Couriers came from the flank guards, and this time there were no rumors. Men riddled with lance and arrow were riding in from the Jordan. They had barely escaped the Saracen column that came from the east to ford the river and march along the Sea of Galilee toward Tiberias.

Taki-ud-Din, Saladin's nephew, had arrived with a second army of Kurdish mountaineers, bearded Bedouins, the atabegs of Mosul with their horse-tail standards. All Islam was in motion and moving swiftly.

The council of the Franks temporized. "Wait for reinforcements!" was a many voiced demand that drowned the impatient clamor of Sieur Raynald, and de Courtenai's taunt to Count Raymond: "Coward! Your wife and your castle besieged—and you wait for men!"

* * * *

Days passed. June ended, and July's flame burned the land. Troops, Templars, Knights of the Hospital, lords of outlying fortresses had come to Seffuriyeh to reinforce King Guy's army. All the power of the Franks was massed; but valor and strength were weakened by dissension.

Sieur Raynald and de Courtenai forced the issue. That was when a haggard courier came from Tiberias. Lady Eschiva could not much longer hold the beleaguered city.

"God's death!" stormed de Courtenai. "We can cut through! Ask Sieur Raynald!"

But Count Raymond, though haggard from brooding over his wife's peril, shook his head. "No. We've waited too long. There is not a well between here and Tiberias. Not a drop of water. Our men would be dead on their feet before we met the Saracens."

"How many times can a man die?" mocked grim de Rideford, the Templar. "Or have you made another private bargain with Saladin?"

Count Raymond's sharp face whitened with wrath. He gripped his sword-hilt, but King Guy intervened. The count answered, wearily, "By God and the Holy Cross that goes before us into battle, I would rather lose my wife and castle than doom an army. You, de Courtenai—would you give all these men to the sword to save Lady Elinor —do you love her more than I my wife?"

"All these and as many more!" flared de Courtenai.

"And I'll lead them!" Sieur Raynald thundered.

They turned blazing eyes to the king who gnawed his blond moustache. He glanced helplessly from face to face. The rumble of voices dizzied him; some seconded Count Raymond's heroic sacrifice, some damned it as treachery, cowardice. And then de Rideford, Master of the Templars, advanced a pace.

"My lord king," he said, "I gave you the treasure I held in trust for the King of England. It has paid all these troops you summoned in this extremity."

"Lead us!" stormed the wolf of Kerak. And de Courtenai added, "Through hell if you will—let thirst drive us to Galilee!"

Count Raymond raised his hand, but de Courtenai's voice was a contagious fire, and so was the gleam in the Templar's eye. Though King Guy gestured for silence, it was his white face that stilled them.

"Lords, knights, burghers—we advance at dawn!"

* * * *

From the hills about the well of Seffuriyeh they marched east toward Galilee. And the sun that baked them that day made all former heat a coolness; a slow torment of choking dust and parched lips. Men lagged, stumbled, rose again as the horsemen smote them with the flat of swords.

But de Courtenai and the wolves of Kerak mocked thirst. This was no worse than any desert march. Elinor was beyond the steep ridge that blocked the view of cool Galilee. Her welcoming arms seemed to reach out, urge him on.

Midway across the Plain of Turan, Turkish archers swooped from the flanking hills, taunting the advance guard, halting the main body while the wolves of Kerak met them in their own game. Harassed on the entire front, backing and filling, the Frankish army wore itself out, making no progress, nor yet closing with the elusive horsemen.

In camp that night the last water skin was emptied. Haggard men dropped in their tracks to sleep. Weary horsemen patrolled to guard against surprise. And priests moved softly to and fro, administering the sacraments to those who would die in the morning.

"Pardieu!" De Courtenai's dry lips twisted, but he refused to touch the water he had hoarded against the next day's march. "We were wrong, Sieur Raynald! These poor devils will die of thirst. We might have known they couldn't stand it."

The old wolf laughed as he sucked a cross bow bolt to save water. "God's blood, Jehan! Is that girl making you a weakling?"

"No. But the lives of these men are on my head and yours." Too late, de Courtenai realized that Elinor should have left Tiberias with him. But who could have foreseen Taki-ud-Din's army, the last fatal reinforcement to Saladin's horde?

A red sun rose into a brazen sky, fierce promise of the torment ahead. Trumpets blared down the long line of spears, and pennons drooped in the still air. De Courtenai and the wolves of Kerak were the king's body guard; and with them went the True Cross, encased in gold. They trotted out, and as the ranks wavered from the broken ground, Sieur Raynald gestured to the dust cloud far ahead.

"God's death! They've come to welcome us!"

Cymbals clanged. Saddle drums muttered. The hills flung back the sonorous war cry of the Moslem. The Saracens had cut down the outposts; and the battle began before the march was half under way.

The two forces clashed in the deserted village of Lubiyeh. Dust clouds obscured the sun, and companies lost each other in the confusion. De Courtenai led the charge to the center of crescent. Lance shattered, he hewed with his blade.

Yard by yard, sheer weight of horse and man ploughed into the whirlpool of swooping horsemen. Arrows peppered de Courtenai like hail, lances bit his hauberk; but Sieur Raynald and the wolves smote home. Water and Tiberias were ahead. Death was behind.

"They're breaking!" He spurred his wounded horse into that hell roar of drums and thundering hoofs.

But as they advanced, the tips of the crescent closed in. Exhaustion killed more than did Turkish arrow or scimitar stroke. And narrow gullies broke the front of the advancing pike men. The battle became raging clusters of unorganized combat. Saracen cavalry swooped through gaps, diving to attack, then swiftly retreating. They had water at their backs and they were fresh.

"Once more!" roared Sieur Raynald, pausing at the king's side. "We're through the village! Guilford—de Courtenai—over there—"

Courage flamed anew. Men half dead of thirst took life from desperation. Scattered companies formed, aligned, shoulder to shoulder. Knights massed to lead the way. Over the next crest, then down the steep slope to the fresh waters of Galilee—

But a new foe met them. They saw too late why the enemy fled. The tamarisk brush of the gullies was aflame, and dense smoke billowed to join the dust. The hollow beyond the village was a furnace. Sparks rained, and arrows beyond number hissed through the enveloping curtain of fire.

Back—around—flank exposed—they formed again, those who were not cut down. Ahead, above the blazing gullies, was barren ground. De Courtenai toiled up the slope of the crescent shaped hill. There, on the Horns of Hattin, what remained of the Frankish army gathered around its king and the True Cross. Only a handful; the wolves of Kerak, and Templars pledged to accept no quarter—though none would be offered here.

King Guy wielded a broken sword. Shoulder to shoulder they stood, notched blades and axes, hacked armor still turning the Saracen charge. Then footmen closed in, driven ahead by the cavalry to overwhelm the king and his standard, whatever the cost.

Sieur Raynald went down. De Courtenai whirled, sword in both hands. It bit deep, slashed wide. But the Templar guarding his back caught a lance between the teeth. A mace smashed down on de Courtenai's dented helmet. He stumbled, dazed by the shock. And a surge of Turks trampled him into the ground, stifling him, weighting the blade he strove to recover. Another blow—the red sunset became black—

Night had veiled the Horns of Hattin when de Courtenai crawled from among the dead. Ahead of him were the fires of Saladin's camp, and above was a moon that picked out the armor of the dead. Bit by bit he remembered, and as his strength returned, he dug into the tangle of Frank and Moslem about him. But he did not find Sieur Raynald nor the king.

A water skin from the saddle of a dead camel gave him fresh life, and with it, fresh woe. All this slaughter was on his head; his strategy had brought this to pass, and Sieur Raynald was a captive.

Desperation moved him. What he had done in Cairo, he could do again. He unbuckled his armor, stripped a raw boned Kurd he found at the foot of the slope. He bandaged his wounds, armed himself anew. His brain was a fevered maze; he knew only that Elinor was in Tiberias, and Sieur Raynald in the Saracen camp. Perhaps he had thus far escaped Saladin's notice.

De Courtenai moved without plan or stealth. Madness succeeded where reason could not. He passed the lines, stumbled among the Moslems who squatted about guard fires. A word here—a word there—a battered, reeling Kurd was no novelty in that camp. Thus he heard the last heavy word. Tiberias had capitulated; with the Franks doomed at Hattin, the countess had no other choice. Elinor, captive again—

He was now too numb to move except by instinct. Find Saladin, assume Sieur Raynald's guilt. Ransom Elinor. Meet Saladin, stab him, and go down in a whirl of blades. Everything was confused, chaotic.

He halted near a pavilion lit by many torches. There were guards in yellow khalats, emirs in gilded mail, bearded scribes and clerks; slaves and musicians. He knew that he was right, even before he saw that thin man whose weary face was darker than his beard; a frail man in black, older than El Adel, governor of Cairo, but with features like his.

Saladin, seated on a rug spread on the earth. Picked swordsmen about him, and others guarding the captives he faced. There was the blonde King of Jerusalem, and Sieur Raynald, sword-slashed but arrogant. The Sultan clapped his hands. A slave stepped to his side, presented a flagon of sherbet chilled by snow from Lebanon. Saladin rose, took the flagon and with his own hands offered it to Guy of Jerusalem. De Courtenai relaxed. No man who tasted the Sultan's food and drink would bend his neck beneath the headsman's sword. The King, lips black with dust, could scarcely speak his thanks. He took a swallow, turned to hand the drink to Saladin's mortal enemy, the wolf of Kerak.

"Thank God!" muttered de Courtenai. "Merciful in victory—maybe he doesn't know about Zayda—maybe—"

He trembled, watching the flagon rise to Sieur Raynald's parched mouth. No one dashed it from his lips. And then de Courtenai's blood froze. Saladin said, "Drink, lord of the wolf pack. But your king gave it to you, not I."

Sieur Raynald started. Strong arms seized King Guy, who understood. Saladin's thin scimitar hissed from its sheath. De Courtenai's yell shook the wits of the bodyguard. He leaped into the pavilion, his own blade dancing.

But he was not quick enough to block the sultan's stroke. The keen crescent slashed through flesh and bone, shearing the right arm Sieur Raynald raised. He sank beneath the flailing steel of the guards who closed in to finish what their master had begun; and rough hands gripped the madman who cursed the grim faced Sultan.

Weight and weariness overpowered de Courtenai. King Guy was pale as he stared at the red heap that shuddered on the ground.

Saladin smiled. "You are a king, and under my protection. But that man affronted the honor of my house and broke a safeguard." He turned to de Courtenai. "Another wolf, and loyal to the end?"

"Strike again!" challenged de Courtenai. "They kept me from you."

"A madman is in the hand of Allah," countered Saladin. "And you came tonight as a Kurd. As you came to Cairo and my brother's palace. Your life is yours, de Courtenai."

De Courtenai scarcely heard for the drumming in his ears. Saladin reassured him. "The power of the Franks ended this day on the Horns of Hattin. Others may come, but Islam is ready and waiting. So go your way. And take with you the red-haired girl who was my sister's maid." He gestured to the curtain that divided the front of the pavilion from the back. De Courtenai bowed to the conquering king and the conquered; then he followed a *mamluk* down the silken passageway to the rear.

He still could not believe. Not until he saw Elinor and the tears that gleamed in her incredulous eyes.

"You—Jehan—but they told me," she sobbed against his dusty mail, "you were dead—Saladin sent men to capture you alive—"

"I cut them down before they could tell me!" He laughed exultantly, and his arms closed about that white loveliness which had led him to the Horns of Hattin.

SCORCHED EARTH

Originally published in *Speed Adventure Stories*, July 1944.

When Mu Lan fingered a curl which was already faultless, and paused for a moment to admire the hair-do which she had invented, a blend of Chinese and Manchu styling, plus a touch of her own. All her life, Mu Lan had been revising rules to suit herself, but this was the first time that the freedom of a sing-song girl promised to have real meaning.

Her *amah* stood behind her, watching with pride and apprehension; Yu Tang was glad when her mistress smiled and said that all was perfect. Then Mu Lan twisted a jade pendant of her ornate head gear. The jewel separated into hollowed halves, into whose cavity she put several small pellets. This was not her first invitation to appear at General Yasuda's quarters, but it might be her last.

General Yasuda was Japanese, and a gentleman, and so, particularly disliking his guest of honor, he had outdone himself in arranging the dinner to welcome Gunther Dreckhauffen, who had come to observe the workings of Co-Prosperity in the Rice Bowl. The bullet-headed Nazi, on the other hand, true to the training of his kind, was not content with being as boorish as nature had made him: he pointed out how German efficiency would have improved every course from bird's nest soup and steamed sweet doughnuts to the flattish and sticky champagne.

"General Yasuda—" Dreckhauffen consistently ignored both field and company officers, his gesture including them with the litter on the table. "It is already plain that instead of occupying China, and then breaking the Russian truce, you are becoming as Chinese as your cuisine."

Yasuda smiled. He was a delicate-looking little man, as frail and unsubstantial-seeming as the evasion which he offered, instead of a retort: "After all, the Chinese are better cooks than we are."

The Nazi was so shocked that his monocle dropped from his eye. *Um gottes willen,* what kind of a man is it who can see good in another nation? Not a bit more character than the *Dagos!* With such allies, no wonder that *der Fuehrer* had to save the world single handed.

Yasuda had a fair idea of what passed behind the envoy's fat face, but his amiability did not waver. "Mr. Dreckhauffen," he went on, using the English which served as a common tongue for the two, "when you see the final Chinese touch, I think that you do not blame me for—for—making concessions to art."

"Eh? More food?"

He mopped his dripping face, and ran a thick finger inside his collar, over which his neck made a red bulge.

"Oh, not at all. Now that we have titillated our palates, we have a feast of wit and reason. Chen Mu Lan, the Shanghai sing-song girl, consents to entertain us."

"*Consents? Herr gott*! Could she refuse?"

"Of course not. But one can hardly be entertaining, witty, and charming by command."

Dreckhauffen snorted. "In Germany, one can, and one does."

And then the Number One announced Chen Mu Lan. Yasuda nodded, beamed at his guest; the general, having the soul of an artist, took pride in being the patron of China's loveliest sing-song girl, and ignored the possibility of her having had unusual motives in leaving Shanghai.

She moved with a mincing pace, artificial as it was graceful. Jade ear pendants, and the jade pendants handing from her satin hood made a thin, sweet tinkling, fragile as the conventional twitter of her voice when she kowtowed, greeting host and guest of honor.

Dreckhauffen eyed her from tiny embroidered slippers to the arch of close-packed curls which framed her forehead. Mu Lan was neither tall nor as slender as she seemed, for the knee length tunic combined with her silk trousers and prim, high collar to exaggerate her slimness, while the Manchu styled headgear increased the illusion of height.

The Nazi grunted, and with not quite his usual disparagement. "Nimble enough, for her crippled feet."

Yasuda hissed, somewhat out of politeness, and somewhat to conceal his amazement at ignorance. "Please, begging pardon, those are naturally small. Sing-song girls never binding feet." Mu Lan's training had taken more time, and covered more ground than an American debutante and an American Doctor of Philosophy could claim between them; she knew how a wine glass should be touched, and how even the incorrect inflection of her smallest finger could detract from the perfection of the gesture: and so with her repartee. But none of the company knew enough Chinese to be worthy of her talent, so she sang in that studied falsetto, and pantomimed with all the finish developed in forty odd centuries of training sing-song girls.

The *sam yin* wailed. The drums muttered; drums, and the shivering, hissing brazen gongs. Dreckhauffen shuddered, and growled, *"Herr gott! This is worse than those stupid geishas!"*

Between songs, Mu Lan drank tiny cups of *mui kwai lu,* which tastes like sewing machine oil flavored with attar of roses. Though she wheedled Dreckhauffen into emptying cup after cup of orange-red *ng ka pay,* her glance slid always to Yasuda, a glance which, as to angle and the droop of eyelids, had been prescribed a thousand years before the ancestors of both Gunther Dreckhauffen and the Son of Heaven had quit raw meat and smoky caves.

The general smiled his appreciation. Of the girl, the Nazi thought; he didn't know that the Jap relished the triple-edged mockery of Mu Lan's song about the foreign devil with the eyes of a pig and the manners of a buffalo, sweating and grunting and fingering his tight collar.

Mu Lan knew now that she had not wasted those weeks of establishing herself in Cheng Teh, to make her presence the touch without which a dinner would merely have been a meal.

To impress the Nazi observer, Yasuda had inevitably to make an important move to convince him that the failure to complete the seizure of this sector of the Rice Bowl had been according to plan. Sooner or later, such a gesture would have had to come, if only to maintain Yasuda's "face" in Japan. Dreckhauffen's presence had merely hastened the climax.

The next move would be toward Ching Pao, Mu Lan's native village; so she was going to her own people. The same instinct which once made Chinese section hands arrange to have their bones shipped from California to the ancestral burial ground, now drove Mu Lan to Ching Pao, "Precious Gold," as the dumpy little village called itself, to sound more impressive than its neighboring rival, Yin Pao, Precious Silver.

She seated herself, smiled dazzling at Dreckhauffen, and proposed a game of *chai mui.*

"Like this," Mu Lan explained, thrusting out three fingers. "I call *three!* You answer, seven, and put out enough fingers to make ten. A mistake, and you lose."

"What do we bet?"

"You have to drink a cup of General Yasuda's brandy. And if I lose—"

Dreckhauffen brightened some more. "You drink one, eh? Very good."

But it wasn't what he expected. Voice and fingers tricked him, and when it came his turn, he could not catch Mu Lan off guard. Though the general lost, he took it good-naturedly, while the Nazi considered that honor was being affronted.

The more bets he lost, the more *ng ka pay* he drank, and the more he fumbled. Yasuda began to enjoy the thus far unpleasant dinner, and so did his officers, until they fell on their faces to snore into the banquet remnants. Food rather than brandy had overcome them, since years of short rations had made them unaccustomed to hearty eating.

The amiable little general blinked owlishly through his misted glasses when Dreckhauffen crumpled in a heap, knocking down bottles and jugs and glasses.

"The foreign devil cannot even pass out like a gentleman," Mu Lan said, laughing. "Now with your permission, worthy general?"

Though Yasuda handed the sing-song girl's maid an envelope containing more than the customary fee for making an appearance, his enjoyment of his triumph made him reluctant to dismiss her; and Mu Lan, after pleading another engagement, let herself be talked into staying.

She did not stay long. A song and three drinks settled Yasuda, and without the assistance of the opiate in the hair pendant.

Yu Tang gathered up Mu Lan's cape and fan and discarded bracelets. The musicians had long since left. Then, as the *amah* watched at the door, Mu Lan searched first the general's pockets, and next the living quarters. She returned with a sheaf of orders, all in Japanese, which she could not speak; but since the monkey men had cribbed their hieroglyphics from the Chinese, lacking any writing of their own, the significance of many of the characters was clear to anyone who could read.

Rumor had been right. There was an order to make a demonstration because of the Nazi's presence.

Once outside the house, Yu Tang awakened the coolies who snored in a corner. Mu Lan got into the sedan chair; her *amah* followed, then drew the curtains. The coolies shouldered their burden, and set out at a trot.

The pass which Yasuda had given Mu Lan to smooth her late return from his quarters was more than enough for the sentries posted at intervals beyond the outskirts of Cheng Teh. All night long the knotty-legged coolies trudged down the yard wide trail which wound and snaked among the rice patches.

During the hours of darkness, little more than instinct kept them from stumbling over slabs placed lengthwise to bridge ditches which led water from higher to lower terraces. There was no shoulder, nor any allowance for swerving; once off the paving, a pedestrian dropped into the knee-deep mud of the fields on either side.

When the moon rose, Mu Lan looked between the drawn curtains, and out across the headed rice which swayed in the hot breeze. Some of the terraced plots were no more than a few yards square; other reached a *li* in every direction.

Irrigation had for the time ended. Only here and there was the moonlight reflected from a dyked field. When once the waters sank, invaders and harvest time would come to the unoccupied stretches of the rice bowl.

Mu Lan had no reason to hope that her warning could put into the field enough guerillas to block Yasuda's troops. The best she expected to do in Ching Pao was to persuade the villagers to destroy their crops rather than to harvest for the enemy. Now she wondered how any argument of hers could succeed when all others had thus far failed; for, seeing again, after those years of absence, how much backbreaking work went into building dykes, and ploughing knee deep in mud, planting rice shoots by hand, and ladling fertilizer to each cluster, she understood why the peasants stubbornly held out against scorched earth.

And the loneliness added its bit. She was in another world, a rural world cut off from news, from cities, from the rest of China. Her parents, if they still lived, bending in the mud of rice fields, could not see beyond local feuds, and the rival village, Yin Pao. To them, an enemy in Cheng Teh was an enemy in the moon.

Unless she could convince them, they wouldn't learn until it was too late.

At times shelters loomed up, dark and massive: brick columns, supporting a tiled roof, flanked brick benches. Here the coolies rested, smoked a few pipes of finely shredded tobacco, and trotted on.

Mu Lan was not afraid. There could not be any pursuit until Yasuda emerged from his stupor, and had occasion to refer to an order whose contents already formed an unpleasant part of his memories. And though suspecting Mu Lan, he would hardly issue an order for her arrest, for to do so would make him lose face with whatever subordinates he detailed to execute his commands. Having been outwitted by a sing-song girl was not a subject he would care to mention, all the more so since the inevitable rumors which no vigilance ever prevented would certainly have warned the villagers. Every Japanese plan was so sure to become public property before being put into effect that Yasuda as a matter of routine included precautions to offset leaks.

Yet she craned her neck, and begrudged the coolies their short rest, some time after sunrise, at a grimy little inn, a hovel of brick and timber, where pigs and chickens shared quarters with the proprietor and his family.

The day's heat was made worse by steam exhaled by the drying rice fields. In some villages, farmers were already cutting the clusters, and beating the grain out of the heads. The continuous drumming and thumping was like the far off rumble of thunder.

Toward evening, the coolies waded ankle deep. Premature rain, falling in the far off hills, had flooded an area before the harvesters could gather the crop, No need here for scorched earth. Famine was already on the way, and men and boys plunged into the mud and syrup-thick water, salvaging what they could. Sunrise to sunset, from year's beginning to year's end, there was rarely a day not given to outwitting hunger.

Mu Lao's shoulders sagged, and more from the weight of her task than from weariness. Seeing these men fight to save the shreds of a crop made her mission in Ching Pao seem impossible.

* * * *

Near sunset of the third day, the coolies stumbled toward the wall which enclosed the rammed earth houses of the families who owned the surrounding acres. This was home, and the sight and smell of it made her for a moment regret Cheng Teh. Then, as the tea shop loafers set down their cups to gape and point, marveling at the gilded sedan chair and the splendid person it sheltered, Mu Lan smiled a little, and held her head high.

She had left this grimy village afoot, and to avoid marrying the village idiot. Far from postponing flight until her wedding day, she had shaken the dirt and dung of "Precious Gold" from her unbound feet the day after the betrothal feast, making her parents lose what little face they might have had. Nothing but instinct brought her back; instinct, and the urge to show her one-time people how to outwit the vicious barbarians from Japan.

Mu Lan's parents, driven by famine and revolt, had not been able to encumber themselves with a daughter agonized and helpless from bandaged feet and when the times finally permitted the family to return to Ching Pao, the girl's feet had grown beyond binding. They could have sold her as a slave girl, rather than lose face by keeping their big-footed disgrace, but they had managed to avoid that solution, for, luckily enough, there was a neighboring family which would accept a bride who did not have "golden lilies."

Since the son was a half-wit, and the parents were as poor as Mu Lan's, they had snapped at the chance.

Thinking of these things, she smiled a little more and said to her *amah,* "Yu Tang, ask that yokel where the house of Chen Ah Tien is."

The *amah* had some difficulty in making herself understood. A crowd gathered, gaping, chattering, and spitting. They shook their heads, and marveled, saying, "*Hai!* What is this? Chen Ah Tien pretends to be poor, and see the concubine he's buying!"

The local money-lender brightened. At this rate, it wouldn't be long before he'd get possession of Chen Ah Tien's acre, for when the number one wife is dead, it doesn't take a young successor very long to settle an estate. He followed the village elders, when they called to give Chen Ah Tien indirect advice. Like them, he was shocked to hear that Mu Lan was not a concubine, but the village disgrace coming home to roost.

There was even a greater shock when, upsetting the final shred of rice belt propriety, she boldly addressed her father's callers. "The monkey men are coming, but there is still time to burn the rice and wreck the granaries and drive away the buffalo."

She had fully expected an outcry of incredulity, then of horror, and was prepared to explain herself: but this was needless. A hard-eyed young man with a bandaged arm and ugly scar which twisted one side of his face addressed Chen Ah Tien: "Honorable First Born, this lady brings from Cheng Teh the advice I bring from commander of the night-marching army. Burn what is dry, flood what is wet, break down what stands, drive away what can walk, and carry what you can. The barbarians come for food, and having not enough guns, we must starve those we can't ambush. They come for rice, and without rice, they can't march."

Like face and eyes, his voice was iron. Mu Lan, though used to monopolizing the spotlight, was grateful for an unexpected ally, particularly a man, and above all, a fighting man. But she had overlooked rural wit. An old man with stringy mustaches got up, bowed ceremoniously, and said, "Young Brother, we also will starve. And this young lady does not look hungry, she ate enough rice among the monkey men. Far better that we compromise."

Mu Lan's jewels and silks and sleekness had betrayed her, and worse yet, she saw the cool amusement in the glance of Zeng Hai Wong, who as much as assured her, with a look, that despite her bungling, he was not whipped.

Nor was he. Zeng's wounds and scars and voice commanded respect, and so did his uncouth rural accent. A one-time farmer, he now harvested Japanese heads. Yet these were stubborn people, who could see no further than the neighboring village.

"*Gung ho!*" he concluded. "Work together!"

"Starve together," they retorted, not mockingly, but rather, regretting the necessity of their logic. "When we leave with fire behind us, and what rice we can carry, will we be welcomed at the next village?"

"The Generalissimo will feed you."

Zeng said this in good faith and certain truth, yet the retort was not slow: "But if the next village, and every other village destroys its crops, where does the Generalissimo get rice then?"

He could not make them believe in the extent of China. He described, but they could not conceive of a land so broad that by dint of advancing into newly made desert, the invaders would finally have to halt or go beyond their own lines of supply; yet it was not amazing that farmers could scarcely picture the needs of an army, nor believe that anything so powerful was also vulnerable.

"Fight them with scythes, that is good, and if we die, we die," they agreed. "But that is not famine."

Simple enough, to be faced stoically, but they could not gulp the nonsense of a sing-song girl and of a guerilla agent who had more valor than sense. However much he told of what he and his kinsmen had endured in occupied areas, they still held that famine was the ultimate enemy, and particularly, self-made famine.

The money-lender, having a stake in many a plot of rice, led the outcry, and then the old feud came into everyone's mind, for Zeng had slipped sadly in mentioning the adjoining village.

"We destroy what we have, and in Yin Pao, they do not destroy. And they eat what the little monkey men allow them, while we eat the nothing we have made ourselves. That is not wise."

Their bitter logic dismayed Mu Lan. No rapier play of wit could serve where the grim sincerity of Zeng Hai Wong failed. Then she rushed from the smoky room, and came back with all the money she had hoarded. She flung it to the rammed earth floor, and added her jewels to the heap. "This will buy your fields and your crops. Gold and may it choke you!"

Her father jerked to his feet, regained his poise, and said, "My disgrace has become an idiot, do not listen."

She was Chen Ah Tien's daughter, and her hoard belonged to him, and to whatever kinsmen might hear of it and come to town to share the family fortune. This was so well established, though long independence had made her forget it, that not a man of them considered her offer.

But Zeng Hai Wong addressed Chen. "Consider, Prior Born, how much face you will gain, buying all the village lands and offering them as a sacrifice to the ancestors. And how much face the misers of Yin Pao will lose if they don't make an equal sacrifice."

There was a growing mutter, first of wonder, then of approval as they saw the possibilities. The village would win either renown or cooperation.

Mu Lan was thinking, triumphantly, "My jewels, his wit." For the first time in her life, she had met a man whose thought kept ahead of her own.

But she had not reckoned on Confucius. The eldest of the elders announced, "The Master Kung said, think before you act, and act before you speak. I would not willingly associate with a man who would empty-handed fight a tiger, or cross a river without a boat, or die without regret."

Mu Lan flared up, "And the Master Kung also said, First Born, a man must have humiliated himself before he is humiliated by others: A nation must have defeated itself before it is defeated by others. And how can you better defeat yourself than by feeding your enemy? The ancestors of any of you would have committed honorable suicide to call to heaven's attention the oppression of an unjust mandarin. Why not a village destroy itself to bring heaven down on the monkey men?"

"Heaven has no favorites," the village wise man retorted. "And if we join the monkey men, perhaps we can each of us cover our floors with gold."

The ironic quirk of his voice brought laughter. She lost face, and so did Zeng Hai Wong for having supported her argument. Ridicule drove Mu Lane from the room, and according to tradition, it should have silenced Zeng Hai Wong, but he stood firm, and he said, "I will prove this for heaven to witness. My honorable suicide, going to the enemy's camp to kill their general. Then perhaps you can kill a field."

The silence which followed his leaving told Mu Lan that he had won, and that through him, she also had won. Then her victory became a coldness and an emptiness: for they had believed him because they had not been able to doubt that he had devoted himself to death.

There was no smoke to redden the sun on that day, or the day which followed; whatever Zeng Hai Wong's fellow-agents had said and done, they had not succeeded in scorching any earth belonging to the villages between Ching Pao and Cheng Teh. And the Japs were on the march. Swift-racing rumor, and the flights of bombers and fighters coming out of the southwest to harass the enemy made that clear enough.

Zeng lounged in the tea shop and played *mahjong*. The failure of his fellows to the east had apparently pulled the teeth of his resolution. When he went to keep his word, it would be too late. There was nothing he could do: for if he went to meet the invaders, already delayed by guerilas, he would find his fate too far from Ching Pao to convince the skeptical farmers.

And he might escape alive, in which case, heaven would not be the least interested. The sensible thing to do about radical proposals was to let the other fellow try them.

But Mu Lan had her thoughts. In the first place, a wounded man could not possibly get through the enemy lines. He'd be suspected of guerilla activity. They'd not even bother to question him. A sing-song girl, however, had a chance to do her work, and escape. Since a woman amounted to nothing at all, her survival would not affect the issue any more than would her death. Heaven simply wouldn't notice.

But the villagers might; and if she settled the commanding officer, there would be no occasion for Zeng Hai Wong to make a sacrifice which she now felt would be useless. Had the enemy approached only a few days sooner, Zeng's resolution would have had weight, but now time had dulled the edge of his words.

Zeng was useful. He should not waste himself.

She went to the market, and made a great show of buying red bands. It was noised about that Chen Ah Tien's disgrace was going to make the gesture of binding her feet. While she could hardly cripple them at her age, they were exceptionally small, and only a little cramping would satisfy convention.

The coolies, homesick for Cheng Teh, trotted eastward with the empty sedan chair. It gleamed bravely, all gilt and red and tasseled, exhaling the perfume of its one-time occupant. The villagers said, "So she didn't own it, after all." Others laughed and said, "She sacrifices a chair, we sacrifice our fields."

But Mu Lan was not there to hear their irony. She was one of two ragged women who trudged eastward along the flagstone trail. Both were bent double under bundles. Her father would not miss her for some hours. Then let them all guess.

The coolies lagged. That night, Mu Lan and her *amah* overtook them at the first inn, a good many *li* to the east.

In the morning, Mu Lan wore her silks and her jewels; her hair-do was perfect. She was exactly as she had been on her arrival at her old home, except for one detail —her feet were bound, mercilessly, torturingly, a sample of the three years of torment she had escaped in childhood.

Well, she'd avoided marrying the village idiot, and now it was nice to think of Zeng Hai Wong. She'd often think of him. She might even see him, some day, though a guerilla's grave was always open.

The coolies were not worrying. The worst that could happen to them would be some forced labor, and there was always the chance of escape, and flight to Cheng Teh, where their advance pay waited at their *hong*. Their only complaint was the jam of refugees on the flagstone trail. There was no shooting. The guerillas worked from the flanks, chewing off unwary detachments, luring them into blind ravines, or knee deep mud.

Finally Mu Lan had a chance to try the pass which General Yasuda had given her that night in Cheng Teh. A non-com, recognizing the official seal, did not bother to read the details. As for the interior guard, her presence spoke for itself.

She demanded to see the general. The splendor of her dress and polished haughtiness of her manner protected her.

Yasuda, despite his rank, was well to the front. Since he had to make a showing, it behooved him to leave little or nothing to subordinates, and thus Mu Lan faced the ultimate test sooner than she expected.

While waiting at his headquarters tent, she lost, as she expected, both coolies and the gilded sedan chair. Then, in the private tent, a slave girl searched Mu Lan, and finding no weapons, took the long pins from her head gear. When she went to greet the general, she had not even her maid with her.

Yasuda had to deny to himself that Mu Lan had once outwitted him, even though the information she had gained had been useless. She wondered where the Nazi observer was, and what he would have done in Yasuda's place. And then she said, "I have canceled many engagements to sing for your excellency."

"So now you have golden lilies?"

"I am retiring. This is my farewell performance. For you."

"Thank you. But this time, if you insist on playing *chai mui,* the forfeit is hot *saki* and not rice brandy."

She laughed, and spoke of the pig-faced man and the murderous headache he must have had: and Yasuda was happy, remembering how the Nazi had been the first to collapse.

An orderly gestured to the attendants, and then drew the tent flap. Outside, an army; inside, a gentleman of Nippon, who wondered whether he had become as Chinese as his favorite dishes.

She sang, and without musicians. Her pantomime made him follow the slender hands, each of which seemed to have a life of its own. It took an artist to appreciate art.

He found an interpretation for the dainty gesture toward a jade pendant, and ignored the possibility of a second meaning. The hands rippled on, weaving their part of a story told by face and voice and step.

His glance followed her as she shifted. Though he did not know it, Mu Lan had designed for him to turn, and upset the porcelain *saki*-jar. And she was ready, catching it by the neck before it broke or even spilled more than a gulp.

"And now," she wheeled, "see if you can beat me at *chai mui."*

He could not. He had never taken that strenuous course of charm, which included the finesse of beating wealthy aristocrats at that popular after dinner game; sober on *saki,* he was no more skillful than when drunk on *ng ka pay.* If for no other reason, eye and hand and voice were always a little out of step for he was distracted by the concealment and primness of that high-collared silken tunic, far more devastating than any décolleté.

And the opiate she had not needed in Cheng Teh now served its purpose. He had lost five games to her one, and he could not stand five times the drug.

Mu Lan continued her mirth and her gestures, mimicking the male falsetto and giggle of the unconscious Jap. The lights were low, and there would be no betraying shadows against the canvas. So under cover of the noisy game, she had one hand free to unbind her tortured feet.

Still calling numbers, she twisted the bands to make a cord, and she did her work to a double take of laughter. Strangling does not take great strength or much time.

Then she glanced about. The final thought which came to her at the end should have come from the beginning, yet she was still glad that she had used foot bindings. Her search was short. Habit and tradition favored her. A Japanese gentleman's sword can never be far from him. She found it, drew it, cut once, and put out the light.

Now that it was done, her feet claimed their due. Better even have married an idiot than be a lady!

Finding her *amah* was beyond trying, so, since Yu Tang, who might have carried the unexpected head back to China Pao, was not there, Mu Lan had to hobble with it as best she could.

She took off her conspicuous head gear and jewels. Muffled in a long quilted jacket, she set out, pass in one hand, and a compact bundle in the other. As verification, she had even taken Yasuda's insignia.

Her luck held until the interior guard was well behind her, but as she approached the outposts, there was a shot, followed by a challenge, and the groan of a man mortally wounded. Sentries at adjoining posts quite needlessly passed on the alarm. A non-com answered, and brought a detachment of the guard. A large disturbance about nothing at all: not a raid but a solitary prowler, who no longer made any sound.

Either he was dead, or had taken cover.

An officer wanted to know all about it. While listening to explanations, he sensed rather than saw the vague movement when Mu Lan made the mistake of trying to slip past under cover of the distraction. Zeng Hai Wong would have waited.

A yell—a challenge—the blaze of a flashlight, and the thin, spiteful snap of a six millimeter pistol. A second and a third shot. She felt the bite of the puny slugs. Her stride broke, but she recovered, and prayed for the life to return to her aching feet.

The blundering pursuit was brought up sharply by the officer, who said, "Just another camp follower. Woman. Get back to your posts."

By now Mu Lan knew where she had been hit. She coughed, and the taste of blood was plain in her mouth. What worried her most was that leg. Given time, she might get to Ching Pao, but she had no time, for they would miss the general's head in the morning.

"Mu Lan," someone said in an iron whisper. "Mu Lan!"

Zeng Hai Wong came out of the darkness and found her; groping, he found the bundle and guessed from its shape. "You—you did it—"

"You came to do it? Did they hit you?"

"No, I groaned to fool them, I wasn't where the sound seemed to come from, I thought they were shooting at my false voice. What's this—you're bleeding—?"

"No, it's his head."

"It's not. This is warm."

"Just a scratch."

But her cough betrayed her, though she choked it to a gasp which carried no more than a yard. "How'd you know me?"

"I knew you'd left. And then that flashlight, though the perfume made me sure." So he remembered her perfume, what little of it he could have picked from the reek and smoke of her father's house. That was the happiest of all her extravagances.

"It's my feet," she explained as she stumbled. "I bound them."

Zeng Hai Wong half-dragged, half-carried Mu Lan and her proof of victory. When she lagged hopelessly, he set her on his shoulder, and jogged along like a porter. He knew what a race he was running with the enemy, but he was too intent to realize what a race Mu Lan was losing.

At the dawn rest, she toppled, and would not mount his shoulder. "You can't go fast enough. Unless you go alone. Hurry, Hai Wong, take the proof or we both lose face—" The feigned rattle in her throat tricked him. Without a backward glance, he swung into a trot. When he was almost beyond her sight, she struggled to her feet, and tottered on. She knew that she could never reach Ching Pao, yet she had to walk as long as she could.

The small bullets lengthened her torment, yet in the end, she blessed them. Had they been larger, she would have dropped many *li* further from her goal. There was no chance of being buried among her own people; that was clear, and she was resigned to reality when she knew that she could not again pick herself up.

Finally she raised her face a little from the flagstones. The height of the embankment above the fields gave her a small advantage, and the rise of a crest furthered it.

Though she could not see Ching Pao, she saw smoke, and ever spreading flame. Mu Lan twisted a little. The men of Yin Pao were not being shamed by their rivals. She saw the smoking fields of the neighboring settlement, and she had even a moment to be glad for that, and for Zeng Hai Wong's fast march.

VENGEANCE IN SAMARRA

Originally published in *Short Stories*, June 10, 1940.

CHAPTER 1.

As the raft floated downstream, there was nothing for Deever to do but sit and smell the cargo of baled wool and rawhides and apricot paste from inner Kurdistan. Nothing to do but watch the rocky bank, the two sleeping raftsmen, and the two who steered with their long sweeps. Nothing to do but nurse a rifle and think.

Thinking. That was what made Jake Deever's long face lengthen a little more. Twelve years now, and he could not go back; some witnesses were still alive. He was homesick from thinking of corn whiskey, the smell of baking corn bread, the fumes of frying ham. But if he had a chance to do it over again, he'd fire that shot without hesitating. A man's duty.

There was neither port nor starboard on a raft; no way of designating Ayyub and Ilderim, who manned the sweeps. It turned slowly round and round, so that Deever and his crew were evenly toasted by the sun. But it wasn't a bad life, living in the mountains, and freighting goods to Bagdad.

Ayyub shouted and gestured toward the dust cloud that filled a granite floored pass, high up and some distance ahead. A caravan was filing down the trail toward the broad shelf which skirted the Little Zab.

The two sleeping raftsmen sat up, and blinked in the shade of their scanty awning. Deever said, "Wet those hides before they bust!"

Still groggy, the two obeyed. They took long-handled dippers and ladled water over as many of the two hundred inflated goatskins as were exposed to the sun. The cargo was not heavy enough to submerge more than a fraction of the blown up hides, much less the poplar trunks and planks that held them into place.

"An old man is riding with Jawan Khan," Ilderim said, squinting through the mirage that danced between the bank and the barren hillside. "A man with a white beard."

"Jawan Khan's uncle," one of the men with the dippers cut in, for the raft had turned enough to spoil Ilderim's view.

Deever frowned a little. He wondered why feeble Tahir Beg had come down from the mountains. No one knew how old he was. Tahir Beg hated infidels.

For several years he had preached against Deever, recommending a blood feud with whatever tribesmen harbored an infidel who dressed like a Turk.

Deever, however, had not changed his way of dress. Instead of the high, conical cap and bulky turban, the baggy pantaloons, and shoes with upturned toes, Deever wore a hat, a Norfolk jacket, trousers that did not match, and a pair of brogans. He had a collar and a necktie, the final abomination in native eyes; all purchased in Bagdad. He would be damned before he would put on the outlandish dress of Kurdistan.

This came somewhat from stubbornness aroused by Tahir Beg's antagonism, and somewhat from that same decent conservatism which had compelled him to shoot a neighbor, back in Pine Ford, North Carolina.

The slow *bong-bong-bong* of camel bells became louder. Dust choked men who thumped donkeys on the rump and cursed the grandfathers of the animals. Tall horsemen all agleam with silver dagger sheaths and crossed bandoliers of cartridges rode slim-legged Turki horses, guarding the caravan from enemy tribesmen.

Already, Deever recognized Jawan Khan; not his face, at that distance, but his figure and his way of sitting a horse. The khan was a shade under six feet—about Deever's height, and definitely runty for a Kurd—but he had magnificent straw-colored mustaches that reached out past his ears, and they somewhat made up for lack of stature.

The khan drew a rifle from his saddle boot and pumped five shots into the air. This was a needless formality to indicate that he waited on the bank with an empty weapon. Deever rose, long, lanky, and magnified by the sun behind him. He emptied his Mauser. And instinctively reloaded it, just as Jawan Khan was doing, ashore.

By the time Ayyub and Ilderim maneuvered the raft past jagged rocks, outwitted whirlpools, and slowly edged her toward the bank, the caravan men had unloaded the animals. Jawan Khan was stamping the caked dust from his scarlet boots. The khan's uncle had no energy to waste. He stood there, very thin, lean-faced, sunken-eyed; top heavy from his oversized turban, and seemingly on the point of toppling over.

There was an exchange of salutations. Then tea was served in a shadowed angle, and cigarettes. Deever felt the old man's disapproving, deep set eyes, but beyond inquiring about Tahir Beg's health, there was no question that could be asked. Barring the lack of Christian food and drink, the way of these mountain clans was very much as it was back home.

Finally Jawan Khan said, "My uncle is making a pilgrimage to Samarra. In this weather, riding is too difficult. But it will be easy for him, on your raft."

Deever had not counted on a passenger; only on merchandise. There was always danger of Arab raiders, attacking when the raft was moored by night. Tahir Beg would be a heavy responsibility. Deever said, "There is a feud between me and the Arabs, just north of Tikrit. I shot some of them instead of paying for the right to pass down the Tigris."

Tahir Beg smiled bleakly. "That is why I want to go with you. You guard whatever you carry. And I must reach Samarra before I die. A saint came to me in a dream and commanded me."

He folded his skinny old hands. Take it or leave it.

The men were loading Jawan Khan's goods on the raft. Ayyub went around with a tube, blowing up goatskins which had leaked. Ilderim was directing the arrangement of the bales, so that there would be a sheltered place for a cooking fire, and a clear space amidships for free play of the sweeps.

Deever did not like the responsibility. A raft might break up from being swept by a treacherous squall against the bank. Raiders might overtake it by stealth, cut its lashings, and float ashore what little they could, while the crew scrambled. Even if the old man sickened and died from the murderous heat of the Tigris flatlands, that would reflect on Deever. He remembered his own kinsmen back home.

Someone would brood over the old man's death, and finally take a shot. And since he could not go back to North Carolina, Deever wanted to stay with these people. They were white folks. Some had yellow hair, some red. They were blue eyed or gray-eyed, and many looked like Norsemen. Though Deever had no book knowledge of the kinship between Anglo-Saxon and Kurd, he instinctively knew them for kinfolk, and knew that his wife, Asima, was as white and proper a woman as any back home.

"Uncle, how will you come back? We break up the raft and ride. You know that."

Tahir Beg had an answer. "I am not coming back. I am hurrying to Samarra to die, and be buried in holy ground."

This was ironic. Samarra, the filthiest, most contemptible city in Iraq. More cutthroats, more thieves, more harlots, more ruffians. Yet, a place of pilgrimage; holy, from the burial of saints, to Shi'a and Sunni Moslem alike. As Deever put it, not with any great inaccuracy, "For Catholic or Protestant Mohammedans, it don't make any difference."

Jawan Khan seemed to read what was behind Deever's long, narrow face, behind his bleak gray eyes, his slowly tightened, thin mouth. He said, "After what you did to that tax collector, we know that you do not fear any Jabaur Arabs!"

They had him there. A man can be forgiven fear—Allah does not make all men equally valiant, nor equally strong—but a man has an obligation to his neighbors. Obligations of doing, as well as not doing. The shot that had made Deever an exile had been fired purely as the fulfillment of a man's duty to punish a breach of neighborliness.

"Your uncle has many enemies. He used to be a great raider. Someone may try to kill him before he can die peacefully."

"We cannot get him to Samarra on horse," Jawan Khan said. "And a saint commanded him to make the pilgrimage."

All that Deever could say was, "Then come with us, Uncle. You are right welcome."

CHAPTER 2.

It took two more days, going down the Zab. Two days of pitiless roasting. Whatever the position of the sun, the slow turning of the raft put the passengers so that both sides were exposed to whatever cliffs reflected the glare. At intervals, tiny melon patches were green against brown hillsides. Here and there, a water wheel creaked. But there was little cultivation. The people of the foothills feared the Kurds of the mountains.

At sunset of the second day, a forbidding range of red hills blocked the view. The sun sank red through a haze of dust, and the heat surged in quivering blasts to dry Deever's eyeballs, sting his shaded cheeks, oppress him as a choking hand and a crushing weight. Old Tahir Beg was soaking cheese in river water. It was aged for two years or more, until it was like lumps of gray rock, so that it would not spoil. Half an hour's soaking, however, would soften the cheese and extract the salt.

Deever asked, "How is your appetite, Uncle?"

"Well, praise Allah," the old man said. The malicious twinkle of his eyes betrayed his pleasure at seeing Deever roasted.

The Zab was joining the Tigris, a very lake of a river, broad and muddy, and skirting the Jebel Hamrin range. Tahir Beg squinted across the water, and into the desolation of the red stone hills, "Verily, from hotness we go into fire, and out of fire into hell," he cackled. "Pray, O Man, for Allah's mercy."

A thoroughly unpleasant fellow, this Tahir Beg, who was going to Samarra to die. There was a promise in his words. Deever became more and more uneasy. He fingered the simmering bolt of his Mauser, and narrowly eyed the hills that harbored the Jabaur Arabs. Deever's blond wife, Asima, had predicted disaster. She blamed it on an evil dream, and begged him not to go to Bagdad. Let Ayyub take charge. Ayyub and Ilderim did all the work anyway. Now Deever began to feel that Asima was right. He should have followed her premonition. Some vague bit of gossip might have warned her of Tahir Beg's plans, and without quite knowing just why, she had sensed danger.

That cackling old fellow with his sour mouth and hooked nose and deep set eyes. A doddering hawk. A falcon too old to strike, yet maliciously pecking at whatever was near. Deever said to himself, "He'll outlive us all. He's like grandpappy, taking more than forty years to die when he was a hundred and one."

He wished the old man long life, but he was uncomfortable. He did not like that jingling proverb, "*Verily, from hotness into fire, and from fire into hell.*" It had a personal dig, the way Tahir spoke it. The old man knew he was unwelcome, and he resented it.

Deever began to see how true the words were. First that shooting back home. It had done no real good; the man's testimony, even though not yet given in court, had nonetheless sent Uncle Stinson to Atlanta, for a bit of moonshining. But putting a bullet through the treacherous neighbor had been a man's duty; a family that let other folks push its members around might as well be dead.

Then flight, and borrowing a distant relative's papers, taking his place on an oil tanker. It docked at Bushire, and Deever jumped ship, as by then he had to. Shooting a Federal witness was a serious matter. He could not go back, so he went up the Tigris to Bagdad.

Mountaineer's instinct and simplicity somehow got him past Bagdad, and into Kurdistan. He knew not a word of their language, but he looked like the rawboned Kurds, he had their temper and their stubbornness.

But a chain of vengeance never stops with one link. That was what Tahir Beg's wry speech really meant. From hotness into the fire, from fire into hell. As grandpappy had put it, "When things get just so bad, they finally change. And get worse." An unpleasant old cuss, very much like Tahir Beg; a hellion for seventy-odd years, then he got religion and spent forty more as a saint.

Up the Tigris, a dozen years ago, to Jazira. Right where Syria and Turkey and Iraq met. A squad of Turkish soldiers came with a tax collector. One of Deever's newly found friends lost some sheep and gained a fractured skull in the course of the collecting. So Deever went out with a borrowed rifle. He picked off the tax collector—which makes any mountaineer a hero, whether in Kurdistan or elsewhere—and six soldiers for good measure. Then Deever emigrated back into Iraq.

More than ever, he was a man of honor, but a price was on his head in two countries now. And Deever began to feel like fate's tackling dummy. Doing the manly thing kept a fellow in hot water. If Tahir Beg was not a parcel of ill omen, nothing was. Already, the crew ceremoniously washed, gargling, sniffing, dabbling their ears with water; getting ready for prayer, even though travelers can claim exemption.

Tahir Beg's presence was responsible for that.

And as the sun dipped behind the Jebel Hamrin, Tahir Beg droned his "intention" and so did the others, letting the raft float free; which it could, safely, at that point.

Then Deever saw the three little *kuffas* that shot from the dancing shadows of the western bank of the Tigris. They were tub-shaped boats, woven of the rushes that had concealed them, and caulked with the asphalt and bitumen that had for centuries vainly spoken of the presence of petroleum in Iraq. Lean, butter-smeared men with headcloths and headbands paddled out into the shadow of the Jebel Hamrin; they had rifles, and there was robbery in their hearts. They were Jabaur Arabs, and no one has found any Arab lower than these.

Deever, sitting in the shadow of a bale, saw the silent approach of the *kuffas*. "Damn my hide," he always said when he looked at such a boat, "it's like the Sunday school story about Moses in the bullrushes. Same kind of ark, all right."

He grinned, cuddled the Mauser to his cheek. Just as Tahir Beg touched his forehead to the rug he had spread, Deever cut loose. A man jerked upright in the *kuffa*, toppled over the side. His companion yelled, and the boat capsized. The survivor swam under water. The two in the other *kuffa* opened fire. A third one pulled from shore.

The crew of the raft scrambled for guns. Tahir Beg continued praying. No Arab was going to nullify his start. In a way, he was right. Before Ayyub and the others could lay hold of a weapon, Deever's second shot smacked over the water. That broke the raid.

When Tahir Beg finished the four-genuflection prayer he had "announced," Deever said, "It is better not to pray when traveling."

Tahir Beg answered, "They were slipping up on men at prayer, and Allah punished them as he saw fit."

Except for Deever's watchfulness, the old fanatic's punctilious devotions would have caused a massacre and looting; the raiders had not challenged or demanded a "present" as they usually did. But Tahir Beg had justified himself with an argument that no one could refute. Ayyub and the others were impressed. Their respectful looks, not at Deever, but at Tahir Beg, indicated that it was better to trust Allah than marksmanship.

The next day, the bare red rock of Jebel Hamrin was behind the raft, while on the eastern bank, a similar bulwark rose out of the brown plain—a continuation of the range whose break made a gate for the Tigris. But ahead, as far as Deever could see, was flatness whose only trace of life or motion was the dancing of heat devils between baked earth and brazen sky.

Finally a great cliff cropped up out of that otherwise unbroken expanse of scorched brown. On its lee slope, Tikrit looked down on the broad Tigris. Tikrit, the fortress not even Hulagu Khan had captured, was now not worth sacking. A dozen tawdry shops, a few coffee houses; straight walled mud houses, rising in steps on the sloped crest of the cliff. Arab girls filed down the narrow path to the river. Their golden bracelets gleamed, their robes trailed in the dust as they glided with water jugs balanced on their heads.

Desert telegraph could easily outrace a horse, so Deever was not amazed when white smoke puffed from a parapet, high up on the cliff. Two hand cast slugs, weighing an ounce apiece, thudded into a bale of apricot paste. Another whistled overhead, and plunked into the brown water. Deever had not a chance of hitting the snipers; so he rose, fired a shot straight into the air, and turned his back to Tikrit.

Tahir Beg's sour smile was begrudged appreciation of the contemptuous gesture. The infidel in the improper clothing did have his points.

They kept the raft in midstream that night, instead of pulling ashore to sleep. "It is cooler," Tahir Beg said.

Deever corrected him. "No, Uncle, it is safer. Your life is on my head."

The old man's leathery face twitched, and would have reddened had there been enough blood in him. Deever was pleased, having finally made this irritating passenger uncomfortable, and without a violation of hospitality. It took a lot to get under Tahir Beg's skin, and shake his complacence, his smug piety, his droning proverbs and his quotations from the Koran.

At dawn, the tall spire of Imam Daur reached high over a mud wall and the parched crowns of sickly palms. Here Nebuchadnezzar had made his golden image, someone had told Deever, and bade Shadrach, Meshach, and Abednego to worship or be thrown into the fiery furnace. As he came near, Deever always grinned thinly and cursed the barren plain and said to himself, "Don't know as it took much gumption after all, Daniel telling his friends to walk into the furnace. Probably couldn't tell the difference no-how."

At times, miserable settlements broke the desolation. A clump of palms. A saint's tomb, of whitewashed mud. Patches of melons. Things noticed only close at hand, for the eye had to cover too much emptiness to accommodate itself to variations. It was close to evening when a small coracle came from the second hamlet they had passed that day. Deever shouted, *"Rub, ya kilab! Get desharda! Keupek ogblu!"* It was doubtful that the man paddling the tub-shaped boat understood either the Turkish or the Arabic words that called him a descendant of dogs, and the son of a lewd mother, and advised him to go away quickly. Before Deever could make it clearer, Tahir Beg stayed his hand.

"He has cucumbers. Let us buy some."

Ayyub looked up from his rice. "Cucumbers, by Allah!"

Ilderim did not speak, but his face was eloquent. Deever shrugged. One scrawny Arab, living with a starved family in a hovel near some stunted trees. Deever beckoned.

The pockmarked Arab was too servile to be convincing. Neither did he haggle as long as he should have, though he had plenty of time, having made his *kuffa* fast to the raft. But the cucumbers were cool, and the melons the fellow had were sweet. He made his sale, and paddled back to the bank.

Darkness came swiftly, with little twilight. Stars cropped out, large and very close; the lake-width of the Tigris made the evening cool. Deever was well fed and content. Two more days, and the old pest would be in Samarra.

Then Ayyub yelled. There was a creak, a snap, a surge of water. The deck sank beneath Deever. Tahir Beg screeched, and a blurred something threshed in the river. The raft was coming apart. Some of the carefully piled bales were separating, sinking, bobbing about in the water. Goatskins were escaping. A greasy, naked man flashed past Deever, who had scrambled toward more certain footing.

That wet contact in the gloom, and the momentary glimpse by the glow of the brazier further amidships told him the story. The *kuffa* had concealed one or more swimmers, river Arabs who had breathed through reeds thrust up through the woven rushes of the "tub." During the peasant's brief haggling, they had easily slipped to the shadows of the raft, and there waited for darkness.

"Watch out!" Deever shouted. "Arabs! Cutting the raft apart! Over there, Ayyub!"

He drew his revolver and fired at the first mark. A knife, gleamed, then was swallowed up by the black water, along with a man's bare, buttered body. Eddies pulled the raft toward the bank. With all hands scrambling about, sometimes on firm footing, sometimes on a bale that sank underfoot, the sweeps were no longer manned.

Tahir Beg was threshing and screeching. His white beard marked him for a moment. Deever lunged, but a bale yielded, making his move fail for lack of footing. The brazier tipped into the water. A billow of steam, and a gust of ashes swallowed Deever when he bobbed up out of the water, just astern.

Two men were swimming toward the bank. Ilderim was cursing and blasting away at them. Deever shouted, "Never mind them, where's Tahir?"

When he boarded the raft, he repeated, "Where's Tahir Beg? Where's the old man? Hold her in place! Get to the bank if you can!"

Ilderim and Ayyub manned the sweeps. The others took to the water and used the bindings of bales to secure what timbers and replace what goatskins they could. As long as too many of the blown up hides did not escape the confinement of the poplar trunks, the raft could be beached before she fell apart.

Deever peeled out of his wet clothes, and took to the water. His heart was heavy enough to pull him under. He was already certain that he was too late to help Tahir Beg. But he swam about, looking, until he was too tired to do anything else but return to the raft. Beyond any doubt, the old man had been pulled under by a whirlpool. Certainly there was no chance of finding and reviving him.

By then, Ayyub had learned that there was no need of pulling ashore and perhaps risking another encounter. "By Allah," he said, "the load broke too fast for them, we were not surprised as they expected, we frightened them instead, and by Allah, they failed."

No one asked about Tahir Beg. Finally Deever said, "Work toward the bank. And wrap up a bundle of food for me."

When he stepped from the raft into shallow water, he said to Ayyub, "Sell the cargo in Bagdad, and on the way home, tell Jawan Khan I am looking for the men who caused his uncle's death."

There was a moment of silence, unbroken except by the sounds made by men who wanted to speak but did not know what to say. Finally Ayyub asked, "Which way will you hunt them? Toward Samarra, or back toward Imam Daur?"

Deever answered, "I don't know yet. It all depends on what I find out there." Here was vengeance carried to the ultimate. As a foreigner, Deever felt that he had to observe the traditions of the hills more scrupulously than the Kurds themselves would. The venture was suicidal, but there was no help for that.

CHAPTER 3.

The start was easier than Deever had expected. He went upstream, toward the hut and the vegetable patch and the scrubby trees. Presently, he recognized the bend in the bank, and caught the smell of irrigated soil, the odor of dung drying for fuel. He could just hear the sleepy cluck and chirp of roosting chickens.

The mud hut was dark. The inhabitants of this stretch of desolation have little use for artificial light, and no money to waste for that luxury. There was not even a dog. Thus there was no alarm until Deever had stood for some moments, listening to the breathing in the garlic scented darkness.

Two occupants. One must be a woman. The reek of palm oil and perfume suggested that. Probably no children. Deever, standing at the low doorway, hailed the house. The sleepy answer had hardly come when he commanded, "Outside, both of you, or it will not be well with you. Tell me who you brought out to my raft to loot it. From where did they come? Where are they going? You know. You opened the way for them."

The man recognized the Kurdish accent. He stuttered and could not answer. His wife wailed and protested ignorance. Deever went on, "Tell me the truth. I have to find them. If I lose too much time, I'll come back and kill you. Where can you hide if you leave this green spot?"

The peasant had no answer to that. He had no refuge, and the fear of a mountaineer's wrath made him speak. He told of the two Arabs who had come from Samarra to wait for the skipper who refused to pay tribute. "And by Allah, *sahib*, they made me go out and offer you melons," the peasant concluded. "My life, or your goods!"

"This must be the truth," Deever said, "because it is their lives, or yours. Either will do, but the fault is theirs more than yours."

The peasant had no changes to make in his story; so Deever went downstream. He could have had his raft wait for him, but he had not expected such an easy start. His problem was merely a matter of getting to Samarra and finding Amru, the son of Musa, who was thin-faced, thin-lipped, and had a white scar that started above the left eyebrow and reached down to the jaw. And Amru's accomplice was Saoud, short, fat, and red-bearded.

Late that night, Deever camped. At dawn, before the sun made the brown expanse reel and shimmer, he picked up a trail—two camels, heading south. The blurred edges of the prints indicated that they had passed about twelve hours previous; shortly after the unsuccessful attempt to loot the raft. The tracks headed somewhat west of south, instead of following the Tigris.

That made Deever stop and frown. There might be little settlements in the flat waste between Samarra and the Euphrates, a hundred miles or so west. Then he saw the slow wheeling of vultures. The scavengers circled above the path of the two fast moving camels. Why would the riders prod their beasts to such a pace? Certainly not for fear of pursuing raftsmen! The vultures, Deever thought, answered the implied queries.

"One of the pirates was wounded when the shooting began," he reasoned. "The other one tried to get him to where he lives, or to a doctor, or something."

Deever wanted to know which man was dead; whose shallow grave already attracted vultures. Mountain, not desert, was his terrain, but camel tracks were no novelty to him. Soon he licked his dry lips and said, "Here's where one couldn't sit his saddle, and the other one gave him a lift. One camel carrying double now."

God, it was hot! That goatskin water bag became heavier every minute, and his hat was far too light for the terrific sun of Iraq. The plain was no longer deadly brown, but a dancing glare. White, salty spots tormented his eyes. Deever took off his shirt and underwear and cut them into wide strips. These he wound into a crazy turban about his hat, and so protected the back of his head. Luckily, his feet were tough.

It took him two hours to reach the spot where the vultures wheeled. A small cairn of rocks encouraged him. When he began tearing it down, the birds of prey settled in a black circle. Well beyond his reach, but close enough for him to see their reptilian eyes, their featherless heads and necks; featherless, since nature had adapted them to their horrible purpose.

Deever had never seen anything quite so sickening as the intentness of those vultures. Something about their expression said to him, "You're really one of us, you're helping us, we can't move those rocks."

The company did not help Deever appreciate his mission, but he persisted. Presently, he saw that the man under the cairn was fat, red-bearded; a town Arab, and a filthy one. The peasant had told the truth, then.

Deever took the dead man's turban. Without it, his brain would soon be too nearly cooked for any thought of finding Amru, who was thin-lipped and had a scar on his face. He cursed dead Saoud, bitterly.

Then he saw that he hated him less than he did the vultures, so he replaced the rocks.

This burial of an enemy troubled Deever. You let them lie where they fall, and if the pigs get them, all the better. But as he trudged back toward the river, he was muttering to himself. Sometimes he grinned, and once he laughed outright.

"My brain was frying. Saoud's turban cools me off. If it weren't for Saoud, I'd be dead soon. If it weren't for him, I wouldn't be sure where to hunt Amru. Supposing I find Amru and settle him, would Amru's kinfolk have a feud with Saoud's kinfolk, account Saoud helped me and betrayed his partner?"

Why not? He, Deever, was hunting Amru because, mainly through ill luck, Jawan Khan's uncle had drowned when a raft broke up. Uncle Tahir was on the way to Samarra to die. Having drowned, cool and clean, a few days short of his destination —Deever started laughing.

Then he stopped. "Shut up! Get some sense, right now."

When a man finds something funny about a feud, that man must be sun-struck. It said in the Good Book that you demanded an eye for an eye. It also said, vengeance is Mine. But a man with a gun was an instrument of God. Anyone could figure that out. God couldn't run around dishing out small scale vengeance. Not when He was busy making up earthquakes, floods, pestilences, things that a man couldn't possibly devise.

"Ain't a bit funny," Deever said aloud. "When men ain't got honor left, God'll uncork a calamity that blots out a whole nation at once. So I got to get Amru. There's nothing else a decent man can do."

He had it all reasoned out when he was once more on the bank of the Tigris, a reeling figure in tweed coat, homespun pants, soldier's brogans, and an incredible turban such as neither Arab nor Kurd had ever tied. Offhand, he'd be taken for a Turk.

All that day, Deever thought of Pine Ford. Perhaps it was the danger of exhaustion, of hunger, of being set upon by river Arabs who would murder a man for a pair of shoes. Perhaps it was because this quest, fantastic even to one nurtured on a grandfather's feud traditions, was making him grope for precedents. While he scarcely realized it, he was no longer asking himself what his fellow villagers would say if he returned without vengeance, but what his folks back in Carolina would say.

Old fashioned, that's what it was. In Grandpappy's day, people had honor. They had to have. Life was too tough and too short to furnish much fun. A fellow didn't have much beyond honor to live for.

Nowadays, it was different. A farmer got paid for not raising corn, not raising cotton. Suppose Grandpappy had been paid for not making moonshine? Suppose the Hatfield's had been paid for not raising hell with the McCoys? Deever blinked the hot dust from his eyes, and said, "Uh-uh. I'm old fashioned. Getting more so, hanging around those ignorant fellows up in the hills. They're just like our folks in Grandpappy's time. No radio. No cars. Nothing but horses and guns. But they're nice people."

Getting back to the States would be practically impossible, unless he went to the U. S. Consul General at Bagdad and surrendered. One of these days he'd write, and find out, though he wasn't sure but what he'd forgotten how. Maybe not enough witnesses were left to make a case.

Deever had five more days skirting the Tigris. Five more days of solitude, blistered feet, eyes that throbbed and grated even after a night's sleep. Ayyub and the raft must be in Bagdad by now. A man could not begin to march as fast as the sluggish Tigris flowed. He could for a while, but the river had been at it when Abraham left Ur of the Chaldees, somewhere not far from here.

"Old settlers, those Chaldees," Deever said aloud. "Four-five thousand years ago, and there's still a few of them running around here."

This was the first time he had a chance to ponder on his surroundings. He was doing more thinking in a few days than he had ever contrived in the entire preceding thirty years. Back home, a fellow never had to think. His elders told him what was what, just as theirs had told *them.*

By the time he reached Samarra, he was hungry, dizzy, and aching for a glimpse of Amru.

Right now, nothing looked finer than those great golden domes. *"Surra-man-ra,"* someone told him, was what the name originally was. It meant. *"That-which-maketh-glad-the-beholder."* A tawny cliff rose up from the desert, jutting up and out into the Tigris. Samarra looked clean. The clear dry air created that illusion, and the intense light.

That biggest dome seemed to float above white walls, cream-colored bulwarks, lime-daubed houses. Then in the smoldering red of sunset, Deever saw the gleaming bayonets of soldiers. Some river Arabs were being turned away from the ascent to Samarra. He heard wailing, the shrilling, quavering cry of professional mourners. Out in the hell glamour of the desert, he saw a burial party, and there were no tombs; just men digging in the sands, and soldiers standing guard. A wagon, camel drawn, went with creaking axles past the sentries.

Deever saw all this from the shelter of an irrigation ditch bank. The scent that the shifting breeze brought explained things. The town was quarantined. Probably cholera. God was taking a large scale vengeance, for the murder and thievery that made Samarra a stench on the Tigris.

"Don't reckon God needs me butting in," Deever said. "First class pestilence'll do more in a day than I could do in two-three years of steady shooting. Bet Amru got here just in time to get caged up."

The plague had just broken out, and this must be the first organized move to bury the dead, for people were still trying to get into town. Clearly, the news had not yet spread. Amru must be in there.

Deever lay in the ditch until darkness, and watched the sleds and wagons haul the dead. He was worried. Suppose Amru were among those to be buried tomorrow? All the more reason to get into Samarra to find out.

CHAPTER 4.

They arrested Deever before he had got far past the outposts. One of the khaki clad Iraq soldiers said, "Five rupees, O Man, and we will let you go. It is forbidden to enter the town, there is cholera."

"How long?" Deever's Arabic made them think he was a Turk.

"Since this morning. It is spreading fast. Not enough medicine has come from Bagdad, not enough doctors. Until supplies come from Damascus, it will be very bad. Five rupees. Quick, before the captain comes to inspect."

An Arab trick, letting him get past the lines, and then arresting him. Deever said, "*Mafeesh!*"

They did not believe him, and said they would settle for three rupees. Once more he said, "I have no money."

A corporal came up and heard Deever say *"mafeesh"* to a rupee bid. He said, "The man's a fool and a liar! Kick him into town and let him see how it is, he'll find money when he wants to get out."

The Arab of it again. Only, it was over-played. An officer came along, and broke into the bargaining. Deever said, *"Ana inklesi."*

The officer, himself an Englishman, said, "My word! You speak like a foreigner. Unusual outfit you're wearing, too."

Deever explained, "You see, sir, I'm really an American missionary. Up there in the hills. I came down to help. With the cholera epidemic. Lost my horse. Men deserted—"

Deever, feigning a little more fatigue than he felt, staggered and would have fallen. The captain caught him. Later, brandy and broth revived Deever. A haggard medical officer said, "You have the devil's own nerve, but if you mean it, you can jolly well help. You missionaries should know how."

Deever's imposture succeeded simply because no proper Britisher ever could predict what an American would do next. Deever's English, halting and a little labored from long disuse, was considered natural enough for a missionary, or for a man on the verge of exhaustion. Also, the few medical and hospital corps men which the Iraq army had been able to hurry from Bagdad were too busy and too tired to be critical.

The man said he was a missionary. Doesn't look it, but who ever had any reason to impersonate one of those bigoted chaps anyway? Who would ever come into a filthy hole like Samarra, and when there was cholera, unless he did have some silly notion of obligation or something like that?

Blast it, he probably is incompetent, but any white man is worth something. Moral effect, you know, on these beggars.

Deever diffidently said that he knew very little about medicine. Cobwebs or plug tobacco were good for staunching bullet wounds, and he could set a broken limb. Surgical skill, however, was at a discount in Samarra. Maybe he'd better just help the orderlies.

In a very few minutes, the doctor learned that Deever had a strong stomach. Grudgingly, he said, "You'll do, I fancy."

The hospital was a tavern whose courtyard and stalls and traveler's cubicles had been hastily cleared. The patients were laid out on pallets of straw. Torches flared in the still, reeking air. Arab orderlies, wearing gauze masks over their faces, were doing their best to give water to those who were blazing in the fever of the third stage. These might live; they had passed that fatal second stage, and had a bare chance. The doctor looked up from a patient who had just got an injection of saline solution. "Deever, never mind cleaning up. God man, you can't, not now." He gestured. "Get them out! Over there!"

"Uh—um—how'll I know for sure that they're dead, sir?"

The doctor cursed and went to the next pallet. He was too busy with those who might pull through to have much thought for those who were cold, turning blue, losing their voices. As an afterthought he turned and croaked, "Do your best, if you make a mistake, it won't be bad—those poor devils in that row haven't a chance anyway!"

Deever soon learned to tell which were finished, which were in a coma and might live until the reaction, high fever and a fair chance of recovery. He became used to the odors, used to seeing those blue-brown corpses trotted out by stretcher bearers. He finally became as numb as the haggard doctors, and ceased wondering when the sanitary corps men would stop bringing in new cases.

All he knew by morning was that more space was needed. They were collapsing, out in the town, faster than they were dying in the tavern.

A warehouse was cleared. Planes from Iraq brought more supplies. Trucks roared in from across the desert, with cots, sterilizers, water purifiers. More soldiers came in, to quell riots that started when orthodox Moslems protested against mass cremations with petrol. The burying squads could no longer dig trenches deep enough nor rapidly enough. And Deever, just from watching, learned how to do doctor's duty; the routine was simple enough, after all.

If you made a mistake, the poor fellow would die anyway, nine times out of ten. If women refused to unveil, refused treatment from an infidel *hakim*, what difference, maybe they were right. If terrified orphans stole water from condemned wells—and every well was condemned—cholera was quicker than starvation! It was grim, it was horrible, it was quite unreal to Deever. He could understand dying from knife or gunshot wounds; from infections following compound fractures, up there in the mountains, when a horse slipped on a narrow trail or an icy ledge. These were chances a man had to take, and the odds were decent. But now: terror, hunger, sudden collapse, and no defense.

Soldiers shooting looters. Short tempered, frightened soldiers shooting instead of bothering to challenge anyone trying to slip through the cordon about the accursed town. What difference did it make? *"Ya* Allah! If they all die, then we'll march away, if we do not die." That was what the soldier told Deever, and Deever said, "That is true, O Man! And you are afraid, so you will die before they do."

Half an hour later, he returned. The soldier was doubled up with cramps. His rifle lay in a pool of filth. Dogs were gathering about him. They were hungry, and would eat him, if no one came in time.

Deever was no longer sickened, and he had ceased to be afraid. He despised Arabs. Since they were afraid, he was too stubborn to let fear get even a secret hold on him. And then, he had to find Amru. He was too tired to see the monstrous jest of it all, hunting a man down to shoot him so that the plague would not first kill him.

This intentness made him scrutinize every warped face, and question those he was now treating in their houses. There was no longer any place that could be cleared up to receive new cases. Deever lost track of sunrise and sunset, dusk and dawn. The medicines he gave, the dead he marked for taking away, the living took from be-fouled houses, the water he sterilized and distributed; these things now became the way of vengeance.

"No, that's not Amru. Isn't this one, either." Another shot of saline. Was it calcium chloride, sodium chloride? Potassium chloride? What difference? "Huh—no, no scar on his face!"

Adrenaline. That's what they needed over in this section. All sorted out. You don't have to think. It's routine here. Once, crossing a torch-lit square, he saw a white-bearded Arab with rolling eyes. The old man gestured at Deever, and called, "Behold, O Men! The *hakim*—see his look, see its madness! Allah is upon him. O Madman, touch us and we will be healed!"

Deever understood only a few words, but they were enough. The Arabs thought that his wits were in Paradise, that Allah loved him, and had given him strange powers. The old man reminded him of Tahir Beg. But the old man did not know anyone named Amru.

Deever did not know when it was that he saw a thin-faced man hauled out of a hovel and toward a sled. He did not know exactly in what quarter of Samarra he was at the moment. He was not certain why he had left the hospital. But he was certain that this man was Amru. The scar, to be sure, was a strong hint; but Deever *knew.*

He said to the one who crouched, not ill but feigning illness, "Who is that man?"

For answer, a stare. Who cared about names now?

Deever booted the fellow to his feet. "Who is he?" He drew his gun. He had kept it, without any good reason beyond instinct. "Speak!"

"*Wallah, sahib.* That is Amru, the son of Musa!"

Deever raised his hand. "Steady, you two! Don't stack on another one."

"But he is dead, *sahib,"* the porters protested. "So are these."

Deever stooped. There was no pulse. The wrist was ice cold. The scarred cheek was cold. Amru the son of Musa had outwitted vengeance. Deever gestured, and the sled dragged on, *bump-bump-chunk.*

"I'm in this pest hole. Can't get out. Got to help these folks, anyway. Maybe that's why it happened, they needed help for a spell."

He watched the sled go down the cobble stone paving. One of the grisly cargo fell off. He shouted at the driver. The man did not hear. Deever cursed, would have run after him, but he was too tired. He watched the vehicle round the corner.

Better get back to work. An orderly stood there, listlessly, like a dead man who has forgotten to drop. The fellow had Deever's kit, and was waiting, masked, fatalistic, weary.

"None in here, *sahib,*" he reported, coming out of the next house.

A second, third; and with the same report. Deever scarcely heard. The orderly stared at him, suddenly alert, and backed away. Abruptly, Deever said, "Wait here—no, come with me! Hurry, hurry, *ya kalb*!"

He staggered, then ran, stretching long uncertain legs. He knew the route of the sleds, and he overtook the jouncing vehicle before it passed the lines. He stopped it. Amru was on top of the heap. Deever said, "Get a stretcher bearer."

The orderly grumbled, "He's dead."

The men who attended the drag said, "By Allah, the dead are dead."

"Look, brother of a dog! His leg moved," Deever shouted. "Take him off, take him off!"

The leg had moved, up, up, up; it touched the man's chin. The attendants shook their heads. "Allah upon you, master! The dead often move, the soul is gone a moment before the life of the body, it is not well to bring back life into what is left. *Wallah,* we must bury it."

Muscular contraction, a purely mechanical thing, was terrifying to the uninitiated.

"Take him off!" Deever's voice rang, deep and commanding now. New life came to him. "Take him to the hospital!"

Wide-eyed, the man obeyed. They could not help but obey, for this infidel had strange powers and the light in his bloodshot eyes was fearsome. He was looking beyond the veil between life and death.

CHAPTER 5.

Two hours later, Amru the son of Musa developed a high fever. The chill of death had yielded; reaction set in, and internal fires parched the patient. But Deever scarcely knew this. He scarcely understood when the surgeon said, "By Jove, you were right!" His vision blurred. He began groping for support, trying to reach the wall of what had once been a stable. "You need rest, old man—the worst is over—fewer cases."

Deever wanted to yell for help, but he was afraid to. If he needed help, then he had been finally stricken by cholera. If his weakness left him in a few moments, then he'd know it was merely rest that he needed; rest which he could now take, since the crisis was over, since Samarra would not be entirely depopulated. Legs were numb. "God, I'm stumbling!" He was afraid now. Mere uneasiness gave way to fear. He tried to yell, but cramps doubled him, and he did fall, into blackness interwoven with knives. They reached into his vitals.

He scarcely knew when they picked him up. The avenger and his victim were the toys of cholera. Vengeance had become a silly thing. Deever in the first stage, Amru the son of Musa in the last; either to live, to be burned to death by fever, or frozen in that cold blue stage.

When Deever finally realized that he was alive and in Samarra, the pestilence was under control. No new cases were coming in. And a rigid quarantine had kept river or caravan traffic from carrying the disease downstream to Bagdad.

In the days that followed, he gathered his strength, and collected his wits. Ayyub and the raft men must long since have sold the merchandise and set out on their return to the mountains. They must for some days have been home, and telling of his blind quest of vengeance in the desert.

Asima would be worrying. She probably considered herself a widow. While no one would know that the pursuit had led him to pestilential Samarra, it would readily enough be assumed that he would by now have returned, unless a desert ambush had accounted for him. Asima would be proud of him, and so would all his adopted tribesmen. He had died upholding a tradition, and more zealously than any native Kurd.

To correct that error, Deever dragged himself through the desolate streets of Samarra, asking each survivor for news of Amru the son of Musa. Somehow, he remembered the fellow. That sharp, thin face; that long scar, those large front teeth.

He had pursued him and he had overtaken him. Here, in Samarra. It was all hazy, confusing. Doctors had been relieved, new ones had come in. There were no records which would help. Deever's only way was to hurry, hunt, find; and before the quarantine guards were disbanded, and the survivors were released.

The natives remembered Deever. They salaamed when he passed. *"Ya sidi,"* a woman cried, and tried to kiss his hand. "O my Lord! O Favored of Allah! My son lives!"

Deever gathered that she was trying to thank him for finding her son, who lay unconscious in an alley, unable to cry out for help. For the first time in his exile, he lost some of his contempt for Arabs. The woman's tears were wet on the back of his hand. An old man knelt, kissed the skirt of Deever's coat. "O thou servant of the Life-Giving! Thou servant of the Living!"

"Quit it," he muttered in English. "Damn it, that's not sanitary."

Well, maybe it was. The coat had been disinfected and was all shrunk and wrinkled. Everything was sanitary. Creosote, chloride of lime, they made the air sting and reek. Every corner, every drain was sterile. But you can't have people running around kneeling and slopping over like that. It embarrassed him. He had a man to kill, and he wanted to get it over with. As he broke from his grateful patients, he said half aloud, "Too much rumpus about it all. Damn fools, don't know I didn't come here to help them."

A few paces brought him to the square, near the mosque whose golden dome he had seen from afar, days previous, guiding him to vengeance. Coming from a narrow alley, the sudden glare blinded him a little. He squinted, looked around for a place to sit down and rest. His legs were wobbly. To the right was the *serai,* and the horse market. First get a mount, then find Amru, then wait for the quarantine to end.

Another man was kneeling at his feet. Others, who had come with him, were still pointing at Deever and saying, "This is the *hakim.* Here he is, he who brought the dead back to life. Yea, this is the Servant of the Life-Giving, verily, *Abd-ul-Hai!*"

Then it came back to Deever, and all the confusion became order. He remembered the man he had taken from the sled. This was that man: Amru the son of Musa. Deever raised him to his feet. It was strange and rather dizzying, looking at that peaked face, that parchment skin stretched over high cheek bones; a beak of a nose, and sunken, dark eyes. Lips still black and cracked from fever. Deever thought, "He looks a lot like me. I ought to look worse, but I guess it didn't hit me so hard."

Amru said, "My kinsmen in Samarra are dead, all dead. But I have a brother in Imam Daur. Give me the hire of a camel, *ya hakim.*"

This was the tradition and the custom: whoever directly saves a man's life is henceforth responsible for his welfare. There was a difference between all those whom Deever and the doctors had treated as routine, and this Amru, whom Deever had singled out for an especial salvation. Thus, it was proper to demand food and necessities.

"I am going north," Deever said, "when the guards let us out. I'll get an extra donkey. Have you eaten?"

Amru pointed toward the field kitchen where rations were served to the survivors. Deever handed him some coins. "I have just eaten at the loqanda. There are cucumbers and *pilou* and eggplants stuffed with mutton. Go and eat, then wait at the *serai.*"

There were two reasons why Deever gave him coins. If he broke bread with him, he could not kill him for at least three days thereafter. This also was the tradition. Then, as a white missionary, he could not eat with an Arab. The emergency was over, and the officers would shake their heads and frown.

The following day, the quarantine was discontinued. The only mounts available were sorry specimens, and the demand was so high that Deever and Amru dared not waste any time bargaining, or looking for better donkeys. Most of the survivors, it seemed, wanted to get out of that ill-omened town. A haggard horde filed down the headland, then parted, some going toward the boat landing and Bagdad, others upstream, toward Tikrit, Mosul, or north into Armenia.

Deever was worried from the start. First, the crowd. Settling a true believer would be an insane trick. He could not risk it. He told himself this, and added, "And I can't push these donkeys. They'll drop in their tracks."

He was weaker than he realized. He clung to the high pommel of the saddle, and with difficulty kept his seat. Amru was not faring much better. Men and beasts were hardly fit for travel. So Deever and his companion lost ground, for being among the last stricken, they were the last to recover. Bit by bit, the crowd thinned, going in twos and threes. Some followed obscure trails toward unmapped settlements in the plain between the Tigris and the Euphrates.

That evening, Deever had his chance, for no travelers were within sight or earshot. He drew his revolver. Amru watched, being too weary for much curiosity. "O Man," Deever said, resting the heavy weapon on his knee, "there is a feud between you and the Shuan Kurds, for the death of one Tahir Beg, the uncle of Jawan Khan. You and a certain Saoud cut my raft apart. Tahir Beg drowned and his life is on your head."

For a long moment Amru sat there, staring, color slowly receding. His skinny hands clenched, and he swayed a little. He looked about, wildly, scanning the gloom and finding neither light nor friend. He understood now that this was no missionary, but one of those merciless wild men from the Zagros Mountains. He knew all but one

110

thing: whether he would die at once, or whether he would live until some kinsman of Tahir Beg could strike the stroke.

"There is no might and no majesty save in God," he said. "Verily, Allah gave me into your hands to save me, and now he gave me again into your hands to slay me, and there is no help for it."

A small bed of coals separated avenger and victim. He did not beg a moment for prayer, nor did he ask if the old man's kinsmen would come to meet Deever and the victim of vengeance.

"The man who came out in the *kuffa,* hiding you and Saoud," Deever went on, "told me, and it was easy for me after that. But do not curse him. He knew that if I did not find you quickly, I would return and kill him."

Slowly Deever rose. The whole thing was crazy. He could not for a moment deny that Amru's death was in order. That would be justice and honor, among his own people as well as among the Kurds who had adopted him. But now Deever knew that he could not deal justice; that he had himself blocked justice, by keeping Amru from burial, and by having that lingering flicker of life flame again.

He had faced the desert and he had faced pestilence to win this moment, and now he was wasting it. *"Out of hotness into fire,"* old Tahir Beg's words rang in his ears. *"Out of fire into hell."* Vengeance leads to vengeance, blood cries for blood, and there is no end to it. Pestilence and famine, flood and war, they do their work, and why need one man exact eye or tooth? Plague in Samarra, Deever decided, wiped out the feud between him and Amru. They had both been in the hands of Allah, and he had spared them both.

So he said, "Take this gun. It is well known among the Shuan Kurds. Give it to them and say that I, Yakoub, was still alive when you found me, after I had taken vengeance on Amru. Alive, but that no doctor could keep me from going where I was bound to go."

Amru could not understand this. Deever went on, "No one knows but what I died honorably, slaying you as my duty ordered. Now rub your head and go your way, for I cannot kill you, since Allah spared us."

Amru went. He was more than ever convinced that a saint or, what to him was the same, a madman had twice saved him. He would be afraid not to execute his mission. And Deever knew this, so he turned and went toward Bagdad.

The chain of vengeance was broken by the shattering of this one link. He was free again. And he would surrender to the United States Consul in Bagdad. He was hungry for the fumes of frying bacon, the odor of freshly baked corn bread, the tang of corn whiskey. And these would be waiting, finally. The music would not be too hard to face; not with voluntary surrender following twelve years of the freest life on earth. Perhaps the witnesses against him were scattered or dead. Perhaps the only charge that could stick would be one of obstructing justice.

Though these details scarcely occurred to Deever. He was not planning or calculating. He had qualms about leaving Asima, but after all, she was to all intents and purposes the widow of a man who had died upholding tribal honor. So his head was high and his heart was light as he rode south. He had news for his own people: a way of getting rid of the burden of vengeance. Grandfather was wrong, and someone had to set him right.

ISLAND TRAMP

Originally published in *Spicy-Adventure Stories*, December 1940.

McCabe was pleasantly dizzy, and he nearly toppled over as he squatted there, beside the homemade still from which palm toddy gin was dripping. When Barney McCabe heard the rustling of the banana leaves behind him, he started, apprehensively, his rugged face in a scowl, his unshaven chin thrust out. Then he recognized the girl who stepped into the moonlight.

"Oh, hello, Malia—what are you doing here?"

Malia's red calico gown was drenched by the spray of surf; it clung to her splendid body, boldly displaying her beauty. Her brown skin gleamed from palm oil, and so did her heavy black hair. She was the loveliest creature on the island, unless one counted the newly arrived trader's daughter, who was blonde and slender.

"I don't hate you like the rest of them do," Malia said. "And neither does my father. He just pretends to, so the trader gives him presents."

McCabe chuckled; the sound was merry, but his eyes were bitter. Then he realized that the childlike Polynesians, most of them anyway, were merely trying to be agreeable to both parties of a feud.

"You'd better go home—" He gestured toward the village, which was beyond the headland that jutted into the Pacific. "Beat it!"

Malia's presence disturbed him. A glamorous, splendid creature, but he was fed up with women. So he told himself, even after the moment of weakening caused by the gleam of her shapely legs and shoulders. He turned toward the primitive still, which was close to his palm thatched shack.

Two blocks of coral held a kerosene can over the fire; a short length of rusty pipe, supported on sticks, slanted downward from the can. When the cold metal condensed the vapors from the boiler, palm toddy gin dripped into the coconut shell bowl. Staying drunk in Pakalafa was just that simple; and as long as McCabe's head reeled, he forgot what a fool he'd been, losing his bankroll in Papeete, and then getting a laugh from the dame who had grabbed the dough.

And now, a white trader had arrived and had warned the islanders against associating with a tramp.

Malia's eyes widened at his brusqueness. Then she came nearer, laid a soft hand on his shoulder, and fingered the tattered shirt. Being fed up with women had its limits. He sat down on an outcropping rock, and caught Malia in one arm. The jasmine blossom in her dark hair exhaled a heavy sweetness, and Malia, her head now pillowed on his broad shoulder, looked up contentedly. He did not need any more gin to intoxicate him. Her generous lips did that.

That kiss made him forget his grudge against women. As he held her closer, and squeezed her until she gasped, he was thinking. "It's white women that're no damn good… Malia's grown up since I landed here…"

There was little doubt as to that last. The branches overhead swayed in the wind, and the leaves made splashes of silver and shadow on Malia's drenched gown and sleek legs. She snuggled closer for another kiss, and McCabe forgot the hissing still…

* * * *

Later, she asked, "Aren't you going to give me a drink of that stuff you're cooking?"

"You won't like it," he said, gruffly. He fumbled under the wall of the thatched hut, and found a bit of carved coral which he handed Malia. "I made this for you."

She got a close look at the little image. "Oh, isn't it funny! Just like the trader— that awfully long nose and long jaw! But I want a little of what's in the bowl. He says it's not good for us, but you drink it, don't you?"

"All right, try it."

Malia sputtered, spat out the gin, and made a face. "It's awful!" McCabe drained the bowl. To hell with Sam Parrish and his high nosed daughter, who thought an island tramp was a bad influence on the natives. His frown relaxed; he was forgetting that he had squandered the stake his father had given him to go to Papeete and open a plantation; he forgot for the moment that he was ashamed to go back to the States and confess that a glib dame in Papeete had taken him for a sucker.

Malia murmured in his ear, "Barney, isn't it funny, when you came here, half drowned and hanging to a piece of driftwood, I thought you were a funny old man, but now you don't seem old at all, and—" She shivered delightedly. McCabe was fully twenty-six.

But Malia's visit made McCabe's resentment rise again; bit by bit, the new planter was robbing him of the friends he had found. Nito, the chief, had turned against McCabe when Sam Parrish with trinkets and trade tobacco and medicine demonstrated the advantages of civilization and proved the worthlessness of tramps.

Then McCabe got a brilliant idea. He sat there, looking at the lovely girl who now lay stretched out on the white sand, her fingers laced behind her head. She was smiling, and saying, "I don't hate you, do I?"

He caught her hand, drew her up beside him. "Look here—we're going to the island, just you and me."

He referred to a nameless atoll some sixty or eighty miles away; the little green ring in the ocean had not enough soil to support a permanent population, though in times of food shortage, the natives of Pakalafa sailed their long canoes to the atoll to get taro and bananas.

"Oh, won't that be *wonderful!*"

With that moon, and that girl, McCabe had to agree. Going native was easier than it had ever seemed; and more pleasantly than going home and telling his grim father how a hot number in Papeete had gotten him drunk and then picked his roll. Disappearing with Malia—getting away from Pakalafa, where trading boats, which would soon arrive, would leave with Sam Parrish's gossip about a beachcombing bum.

Then Malia cried out and broke from his arms. Half a dozen natives emerged from the foliage. Petelo, the chief's brother, led them. They were proud of their shirts and hats and canvas pants, and full of borrowed authority.

"What the hell you want!" McCabe stumbled to his feet. "Get out of here!"

Malia bounded toward the beach, her skirt all a-flurry. One of Petelo's companions took after the girl. The big fellow caught her arm and spun her about. Then McCabe got into action. He sidestepped, eluded the handful of huskies who had moved toward him, and overtook Malia's captor, who for all his size, had his hands full.

Malia was kicking and screeching and squealing. Her hair streamed, her red calico dress was in shreds that trailed to her waist. In the moonlight, it became charmingly plain that she wore coconut oil from head to foot. McCabe got all that at a glance, just as he closed in.

Sock! He was as big and heavy as any of the six-foot natives. His solid fist knocked the fellow stiff. But that was wasted effort. The others landed on him, and caught Malia before she could improve on her chance of escape. Numbers and gin handicapped McCabe.

His former friends were kicking and choking him senseless. They dragged him to the village, and half conscious, he saw Malia was also a captive. Bruised and peeled down almost to her gleaming skin, she had given it up as a bad job. Then McCabe's captors bound him hand and foot with coconut fiber cords, and flung him into a hut.

Somebody, it seemed, objected to his plans for Malia.

* * * *

The following day, Petelo brought McCabe before the chief. Malia was there, unhurt except for a few scratches, and unbound. As long as her lover was a captive, they reasoned that she needed no bonds.

Nito had become a figurehead of a chief. Parrish, the planter, was plainly in charge. He rose from his chair on the verandah of his palm thatched bungalow, a temporary building which was to serve until he had the natives erect a coral block house.

"Untie him!"

McCabe could scarcely believe that this stern, long nosed man was the same person whose easy amiability had won the native heart. Parrish was tall enough, but he seemed frail among the powerful islanders. For a moment he fingered the little coral image which Malia's captors had taken from her.

"I found this amusing, McCabe," the trader said. "But Petelo thought you were practicing a witch doctor trick. Planning to burn the image, or drive nails through it, or the like. That worried him, and I couldn't convince him that damages to the image wouldn't hurt me a bit."

"I'm an American citizen," McCabe growled. "I'll have the commissioner take your hide. What the hell is the idea of setting these fellows against me? They were my friends before you came here, you blue nosed heel! You ought to get a job as a missionary!"

Parrish chuckled. "I think your not having a distiller's permit would also interest the commissioner. Giving hard liquor to the natives is forbidden, you know."

"Nuts! I've never heard of a trader who didn't get them pig drunk so he could rook them."

"They seem pretty well contented with my way of doing things." Parrish gestured toward the heaps of newly cut coral. "They're going to build me a permanent house, a trading post."

Through the mosquito netting that screened the front door, McCabe got a good look at the trader's daughter. Her blonde hair found all the light in that shaded room; and while she wore a good deal more than the native girls, her print dress could not conceal her array of smooth lines. Lydia Parrish was not as hefty as Malia, but she was all woman, shapely for all her slenderness—as McCabe recollected from one good glimpse of the blonde newcomer swimming in the lagoon.

McCabe reddened when her glance met his, and his eyes dropped. He was barefooted, unshaven, and without more than a scrap of shirt. Bruises on his tanned skin showed how he had been mauled. Worse than that, this first eye-to-eye look told him she was sorry for a white man on the beach.

"Why can't we," her father was saying, "try to get along? I did warn them against your gin, but I didn't tell them to tie you up."

"Be damned to you!" McCabe thrust the natives aside. "Touch me again, and I'm breaking some heads!"

Nobody tried to stop him.

* * * *

He spent the day sitting in the shade near his shack, and moodily stared at the green lagoon, and out at the blue expanse of ocean. For all Parrish's fair approach, McCabe could not meet him half way. He did not want white people about him. They might not know the details, but they would soon enough, and they already had guessed he was a chump who had found refuge from folly. He would not feel right until his father finally concluded that a shark or a hurricane had settled the missing son.

Until then, McCabe wanted to evade all inquiry.

He had to steal a canoe, and take Malia with him to the distant atoll. And now her continued absence sharpened his resentment against Parrish and the fickle villagers. They had frightened her, or she would have come back.

A second day, and a third; no sign of Malia. So McCabe took the initiative. He wiped the warm gin from his lips, and grinned. "I'll show this moral influence, I'll show him what it's like when someone really is giving the boys gin!" He put a number of calabashes and coconut shells, all filled with freshly distilled liquor, into a net of coconut fiber, and set out into the jungle. He clambered up rocky paths, plunged through pandanus thickets whose thorns raked and scratched him; but finally he reached the native village from the landward side. This approach was not as conspicuous as the easy way would be, along the beach and past the trader's house.

Malia's father, gray haired Nikusa, was the man to see.

He found Nikusa at the men's clubhouse, well behind the village. There no woman was ever allowed. Some of the younger men eyed McCabe suspiciously, but Nikusa and his gray haired friends greeted him amiably.

McCabe's watch had survived his long swim when he went over the rail of the boat that would have taken him home. He handed this to Nikusa and said, "This is for you."

The old man beamed. "You could have the girl anyway. I did not send them to keep you from going to the atoll. She's raising such a fuss that I wish you two would get away from the island."

"What's keeping her?"

Nikusa answered, "Nito and Petelo. They like Parrish."

McCabe took a calabash of gin from his net. "Look here, Nikusa! You men all elected him chief when his father died. Malia told me that. Now Nito makes you do things you don't want to do."

"*Aué!* That is true." The easy going natives frowned, then sighed and shrugged. "Still, a chief once elected is a chief, even if he does wrong."

That was just what McCabe had waited for. He took a deep drink, and passed the calabash to Nikusa, saying, "I make this myself. It's good, and never mind what the long faced fellow says."

Nikusa took a long pull. Tears were in his eyes, but he stuttered, "F-f-f-fine!"

One of the other elders demanded a shot. Then a second and a third. Nikusa was now rubbing his stomach; his eyes gleamed, and he said, "Powerful medicine, no devil doctor makes stuff like this."

The calabash circulated. Presently McCabe said, "Now that we know Nito isn't a chief, that he's just a flunkey to a trader, working the life out of all you people, I'll tell you what to do about it."

"We could kill him," someone suggested.

McCabe did not want that. "No. Just quit work. You're crazy, working all day, picking and splitting coconuts. What for? He gave you presents, he has bought your souls. Next thing you know, he'll have a missionary here, and a school. To make slaves of you. To make money for him, for the trading boat captain."

Nikusa and the elders, now glowing with gin, began to see how their chief had sold his people into slavery, how he was putting on airs. *"Aué!"* they muttered. "He does no work, he gets all the presents. It was not that way in the old days, when a chief shared with his men, all alike."

At this point, McCabe headed back over the hills. Once the natives stopped work, began drinking and muttering, and became surly, Parrish would get off the island quickly enough. The natives had welcomed him, else he would have left on the very trading boat that had brought him; if they rebelled against routine work, Parrish could only do as he would have done had he gotten a repulse at the start.

McCabe quit drinking. He found a chunk of volcanic glass and used it as a razor. This shave was a painful business, but the next time high nosed Lydia Parrish saw him, she would not display so much pity.

The next day, Nikusa came for more gin. The devil-doctor, who had been sulking in the heart of the island, for he felt that the new regime had made him lose prestige, came with Nikusa.

"Once you win the young fellows," McCabe said, "show them the gadgets they get aren't worth the work they do, the trader is finished."

"Aué!" the witch doctor said. "I knew you were a smart man, and the trader's friends will be sorry they beat you."

McCabe looked at his bruised fists. "Some are sorry already. But listen, Nikusa. Don't get rough, don't damage anything, and for God's sake, don't hurt Parrish or his daughter, or you'll get marines dumped on the island."

"What is a marine?"

"Worse than a trader, worse than a missionary. So take it easy."

* * * *

116

The revolt some days later—for it took time to undermine the loyalty that Parrish had built up—caught McCabe quite off guard. He had expected loafing, sabotage, until Parrish's persistence crumbled; but the shouting from the village, nearly a mile away, told him that the lid had blown off. Flames reached as high as the palm grove which girdled the settlement.

McCabe broke out in a sudden sweat. He rose, wiped his forehead, then seated himself again. "They won't hurt him," he said. "They're just a little lit, that's all." But he felt as if red ants were crawling all over him. He heard the howling, the click of rattles, the fearsome booming of bullroarers; he had not been in the islands very long, but he knew that hell was popping for fair. And for the first time in his life, McCabe was mortally afraid, with a sickening fear quite other than that of going home to face his angry father.

A white girl, even though she was high hat and superior, was in the midst of that riot. The idiots had gone crazy, crazy drunk on the gin McCabe had expected would make them sodden and lazy and sottishly agreeable to anything but work.

He snatched the rusty pipe and sprinted down the beach. His heart was in his throat before he had covered a hundred yards, and red spots danced before his eyes. He was ready to drop before he had put a quarter of a mile behind him.

McCabe stumbled along, for his legs were numb from that first exhausting sprint. Time and again, he fell, cutting his hands on the coral that cropped out of the beach. His bare feet were bleeding, but he did not feel those slashes.

The copra shed was ablaze. Parrish's house was not afire, but a ring of howling natives surrounded it. The devil doctor and Nikusa's hardshells had brought their masks and plumed headgear out of hiding.

Parrish was on the verandah, fully dressed, including his hat. His daughter was at his heels. He turned, gestured, and she went back into the house; but McCabe's first glimpse told him that Lydia had her share of courage. It seemed to run in the family.

As McCabe staggered toward the howling group of natives, Parrish raised one hand. Boldness and dignity won him a moment's silence.

"Go your way. Nito has come to my house. I will not turn him out. When you are sober, you will know this is wrong."

They were out to finish their deposed chief. Some, still sober, blocked those who threatened Parrish with fish spears and clubs. McCabe broke through the line and yelled, "Go back! When Nito has to hide from his people, he is no chief. You've won."

Silence followed, but the circle closed in on the sides and rear. The rebels hesitated to lay hands on a white man or his house. Then from inside came a native's yell. That must be Nito; and the sounds from the rear indicated the crowd was trying to break through the laced wicker to which the wall thatching was found. Smoke rose; fire spears made arcs of flame, and landed on the roof. The rebels reasoned that the taboo which protected the planter's house against breaking and entering would fall on the burning spears, not on those who threw them. Their witch doctor had not overcome their scruples.

At the sound of Nito's voice, Parrish turned to go into the house.

"Cut it out!" McCabe yelled. "They'll spear you, sure!"

His sudden move and cry checked Parrish. When the trader saw who had arrived, he said, "Keep out of this. Your gin has done more damage than you can repair."

He turned back toward the door. Lydia came running to meet him. "They've set the roof on fire!"

Then Nito broke from hiding, and met the missionary well inside the doorway. He groveled at Parrish's feet. Lydia caught McCabe's arm and demanded, "Can you talk some sense into them? They'll kill Nito."

Her cheeks were white, and he could feel her nails sink into his forearm. But she did not seem afraid, in spite of the choking smoke that forced her out of the house."

"Too late," McCabe said. "This is a native feud. You're safe. Your father is."

Parrish got his ankles away from Nito's grasp. "This man came to me for protection. I cannot turn him out."

McCabe jerked Nito to his feet. "Get up, you big ape! I'll club a few, and you run for the beach and get a canoe!"

Nito, trembling and sweating, was a sorry chief he stumbled toward the door, but McCabe caught his shoulder. "Wait a second! Not yet." His strength was returning, and he hefted the rusty pipe. "Parrish! You get clear. I'll get Nito through, somehow."

But it was not the fire that forced the issue. A handful of the boldest rebels charged in through the door.

McCabe's pipe knocked a spear man to his knees. But Parrish was turning to interpose, and some of the bone tipped lances reached him instead of Nito. The chief broke clear in the confusion and blinding smoke, and bolted for a window. McCabe parried a club and splintered one of the fishing tridents. The thatch was roaring overhead. The natives, believing their work done, bowled him over as they ran for the door.

Lydia was knocked into a corner by the rush. McCabe recovered and cried, "Give me a hand!"

The blonde girl scrambled to her knees and caught her father's feet. They stumbled to the verandah, just ahead of the flames. When the natives saw the wounded man's white face, and the blood splashed on his shirt, they recoiled, and offered no opposition. They had not noticed Nito's dash for freedom, and when the roof collapsed, they did not doubt that he was finished. There was no one to check his flight from Pakalafa.

"They're scared silly," McCabe explained as he and Lydia laid Parrish on the beach. "Afraid of a taboo. Or a battleship to punish—"

"I'm not interested in reasons," she said, thin lipped.

She knelt there, swaying a little. McCabe examined her father's wounds. "There's a chance—they didn't run him through—"

* * * *

The first aid supplies were burned. All that could save Parrish was gin to sterilize his wounds, and perhaps herbs gathered by some loyal native.

McCabe had scarcely voiced this hope when Lydia cried, "They're taking to their boats! Stop them! We need their help. We might get to Papeete."

McCabe yelled as he ran, but no one heeded him. The leaders were already crossing the reef. Facing Lydia was worse than returning to the states and his father's wrath.

By torchlight, he used his pen knife to extract several barbed spear heads. Parrish was half conscious, in spite of the pain. He said through his teeth, "Go ahead! I can stand it."

Lydia was looking the other way. McCabe wiped the sweat from his forehead and said, "This one is the worst. Better take a slug of gin. I need one myself."

The planter's gray lips twisted in what he intended for a smile.

When McCabe handed him a bowl of gin, Parrish choked it down.

"Get to work," he coughed. "But you might have aged the stuff."

Fever and delirium followed that crude surgery. During the worst of it, McCabe had to help Lydia hold her father on the palm leaf pallet they had made in one of the deserted huts. But finally Parrish's vitality won, and then McCabe had nothing to do but forage for food.

At night, he spread nut meat on hot rocks, to trick the robber crabs from their homes in the rocks. Later, by torchlight, he returned to catch them as they snapped at the savory bait. He lacked the native's skill in snatching the savage creatures. They had claws strong enough to cut coconuts open. This was their customary diet, but they seemed to relish bites of his hands and forearms. Whenever he returned with his catch, he was bleeding from elbows to finger nails.

Every so often, during the days following the crisis, McCabe would say, "Anything I can do?"

Lydia's toneless "No" meant, "Yes, get out!"

Then he would pace up and down the beach, or sit on the headland to look for the trading boat that was not due for some months. He ended by burning coral rock to make lime. When this was done, he set to work on the foundations of the permanent house that Parrish had started. Wrestling the cut stones into place, sweating and straining as the increasing height of the courses made his labor harder, kept him from being sorry for himself.

The wall was shoulder high when Lydia asked, "What's that for?"

McCabe reddened under his tan. Parrish cut in. "A man needs exercise. I wish I could join him."

Lydia smiled for the first time in two weeks and said, "I don't think you really intended for Nikusa's clique to go wild the way they did."

"I didn't, but I never had the nerve to tell you that."

Parrish chuckled. "You don't have to do that work to square yourself. When the natives are good and homesick, as they will be, they'll return and finish the job."

McCabe squinted out into the blistering sun, and chewed on a smoked flying-fish. When he went back to work, he felt a little more like a white man.

* * * *

A few nights later, Lydia joined McCabe as he sat up on the headland, staring out to sea. She smiled at his startled expression, and seated herself on the rock beside him.

"Why did you come to Pakalafa in the first place?"

He regarded her for a moment. She was ragged, and her hair was twisted into a knot at the nape of her neck, and there was not a trace of the wave she had brought from Papeete. But if Lydia had ever been high-nosed, she did not look it now; so he answered, "My old man staked me to some dough. Most of what he'd salted down. So I could get a start out here, like you folks. Well, I lost the roll, in Papeete."

"I guess a girl was to blame?"

"Huh! I don't blame her. I was a chump and I asked for it."

"So you came out here to hide, and resented us?"

He met her gaze, squarely. Once he could not have done that, but having faced the ruin his resentment had brought on Parrish and his daughter, having been unable to dodge the issue, McCabe had gained courage.

"That's it. I didn't have the guts to tell the old man I'd shot the roll, he'd taken a long time saving it up. I guess he thinks I'm drowned or something. Anyway, I hoped he would, when I went over the side and swam to this island. And I didn't want you people crabbing my hideout."

The moon made Lydia's hair a twist of gold and its glow modeled her cheek and the graceful line of throat and shoulder. She was lithe and supple, sitting there with her arms clasped about her knees. Her eyes were friendly, and so was her smile; he wondered what had become of the frozen-faced, haggard girl who had watched him tend delirious Parrish.

"But why this interest?" he asked, after a moment during which his heart beat seemed to shake him, and he fought a crazy urge to take her in his arms and hold her closer than he ever had Malia. "I played the devil with you folks, even if I didn't mean to go so far."

"Because you faced the music, Barney. It's not as hard as it seems. You might even go home and face things. Don't you think so?"

The softness of her voice was the last touch. In a flash, he had both arms about her, and he sought her lips; he found them, and his kiss cut off her little cry of surprise. For a moment, she yielded, and he could feel her heartbeat, the warm pressure against his chest.

Then a gasp, a sudden wrench, and she was jerking free.

"Don't—" Her voice was cold. She rearranged the skirt which had crept up to her knees, and pulled her blouse into shape. "Do you have to paw me the first time I'm friendly?"

"Don't you think that your being friendly, after all that's happened, is enough to make a fellow dizzy?" He leaped to his feet. "Keep away from tramps, and thanks for the kind words."

Lydia snatched his hand and detained him. "Sit down, Barney. You're not really a bum, you're merely trying to make one of yourself."

He pulled loose, but did not leave. She went on, "After all, I couldn't help but know all about you and Malia. You're putting me in a rather flattering position, aren't you? Seconds to a native girl?"

"Oh, high-nosed, huh?" he flared up. "Listen, snooty! Malia's twice the woman you'll ever be, and you and your old man can go to hell with your pats on the head, who do you think you are, rooking the natives?" he stalked down the steep path, ignoring whatever she may have said. And as he went, he knew he had played the fool once more, instead of facing the fact that any white girl would have reacted as Lydia had.

Down on the beach, he noticed how cool the wind was, and how brisk; how unnaturally bright the stars were. "This damn place," he muttered, "is in the hurricane belt. It may be, anyway."

* * * *

And for the next few days, McCabe gathered coconuts, and breadfruit. Lydia helped him, and her father, now able to get about, stacked the loot in a corner of the coral wall, along with the dried flying fish, and the turtle's eggs found a mile up the beach. The wind had become stronger; there was never a moment's cessation of its howling. On the following day, the native huts were stripped of their thatch.

On the fourth night, heavy rain fell, and the wind came in short sharp puffs. It twisted, driving the big drops into every corner of the coral wall which McCabe had built.

Thunder barely made itself heard above the roar. Lightning blazed through the gloom, and touched the water that flowed about the huddled three. And then the full force of the hurricane reached the island. Trees splintered. The wind drove coconuts against the coral wall. He had Lydia in his arms now, but terror kept this from being any triumph.

Speech was impossible. Whatever it was that Lydia screamed into his ear, McCabe could not hear. The skeletons of natives shacks were disjointed and hurled through the doorway openings. Flying splinters probed the corner where they crouched. And at dawn, gray and ghastly, the wind whipped up and scooped wet sand from the beach, rolling it in a solid wave of cutting particles. Some of the upper courses blew out of place, for their mortar was green. Only McCabe's foresight had kept his companions from being crushed by a fall in one corner.

When sickly daylight filtered through the thick air, McCabe saw the shells and sand that had drifted like snow. Coconut trees, uprooted, lay half buried; others snapped off a few yards from the ground, reached up from earth stripped of vegetation.

For a while, the wind slacked off; in a few hours, it was scarcely more than a stiff breeze. Lydia cried, "Thank God, it's over!"

She was drenched, shivering, her face and legs slashed by flying sand. And her hair, whipped free, clung in a sodden mass. McCabe said, "This is only the start. I'll try to find some fresh water at the spring."

Half an hour later the return trip of the hurricane lashed the island. Now it found whatever had been protected from its first lashing. The food cache was buried under tons of sand. McCabe and his companions shivered in a corner until exhaustion finally made them sleep.

The cessation of the uproar awakened McCabe. For a long time, he sat there, cramped and cold, not wanting to disturb Lydia and her father. He wondered if the old man could endure the prolonged exposure. A heavy sea broke over the lagoon, and rolled almost to the foundations of the wall; but all was clear, and the sky was brightening.

There had been no matches on the island since the burning of Parrish's bungalow. McCabe rigged up a bowstring and spindle, and set to work. The bit of glowing sawdust that rewarded several hours of hand-blistering effort was the biggest triumph of his life.

"Look! Lydia! It's burning!"

She knelt and blew till her cheeks puffed, and fed bits of fiber while he twirled the spindle. Once a blaze was crackling, she said, "Do you know what I found up the beach?"

"What?"

"A canoe. It isn't damaged. It must have been hidden in a cove, and washed out by the storm.

Once the fire was crackling, they ran along the sand to inspect the derelict. "What's wrong?" Lydia asked, seeing him frown. "What's the matter, Barney?"

"This is Nikusa's boat. I can tell from the carving. It must have been blown adrift, from whatever island they found. If they went to the atoll, they've all drowned, with the water breaking over it, and no shelter."

"Afraid Malia is finished?"

"If you're trying to rib me, you're wasting time. She checked out, didn't she, with the others?"

"She did," Lydia said, very slowly. "And you could have."

"I couldn't." He caught her by both arms. "Listen, I've got enough to think about now. Without you rubbing anything in."

"Why—Barney—" She frowned, perplexedly. "What do you mean?"

"Those poor devils drowned on some low atoll, where they didn't have our chance. My fault, too."

* * * *

That evening, McCabe told Parrish that the canoe was seaworthy; that rigging a sail and steering by the stars for Papeete would not be difficult.

"I'm sure it could be done," the planter said. "But if any of the natives return, I want to be here. To tell them that they are quite safe, even though the hurricane did not drown me. There are enough palms and taro in the sheltered ravines to feed the whole crowd if they come back."

"That's right."

"So if you want to leave, the boat is all yours."

"I could make it alone, easily enough." McCabe tried to get Lydia's eye, but she was looking the other way. "I'll think it over." He went across the rubbish strewn beach, and climbed the headland that overlooked the reef. Moonlight and calm water tempted him. The thing to do was to get out. He was so firmly established as a tramp that he could not redeem himself in Lydia's eyes.

He heard pebbles clatter down the slope, and turned. A brown girl with gleaming legs and arms came up the path; a shapely girl whose oiled body peeped through rents in her bedraggled calico dress. It was Malia; he rose, and exclaimed, "Where'd you come from? I thought you were dead!"

She ran to him, arms extended. Breathless, she clung to him, kissing him. Her eagerness nearly crowded him off his feet, and he seated himself on the rock, drawing her to his side. Finally Malia explained, "I came back in my father's canoe, we are all going far away—"

He shook her loose. "What about the storm?"

"Oh, the storm?" She laughed. "It missed us, the way hurricanes do. We were safe, we planned to go far away, so we'd not be punished for killing the white trader, but I came back for you, you'll go with us."

Warm and lovely in his arm, Malia was the final argument. A shapely temptation, looking up at him, eyes misted, lips half parted. He wanted to go native, and now a tribal immigration was waiting for him.

Then he remembered how the childlike natives had turned against him; how he had managed a painful shave so that Lydia would not look so sorry for him. It had never occurred to him to wonder what Malia thought. It only mattered what his own people thought.

He said to the brown girl, "Go tell your father and his people to come back home. Parrish won't make any trouble. I doctored him and cured his wounds, and there are no grudges."

She eyed him dubiously.

"I mean it," McCabe insisted. "Parrish is a fine fellow. You can come home, all of you."

Malia brightened. "Oh, then you and I won't have to go to the atoll!"

Her arms tightened about him, and she pressed closer, until he wondered how much longer he could resist her ardent invitation. Suddenly, he broke her grip, and said, "Listen, Malia—you and I can't go to any atoll—or anywhere else—I have to go home—to see if my father has forgiven me—for a foolish thing I did—I won't ever come back—now go and tell your people that Parrish wants them back."

She rose, and looked at him as though dazed. "I understand, Barney. You ran away, now you are brave again, and you go back. Or maybe the yellow haired girl has taken you from me."

She turned and went down the path. Moments later, he saw the canoe dart out across the lagoon. McCabe was glad that he was not going native. He was thrilled at the thought of going home to face the music, like a man.

He had scarcely come down to the beach when he saw Lydia step from the shadow of a rock. "I didn't know who it was," she began, breathlessly. "I thought perhaps they had come back to finish us. The natives, I mean. Finish us to keep us from mailing a report. And then—"

"Then you got an eyeful?"

Her chin rose, defiantly. "Yes. I looked, and tried to hear as much as I could."

He grinned ruefully. Surf makes too much noise, but you could sure see plenty, with us up there against the moon. "She said they were afraid to come home, and they were migrating."

"She came back for you?"

"She did, and I told her they didn't have to migrate, that they could all come back home, that I was going to the states to face my music. I had to face you and your father after the dirt I did, unintentionally. Well, it wasn't as bad as I thought, not when it was over. So I'm going to tell my old man. I think I've learned how to look things in the eye."

"Facing me, and hurricanes—" Lydia's laugh was unconvincing, and he thought her fingers would sink all the way into his shoulders. "And native sweethearts—you can face anything now, Barney—"

It did not take him long to understand that. "The devil I can!" he said hoarsely, and caught her in his arms. "The idea of leaving, when I'd rather have you around; when I'd rather help your father build up this island—"

Neither could speak for a moment, but Lydia's arms and hungry lips told him that she would agree to anything rather than parting. Dawn was touching her hair, and pearling the lagoon. Far out, McCabe saw a black speck. He said, "Look, way out there. The trading boat. See the smoke? I'll be gone by evening, I guess."

"You don't have to leave! You've found yourself right here, facing us was harder than facing your own father, you silly. You don't have to prove yourself any further, do you?"

So she wanted him to stay. He had to believe that now. He said, "I'll be back, when I've squared things up."

"Do that here, right here. I know dad needs help. A partner."

"How do you know?"

She looked up through drooping lashes. "Do you think I've not asked him?"

"You had your nerve, asking him how he'd like an island bum for a partner. Can't believe it, honey."

She tugged at his arm. "Come on, you ask him then."

"Nuh-uh! It's too early." He sat down and drew her toward him. "Way too early. Let's sit here and watch the boat come in."

"It'll take an hour or more," Lydia decided, and snuggled closer to the island bum. She sighed contentedly. "We'll have lots of hours all to ourselves, but this will be the best of them all."

YOU CAN'T EAT GLORY

Originally published in *Short Stories*, October 1946.

Cartridges cost one rupee apiece, and all a man got for burning them was honor, if he lived to get home again. Gul Mast Khudayar fingered the loops of his crossed bandoliers and groaned in his dusty beard. A slug spattered to bits against the smoking-hot sandstone ledge.

He hitched himself a little further back into cover, squinted along the barrel of his Mauser, and for a moment, he had the reckless sniper lined up for a bull's-eye.

But he held his fire; Afghan volunteers furnished their own weapons, and *rupees* did not grow on bushes.

Shir Dil, the fool, was blazing away on the right, and Wali Dad's old Martini-Henry roared from the left. Then a machine-gun opened up, spitting out *rupees* at a rate that sickened Gul Mast, even though the king did pay for its cartridges, and for the 75 millimeter shells for the field gun whose shrapnel made white puff balls of smoke high above the rebel lines.

This continued all day, while Gul Mast, safely under cover, considered the worn soles of his campaign boots. Hardly a hob-nail was left. They would have lasted years, but for this accursed campaign; little food, and less loot, for the rebels sacked every town in their deliberate retreat into the mountains.

By noon, the skirmish became a battle. An enfilading shot drilled Gul Mast's goat-skin canteen. This infuriated him, so he leveled the Mauser, squeezed the trigger on a whole *rupee,* and sent the sniper to the mercy of Allah. Then, as the sun blazed down, and the nitrous fumes thickened on both sides, Gul Mast settled down to calculating the interest on one *rupee* at fifteen percent per month; he was no longer certain just who had been hurt the most in that moment of uncontrolled wrath.

Later, the Sardar rode up, his wiry horse agleam with sweat, foaming and puffing as it scrambled over the rocks. His medals and gilded saber made him conspicuous. The shaggy mountaineers cheered when he deliberately focused his field glasses, and ignored the slugs that crackled past him. The staff officer at his heels tried to look unconcerned, but he was glad when the Sardar took cover, and began to address the volunteers.

"Oh Men! It is written that Paradise is in the shadow of spears—"

Gul Mast had heard these things before, but now they were becoming pointed and personal. The Sardar was not addressing the army; this time, he was concentrating on the survivors of the company which had come from Gul Mast's village, some miles east of Ghazni.

Shir Dil leaped up before the harangue was half over. He said to the Sardar, "By the Four Companions! It is already as good as done! We, the men of Darabad, will capture the gun for your highness."

"Victory and honor depend upon it. I know that you will succeed."

The Sardar took off one of his medals and fastened it on Shir Dil's ragged coat, where it blazed against dirt and mutton grease and old bloodstains. Shir Dil, commander of the village militia sent from Darabad in token of allegiance to the king, saluted and led off, apparently not realizing that a suicide detachment had been decorated in advance. This was too much for Gul Mast.

He said to the commander in chief, "*Ya* Sardar! It is not fitting to send me with the others from Darabad. My Uncle Haroun is old, and I am his only kinsman. Is it not written—"

The Sardar raised his hand. "Since half the regiment owes you money at fifteen percent per month, your uncle will inherit enough to keep him in comfort if you are taken to the mercy of Allah. So be of good cheer, Gul Mast." He gestured toward the file that was marching by the flank. "Is it not written: *there is no joy greater than dying with good friends?*"

For all the democracy of the Afghan field force, Gul Mast knew when argument reached its limit. He saluted. The Sardar added, somewhat ironically, "And then the *izzat*—the honor that outlives a man! That is greater than the decoration which I gave Shir Dil. You go to save Kandahar for our king, and for our country."

As he went to overtake the flanking detachment, Gul Mast was certain that the men of Darabad had been given this sacrifice detail mainly to cancel fifteen percent per month, compound interest. On top of that, if Uncle Haroun died without heirs, his estate would go to the royal treasury. Gul Mast was sure that in more ways than one, he was about to die for his country.

He cursed bitterly, and not at the snipers whose shots smacked past his peaked turban whenever his head bobbed up in a cleft of the sandstone. He was a practical man. Spending two years to ambush and shoot Rahim Ali, at considerable risk of life and expense of cartridges, that was something else: a rival money-lender is bad for business. But saving Kandahar! It didn't make a bit of difference who controlled the town, and certainly none to the herdsmen, the water carriers, the eleven bandits, the camel drivers, and the shoemakers who had left Darabad at the king's call. Gul Mast Khudayar's name meant, "Rose-Intoxicated Friend of God," but for all that, he was a practical man.

A rebel battery was checking the Sardar's slow advance. The air was thick with fumes and rock dust, and screeching fragments; high explosive searched the entire line. Heat made the cliffs dance and shimmer. What little grass there was had been burned brown, and the few stunted trees were hardly greener than the grass. For awhile, Gul Mast's party was unobserved; but as they wormed their way up the further wall of the valley, a machine gunner opened up.

Shir Dil dropped flat on his medal, perhaps an instant after Gul Mast. Wali Dad, slow or unlucky, spun twice, and followed the Martini-Henry that clattered to the rocks. Gul Mast got the dead farmer's canteen and took a long drink of goat-flavored water, which tasted better, to a practical man, than the ice cold rivers of wine that flow through Paradise for deceased heroes.

The battery on the reverse slope was the key to the rebel position. Its concussions hit Gul Mast like hammer blows. Protected from the Sardar's shrapnel peppering, it would cover the counter-attack that the rebels were about to start. And now the enemy knew that the Sardar intended to flank those Krupps and put them out of action;

the machine-guns, chattering at the rate of 600 *rupees* a minute, told how valuable the extermination of Gul Mast and his comrades would be.

The men of Darabad resumed their advance, moving so skillfully that the enfilade fire stopped for lack of target. Shir Dil paused for breath, and said to the following file, "The sons of lewd mothers, they think they've wiped us out. Now look—it's not far to the crest. From there, one dash and we'll settle the gunners. We'll take the gun and turn it on them."

Gul Mast inched himself upgrade and said, "First let me look, Shir Dil, and see if this thing can be done. How do we know that they are not expecting us, and pretending they think we're all dead?"

Shir Dil, aptly named Heart of a Lion, had sense enough to see the merit of first looking. "I'll go up," he said.

"No, you are our leader, let me go."

This amazed the men of Darabad; not that anyone had doubted Gul Mast's valor, but because assuming the leader's risk seemed needless.

Up he went, clawing the blistering sandstone. He moved with the stealth of a master horse-thief. Gul Mast knew all the lore, but as a boy, he had been practical enough to see that even the best thieves are occasionally shot, while others were executed; whereas money-lenders, or landlords like Uncle Haroun lived to become old and gray and wealthy, and usually endowed a mosque in order to spite greedy kinsmen. So Gul Mast had decided against the respect accorded a successful bandit or horse-thief.

There was no fire to menace him. It was an easy climb, and he thanked Allah for the slug that had made him heir to Wali Dad's canteen.

Slowly, skillfully, half an inch at a time; his grimy turban, his baggy pants, his brown hands and angular face, they blended with sun-baked gray and tan of the slope. He needed information, the facts, the actual facts, and not a valor-distorted belittling of the enemy, nor a harangue by Shir Dil, who was still light headed from having been decorated by the Sardar.

When he finally did see, he knew that he had been right from the first: a handful of hotheads could rush the two guns, could with luck put them out of action by shooting the cannoneers and then knocking the chocks from behind the wheels and trails; they would roll downhill into a deep cleft on the reserve slope.

The ground was so hard that a trail spade could not be sunk. With each blast, the pieces kicked back against solid timbers. The spades were chewed up from slashing at the rocks. But for all that, the sweating cannoneers were punishing the Sardar's men. Allah alone knew how many *rupees* those shells cost!

So much was good. The rest was not. Once the battery was out of action, a band of heroes would follow. Exposed to view, they'd be cut down to the last man. There was not a chance of scrambling up the slope and back over the crest to comparative safety. This was something that hot-headed Shir Dil would never think of.

Gul Mast went back to report: "The Sardar is crazy. This thing cannot be done."

He began to explain, until the medal-intoxicated Shir Dil shouted him down. "Some of us will come back. Those who stay—consider the glory! The king will honor us."

"I do not see," Gul Mast pointed out, "what a dead man does with glory. He can neither eat *izzat,* nor borrow money on it, nor kill an enemy with it, or buy a wife with it. This whole campaign is fool's business. Look at the cartridges we furnish, one *rupee* apiece, and so far we are not humpbacked from carrying loot. Is one king different from another king? In our lives have we ever enjoyed the Gardens of Kandahar? Will we enjoy them any more for going like fools for the Sardar's glory and our own?"

But *izzat* had the advantage. Shir Dil's medal would fill a man's hand. That it contained no more than ten *rupees* worth of silver had no force with anyone except Gul Mast. Yet he followed his leader. He was practical enough to know that if anyone did survive, and all things are possible to Allah, every one of his debtors would default principle and interest when it was noised about that he had been hesitant about dying for his king.

He did very well, once they cleared the crest. He spent five *rupees* worth of cartridges, firing from cover he had picked in his reconnaissance. And he did not waste a single shot. Neither did he join the rush. Prudently, he stayed in a position from which he could retreat, and watched Shir Dil and the others rush the battery of Krupps.

The guns had barely started on their backward course when rebel riflemen noted what had happened. A *yuzbashi* bounded up, sword in hand. Sniders and Enfields blazed. The nearest squad left cover and charged, firing as they ran, and others followed. Shir Dil and his men had their chance to learn whether or not Paradise was under the shadow of spears.

It did not last long. Two shoemakers from Darabad stood with empty rifles, facing knife-armed herdsmen, and camel drivers.

Shir Dil justified his name, and there was so much blood on him that the enemy did not see his medal.

Meanwhile, Gul Mast saw the Sardar reap the crop of *izzat.* The insane rush by a few men had convinced the rebels that they had been flanked. They left their lines to face the non-existent menace. There was a moment of uncertainty; there was dismay at the destruction of the guns a hundred feet below, on the ragged bottom of the cleft. And from the other flank came the Sardar's reserves, perfectly timed, set in motion by signal flares.

They rolled up the rebel line, making the most of that shocking surprise.

Gul Mast, skulking under cover, found his chance to retreat, but not until he had taken Shir Dil's big medal, ten *rupees* worth of silver.

The rebels were scattering in every direction. Since their leader had allowed himself to be outmaneuvered, they changed their minds about fighting to the end. As Gul Mast saw it, he had merely the advantage of foresight.

Now that there were no witnesses to tell of his prudence, he would readily enough collect his fifteen percent per month from half the regiment. Once certain that the rout was ensured against any rally and counter-attack, he ran forward in the general direction of pursuit, yelling and occasionally firing his Mauser.

There would be a certain amount of *izzat* gained from being the only survivor of an heroic attempt. Gul Mast was definitely pleased, until he heard horsemen at his right, and somewhat to his rear.

The Sardar, with one staff officer, galloped along the advancing line, directing the pursuit. Couriers were riding in every direction, carrying orders to the *yuzbashis,* and the higher officers.

When the Sardar saw Gul Mast, he reined in, sweaty and scowling.

Gul Mast saluted. "Allah in his mercy spared your servant to bring a report—"

Then he saw that something was wrong. The Sardar shouted, "Father of many pigs, I was watching through these glasses—I saw—"

Gul Mast was ready when the staff officer drew his pistol in anticipation of the next command. It seemed that they had both seen why one man had survived.

Gul Mast's shot cost a *rupee,* and it was the one un-regretted expenditure of the campaign. The blast knocked the officer out of the saddle. The Sardar, hampered by field glasses, lost time fumbling. Gul Mast dashed to cover, for his magazine was empty and it was quite too late to shove in a clip.

When the Sardar's pistol opened up, he wasted ammunition. Glare, dust, a zig-zagging target, and a startled horse were too much for him.

Gul Mast found refuge where no horse could follow: and the Sardar still had a victory to consolidate. Orderlies came up with messages.

That evening, Gul Mast realized the need for going to India for a long stay. He decided to forgive his debtors, since there was no chance of collecting. After the sunset prayer, he recited from the Traditions, *"Allah loves the just, the generous—"*

* * * *

By forgiving debts, a man won merit in the sight of God.

But it was hard, thinking of old Uncle Haroun, and those chests of coin squeezed out of the tenants of Darabad. An exile could not inherit, no more than an outlaw or an apostate; the learned Fakhru'l-Sabikani was very explicit on that point, in a manuscript whose transcription had been completed on Friday, one of the four nights at the close of Shewal, in the year of the flight 712, in Damascus. And the learned Shaykh Siraju'd-din, to say nothing of Sayyad Sharif, left no doubt on the matter.

No more doubt than there was about Gul Mast's exile being permanent.

So he found refuge in Peshawar. He sold the big silver medal, and became a money-changer. He slept in an alley near the coppersmiths' bazaar, and to protect his slim capital, he ate little. It was very much like war, except that no one was shooting at him, and no one promised him *izzat.* And after the first caravan came down from Turkestan, his ten *rupees* began to show a profit.

The Uzbek merchants rarely complained when he short-changed them. First, they were thick-witted, and seldom suspected until it was too late. And then, Gul Mast Khudayar was large and lean and hard-eyed, quite unlike his poetic name; so they did not care to quarrel with him.

Months later, he bought back Shir Dil's medal. The silversmith asked, "Why didn't you borrow from me? I might have sold this token of your valor."

Gul Mast grinned and took a fresh chew of *pan.* "Oh Man, had I borrowed, I would be thy bond-slave for life. As it is, I start today as a money-lender. And look —I have not charged you for the loan of my *izzat,* all these days."

Then from the north came the news of Uncle Haroun's death. His coffers of *rupees* and his lands were waiting for his heir. This took all the joy from life in Peshawar, the largest town Gul Mast had ever seen.

At first, he thought that it was a trap. But as the months passed by, he became convinced that while it might be bait, Uncle Haroun had really died, and the estate had not been turned over to the royal treasury. Apparently, the Sardar was cunning;

instead of reporting Gul Mast's logic and having him outlawed, the Sardar had held his peace, perhaps trusting to the dead officer's kinsmen to exact vengeance.

Day by day, Gul Mast weighed the chances. He would have to spy out the Darabad district, and learn just why he had not been outlawed. The thing to do was to go in disguise, and not reveal himself until he knew what was behind this curious oversight. Neither the Sardar nor the kinsmen of the staff officer would forget that *izzat* demanded payment of the blood debt.

Gul Mast went, finally, after considerable expense. The disguise was arranged in this wise: there was a Kashmiri woman who curled and bleached and dyed the hair of the infidel women, and painted their nails and their faces; and it was easy for her to bleach Gul Mast's black beard until at last it was a venerable white.

He spent hours thus, at night, after the *memsahibs* had gone. When it was complete, he had aged forty years or more, until he looked as Uncle Haroun must have looked. Now he could spy out the district, and if all was well, he had only to wait for his beard to grow black again, and then reveal himself. Meanwhile, he could readily enough kill whatever fools carelessly admitted that they were waiting to settle Gul Mast, renegade, coward, traitor, and assassin: which was what they would consider a practical man who reasoned that it was manifestly silly to die for benefits which would be enjoyed mainly by non-combatants.

So he set out on foot, carrying his rifle as he would a walking stick. He had Shir Dil's medal. He enjoyed looking at it, of an evening, as he drank his tea; it consoled him whenever he shuddered from thinking that perhaps something might keep him forever from inheriting Uncle Haroun's *rupees*. It reminded him that he was alive, when with a less practical mind, he might be with Wali Dad and Shir Dil, and all the other *izzat*-drunken comrades.

When he reached the final crest, and looked down into the bowl-shaped valley and the town where his uncle had been an important man, Gul Mast was bewildered. There were the same scrawny fields, with outcropping rock and stumpy watch towers, the ugly little houses crouched inside the wall of earth and stone, the brush-roofed market booths baking in the sun. Yet something had changed: there was greenness in the square which once had been sun-blasted and dusty, and a water carrier went about, sprinkling the street which led to the Ghazni Gate.

This extravagance was hard to understand until he saw the streak of green which led up into the hills. Grass marked the leakage from an aqueduct made of masonry. Times had changed in Darabad. Gul Mast was not quite sure whether he was stirred by seeing his old home, or by the impending contest for a dead man's *rupees*.

He spread his coat on the hot earth and gave thanks to Allah for the foresight which had preserved him until this day.

He began to wonder, as he came nearer, whether his bleached beard and artificially aged skin were necessary, or worth the money they had cost. There were no familiar faces to fear; the *maidan* was crowded with strangers.

Gypsy women with golden coins festooning their hair flounced about, shamelessly eyeing the caravan men. Gul Mast, a stranger indeed, began to resent being cheated of the chance to see without being recognized, to bait old friends and old enemies and old debtors, cunningly pumping them dry. Darabad, the forgotten of God, had become a trading town, a town where there was water and coolness to the eyes: so that the caravans stopped instead of passing on.

In Peshawar he had been too busy to keep posted on what went on in the hills. Now he would learn by loafing at the big fountain in the middle of the *maidan.*

There was some difficulty in getting to its edge, for all the women of the town were there with earthen jars. Instead of drawing from a lean and brackish well, with a hoist of a hundred feet, they had only to dip, and they could spill all they pleased: no wonder the wenches were chattering.

An inscription decorated a white slab of the masonry. The gilded letters gleamed bravely in the ruddy sunset. They were elegant as the script in the *mullah's* Koran, and Gul Mast wondered what the lines said; he could not read the ornate characters, for they were as much an arabesque picture as a text, and his knowledge of writing was confined to necessities such as noting the names of debtors, and calculating interest.

He wiped the cool drops of water from his beard, and stalked down the street. Old Yusuf, the gunsmith, squatted in his booth, filing a breechblock into shape. In back, his son operated a creaking lathe, foot driven, slowly turning a rifle barrel that would some day settle a feud, or start one. Gul Mast was so glad to see a familiar face that he almost saluted Yusuf; then he checked himself, for the gunsmith owed him fifty *rupees,* with interest compounded for nearly a year.

Better not depend on Yusuf.

He ate grilled lamb and cucumbers and sour milk at a restaurant which was crowded with dish-faced Uzbeks. Their barbarous Mongolian chatter told him nothing, and made him feel even more a stranger.

Next he went to the cobbler, a newcomer, to have a worn sole patched. It was dusk now, and men gathered about the fountain to drink tea, and gamble, to tell monstrous lies, to sing ballads and to play droning tunes on reed pipes. Gul Mast was shocked at hearing someone pronounce his name; he whirled, catching up his rifle, and he cursed the devil who had inspired him to take off the boots he needed for fast action on foot.

The shoemaker, fortunately, was intent on his work, squinting by the light of a rag floating in a dish of tallow. Then Gul Mast heard and saw: an old man, pious and learned, judging from his Persian tunic, was pointing toward the inscribed block, and saying, "Gul Mast, may God be gracious to him, gave us this."

Barefooted, he went across the street, and saluted the group. "Uncle," he said, "out of your kindness, tell me of the generous and saintly man who brought the blessing of water to this town."

The *mullah* was not amazed to hear a white-bearded man address him, very respectfully, as "uncle," though for a moment, it seemed to Gul Mast it had been an error to forget his assumed age. The scholar answered, "Brother, this is the memorial to a hero, the nephew of Haroun. The lines are in Persian—I composed them myself— telling how Gul Mast Khudayar inspired many companions to valor, and died with them to win a battle."

"Allah requite you," the disguised hero stuttered, when he swallowed his horror. "Did the sorrowing uncle spend his whole fortune on this father of fountains?"

The mullah stroked his beard for a moment. "Allah is the Knower. Though it is said that Haroun kept a small parcel of land and perhaps ten or fifteen thousand *rupees* for his old age. But he did not outlive his grief."

Gul Mast wondered if he would outlive his own. He stumbled across the street to get his shoes, and he did not have to feign the stoop of old age. His heart was hardly in it when he haggled, for the ensuing half hour, about the price of the repair work.

Later, in the gate of the darkened *serai*, he stood listening to the gurgle of the fountain. He whispered, fiercely, "God curse Haroun, God curse his ancestors and all his kinsmen, the goat-bearded old fool did that to spite distant relatives, and may Satan damn them also!"

He spat in the general direction of the fountain, and then went to his cubicle in the second floor gallery which overhung the compound of the *serai*. And weary as he was, his sleep was not restful. Time and again he awakened from the sound of the fountain; every gurgle, every splash was a *rupee* out of his pocket.

The following day, he went about his spying; and very quickly began to realize the difficulty and danger of the task he had approached. First of all, there was the chance that in spite of his white beard, some shrewd person would become suspicious: for the woman in Peshawar had neither the art nor the science to put wrinkles into his face; none of her clients had ever made any such outrageous demands! So Gul Mast, subjected to the scrutiny which all strangers got when it seemed that they had come to Darabad to stay, spent uncomfortable hours wondering when someone would remark about the lack of wrinkles in his weathered face.

Caravan men and traders, who came and went, got little attention, but with Gul Mast, it was different. Everyone was eager to know his business, his intentions, his place of origin; he was quizzed about his kinsmen and offspring; and he was in constant unease lest someone pick a contradiction in his carefully rehearsed story. More than that, he spent most of his time answering rather than asking.

True, evasion had its place. A certain vagueness, a judicious changing of the subject: these helped establish him as a man who had taken a sudden trip for his health. But there was always the chance that he would forget to walk with an old man's stoop, or that someone would wonder why the backs of his hands were not puckered from age.

And the agonizing expense of it all! Where the real Gul Mast had haggled for an hour over two *pais*, the disguised Gul Mast had to be careless of *rupees*. Instead of telling a beggar that with frugality and good investments, he would have been prosperous, he gave an *anna*. The whole town was fleecing him.

But finally he learned the details of Gul Mast's valor, though this took patience, for a stranger would not normally be interested in more than the bald facts. The Sardar, it seemed, had been shot from his horse, early in the pursuit, and the second in command had driven on to final victory.

"When an orderly came up beside him," Taimur the pipemaker said to the white bearded stranger, "the Sardar spoke the name of Gul Mast. He said that name before he died, just that name, and pointed to his tunic where he wore many medals. From others, we learned how the men of Darabad had been sent to save the day, so we knew that the dying Sardar meant to decorate the bravest of them all, Gul Mast, the Friend of God. His body was never found-doubtless he fell into a cleft."

The tobacco which Gul Mast bought became rank and bitter in his nostrils. The Sardar, intending to denounce him, had inflicted the worst possible punishment. Allah alone knew how many thousand *rupees* that accursed fountain and aqueduct had cost!

He had come to bushwhack whatever witnesses there were against him; now this was unnecessary, seeing that he was not an outlaw. But there was a new problem, that of sifting all the stories, and from the details building up a plausible yarn to account for his resurrection. His death had brought *izzat* to the town, which was more than his life had done. Planning was needed, and each day's spying cut deeply into his supply of cash.

Meanwhile, the administrator of Uncle Haroun's estate pilfered all that he could. Ahmad, called Hafiz because he had memorized the entire Koran, had begun wearing silk pants and a silver-embroidered jacket; the old scoundrel had married two new wives. If Gul Mast did not act soon, there would be nothing left to claim.

Nor was a resurrection so simple to arrange. Revealing himself at once would require an explanation of his having taken the precaution of disguise. While a dead hero was sacred, a living money-lender was something else. His debtors might profitably pick holes in the story.

That memorial fountain fascinated Gul Mast. He sat there, day after day, watching his *rupees* gurgle up and flow over, refreshing men and dogs and camels and women. At times he felt that his hair and beard would soon become naturally white from sustained misery, but for all this, he took a certain wry pleasure in hearing the old men speak of Gul Mast's valor.

The thrill, however, became a chill whenever the new wives of Ahmad Hafiz came to draw water. They clanked with golden anklets, they reeked of costly perfumes; every day, the residual legacy was fading, and the administrator became greasy from over-eating.

Meanwhile, there was a small sprouting of black at the roots of Gul Mast's beard. It was time to leave, for he could not return too soon after the departure of the venerable and generous "Abdul Karim"; someone would suspect. Though he had by now learned sufficient details of the battle to shape a logical tale of lying wounded and too helpless to call for aid as the victors rushed by, the story had to be seasoned and ripened, lest some debtors pick holes in it.

Several times, when Gul Mast was on the point of leaving, that splendid fountain drew him back, though he did not know why. He had ceased cursing it and Uncle Haroun; he saved his damnation for Ahmad Hafiz and the perfumed wives. He had ceased to resent the Sardar's farewell gesture, and the fatal story which the orderly had brought back.

Then, of an evening, he saw a man from a neighboring village, one Usaf Abbas, who had served in the other company of that same badly riddled battalion: an onion-nosed fellow with an unpleasant sneer, an ungenerous man who never borrowed money for *hasheesh* or tobacco; all in all, not the sort of man one would trust.

Usaf, squatting by the fountain which had refreshed him, did not recognize the dead hero. He was grinning when he looked up from the shining *na'astalik* script, and he said to Gul Mast, "It is well that Haroun died when he did. Verily, his nephew, may pigs defile his bones, was too stingy to burn a cartridge in self-defense."

A passerby heard this statement, and halted near the group of old men. "Doubtless Gul Mast was not extravagant," was the fair-minded answer, "but in his death he made up for his life. Many of us repaid our borrowings to the old man, his uncle. Gul Mast brought *izzat* to the town, and the king once mentioned his name in public prayer."

Usaf's laugh was poisonous. "Oh men! There was one of the dying who cursed Gul Mast for tricking his comrades into charging, while he hid behind some rocks. I speak of Wali Dad, whose fields were seized to satisfy the debt which Haroun inherited from the nephew."

Gul Mast's beard twitched, and he got a firm grip on his rifle. He shouted, "Thou father of several dogs, thou son of a nose-less mother, I marched with the rebels, and I am one of those who saw the valor of Gul Mast. He came like a roaring lion toward our guns. His leader lagged from fear, but Gul Mast came on, shouting his names and titles."

He paused for breath. Spectators gathered to hear these new details about their hero. One said to Usaf, "Rub thy head and go thy way. Is it not enough when even a former enemy praises him?"

Gul Mast could feel the growing indignation of the townsmen; it made him lightheaded as the Sardar's medal had made that fool, Shir Dil. Never given to needless quarreling, Gul Mast bellowed, and with surprising volume for an old man, "We fired at him, we missed, we were surprised. And when his gun was empty, he still came on, cutting and hewing." Then some devil entered Gul Mast and took his tongue. "I myself saw him stand to face three men, after our cannons had rolled down hill. He slew them all, and he fell from his wounds when he went to meet the others."

And another devil took possession of Usaf, who could have rubbed his head and gone his way.

He said, "Gul Mast was a skinflint and a skulker, how could he change? Is it not written, anoint a serpent with rose water for a hundred years and he remains a serpent?"

This was bad enough, and then Usaf spat at the dedication slab. Gul Mast cursed and jerked his rifle to his hip, but he was not quick enough. From his side, so close that the blast fairly shattered his ear drum, one of the villagers had cut loose with a pistol. Usaf dropped his own half-leveled weapon, clawed his sheepskin jacket, and clutched the fountain's edge. His hand slipped, and he crumpled in the dust, and lay there twitching.

Gul Mast bounded forward, cursed the dying man, booted him in unfeigned fury. And his voice sounded strange in his own ears when he gave the corpse a final kick and croaked, "Oh Men! Before we fled, I went to Gul Mast to plunder him, but I could not, for he was a brave man. He gave me a medal, saying that the Sardar had pinned it on him at the start of the surprise attack, since there was little chance that any man would return alive. It was Gul Mast's valor that made the Sardar honor him rather than the leader of the company!"

He fumbled in his coat, and brought out the medal, which he laid on the rim of the fountain. Before a man of the group could say *"Mashallah,"* he went on, "So I waited until the wrath of war cooled down, and I was afraid to tell of my purpose, lest you kill me. But Gul Mast had begged me to send this medal to his uncle. Here it is, and the peace upon you!"

He turned his back on the fountain and the townsmen, and stalked toward the gate with the two stumpy watch towers. There were only a few *rupees* left in his purse; and now that he had buried Gul Mast beyond any resurrection, he realized that he had showed very little more judgment than the late Usaf Abbas.

On the other hand, while *izzat* was certainly not worth a man's life, it was cheap enough at fifteen thousand *rupees:* and a practical man could soon get a fresh start in Peshawar. So he reached out with his long legs, and chuckled as he heard the last faint gurgle of the fountain he had brought to Darabad.

BONES FOR CHINA

Originally appeared in *Speed Adventure Stories*, July 1945.

When Yang Li-cheng recovered enough strength to struggle to his knees, he noted the two men who squatted beside the trail, watching him; his first concern, however, was to look at the sun, to see how long he had been unconscious. He felt better when he saw how little time he had lost. He tried to get to his feet, for there was no time to waste, only weariness and the aching old bones. The fever he had brought all the way from the Burmese jungle bore him down almost as much as did the pack on his back.

The two men had not been in sight when Li-cheng stumbled and fell beside the trail which rose steeply toward the pass. For miles back, the country was barren and rocky, without a village, or any rice fields. Like Li-cheng, the strangers had broad-brimmed hats, mushroom-shaped; dirty blue shirts, worn with the tails flopping outside their tattered cotton pants. Their straw sandals were so shredded as to be little more than tokens of footgear. They were dressed like Chinese farmers, but Li-cheng sensed that things other than tilling the soil occupied them.

"Which way do you go, grandfather?" one asked, as the two helped him to his feet.

"Ming Tien," Li-cheng answered, pointing to the pass.

His destination was the home which he had left nearly half a century previous, to join his grandfather in California.

"It is not good to go to Ming Tien."

There was command in the advice yet also the deference proper when addressing the aged. Farmers did not have the manner of the man who spoke, nor his grimness, nor that purposeful glance. The scars which seamed his face, and showed through the rents in his shirt were unusual; and it was odd indeed for two farmers to be popping up from rocks of a barren slope, so far from any field.

Li-cheng regarded the two, and resolutely said, "My grandfather says I have to hurry to Ming Tien."

They regarded Li-cheng, and the big earthenware jar which weighted his pack. "The Japs are marching up the valley; they'll be at Ming Tien soon."

"I must go on. Grandfather has been away from home for nearly a hundred years."

The men exchanged glances. The scarred one began to understand, and he said, kindly, "Eat first, the way is steep."

They gave him cold rice and cold tea which they brought from somewhere behind the rocks. When he had eaten, they helped Li-cheng to his feet, and set him on his way.

"Walk slowly," they said.

Later, halting on the crest he had so painfully reached, Li-cheng twisted his scrawny neck to say over his shoulder, "Venerable grandfather, it is not far to Ming

Tien."

There was no answer, but by now he had learned that grandfather picked his own times for speech, so, hearing no correction, he was comforted. He knew that his memory was not tricking him, and that the nearest of the mud-walled villages, and its girdle of diked rice fields must indeed be the home he had left so long ago.

When Li-cheng finally reached the gate of the village, he knelt and clawed deep into the dark earth of the street, and smelled it as though it were perfume. His thousand wrinkles puckered into a smile, and he said, "Venerable Ancestor, this is the earth of Ming Tien, you are at home."

Then he gravely saluted the blank-faced farmers who had gathered. "This person's grandfather is in the jar. I have brought his bones from America."

"Ai! From Mei Kuo?"

"Yes, from Mei Kuo."

And he told how, after having shipped grandfather's bones to China, he had learned that there had been a mistake which had caused an entire lot to go astray. "So," he concluded, "when I wrote letters and got no answers, I went to Shanghai to get his bones from the warehouse, to take them to Canton and then come inland, but there was talk of war, and the ship went to Manila and then to Singapore. From there I walked."

Of Yang Li-cheng's four brothers, none remained. As for his nephews, some were dead, others were in the army. It was clear now why there had been no answers to his letters, and it was good that he had himself brought grandfather's bones to Ming Tien for burial with the others whose graves were on the knoll.

They made him tell them of his march, and he said, "Each day I walked as far as I could. Sometimes people showed me the way, and sometimes grandfather told me how to go."

No one considered this improbable. The big wonder was America, and when he told them of the land, they politely concealed their incredulity, for Li-cheng's filial piety made him honorable. Some day, the government would erect a commemorative gateway at the village.

Presently, the *feng shui* man joined the group, for he had heard talk of bones. No one could lay the foundations of a house, or start a journey, or be married, or buried, without first learning the auspicious day. Though the magician was nearly as old as Li-cheng, his eyes were bright, and his wits were young.

After taking into account the phase of the moon, the wishes of the Air Dragons and the Earth Dragons, he said, "Honorable Yang, the lucky day for burial is eleven days from now."

But the farmers pointed to the smoke on the horizon. "The Japs are coming, they ruin what they cannot steal. We leave in the morning, go with us before they kill you."

Li-cheng was so nearly spent that he could not endure the thought of further marching. The *feng shui* man added, "Later, there will be other lucky days. You can come back."

Li-cheng gave the soothsayer a piece of silver, and then took grandfather to the inn, where he spread two straw mats in a corner.

"Venerable Ancestor," he said to the jar, "there will be other lucky days."

Grandfather did not answer, though he had spoken a good deal during that march along a rutted road through Burma. Perhaps, having come back at last to the home he had left almost a century previous, there was nothing for him to say: and so Li-cheng had to make his own decision.

What the villagers had told him began to gain force; while it would be bad if the enemy arrived while he waited for the lucky day, to march on might make him collapse, and who would return to bury grandfather?

In the morning, the farmers loaded their wagons, and tied their pigs to carrying poles, and put their chickens into cages. The granaries were empty, the mud-walled houses were empty; silent and stolid, the villagers filed down the narrow street.

The *feng shui* man said, "Honorable Yang, there is room for your grandfather on that wagon."

But Yang Li-cheng answered, "You have left me rice, and a shovel, and maybe they will not come before the eleventh day."

"Maybe they will not," the soothsayer agreed, and joined the column. The refugees took the main highway which ran east and west, instead of following the steep trail along which Li-cheng had come from the south. He watched them making for the broad pass which pierced the western rim of the valley. He would have remained until the last wagon went over the crest, but a rain of cinders drove him to cover.

The farmers had set fire to the yellowing stalks of the rice they had been able to harvest. As for the other patches, Li-cheng could smell them drying, since the dikes had been cut so that there would be no new growth for the enemy.

Now that the village was entirely Li-cheng's, he left grandfather in the corner and went to the knoll where for centuries the Yangs had been buried. Weeds hid the crumbled coping. Either his nephews had been gone for a long time, or they had neglected their duty. Patiently, he uprooted a stalk at a time, and then he set the stones in order.

Digging grandfather's grave was slow and hard, far more so than Li-cheng had expected. There were no wood-working tools; this detail he had forgotten, and thus he could not make a coffin. The earthenware jar would have to do.

An excellent grave, and a first-rate coping, horse-shoe shaped, to mark it; all in all, grandfather would be pleased. And soon Li-cheng had not long to wait for the lucky day.

He sat beside the jar, that evening when the digging was at last done, and ate his rice. The horizon was red; he heard the steady rumbling, low and sullen, of trucks and tractors and gunfire. Concussion shook the air, and as it darkened, the flash of artillery and the burst of shells made the sky lighten with color.

He had always imagined war as the meeting of men with guns and swords, men shooting and shouting and slashing: this was impersonal as typhoon or earthquake, there was no hiding from it, nor any escaping as from the advances of soldiers, for the sound and fire hemmed him in. Gusts of sound became solid impact, shaking Li-cheng, not sharply as had the army trucks on which he had hitched rides, far back, but crushingly, oppressively. The shudder of the earth made pieces fall from the walls of the inn.

Vibration troubled his sleep and his awakenings. Where he had expected only armed men who could scarcely see harm in one old man, he now felt the anger of dragons; in their fury at the invasion, they would not find him different from the enemy.

"Venerable Ancestor," Li-cheng quavered, "maybe it would be better to go, I have rested, I can walk fast, there will be other lucky days."

Whether chills or fear made his teeth chatter, he could not be sure, though the drumming and thickness in his head might well be the blending of malaria within and the steady grumbling about him; but the faint dry rattling he heard was not that of his teeth. It was a stirring that came from the jar. Where once such sounds had made his skin twitch from fright, he was now glad, for grandfather was about to answer. He listened.

"Heaven does not speak, yet the four seasons come regularly."

Just that, and no more. Li-cheng, though still he twitched from unrelenting blows of sound, felt less alone, and his terror subsided.

"The four seasons come regularly," he repeated aloud, and frowned until understanding made him smile. "Four seasons each year, but not Japs each year."

He got up, for moving about was better than crouching, and shuddering from each concussion. Though far-off smoke made the full moon red, the brightness was as much as Li-cheng needed.

Once out in the diked fields, he began to dig as his people had dug before they made the first plow. Barefooted, he worked, sinking deep into the mud. And after repairing a dike, he listened to the changed voice of water no longer going to waste. Work made it easier to endure the hammering.

Some hours later, he washed the dirt from his feet, and shouldered his shovel, and went back to the inn. There were no voices to break into his sleep. Tilling the earth of his people had given him fresh strength and courage. He knew now why grandfather had to return to that ancestral earth.

Sunrise did not awaken Li-cheng, and neither did the rumble of trucks, the sputter of motorcycles, the chatter of the Japanese soldiers who poured into Ming Tien. He did not awaken until the billeting officer, making the rounds of the deserted village, found and booted him in the ribs. They took him to regimental headquarters where a captain questioned him in Chinese.

"Where are the others?"

"They went, *ta-jen*."

"Which way?"

He pointed to the western pass, and the main highway.

"Why did they go?"

"They are frightened, *ta jen*."

"Why do you stay?"

"I stay because I am not afraid, Excellency."

Captain Tashida was interested. The commanding officer would also be interested to hear that after some years of pigheaded resistance to Co-Prosperity, the Chinese were beginning to see the light. Here was one who waited for the Elder Brother instead of running.

Then Tashida's bristly mustache twitched, and he fingered the clumsy grip of his straight sword. This was just too good to be true! In other words, something was wrong, dead wrong.

"What are you thinking, Li-cheng?"

"Contemplating *ta-jen's* stately presence."

"How do you like Co-Prosperity?"

"This person does not understand."

Tashida wrote on his notebook, "Possibly course of indoctrination and Right Thought for Li-cheng." Only, a Chinese who was able to move, and yet staying instead of leaving with his fellows, might not by any means be a sign that Co-Prosperity had won a friend without bribery.

"Who told you to stay?"

"This person's venerable grandfather, Excellency."

Tashida scowled. "Grandfather? You're nearly seventy!"

"This person has sixty-eight years, *ta-jen.*"

For a moment it seemed sure that the sixty-ninth year would not be completed. Triflers and humorists were strictly out of order. Scouts had brought word of a road block, held in strength by Chinese regulars, in the western pass. Guerillas were harassing the flanks, and the supply lines, not only of this advance guard, but also of the main body. And the lingering smell of burned fields did not put the commander in good humor.

"Where's your grandfather?"

"In the earthenware jar, Excellency." The old man clasped his hands, and bobbed his head. "He died forty-three years ago, so I bring his bones back from Singapore for honorable burial. With my father, and my uncles. I am the last living descendant, no sons, no nephews to do this duty."

Tashida sent an orderly for the jar, and verified the contents. He was about to dismiss Li-cheng when significant questions occurred. "Why have you waited to bury him?"

"For the lucky day, Excellency. The *feng shui* man told me—" Li-cheng counted on his fingers. "Day after tomorrow, that is when my grandfather can rest serenely in his grave."

Captain Tashida made a notation: "Ancient Chinese stated that auspicious time for burial of grandfather would be day of Imperial troops successful forcing of road block west of Ming Tien." He went on, amiably, "Tell me of guerilla activities. What guerilla burned your rice crop?"

"This person arrived in midst of hasty departure, hence ignorant of facts."

Tashida wrote, "Venerable farmer asserts guerillas treacherously and by stealth set rice afire, thereby forcing terrified friends of Co-Prosperity to evacuate."

An orderly came in with water from each of the several village wells. "Drink," Tashida commanded.

Li-cheng obeyed, to prove that the water was not poisoned. He spent the rest of the day opening doors for the billeting officer, who had had unpleasant experiences with home-made booby-traps. Li-cheng was glad when this task was done. An explosion would not only have deprived grandfather of proper rites, but would likewise have kept Li-cheng forever from suitable burial.

This possibility had worried Li-cheng more than any danger or pain or hardship, but whenever he brought the matter up, Grandfather Yang offered him neither hope nor consolation. The voice in the jar recited from the traditions, *"The present is the most important time, the person before you is the most important of men, and doing your duty is the most important of acts."*

140

The Japs booted Li-cheng from the inn, and sent him to join the peasants who had been herded up that afternoon to repair the highway, to drain the rice fields, and to dig trenches for the detachments which were to protect the advance guard, so that it would not be caught from the flank as it forced the road block.

As he set to his task, he remembered the two men who had warned him to stay out of Ming Tien. He began to understand that they might have had urgent business along the ridge.

That evening, as the members of the forced labor party ate their skimpy ration, Li-cheng was startled to see one of the two who had accosted him on his way to Ming Tien. Each, glancing over the edge of a rice bowl, eyed the other, said nothing, and went on eating.

Later, he saw the other, and heard him address the scarred man as Ah Sam.

By what little daylight remained, Li-cheng began to scrutinize his fellow slaves. In each of several groups, he noted a man who looked very much like any other peasant driven into a labor detail; but there was something different, something he would not have observed, except for what he knew of Ah Sam's lurking among sterile rocks.

Farmers, coolies, stolid and weary and cheerless as the others, underfed and ragged as the others; yet Li-cheng could feel the difference, and he wondered why no one else was aware of it.

To read a man's thought is not easy: but Li-cheng had spent so many days and nights groping for the wishes, and listening for the voice of a man dead more than forty years that he was sensitive to that which others would miss.

That night, as he slept beside the jar of bones, grandfather told him plainly Ah Sam was a guerilla, a spy who had joined the labor party, and who had good reasons for coming to help clear the ground in preparation for the assault against the road-block.

By now, Li-cheng had become accustomed to the incessant firing of far-off artillery, and the intermittent glow which reddened the horizon. Holding the Chinese troops in one quarter, the enemy was getting ready to drive to the west. For a farmer, Grandfather Yang had an unusual knowledge of what was going on.

In the morning, Ah Sam and the other guerillas were gone, and without doubt, back to that rocky far-off ridge from which a little known trail led to the Japanese flank…

As the day wore on, and the task-masters whipped Li-cheng and the others to a faster pace, the old man sensed the growing tension. Though the soldiers were neither afraid nor worried, they had become aware that something unusual hung over them, and they faced more than the reduction of a road block.

Toward dusk, Li-cheng learned that rumor of concealed menace had become certainty. The news spread, so that coolies as well as enlisted men had all but the details. Ah Sam, though they did not know him by name, was planning a guerilla surprise. Observers had noted signs of activity on the southern ridge.

There were embankments, rifle pits, fox holes, and irregular trenches on the lower slope. These, though disguised as parts of the uttermost extreme of the irrigation system, had been detected; Ah Sam had slipped.

Digging indicated that the guerillas, in unusual force, planned a stubborn stand, instead of the usual hit and run tactics. The Japs, however, saw even more in these signs: guerillas, they reasoned, were paving the way for a large body, regulars with a major purpose, such as rolling up the flank, and taking Ming Tien.

This dismayed Li-cheng. The far-off sound of war was terrifying enough; to be right in the midst of an assault on the town was beyond enduring. How bury grandfather, in the midst of battle?

Now that Li-cheng was so near the fulfillment of his mission, all hardship he had faced on his impossible march from Singapore became trivial in comparison to the burden of growing apprehension. Fatality loomed up, rather than common-places such as hunger, and fatigue, fever, and the ache of old bones. The accumulation which he had ignored now swooped down at once and for the first time made him fully aware of their crushing weight.

Since it was almost dark, grandfather might speak. Li-cheng huddled against the jar, where it sat in an angle of the wall. The white coping of the laboriously dug grave, not many yards away, was still visible. Soldiers bivouacked about its elevated position. Machine guns were emplaced. An old man, bending under a pack, would not have a chance when the guerillas swept the crest with their fire.

"Venerable Ancestor, the lucky day is so nearly here, must I wait, will not the rites be as good now?"

No answer. When there was a lull in the noise of the camp, he repeated the question. There was still no answer. Li-cheng said despairingly, "Grandfather is like Heaven, he also does not speak."

The old man, abandoned by both gods and ancestors, was desperate enough to rebel against filial piety, and sneak out of camp, and return later, as the *feng shui* man had advised, and as his grandfather had forbidden. He, Li-cheng, saw no chance of having decent burial for himself if he obeyed. But for the fatigue of forced labor, the aching cuts of the task-master's whip, and the swooping-up of the fever which for some days had lain dormant, he would have mutinied against injustice.

Then he heard the voice: "The Japs sneaked out by twos and by fours, to surprise Ah Sam before he can strike. Go, Li-cheng, tell Ah Sam to watch."

The stir and furtive rattle and ghostly clicking inside the jar ceased. But more than grandfather was behind this command. Li-cheng himself had felt the urge but discarded it, being too feeble and worn out. The ghostly prod, however, made him try.

Painfully, he got the pack on his back, and contrived to rise with it. Men intent on what might come into camp had no attention for that which left camp. They did not hear grandfather's advice from time to time as Li-cheng picked his way, avoiding encamped groups; they had no fever to sharpen their senses.

He had taken the jar lest it be disturbed during his absence. Habit had made it part of him, so where walking alone would not have been easy, he was bent by a burden.

Li-cheng cut across the fields, he stumbled over dikes. He sank half way to his knees in mud, and he clambered into and out of dry ditches and canals. For a while grandfather helped him to his feet whenever he fell, until, finally, Li-cheng was beyond helping.

Chills and fever took their turn with him. Shivering made him jerk like a mechanical toy. Rising temperature fried his brain as he lay there, face down in the stubble.

The moon was rising when Li-cheng was again able to move, and tried to remember why he should move. Everything was a confusion.

"Heaven does not speak, yet the four seasons come regularly."

The earth would perish but for the seasons, and doubtless it would become lonely for lack of care. Li-cheng began to remember sayings he had long forgotten. It is not parents we revere when we bury them fittingly, we really pay our debt to the earth by returning that which grew out of it.

"Every spring, the Emperor with his own hands ploughs a furrow," grandfather was saying to Li-cheng. "The Son of Heaven blesses the earth and pays homage to it."

Where tradition had driven him blindly across an ocean, and a dead man's voice had prodded him through Burma and to Ming Tien, Li-cheng at last knew why, as soon as he had warned Ah Sam, he had to go back, regardless of risk, to fill the grave, if not with a shovel, then with his bare hands.

He walked with new strength, sometimes on the dikes, again, cutting across fields, but always bearing toward the rocky sterile ridge. He moved faster than did the soldiers who had set out cautiously, even while covered by darkness. He reasoned that soil guided him, but did not speak to the invader. His logic was as good as that based on the plain fact that each group of soldiers had to keep in touch with the others.

Making no attempt at stealth, he was not cut down by the men who crouched in a spot not noted by the Japanese observers. When these rifle and spear-armed farmers heard what message he brought, they were not interested, yet one went with him, until at last he found Ah Sam.

Moonlight made the guerilla chieftain's face old and bitter and wise and hard as sunlight had not done; the face made Li-cheng think of the men of olden times who had become tigers, and this man was now a hungry tiger. Yet his voice was gentle, and he made Li-cheng sit down, and helped him with his intolerably heavy pack.

"That you go to this trouble makes me sad, old man. We know the Japs are coming. We made them see so that they would come."

The stirring of bones in the jar chilled Li-cheng. It was ghostly laughter. Grandfather's sense of humor seemed out of place, but Li-cheng was too tired to complain.

"You will win, and I can follow you back into Ming Tien," he said, hopefully, "and your victory will make a lucky funeral for my Venerable Ancestor."

Ah Sam now looked very much like a serious farmer, and not at all like a tiger. "No, old man, when they come to get us, others of our men will come out of the east, to hit them where they do not expect it."

Li-cheng, who understood nothing of war, cackled gleefully, and thought that he now understood grandfather's laughter.

"All the Japs dead, and I go to Ming Tien to wait for the next lucky day. And you will come to the banquet. Maybe I can find a duck to roast, even a pig."

"This will be an eating of men, and not many of those you see will fight again. Ming Tien will not be taken. It cannot be. We are too few, and so are those who strike from the east. We will kill many Japs, and so will they. And so will others after us, and in a year, there will be fewer Japs, and in five years, still fewer, and perhaps in twenty years, there will be none of them left, and many of our people left."

And so Li-cheng began to understand war.

"Go away, old man, and wait."

"Twenty years?" Li-cheng said, wearily. "I cannot."

"I mean," the patient guerilla explained, "in a few weeks, maybe a month, they will be far beyond Ming Tien, and then you can go back to town."

A man came running. Ah Sam turned to him. There was a shout, a shot, far down the slope. Rifles and machine guns opened up. Men darted from cover to cover. The skirmish developed. Grenades roared, mortars coughed, bombs rumbled; flame geysered up, and fragmentation whined and screamed and whistled. The shifting wind carried both the nitrous reek of modern cartridges and the sulphur stench of black powder. Men with long swords, men with spears, men with scythes raced here and there, at a crouch, ducking, halting, bounding up again when bombs and musketry covered their advance.

The Japs, fighting it out, from trench to trench, from dike to dike, plugged grimly toward the uncultivated upper slopes. Far off, others were racing to their support. Artillery began to pound and blast the ridge, to pocket the guerillas. Light tanks picked their way over dried fields. Some burst into flame as bottles of gasoline were smashed against their ports.

Li-cheng, in his first battle, had not even a weapon to steady him. The confusion was wilder than anything in his bouts with fever. Grandfather was talking, and the voices of Dragons became clear above the roar and rumble. "You are too old to go back to California...stay here, Li-cheng, when the Japs are gone, get the money you hid under the wall of the inn and buy the land Grandfather Yang used to own, and if you do not hear Heaven speak, at least you will see the four seasons and their regular coming."

In the bitter moonlight, he saw the upturned faces of guerillas with whom he had been working; young men, middle-aged men, boys. Others were sprawled in the shallow trenches. Some still moved. Some were half buried by shell blasts. He did not know which way to go, or what to do, but the voices of Dragons had spoken truth, and Li-cheng was resigned to seeing no more of Stockton, no more of the children and grandchildren who thought him backward for knowing only a few words of the language they spoke so glibly.

These guerillas with whom he had eaten rice, they would lie where they dropped, and their descendants would not find them, nor give them rites, nor blazon their names on ancestral tablets. Far off, he heard the roar and saw the flame of battle, beyond Ming Tien, and it made this skirmish seem like the fire-crackers he had hoped to set off at grandfather's funeral. Ah Sam, offering himself and his men as bait for the enemy, was in that distant attack getting rites as no Chinese farmer had ever got from his descendants.

Having done their best, having taken the worst, the surviving guerillas retreated, skillfully, one group covering the other; and the Japs, having come with a sledgehammer to drive a tack, charged up the slope.

"Get out, old man!" Ah Sam yelled; and then, to all within earshot, "Every man for himself!"

Li-cheng was beyond terror. There was not enough of him to register all that he had endured. He and grandfather were in a world of fever, noise, and voices, a heat that fried the brain, and a chill that made the teeth chatter. He saw Ah Sam spin, and pitch, and drop from sight. He saw bayonet-armed men blend with groups, plying long swords. Not able to run, Li-cheng moved slowly, no matter where.

He stumbled. The bones rattled. He knew now why Ah Sam had vanished: a trench had swallowed him, a guerilla grave. And now the fullness of understanding came on Li-cheng. There was no better ritual than this, nor any ground more suitable.

He struggled clear of the pack. He let the jar slide down the parapet, to rest among men who, though they still breathed, would not ever get up out of the earth of China.

He knew now that grandfather, foreseeing everything, had selected this spot, so he knelt, and filled his hands with earth and dropped it down on the jar, and on those others who had returned their bones to China. His work was complete.

Li-cheng, not able to understand what grandfather was saying, tried to hear, so that he was not aware that three Japs, darting upgrade, came upon him. An eager yell. They jostled each other. Their bayonets bit home, and the force of the thrust drove Li-cheng to the edge. When they twisted their blades clear, and hurdled the trench, Li-cheng thumped against the jar, and his hand touched the wet face of a man who lay near by.

Chunks of dirt slid down, falling on Li-cheng, but he felt them no more than he did his wounds, for what consciousness he still had was centered on what his comrades were saying: "It makes no difference that none of your children are here to bury you, for you have brought your bones back to the earth of Han, and the earth is our ancestor."

DRAGON'S DAUGHTER

Originally published in *Witchcraft & Sorcery* #6, May 1971.

CHAPTER 1

The singsong girl's fingers danced and rippled. Her left hand crept along the neck of the lute, advancing, retreating. The strings laughed and sang; they wailed, and sighed, and murmured. As Li Fong savored her loveliness, he recalled what a poet had said, a thousand years ago, about the girl next door...too tall, if an inch were added to her height...too short, if half that much were taken away...another puff of powder and she'd be too pale...another touch of rouge would be too much...

Stilling the voice of the lute, she handed it to him. Its four strings were stretched over ivory frets. The body, shaped like a pear split lengthwise, was of teak. The sounding board was of wutun wood, all inlaid with mother of pearl.

"*Tajen,* you play?"

As he plucked the strings, Li Fong recited lines snatched at random from Po Chu Yi's poem in honor of the lute:

> *"Loud as the crash of pelting rain*
> *Soft as the murmur of whispered words*
> *Frail as the patter of pearls*
> *Poured on a plate of jade"*

Li Fong gestured. Before he could fairly say, "Another cup!" she was pouring from the bronze jug. And he said, "You sang of the Uttermost West, of the Mountain of the Gods, and the Dragon Lords. Sing more! Tell more!" So the evening carried on, as such evenings will. Nothing was over looked. Not even that hour of whispered planning, after his promise to buy up her contract and take her home to be his concubine.

Nothing for Li Fong to do but pass the examinations, and be appointed to a post in the Imperial Civil Service. And of course, give presents to various eunuchs and other important persons at the court of the Son of Heaven.

Another jug of wine would not cut too deeply into the gold reserved for such gifts, nor into the silver for living expenses and tuition, the final cramming before the examination.

When Hwa Lan realized that Li Fong actually meant what he was saying, she countered, whimsically. "There is a better way for us, Old Master! We'll go to the Taoist magician and learn their art. Then we'll ride the wind, we'll go to the Mountain of the Gods, and we'll kowtow to the Dragon lords—we'll plead for their help! Otherwise *aiieeeyah!* How unpleased your Venerable Father will be when you start with a sing-song girl—when he's most certainly got a wife picked out for you!"

Hwa Lan was practical. Li Fong and the wine were not. So, she sang of the Dragon Lady who lived in the Great Desert...or, atop the Mountain.

At dawn, Li Fong awakened with the city. Considering how massively drunk he had been before Hwa Lan crumpled across her lute and toppled into bed he felt fine. Seeing her lying there, beyond the half drawn curtains of her alcove, he wondered what had happened. She'd been sparing enough, and had been urging him to drink less wine.

Something odd about her breathing. Hwa Lan still wore her jade hair pins. She still wore everything.

The bronze jar was empty. On the table was a small porcelain jug. Two matching cups. One empty. He reached for the other. He recognized the smell of that drug from Hindustan.

He had been so drunk that he had escaped being doped. And, so drunk that robbing him had required no fancy work whatever. Instead of gray silk tunic and black trousers, and embroidered boots and embroidered cap, he wore coolie clothes, ragged and grimy.

He was sure that Hwa Lan had had no part in this.

Storming through the wine shop, demanding his clothes and his money had landed him in jail. He did not look like the sort of person who would be admitted as a patron.

That was the wrong day to be in jail. A recruiting party took charge of every prisoner who could walk, gave the jailer a present, and collected a bounty of one silver *tael* per new soldier, when the detachment arrived at the military commander's *yamen*.

That is how it had started.

The Son of Heaven required a lot of soldiers to fight the Uighur Turki barbarian of the Uttermost West. And now, well over two thousand miles from that fatal wine shop, Li Fong was seeing the glamour-lands of which Hwa Lan had sung. Six months of long marching and short rations brought out the difference between song and fact...

The mountains, even from a great distance, loomed up as monstrous fantasies. More and more, they brought to mind Hwa Lan's music and words. He persisted in his belief, in what he had come to regard as knowledge, that Hwa Lan had played no part in robbing him. His other fixed belief, a growing conviction, no more rational than the first, was that someone spoke to him, usually during his sleep, but at times by day, as he plodded, hour after hour, licking the windblown *loess* dust from his lips, squinting through the yellow haze and at the sky-glare until waking and sleeping became ever more alike. Finally, he could not tell one from the other.

Li Fong never ate all his ration of parched barley or beans. Always, he saved a bit, building up a supply. This added to his burden, but it lightened his spirit. Prompted by his invisible counselors, who persistently asserted that Hwa Lan had seen great adventure and ultimate victory for him, Li Fong was making plans.

And the camel freighters were interesting fellows. They told of buried cities...of sands which spoke at night...and of the Gods who lived on several of the high mountain peaks.

One night Li Fong stole a camel. This was a smooth escape, without a moment of suspense. Since no one could possibly be so insane as to desert, the sentries were far from vigilant. So, he put the army behind him and looked up at the stars he had come to know, during those long nights of sleeping on hard earth.

> *"The Sieve now sparkles to the South*
> *And mostly ill drops through.*
> *Slowly, the Dipper tips and spills*
> *But pours no good for you..."*

The fact of it was that he recited those pessimistic lines to tone down the exultation which dizzied him.

Wind driven sand whispered and rustled, a dry, thin sound. Flying creatures grazed his face as they swerved. Some were feathered, some were furry, and as to others, he had unpleasant surmises.

The bats betokened a mine somewhere. But, how far... Outbound bats, not homeward faring...not at this hour...

Shortly before dawn, he came upon masonry rising a few feet above the drifted sand. There were stunted poplars. Li Fong halted at the ruin. He found a moist spot, as he had anticipated. He scraped and dug with his sword. Soon a brackish pool accumulated in the basin. After drinking, he crawled to the lee of the cornice of a deeply buried building. The drift was a softness such as he had not known for many a week.

Blazing sun awakened Li Fong.

Hobbling a camel so that the beast would remain hobbled was not one of Li Fong's skills. He was alone and afoot.

Li Fong shouldered his gear and made for the mountains.

By night, the mountains wore coronets of stars, and crowns of snow. By day, mirage made them dance and weave. Several times, when hunger and thirst and weariness would have kept him from getting up when he lurched and fell, voices urged him on. He found water, and grubbed roots. He ate the seeds from pods. Once, he found the eggs of a wild bird. Several times, he sword-speared a lizard. When he quit the desert and could distinguish trees on the mountain's upper slopes, Li Fong still had a handful of parched barley in his pack.

Li Fong propped himself upright, with staff of acacia. He tilted his head far back, and stared until finally he could believe that what he saw, so far up, was summit and snow cap, not clouds.

"*Omito fu!* The Mountain of the Gods!"

Water now, and pine nuts. Sometimes at the rim of a pool, he found lily roots. The air became thin and crisp. Mists billowed.

With flint and steel, he would make fire of an evening. Sometimes there were herbs which he simmered, making soup. He had long forgotten hunger, since he could not recall when he had last eaten other than famine-fare.

So, that sunset, with its slanting lances of red and gold reaching through the branches, when he saw a strange bird approaching him, he regarded it as beauty, rather than as food walking to his fire.

No doubt at all that he could throw the staff and clip the approaching fowl, but this possibility did not interest him.

The bird came without fear. In its gold-flecked eyes was a glint as of intelligence as well as curiosity. Tawny-buff and gold, white and scarlet plumage, with a triple crest and metallically gleaming beak, it seemed to be the origin of all the pheasant-kind, all the more so since the color scheme shifted until no variety had been omitted. This, however, was much larger than any pheasant, although to judge size was absurd. The trees, the escarpments which swooped skyward—all about Li Fong was gigantic. Nevertheless, the bird must be larger than a peacock.

It paced somewhat like a quail, flashing quick paces, yet progressing deliberately, always level, as though skimming the surface. This was a curious, a cadenced pacing.

The bird halted, regarding him, the haggard, the sun-seared, the ragged, and the dried-out. The beautiful and the devastated regarded each other, with interest ever increasing and compelling.

The lances of sunlight shifted.

A vast shadow enveloped Li Fong and the iridescent bird. The shadow was that of wings, tremendously outreaching. This was not the shadow of any cloud. The bird's eyes gleamed pointedly. The wings flickered. The tail fanned, the feet moved, a pacing which brought the bird no nearer Li Fong. It was as though this creature perceived, and knew something which Li Fong did not.

Then he understood. He recalled Old Master Wong, the calligrapher, who would close his eyes and with a single unbroken motion, brush never quitting the paper, shape four characters, the final ending in an exquisite long prolongation stroke.

"Soaring Dragon: Dancing Phoenix."

He spoke the words aloud.

There was a blur of gold and red and apricot and persimmon. The shadow shifted and wheeled. Glancing up, Li Fong caught the glint of scales, the gleam of claws. Looking back, he saw neither shadow nor bird.

He saw only a black-robed man who wore a Taoist hat. The man's white beard trailed to his waist. His face had scarcely a line, yet if he had declared himself to be a thousand years old, Li Fong could have believed him. The eyes half-glinted with humor, yet were half-stern, and entirely penetrating beyond the glance of ordinary men.

Once and a second time, Li Fong touched his forehead to the pine needles. Before he could kowtow a third time, the man helped him to his feet.

"Perhaps you should stay here—perhaps it is better for you to go far from here. But first, you will rest and eat. It is very interesting that you thought of *Soaring Dragon: Dancing Phoenix,* instead of roasted fowl."

CHAPTER II.

Li Fong followed the *tao shih* along a path which presently led to a monastery of brick and masonry. It nestled cozily on a shelf of rock which seemed to have an overlay of soil sufficient for a small group of monks, provided they were not hearty eaters.

As though sensing Li Fong's thought, the *tao shih* paused at the entrance. "What you do not know about farming, I will show you. I am Tai Ching, disciple of Master Ko Hung."

Li Fong put his palms together, bowed three times, gave his own name, and begged leave to abstain from stating his surname.

Master Ko Hung's life had ended three centuries ago. Whether Tai Ching meant that he had actually been one of the alchemist-magician's pupils, or merely that he had devoted his life to studying the *Pao P'o Tzu,* the Master's final book, was an open question. In any event, Tai Ching undoubtedly knew, from long ago, all the reasons which might make a man wish to conceal his surname.

Li Fong followed the *tao shih* across a well-kept courtyard. He paused long enough to scrape a bit of barley from his haversack, and put the grains on the altar of the shrine, just beyond the entrance. Having paid his respect to the Gods, the Immortals, and the Buddhas, he resumed his way, until Tai Ching gestured to an alcove in which spring water accumulated in a wall-basin.

"You may wash. Then follow food-smell to the refectory."

Presently, Li Fong joined the *tao shih* at the low table and shared the bowl of millet porridge and a platter of greens.

"Long ago," Tai Ching said, "I made my peace with all living creatures. I eat none of my friends and neighbors. There is only this famine fare."

Presently, he brought a pot of herb soup.

Finally, Tai Ching said, "When you are ready to go your way, I will give you food to last until you reach the Silk Road. Or, stay and work in the small field. When not working, you may study, and learn according to your talents. Scholars have many reasons for leaving home and taking up the sword. Sometimes a man returns, and again, it may be better that a man does not return.

"One more thing before you sleep. When I am not seen, you will not seek me. When I am in my study, you will not ask permission to enter. Otherwise, go about as you please. Nothing is hidden."

In the morning, slanting sun reached into the dormitory and awakened Li Fong. With no more self-intent than a puppet-show marionette, he roamed about. On the natural terrace, he noticed several patches of buckwheat, and scrawny little Turkish melons, peppers, and seasoning herbs. Quail regarded him without alarm.

"Why not stay here?" he cogitated. "Far away and out of sight Father will not be embarrassed by my stupidity. He will merely be grieved, thinking I was killed and robbed. Lucky, not being in jail long enough for name to be entered in the magistrate's books."

Back in the monastery, Li Fong ate cold porridge and drank cold herb soup. Presently, he resumed his prowl, and soon found the Great Book Room.

After bowing to the image of the God of Learning, he stepped to the writing table. The ink-slab was still moist, and for the first time in many a week, be breathed the camphor-scent of ink. There was a packet of fifty yarrow stalks, and the *Book of Change,* the *I Ching,* foundation of all wisdom, and all divination. He would have been amazed had this fundamental book been lacking.

What caught his eye and held his attention, then, was the opened volume near the *I Ching.* He turned the according-pleated strip, fold after fold "*...pass through fire without being burned...through water without being wet...*"

He turned several pages, "*...to ride the wind...see all, yet not be seen...become a Dragon and yet keep the form of a man...*"

Only one chapter was missing: the monograph on making or finding sufficient treasure to permit him to return home, and with honor.

"You don't need any such a writing," a woman said. "Listen, and be patient."

Startled, he glanced about. He caught a flash of shimmering color, the gold of brocade. There was the frail tinkle of jade, and a breath of perfume. When he faced where the woman should have been, he saw only books on shelves.

Shivering, Li Fong decided that he was not afraid. Startled, yes. Perplexed, yes. But afraid not at all!

When he heard softly whispering footfalls, Li Fong was relieved that it was only Tai Ching who entered the Great Book Room.

"Something interests you?"

Li Fong bowed. "My interest is in what you are about to say."

The priest touched the cover of the *I Ching,* with its sixty four hexagrams which symbolized the fundamental Laws of Change. "I have consulted the Oracle. To teach you the elements of magic, so that you could be a helper, would not be an error. You might be useful here, as well as in the field."

The study of magic and philosophy, together with his duties in the garden and in the buckwheat patch, made Li Fong's life as that of a soldier or of a coolie. His outdoor duties included moving rocks about, to build retaining walls, and then collecting and dumping basket after basket of earth, to make a terrace—just in case, some day, there were many students, and more gardens would be needed...

And, hour after hour, chanting sutras. Hour after hour, intoning mantrams, or sitting on the floor, facing the wall. There were the rhythmic inhalation-exhalations, and there were exercises in not-breathing. Then, as a variant, all these exercises were repeated as he paced the perimeter of the combination meditation hall-dormitory, where twenty students could find ample space, or even forty...

From time to time, Tai Ching came to observe the novice for a moment. At long intervals, he would offer a suggestion. During the conferences in the *tao shih's* study, there were cryptic and seemingly pointless questions. Whatever answers Li Fong might give, he could never guess whether he was establishing himself as a hopeless blockhead, or, as a probationer in magic and alchemy.

No praise. No blame. Nothing. Except, the ever present bag of groats and parched beans; four pairs of cord sandals, and a stout staff—just in case Li Fong felt that he had had enough of it all.

One evening, Tai Ching set a mat beside Li Fong's place. The Master seated himself. He had a small drum. He tapped it with finger tips, and knuckles, and with the heel of his hand. At times, with cupped palm, he made curious concussions which sometimes were a popping sound, and sometimes, a breathing. The old familiar verses, the often repeated mantrams became different from being patterned to accord with the moods, the rhythms of that small drum.

To accord with the drum voice, Li Fong changed the depth and the cadence of his breathing. He became light-headed. His pulse began to play curious tricks, as it got in step with the drum. Suddenly, he could no longer feel the tiles beneath him. He was without weight.

He was now above floor level. This queer feeling was beyond belief until he was looking eye to eye at the figure of an Immortal on the altar. Amazement broke the rhythm of his breathing. He toppled, sprawled, entangled in his mat, as he thumped to the floor.

The drum ceased. The *tao shih* stood beside him as he clawed himself clear. He said, sarcastically, "As you begin to suspect, you were several feet off the floor.

When you learn how to keep your mind on what you are doing, I'll teach you the next step. How would you like to bumble this way when you're a thousand feet off the ground?"

He quit the hall.

Problems came with Li Fong's experiments in levitation. Unpleasant creatures began to collect about him, in a circle. They were somewhat human, somewhat reptilian, and entirely contradictory in their proportions, their coloring, and their locomotion as they ambled about the hall. Without any order or system, individuals would pause, gesture, jeer, and threaten. Sometimes he could understand their obscene mutterings. Often, their language was foreign. These apparitions were never extremely noisy. Nonetheless, Li Fong wondered why Tai Ching never came to inquire about the muttering, gibbering, yelping, and scrambling about.

Inquiring seemed to be not quite the sensible thing to do... And, there was activity in the garden. But he did not glance up from his work when the shadow of great wings hovered about him. Again, he caught a glimpse, from the corner of his eye, of gold-flame-tawny-white plumage. He did not let his glance waver.

He suspected at times that the *tao shih* was testing him with diverse illusions.

Another afternoon, with sun quite low, a twisting little breeze stirred the dust into small spirals which caught up dry leaves.

There was a breath of perfume somewhat like Hwa Lan's, yet different.

"...Soaring Dragon... Dancing Phoenix..."

It was as though someone had spoken, except that there had been no sound for the ear to pick up. He straightened, drew a breath. Outdoors as well as within, the entire area seemed bedeviled.

Then came what was speech, beyond any doubt, a voice.

"When he tells you to walk—walk, and keep walking. No fear. You won't fall. I promise you."

The voice cut off abruptly, in a tinkle of jade.

Li Fong finally learned to strike and caress the little drum and at the same time, chant in accord: so that with his mat, he would rise to altar level, and higher. He was curious rather than dismayed when, after pausing for the images to regard him, he drifted toward the end of the hall. His course curved until, finally, he came back to his meditation spot. There, he settled slowly to the floor.

The *tao shih* said, "You didn't know where you were going."

"Yes, I did not know," Li Fong answered.

"Stand on feet," Tai Ching commanded. "Follow me."

Taking the drum, he led the way. *Tummmm—tumpa-tummm—tum tupa-tuppa-tum* and the droning chant which Li Fong repeated until he could feel, inwardly, the vibration of his voice, and of the drumming, and of the *tao shih's* chanting.

The standard routine, except— The floor now slanted slightly upgrade. Presently, he suspected that he no longer trod the pavement at all. And then he was following Tai Ching out and over the buckwheat patch. The mountain slope fell further and further away. He was pacing now, with the tips of tall trees at waist-height...knee-height...ankle height...

Far out, the desert shimmered and danced. It seemed that in the glare and the glamour he glimpsed the ruin where his camel had left him stranded. One recruit would not, positively not, go to Hotien...

Without warning qualm or twinge of apprehension, giddiness and terror closed in and took command of Li Fong. He began to sink. His eyes were now level with the *tao shih's* feet. Little devils leered, jeered, mocked. Below, rocks began to loom up. He sank faster, faster, a dozen paces or more.

"Sing, man, sing your mantram," a woman said. "You won't fall."

She was over-optimistic. Not falling, not really, but sinking, and ever more rapidly.

"Sing!" she repeated.

"Gate, gate, paragate, parasamgate, bodhi, SVAHA!"

The mocking devils thinned, faded in sun glare.

He felt a touch at his elbow.

"Chant with the master," she said.

He found his voice. His wits returned. He caught the beat, the rhythm. He maintained elevation, but could not rise. He was nearly a tree's height lower than his guide as they circled back.

Li Fong stumbled and rolled when he stubbed his toes against the rocky mountainside. Tai Ching called from the monastery entrance. "I told you to keep your mind on what you were doing!"

"Devils and spirits so I intoned—"

"As if I didn't hear you!"

"You heard?"

"You were bellowing like a buffalo."

"What sounds, Master?"

"The mantram I taught you."

"That's all that helped? You didn't—"

"I saw you gain control, so why interfere? A good scare, just what you need to learn wind-walking. Now, fire-walking—waver for the flicker of an eyelash, and you're finished!"

When he finally stretched out on his mat, Li Fong lay awake for a long time, pondering his adventure. The *tao shih* had been aware of his probationer's plight, and had been ready to help, in the event of total failure. On the other hand, he had neither heard nor otherwise perceived the woman-presence.

CHAPTER III.

Li Fong became accustomed to long hours divided between meditation hall and garden. He required less rest, slept lightly, and found it more and more difficult to distinguish between waking and sleep.

One night, a blade of moonlight reached through a wall slot. The brightness aroused him, and then he heard the tinkle of jade, and savored perfume. He said, aloud, "I was afraid that a mantram had driven you away."

The Presence became ever more immediate, more compelling. Li Fong sat up. After a moment, he knelt. From the corner of his eye, he sensed motion in the darkness. And then she stepped into the moon patch. She was slender, silken-gleaming, and because of her stately headgear, the woman seemed quite tall. Medallions of jade and linked clusters of rubies and sapphires descended from a headdress shaped of kingfisher breast-feathers, and heightened with sprays of peacock plumage. "No mantram can ever drive me away."

Jade hair pins gleamed as she nodded, gestured reassuringly, and stood there, half-smiling and splendid. Li Fong put his palms together and bowed.

"This beggar is Li Fong, surname forfeited. New name, not yet conferred. Homeless One, quitting the Red Earth."

"This ill-favoured hag may be called Mei Ling," she said, bowing.

"Your presence has made my days golden," he countered, in words which were a play on her name. "In my heart I have thanked you many times for voice without visible presence."

"Soaring Dragon—Dancing Phoenix."

"You really were there, then?"

Mei Ling smiled. "Perhaps as the Dragon's Shadow?"

"Dragon's Shadow?" he echoed; the implications dazed him.

"How far will you follow me?"

"It would be polite for me to consult Master Tai Ching."

"You can go a great distance without ever leaving this place."

"What should I tell the Master, when I return?"

"Whatever he asks, tell the truth."

Mei Ling beckoned, inviting him into the moon-patch. He moved, hesitated, halted. She said, "Where we are going, coolie's dress and silken tunic are alike."

He stepped into moonlight and into the fragrance which Mei Ling exhaled. She was at once tangible as Hwa Lan, and also, entirely mist-and-moon glamour. Awe and apprehension combined to numb his wits. He glanced along the shaft of light.

Mei Ling shook her head. "Leave that to Master Tai Ching. You and I go another way." Her smile was sweet, most amiable, and also, cryptic, baffling. "I asked how far you would follow me. That was a mode of speaking. Really, you will, you must, lead, far as you dare."

"I—lead—where?" he groped.

She pointed into the darkness, toward the further end of the hall.

"But—but that's solid mountain—"

"Straight on, head-on!" From beside Li Fong, she stepped back, and behind him, laying a hand on his shoulder. The fingertips rippled, as though on the strings of a lute. "Unless you lead, how can you follow and go into my home?"

This went further than the wildest Taoist paradox...

Power trickled from her fingertips and spread into his body, invading his veins. Breathing into his ear, Mei Ling said, "If a leader waits to know where he goes, he will never start."

Borrowed fire made him step forward, and with assurance. A pace, another, and yet another, until he could discern the chiseled heart-rock of the great mountain: a solid, unbroken wall.

Mei Ling moved in such close harmony that there were fleeting contacts of her body, sinuous and rippling. She whispered something which he could not understand. Then came an instant like that interval between wakefulness and sleeping. He should have come up against unyielding stone. Instead, he merged with the heart-rock.

Li Fong knew, though not through any way which he could call "seeing," that the rock was a void peppered with particles of blurred, indefinite shape, and of indecisive position. He himself was equally nebulous, an emptiness in which wandered indefinite shapes. Here and there, pulsing discs made pinwheels of fire.

As he moved, the luminous gray space became ever brighter, and less hazy, until from indefinite emptiness he came into the solid, the shaped. And Mei Ling caught his hand as they stepped into and emerged from wind-driven mist, to enter an area of gardens, of pavilions—a tiny lake, with high arched bridge—trailing willows—peach trees burdened with ripe fruit. He looked about him.

Mei Ling said, "There is neither indoors nor outdoors, neither heaven overhead nor tiled roof. We're not enclosed by walls or by horizon." Dazzling, glowing, she paused, her smile blossoming, as the gradual unfolding of petals. "You experience now what Master Tai Ching has been trying to demonstrate. By wind-walking, for instance."

"Mountain of the Gods—Home of the Dragon Lords—"

"Not bad," Mei Ling admitted, "but any name limits, it restricts, it separates-and that is *maya*, the Great Illusion."

They entered a small villa. Li Fong had the feeling that the corridors and inner courts were settling down and reshaping, to take steady form. Although he saw no servants, it seemed that an entire staff had just quit the place.

As he went with Mei Ling into a cozy reception room, she said, "I arranged everything before I went to find you. The wine hasn't had time to get cool. Do sit down and let me pour a cup." Li Fong wondered whether, in an empire of dreams, he was repeating his experience with Hwa Lan, or whether he would awaken and learn that he had never been robbed nor jailed nor marched across the desert.

As she tuned her lute, he recited, *"... Soft as the murmur of whispered words, frail as the patter of pearls..."*

She smiled fondly, and carried on, *"...dripping on a plate of jade..."*

Mei Ling accepted the cup he poured, and set aside the lute.

He said, "Wine game riddle: Dancing Phoenix, or Dragon's Shadow?"

"Wrong question!" she retorted. "Penalty empty one cup!"

"Wrong answer!" he cut back. "Penalty drain one cup!" Simple compromise: each drank, and Mei Ling poured again from the bronze jar. Then, "The next riddle for you."

"I listen."

"Watch, too," she suggested.

Her words were needless. He could never have done other than watch when, with both arms, and as though making ritual gestures, Mei Ling unfastened her tall and stately head-gear. She raised it clear of her gleaming black hair, and twisted sinuously to set it on a tabouret, well away from a table set with trays of *dim dum,* and bowls of loquats and apricots and peaches.

"Riddle: Dragon's Shadow—or, Dancing Phoenix?"

"Both."

She laughed, mocking him in sweet malice. *"Aiieeeyah!* How stupid, how silly! Correct answer, *Soochow Sing-Song Girl.* Drink one cup!"

Mei Ling coaxed the lute into full voice, and sang,

"A lutist from Omei Mountain
With a single touch of the strings

Brought back memory of a long ago meeting
By the nine-stage pagoda at the Lion Bridge.
Now I sit in sorrow nine stages deep
Facing a broken mirror—"

"Sing-Song Girl, when Master Tai Ching teaches me the secrets of alchemy, I'll make gold by the cart-load, and buy your contract!"

She smiled at him through the dancing flicker of candle flames that stifled behind pinnacles of wax. She snuffed a flame or two, and once more with both arms made the stylized gestures of a sculptured goddess, and flexed her silk-sheathed body. Her finger tips caressed brocaded curtains for a moment, then flicked them aside, to reveal a shadowed and cushioned alcove.

"Even in this place where Time is not," Mei Ling said, "learning to make gold would take quite too long." She stood now, a curtain half concealing her; and she beckoned. "There may be no contract to buy. There may also be a contract cost which you would never meet."

On his feet, he had Mei Ling in his arms as she reached over his shoulders and drew the curtains together behind him. "Where Time is not, it is always now," he said, and tried at once to kiss her, to trace the elegant curve of her body, and to unfasten the loops which secured her gown.

Mei Ling laughed softly. "Even with help, you couldn't possibly tend to all that at once," she said, and deftly plucked the first loop free.

Another candle expired, leaving its lonely companion to stand watch, and coax reflections from the brocaded curtain of the alcove.

CHAPTER IV

"And now," Mei Ling murmured, "what am I—Dragon's Shadow, Dancing Phoenix, or Sing-Song Girl?"

"We began as *yang* and *yin*," he answered, "and now, with nothing left to desire, quietly waking-sleep, we still are *yang* and *yin*. You are Dragon Shadow, Dancing Phoenix, Sing Song Girl, all at once, and who cares because that is quite impossible?"

She looked up through half-parted lashes. "You're not really certain. You still wonder whether a mantram would make me vanish."

He sat up, took her by the shoulders, viewed Mei Ling from arm's length, and sighed. "You didn't ask me. You told me. But my wonderings are not quite as you think. Phoenix and Dragon—*yin* and *yang*—Moon and Sun—you and I, we held each other so closely that there was only one and no longer two of us. Something strange happened to us and we cannot be quite what we once were."

Her eyes narrowed ever so little. She almost smiled. "This is interesting, Li Fong. I'm not your first woman. But, I am different, you tell me. Another wine-riddle? Or do you tell me without prize or penalty?"

"No wine game, now. Maybe I can tell you. If you insist."

"I do insist. Maybe you'll guess, maybe learn why."

"This goes beyond words."

"Try. Even if wrong, your penalty could be a reward."

"You and I—*yin* and *yang*—but finally, we were balanced, neither female nor male."

"Yes…" Not assent, but breathless urging.

"Yin became yang, Phoenix became Dragon. A moment of each being the other, while the entireness remained unchanged."

"Li Fong, you really do know. When I was completely Phoenix, I had to have my moment as Dragon—what else could I become? For I had to change—that is the Law. When the Sun reaches the Meridian, midnight begins—remember?"

"All that, *aiieeeyah,* of course. But you are not like other women. There is some-thing different. You're trying to talk it away from me, but you can't!"

"I am so real that a mantram can't make me vanish. I so intensely female that I re-verse and become Fire and Dragon. And my momentary opposite nature is stronger than your ordinary nature! Drink a cup, Li Fong—that is your penalty, before you drive me mad, drive us mad!"

She twisted, flipped herself, in a golden arc, landing poised on her toes. Balanced, Mei Ling whipped the brocaded gown about her, and parted the alcove curtains. Li Fong followed her to the table. Fresh lights had been set out. Incense fumed anew. The refilled wine jug was hot from its bath of water.

"Aiiieeyah, Li Fong, how stubborn, how persistent! Very well, I'll tell you. My body is no different from the body of an earth-born woman, but I am different. I am fire, Dragon, and Immortal. And until now, never a woman you have known except she was earth, and mortal. You learned this in the only way, at the only moment when it was possible to know the difference." She filled the cups.

Li Fong raised his, no more than half way, pausing to regard her.

"You said I could not lose. That penalty could be reward. Well, now, Dragon Lady, Jade Lady, Woman of All Women, now that I am right, tell me about the re-ward that could be a penalty."

"Another lesson with that *tao shih,* and you'd be impossible! Tell me your thoughts on the matter."

"Since I am totally mortal, the more you are my reward, the greater is my penalty."

"For me, also. But think how much each would have lost, if you had not learned my inner and true nature."

Li Fong laughed happily. "Cannot win. Cannot lose. As long as we stay here, where it is always now, I am immortal."

She looked at him over the rim of her cup. "Old Master, you've not been wasting your time. Next time you see Master Tai Ching, kowtow three times. Tell me—have you really truly forsaken the Red Earth?"

"Master Tai Ching asked for nothing of the sort."

"Odd, wasn't it, how you crawled up out of the desert, and in spite of being starved and dying, you remembered the Soaring Dragon and the Dancing Phoenix. I've told you what I am—now tell me who and what you really are."

So he told her, and their wine became cold as she listened. "Father would be sad," he concluded, "thinking I had been robbed and killed, but he would be ashamed and embarrassed if he learned the facts. So, better for me to disappear from the Red Earth. He will adopt Younger Uncle's son, my cousin Shiu Shen. Younger Uncle died last year."

"That girl, Hwa Lan? What of her?"

"I do not know her as I know you. Nevertheless, I say again, I know she was honest."

Mei Ling smiled. "You have no fear of mockery. That is very good. It would be so easy to blame a sing-song girl, or a flower-boat girl for whatever your stupidity brought. Now, this matter of being mortal. The Way of Fire is the only way to me."

"The Way to you?"

"Yes. This tiny world of mine is real, but only relatively so, not absolutely real. To be here with you, I must have my reality partly veiled. For you to be here with me, your reality has to be, has been, somewhat increased."

"*Aiieeyah!*" He pounced to his feet. He caught Mei Ling by the arms, looked at her as though seeing her for the first time. "Now I know—what happened to us—during a strange moment—"

"That moment will never leave you. But the Way of Fire cannot make you immortal. The most you can do is to risk the next step, and go with me into the next stage of NOW-NESS."

He glanced about, as though seeking a gateway.

She said, "While you work in the garden, I'll shape the next *now.*"

Her voice was a dismissal. Li Fong asked, "How find you again?

"I have never been away from you. So, after this meeting, could we be further apart? But your earth-habit, too wise ever to be sure of a female creature, is it not?"

"The Way of Fire may burn that out of me."

Mei Ling turned to a lacquered cabinet. From it she took an embroidered pouch, opened and thrust into it several jewels which she gathered from the drawer. "Sapphire and rubies," she said, "to keep the gold company," and thrust the treasure into his hand. "This will remind you that no mantram can ever make me vanish—that there is reality between us."

Mei Ling nudged him toward the brocaded curtains. "Many ways into our little world, and many a way out of it, Breathe deeply as you leave—exhale a reminder of me, into your world." Li Fong's merging with the boundary was as incomprehensible in departure as it had been when he entered.

He walked in cold moonlight, near the pool in the monastery garden. He had an embroidered pouch, amazingly heavy for its size. Sweetness lingered in his nostrils. When he licked his lips, the cosmetic taste assured him that this was no hallucination. Whatever treasure a sleepwalker might have found in his prowlings, a smudge of lipstick was impossible.

Li Fong looked up. What he still termed, in his mind, "last night," had been lighted by a full moon. Now the frail sliver of a new moon was rising.

He was still grappling with his perplexity when Master Tai Ching emerged from the dark entrance of the monastery.

"The people of the Red Earth enjoy Moon watching," the *tao shih* remarked. He listened to Li Fong's none too coherent queries and statements, then resumed, "That is the new Moon, and you did surely quit this place under a full Moon. That you still fancy that you left 'last night' is illusion. Harmless, of course, yet, error."

"I apologize for rudeness. I intended nothing of the sort."

Li Fong would have kowtowed, but Tai Ching prevented him. "Please desist. I am neither your father nor your teacher."

"Venerable Sir, I deserve this dismissal."

"This is not the sort which you have in mind," Tai Ching said. "This is recognition. Your return with the perfume of the Dancing Phoenix tells me that you have taken a step along the Way of Fire. She will lead you as far as you dare go."

"Venerable Sir, there is more than I understand."

"The Dragon Lady will clarify."

"But the Way of Fire—is there a point of no return?"

"In this respect, and I know not how much more, your experience has gone further than mine. If you vanish, and I do not see you again, I must conclude that there is such a point.

"Meanwhile, you are welcome to stay here. I cannot accept any of the gold in that purse. Each day, you must work to earn your food."

The *tao shih* bowed, and left Li Fong to examine, by the candlelight of the shrine, the rubies and sapphires from the land of the southern savages, the Indian *mohurs,* and the *staters* stamped with the head of Flavius Claudius Julianus, Emperor of the Western Barbarians...and gold coined by earlier monarchs...

CHAPTER V.

Whether because of fancy, or out of necessity, Mei Ling waited until the full moon to seek Li Fong. This time, she led the way into her world of everlasting now.

"Sing-Song Girl, or Dancing Phoenix?" he quipped, as she made her way into the reception room.

"We'll be all things, all at once, Old Master. And you've brought the gold and the trinkets back with you—you knew, surely, that I offered them as a gift, and not a proving that you and I had met?"

"Your gift raised questions."

"Wine game riddles, with penalties?"

Her brows rose, and her smile matched the sweet mockery of her voice. He shook his head. "While you're still all stately, with your tall headgear, tell me things, before my understanding begins to dance and go wild, or falls on its face. Master Tai Ching says that he can teach me nothing about the Way of Fire."

"Aiieeeyah! So, he knows?"

"He knew, before I spoke."

The spray of peacock plumes swayed as Mei Ling nodded. "So, you don't know whether to study in the monastery, or to come here and take the Way?"

"Yes."

"Those who quit the Red Earth before they are truly ready sometimes have their regrets."

"They cannot return?"

"You mean, whether you could not return." Without waiting for assent, Mei Ling continued, "Was it more difficult to enter, this time, than the first?"

"It was easier."

"Then?"

"I didn't find my own way. You came to guide me."

She smiled tantalizingly. "You're not sure but what I might through forgetfulness, indifference, leave you tramping the dust of the Red Earth, no longer belonging there, but not able to return to the Land of Fire."

"Jade Lady, this is not bargaining," he protested. "This is not distrust of you."

"All you want is to know what you're about to do?"

"Of course."

"Fire," she flashed back at him, "is knowing without reason! Without thought. Without clod-like intellect!"

He got to his feet. "Dragon Lady, I bow three times. I am a clod of the earth."

"With one tiny spark which knows! Tell me, Li Fong, why is all this?"

He slapped the embroidered purse to the table.

"With this, I could repay my father for all that I cost him, just to benefit a thief. There is sufficient more to buy land, so that he could establish the family, before he dies. I am sure he has already adopted my cousin, Shiu Shen, to pay funeral respects when the time comes. And it is said that the seven generations just past are ennobled, when a son quits the Red Earth."

"*Aiiieeeyah!* Inimitable Li Fong! Becoming half-immortal, and sleeping with me to the weariness, in a world without day or night or time, this will make seven generations of ancestors happy?" She sighed, shook her head, but could not keep her eyes from mocking him. "That would make them envious—unhappy!"

"Penalty! Drink one cup! Only the male ancestors would be envious."

"You learn, you learn," she conceded, and moved to the doorway. "See, how lovely-strange the lake!"

Pulsing fire towered without limit. The golden ruddy column became greenish and then clear blue. It expanded until the coping of the tiny lake was in the purple heart. Mei Ling's lips moved. She made an invocatory gesture. The color changed, until it became—to say *white* would have been an absurdity, yet to have called it colorless, nonsense equally devoid of meaning.

Wave after wave of heat billowed against Li Fong, yet his garment did not scorch or smolder, nor did hair or eyelashes curl or smoke. Mei Ling ceased intoning the mantram which came to him, clean out, resonant as a war drum, and also, no more than a whisper. She shaped a final mudra.

And, "*Svaha!*" The pagoda of white-colorless fire stabilized.

Li Fong flipped off his sandals.

"This is the test?"

She nodded. The plume-sprays wavered.

He turned his back to the silent strange flame whose immeasurable heat did not consume.

"Do you lead—do I lead—or do I go alone?"

She regarded him with eyes inscrutable, dark and deep as the gulfs between stars. Whether challenge—warning—or benediction, he could not tell. When, finally, she said, "Li Fong, this is no wine game," he knew that he was on his own. He had neither an ally, nor any second chance.

Deliberately, he took off her headdress. He unfastened the loops of her tunic, and plucked it, so that it crumpled about her ankles. He nudged Mei Ling, and she stepped clear of the garment.

"Dragon Lady, you knew that I knew where your fire is." He did not glance back, since behind him there was only a tiny lake, and no tower of elemental flame. "Nice riddle. No penalty."

"Nice tunic," she said, smiling, and retrieved garment and headgear. Then, as she went with Li Fong, "You know where the fire is, and you know its Way. No penalty."

Darkness and brilliance came and went. When they awakened, Mei Ling would serve rice and bean curd with mushrooms, or steamed bamboo shoots and crisp water chestnuts. And always, after breakfast, the Great Book Room invited Li Fong. Learning the Way of Fire had been only the beginning of study.

Sometimes, she would bring tea and a tray of *dim sum* to the library, and hear him expound what he thought he had learned. Often, she would set him right, and they would laugh, and add to the score of penalties to be assessed at the next pouring of wine.

"Old Master." Mei Ling finally wondered. "I am still far from sure how you learned the Way of Fire."

He set down his tea cup. "Dragon Lady, there was no fear of passing through the flame. Why this was so, I cannot say. I knew simply that the attempt would have been no test at all."

"*Aiieeyah!* Elegant, spontaneous liar! The way you did take, not too long after we quit the garden—*that* was an ordeal?"

She snapped her fan shut.

"That is not what I said. Do not make as though to slice my head off with the edge of that fan. The first time I entered the land of here and now you asked me things, and I answered. After many wrong replies, with penalties to match, I had learned more than I'd realized, at the time. So it came about as it did.

"And we were speaking, you remember, before I faced the flame? Speaking of those who quit the Red Earth, and of those who return to it and what might happen to them?"

Mei Ling sighed, spread her fan made a slow gesture with it.

"I remember, and I have been thinking. There is the Great Law, the all-containing Tao, which has its own order. Neither Gods nor Dragons can evade. At times, they cannot even foresee, and in their own way, they are helpless as any man of the Red Earth. Least of all could they help you upset your karma, the sum total of all the lives you have ever lived."

"You have in mind, for instance—"

"Once it was your fate to be robbed. Once, you were taken out of jail to fight the barbarians in Hotien. What you did not escape, you may meet it again, and be snared. And what you did escape, it may trap you this time, without recourse."

Li Fong hefted the purse of gold. "Maybe I'd not lose this. But there might be an army I could not desert."

She recited,

> "...not one battle famous in history
> Sent all its fighters back again..."

"So, I should forget my obligation to my father, and stay here in the everlasting now?"

"No! That is not the way of the Dragon. I will teach you mantram and mudra to use against whatever assails, whatever traps you. This is not outwitting karma—you will gain only a postponement of it. The enchantment I will teach you is deadly beyond all imagining. I will not tell you its nature. If I did, you might shrink when the time came, fearing that what you set in motion would include you, and destroy you."

She fixed him with eyes dark and smoldering. He endured her gaze as he digested her words. Finally he said, "When postponed karma is finally paid, the interest is heavy. But I accept that, too."

"There is more, Li Fong. This enchantment can be used only once, so it should be reserved for uttermost need, and that can be a hard choice. Worse yet, that half-immortality you have won through the Way of Fire will be forfeited. The Great Law accepts no gifts, and it gives no bounties."

Darkness closed in on Li Fong. Darkness and oppression extinguished all the glow which had built up within him. And when Mei Ling saw the inner blackness come to the surface, she said, a hand on his arm, "Li Fong, it is so simple to avoid all risk. Let me ride the wind, and give this treasure to your father. I will speak your message, and return surely. In this I cannot fail."

"Teach me mantram and mudra," Li Fong said. "I must do my own duty. No Dragon can do this for me."

CHAPTER VI

Li Fong followed the Silk Road eastward. Better, he reasoned, to tramp the Red Earth than ride the wind. In the end, Mei Ling had agreed with him. If he came home with the Dragon Shadow hovering over him, he would be a stranger, not entirely real.

Along the way, he sold his sword, to buy food and shoes. Ragged and dirty, he would not interest bandits. He had only to evade recruiting parties.

As he neared his native village, he learned that the harvest had been poor: and the further he went, the more he realized that his homecoming with gold would be a blessing.

Finally, one evening, he came to the old familiar settlement. He caught the savor of dumplings frying over coals, and the aroma of meat spiced, skewered, and broiling. He followed the appetizing odors to their source, a portable grille, sitting in the alleyway between two shops.

Li Fong ate, and he drank some tea. Finally, after a good suspense build-up, he broke his surly-faced silence.

"Know where Old Man Kim lives?"

The peddler pointed in the general direction. "Know him?"

"Met his son in the army."

"Which army?"

"Fighting in Hotien."

"So Old Man Kim's boy didn't get killed and robbed."

"Aiiieeeyah! Might as well have been, so far from home."

"Wounded or sick?"

"Not too badly, but moving slow. So I said I'd give news he was on the way."

"Cousin Shiu Shen won't be happy."

"How come?"

"Old Man Kim adopted him. Now you tell me, Li Fong is coming home, so Shiu Shen won't be Number One heir. Li Fong will be sore, with a Number Two heir. Old Man Kim will give you a happiness present, but nobody else will be glad."

"I forgot people gave happiness presents," Li Fong grumbled, and took a few cash from his string. "Well, here's some for you, in case I don't see you again."

The advance dividend brightened the peddler. "Maybe the bond-servant, the new one, will be glad."

"Servant?"

"Could be a slave, don't know. I hear the old man took her as part payment on a debt. Anyway, she doesn't like Shiu Shen at all."

"What's wrong with him?"

"Nothing. Nice fellow. She's just a fussy bitch and don't want to sleep with him, and the old man thinks that's funny, and sort of takes her part."

That was just like the old man...

"What she like?" Li Fong resumed.

"Might be nice, with decent clothes." He eyed the stranger. "Bandits making much trouble?"

"Not the way I came. I was busy dodging army recruiting. Been having much trouble with them?"

"Anyone your age better get out of sight by sunrise."

Li Fong decided against waiting for the peddler to alert tomorrow's market crowd, so that one of the servants would go home with a rumor about Li Fong's survival. After all, when you've reached a certain age, there are no real shocks or surprises. You have had it.

So this was the Red Earth. Quicker he fulfilled his obligation and got back to Mei Ling, the happier he'd be, and riding the wind would not be fast enough...depressing mess...

There was a group not far ahead of him, coolies squatting on the ground, gabbling with another peddler: he featured sausages, judging by the pungent smell. When a yard or so from the palaver, Li Fong paused, and knelt, making a pretext of easing his shoulder by getting out from under the carrying pole from which his two packs of clothing and travel gear were balanced. And, he fumbled with the fastenings of his sandals.

As far as gossip went, or rumors of recruiting parties, this was a waste of time. However, Li Fong did get an unexpected dividend and it jarred him. What he heard was a casual reference to the year-name. Now, and for the first time, he realized that more than six years had elapsed since his mishap in the wine shop. This was hard to believe. It would have been wholly incredible, had he not recalled how amazingly long had been the interval between his first entering Mei Ling's world, and his return to the monastery.

In a nearby shop, he verified the date. He bought paper, borrowed a brush, and ground some ink. He brushed three columns, rinsed the brush, and laid out some *cash.* The shop keeper declined the money.

"The moment you dipped that brush, I knew you were a scholar. I cannot let you pay for a trifle. *Omitofu!* Devils rule these times."

Li Fong folded his writing, and went his way.

There was a new gate keeper at the old home. This helped a lot.

"Where's old man Wu?"

"Died couple years ago. Who are you?"

"Got a message for the Master," Li Fong said, and spread out the sheet of calligraphy.

The gate keeper plucked a brand from the gatehouse hearth, took a look, recognized the fine, formal characters, and reached for the paper. Li Fong drew it back. He dug up a *tael* of silver and said, "This is more than the master would give you—especially if the news is bad."

"How bad?"

"Read it and see."

"Do you think I can?"

"Neither can I," said Li Fong. "But I think it's about the son who disappeared several years ago. Look here, it's late and they tell me it's a good idea to keep out of sight. Spread me a mat in a corner of the court, and you get another *tael.*"

"Where's the ounce?"

"Here it is. And you might hustle up a bowl of rice."

"A few cash for one of the maids, and maybe I can."

In a few minutes, Li Fong had a mat spread in the court where he had capered about as a child. Presently, a woman with a candle-lantern stepped from an inner doorway. She balanced a tray on her head. Seeing him in his corner, she set down the light and came forward with tea, a bowl of rice, and some vegetables. Without a word, she went back to her lantern, stood there until he picked up the chopsticks. Seeing that nothing else was required, she quit the court.

Li Fong had no chance to deliver his message. At the first alarm, early that morning, he bolted for cover. The splintering of wood, the yell of the gatekeeper, the screeching of servants, and the chattering of villagers gave him all he needed to know.

Bandits, making a sweep of the village, were closing in on the house of its most important citizen.

Addition after addition, expansion after expansion, had left many an obscure corner, many a hidden catch-all space, often very nearly like a room within a room. Li Fong had to get out of sight. He would be mistaken for the advance agent of the bandits, and killed by an unusually courageous servant. To declare himself, on the other hand, would be a disaster. He'd be seized, either as a hostage, or for ransom. Worst of all, the Dragon treasure was in jeopardy.

Invaders poured into the main court, and faster than servants and farm hands could escape through exits.

From concealment, Li Fong saw his father come out to confront the raiders. The old man wore a gray silk robe, and a black skull-cap. Li Fong could now believe that he had been away six years or more. However firm of purpose, his father was thin, frail, and shaky.

The bandit chief and two henchmen stepped forward from among their men. They went through all the forms of politeness. The old man parleyed: there was the usual bartering, proposal, rejection, and offer in compromise. He beckoned finally to an elderly servant, and gave an order.

The confidential servant quickly returned with heavy bags of silver.

"Where's the rest?" the chief demanded.

"Two bad seasons in a row. You know that. And the tax collector got here ahead of you."

164

"Sometimes he does and sometimes we intercept him." The bandit ruefully added, "This one had too many soldiers to guard him. Now, there must be more than this to divide among my men—you see how many I have—these are hard times!—soon I'd have no band." He grinned, rubbed his neck. "Nor even a head."

"But this is all."

The chief beckoned. A squad of burly fellows with bamboo sticks and lengths of cord came forward. No command was spoken. This was a well-organized party, with all details ordered in advance.

They lashed the old man's wrists, neatly trussed him to the spirit screen, and set to work beating him. If they overdid things and beat him to death, there was the confidential servant, who knew all that the master knew. And he would not be blamed for his ready capitulation. He'd reveal every treasure cache in the villa.

Simple.

Efficient...

Li Fong came from hiding. "This is not necessary," he said to the chief. "This man is my father."

"You are dressed like his heir."

The beating ceased. This was interesting.

"I am an army deserter. Like many of you." He dipped into his grimy jacket and brought out the purse. "I bring ransom from Hotien, from the dog-fornicating Turks." He poured gold and rubies and sapphires on the paving. "You and I, civilized persons, can agree on this."

The chief watched one of his men collect the gleaming loot.

"The army didn't capture Hotien, but wherever you got all this, you did very well."

"You accept my present?"

"*Aaiieeyah!* This is generous." He spoke to the strong-arm squad. They released the old man. He gestured to the others, and they filed from the court. He paused long enough to bow, and to say, "Next year, I promise you, I will not loot your house."

CHAPTER VII

Li Fong knelt before his father, and three times touched his forehead to the tiles. The old man extended his hand, and Li Fong arose.

"Those jewels—that gold—man, where did you get the stuff?"

Li Fong smiled. "Cousin Shiu Shen, that is as surprising as this business of a maid not wanting to sleep with a fellow as good looking as you are. Now, the food and wine—" Before that was well started, there came wails of misery from outside, the voice of crushing dismay. House servants were coming back. Villagers followed. Some pointed at Li Fong, and cried, "He can help us. He dealt with the bandits— great bags of gold—"

Li Fong caught his cousin's arm. "What's all this?" And he got it: the bandits were going to loot the granaries, and, worst of all, take the seed grain, too. Those who could not migrate to a province which had a good crop would stay and starve.

"Those turtle-fornicators," Li Fong said, bitterly. "I talked to them, as one deserter to another!"

"Son, this is all beyond believing. One of the servants told me a strange story last night. I did not believe her."

"What I have to tell you is also beyond belief."

"No, don't tell me a thing until you've eaten, until you've bathed, until you've rested. You look starved. Yes, and let your cousin get you something to wear. Drink a few bowls of wine."

"Father—"

"Do as I tell you."

The old man stalked out of the courtyard. He looked younger already. He was steadier on his feet.

Li Fong eyed his cousin Shiu Shen. Greetings were fraternal, but less than ebullient.

"No doubt Father adopted you. Relax. I am not here to push you out. I'm very likely to go back to where I came from." He darted to the gate house.

Cousin Shiu Shen caught his arm. "Don't be a fool! They might have taken your gold and still beaten Father to death."

"Better flog him to death than starve him!" He shook off Shiu Shen's grasp. "I am telling those sons of female devils a thing or two, and they'll never forget it."

He shouldered his way through the milling pack of farmers, servants, villagers, "Quit your screaming! Where is all this going on?" They pointed to granaries built after Li Fong left town.

They followed him, but at a distance. This relieved some of his apprehension.

The bandits were well organized. They had a wagon train. They had a caravan of pack animals. By putting enough grain in storage, they could sell it, later, at famine prices: it would be as approach. The sun dimmed, as though beclouded. The three bandits noted these phenomena. They ceased their talk about the strange actions of the demented villager, and looked up.

Li Fong approached the chief and his two assistants. They regarded him with interest.

"Honorable Sir," he began, "Distinguished Lords—possibly I could induce you to desist. Many will starve."

"They should keep and eat their buffalos," the chief said.

"Some do not have Your Excellency's foresight," Li Fong patiently pointed out. "I respectfully suggest that you take no more than half."

"Please elaborate?"

"Leave all the seed grain. If you take all that's in the granary, the starving will eat the seed grain now. Then comes total famine."

"Accurate observation," the chief conceded. He hefted a familiar brocaded purse, jingled it. "What inducement do you offer?"

Li Fong kowtowed. "The purse in Your Honor's hand is all that I had. I beg of you, let these people live. Come back two seasons hence. There will be more for you to take. This is the way of civilized folk."

"You are persuasive. But my men and I are doing dangerous work. We are not inclined to consider the future. Tomorrow, each may be secured to a stout frame, and sliced a slow thousand cuts. Or, one of us may be sitting on the Dragon Throne.

"You are amiable, appealing, quick-witted, a man of character. Sir, I respectfully suggest that you join us. I promise we will spare your village."

Li Fong got up from his knees. He brushed dust and chaff from his forehead. "I have been away six years. My father would not be pleased if I left to become a bandit."

He retreated three paces, and bowed.

He retreated another three paces, and bowed again.

He retreated a third time, a like distance, and said, "Sir, I beg leave to depart. Thank you for hearing me."

The courteous chieftain bowed.

Li Fong, glancing about as he withdrew somewhat further, noted those who had followed him. He gestured, and hoped that they would retreat. He hoped that Mei Ling had not exaggerated...

There was one who, instead of joining in the retreat, was approaching him. She wore the dress of a peasant, and her complexion was that of a farm woman—but there was no way to disguise Mei Ling.

"Dragon Lady, you came to help me?"

"That is forbidden. I am here to wish you well. And to see you do what must be done. Without fear, without anger, without pity."

Li Fong raised his arms. Never before had he combined the sound, the cadence, and the gestures. The First staging had to be perfect: mantramic words which had no meaning; the tone, which no untrained throat could shape; and the mudras, which only practiced hands could make.

The chief and his two henchmen were well away from those working at the granary. Curiously, and with a measure of interest, they regarded Li Fong, and his odd doings.

Apart from his own voice, Li Fong perceived other sounds: a curious whirring, a whispering as of a desert sandstorm's. A misty shape swooped down, circling the trio. The mist became a cloud. As the spirals tightened, the cloud became more dense. The three thus enclosed were startled. They eyed each other, perplexedly.

Li Fong's voice rose. His gestures became ever more stately. The bandits, now hemmed in, sought to rejoin their men. This they could not do. They began to strike and claw and lunge, but it was as though they hurled themselves against barriers of stone.

The spirals were dragon coils. Scales gleamed. Teeth glistened. Claws twinkled. The monstrous form began to glow. There was a tremendous roaring as a column of Fire reached from earth to mid-heaven. The bandits busy at the granaries quit their wains and ran for the nearest horizon.

The fire subsided. The dragon coils faded, leaving ash, and molten gold. The rubies and sapphires had endured the heat.

Li Fong said, "Dragon Lady, if I'd known, I don't think I could have done this thing. My first, and my final magic. And that half-immortality you helped me win, I've lost that."

"But no bandit or tax collector will ever loot this village again," Mei Ling told him. "And, all you've lost was your fraction of immortality. We can ride the wind back to my home."

The people were recovering from their awe. Li Fong's father was hobbling along, the elderly servant following.

Li Fong sighed. "Dragon Lady, these are my own people, as they never were before. In your land of here and now, there'd be a few sleepings together and studyings together, and I'd come to the end of my mortal lifetime, before it fairly started."

"I didn't foresee this," Mei Ling said. "I saw only that there was a risk. And from this which has happened to us, you know that Dragon Folk also have their sadness." She pointed as the people came nearer. "See that one over there? In the dress of a servant? That one is your Hwa Lan."

Recognition grew. No cosmetics. No gleaming silks. No jewels. No lute. But, beyond any doubt, Hwa Lan, the sing-song girl. "But—how—what—this is—"

"She is really as honest as you told me. I learned this, last night. In a little more than five years, she bought her contract. She told your father what had happened, and offered herself as a bond-maid to prove her good faith. He was free to keep her as a slave, or sell her to recoup some of his loss."

Mei Ling beckoned, and Hwa Lan came nearer. "Go, Li Fong—" She nudged him. "Always, the Dragon's Shadow protects you and her. Don't look back. I ride the wind alone, to my own land."

"Dancing Phoenix—" Li Fong choked back the words. For a moment, he stood in a circle of aloneness, in the vacancy made by her departure. Then he stepped into the Red Earth, and faced Hwa Lan.

"Last night," she said, "you didn't recognize me, and no wonder! Each time we meet, I'm a slave."

He turned, and pointed to the scorched circle.

"I still don't know what happened," Li Fong said. "Wasn't lightning, but surely fire from Heaven. The strangest thing—the bandit chief and two of his men, burned to ashes. Now, when the gold they had is cool enough to pick up, I'll buy your contract, and we'll find you a new lute."

"And something to wear, and a bronze wine jug," she said, happily. "Just like it was when we met. And I'll sing of the Uttermost West, and the Mountain of the Gods—"

"Hwa Lan— Jade Lady—" He sighed, looked far away, and then shifted his glance to meet her glowing eyes. "Songs of the Red Earth are much better."

www.ingramcontent.com/pod-product-compliance
Lightning Source LLC
Chambersburg PA
CBHW050749250626
47155CB00005B/1984